Across Time • Book 1

FIRES
OF THE
FORSAKEN

STEPHANIE E. DONOHUE

Midnight Tide
PUBLISHING

Published by Midnight Tide Publishing

https://www.midnighttidepublishing.com/

Edited by Meg Dailey https://thedaileyeditor.wordpress.com/

Cover art by Mila https://www.milabookcovers.com/

Map created by Hannah at Centaur Maps https://linktr.ee/centaurmaps

Character sketch by Kalynne https://www.instagram.com/kalynne_art/

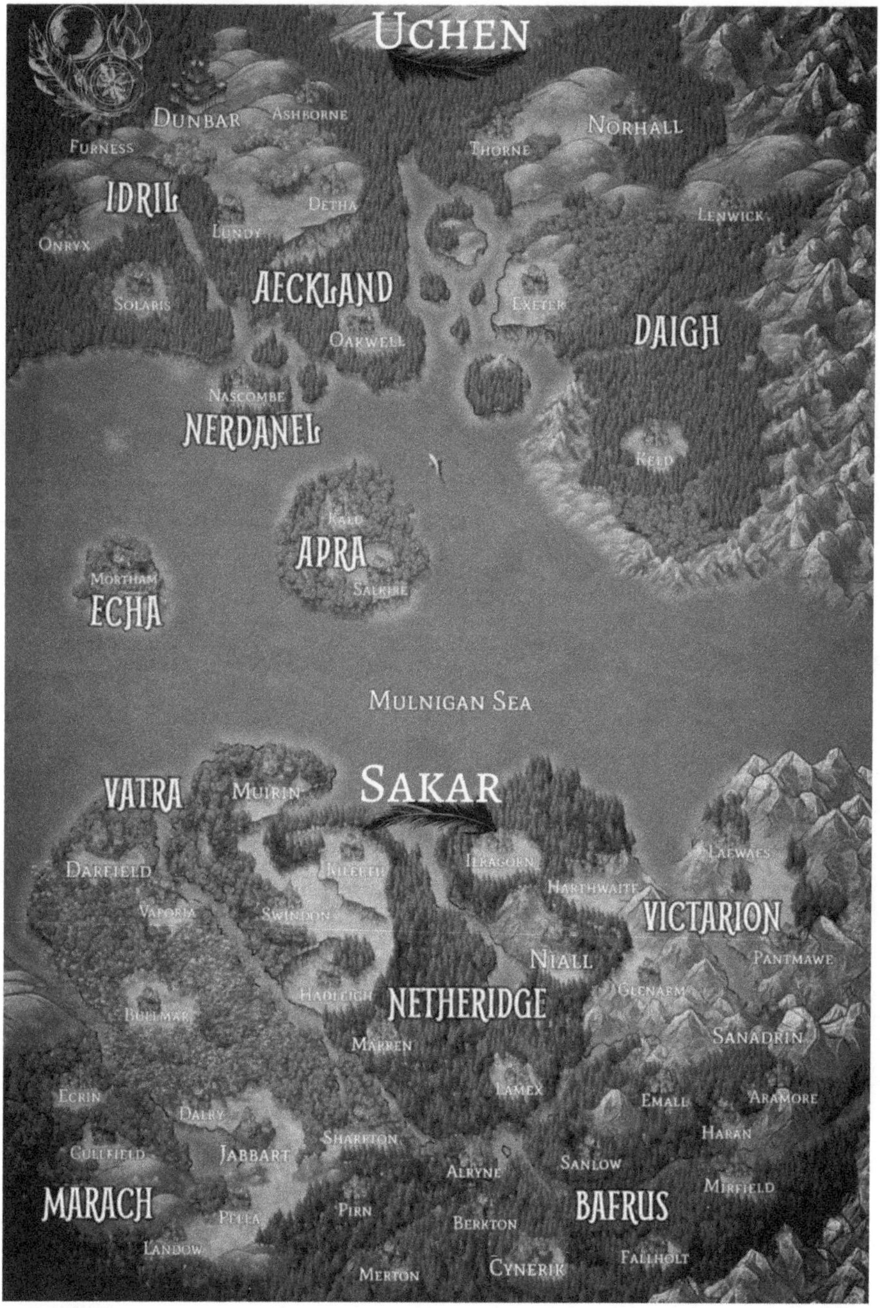

Uchen
Dunbar
Ashborne
Furness
Norhall
Thorne
Idril
Detha
Lenwick
Onryx
Lundy
Aeckland
Exeter
Solaris
Daigh
Oakwell
Nascombe
Nerdanel
Keld
Apra
Mortham
Echa
Mulnigan Sea
Vatra
Muirin
Sakar
Laewaes
Darfield
Harthwaite
Victarion
Vaporia
Swindon
Pantmawe
Niall
Glenarm
Hadleigh
Netheridge
Sanadrin
Marren
Lamex
Ecrin
Emall
Aramore
Dalry
Haran
Gullfield
Jabbart
Sanlow
Alryne
Mirfield
Marach
Pirn
Berkton
Bafrus
Landow
Fallholt
Merton
Cynerik

CONTENTS

PLAYLIST

1. I Dare You – Shinedown
2. All Star – Smash Mouth
3. Thriller – Michael Jackson
4. Mad World – Gary Jules, Michael Andrews
5. Superstition – Stevie Wonder
6. Disturbia – Rhianna
7. Monster Made of Memories – Citizen Soldier
8. Long, Long Way from Home – Foreigner
9. Man In the Wilderness – Styx
10. I Won't Let Go – Rascal Flatts
11. Believer – Imagine Dragons
12. Hungry Like the Wolf – Duran Duran
13. Zombie – The Cranberries
14. Land of Confusion – Genesis
15. Knocking on Heaven's Door – Bob Dylan
16. Vienna – Billy Joel
17. This is Halloween – The Nightmare Before Christmas soundtrack

CONTENT WARNING

This book contains violence, graphic descriptions of blood/gore, mentions of sexual assault, mentions of abuse/assault to a minor, a vague hint of an abortion, general language (lots of F-bombs), and occasionally crude jokes. Also includes scenes depicting the loss of family members/loved ones and scenes showcasing mental health issues, including (but not limited to) anxiety and depression.

Life's short. Eat more pizza.

PROLOGUE
PORK CHOPS

B urnt human flesh smelled like cooked pork fat.

Well, at least I thought so.

I was five years old the night my parents died in a house fire. The night I first caught a whiff of burning flesh.

My bedroom had been next to my parents'. We lived in a tiny rancher with paper-thin walls—my poor parents literally couldn't have sex without me hearing them. And, as a kid, I didn't realize it was inappropriate to ask why mommy sometimes sounded like she was grunting in pain.

Anyway, those thin walls also meant I had to listen to them die.

I was awake when the fire started. Awake and crying and spitting mad.

I'd been grounded earlier that day because Mom had asked me to clean my room and I'd refused. Actually, I'd told Mom my room could "go fuck itself."

I started young, okay?

And Mom, at her wit's end with my ever-running mouth, had snapped, "That's *it!* Go straight to your room, Adelaide. If it's not clean in the morning, you've lost your Kandy Kakes for a week."

So what did I do when at risk of losing my all-time favorite snack?

I trashed the rest of my room.

Look, to kid me, this somehow made sense. Like I was exacting vengeance against Mom's cruel and unusual punishment. And after my parents went to bed, I'd flopped onto my unmade mattress and bawled like...well, like a baby.

I didn't even notice the fire until Mom started screaming.

I'd never heard a sound like that before; a long, agonized wail, almost too animalistic to be human.

By then, the flames were climbing up my walls and stretching across my ceiling. I remembered calling out for my parents, figuring they'd know what to do. Because I used to think they were superheroes (or supervillains, depending on my mood). Faster than speeding bullets, stronger than locomotives—nothing hurt them, right?

Yeah, well, everyone has to grow out of their silly fantasies eventually.

My parents couldn't help me. They were too busy being burned alive.

And I was helpless. My skin itched, my muscles twitched, and every instinct screamed at me to *run*. But I didn't.

I stared at the flames, hypnotized by their flickering light.

The scent of pork chops wafted into my room. Which had

my muddled, terror-stricken brain thinking, *it's past Dad's bedtime. Why's he grilling pork chops?*

I didn't realize he was the one being flame broiled.

He pounded on the wall that divided our rooms, trying to bust it down to get to me. Or maybe he was lashing out in pain.

The fire grew and grew, scaling the walls and roaring across my bedroom floor, devouring everything it touched. My Barbies? Gone. The drawings I'd done in kindergarten? Didn't stand a chance.

The flames would eat me next. I cried but didn't move.

Or, at least, I didn't *remember* moving.

The next thing I knew, I was outside, the sky above me gray as the sun rose. A firefighter sat on the curb next to me, stroking my back. "You're a lucky girl," he kept saying. "Everything's going to be okay now."

Dissociative amnesia, one of my (many) psychologists had called it; the human brain's ability to forget traumatic events. I'd escaped—likely by jumping out a window—and I didn't remember.

It made sense. But it wasn't the truth.

I was five years old on the night I became an orphan. And it wasn't until twenty-five years later that I learned why.

LASS

FIRE IS VERY HUMANLIKE.

It has humble origins—a spark, no bigger than a fingertip. And then it grows. Innocent, at first, but often becoming more

~~malisious~~—malicious as it develops. Anger will cause it to fume and swell. It will consume land greedily but will never be full nor truly satisfied. It is capable of taking life, of causing pain, but also capable of creating.

Very much like humans, yes?

Well, perhaps not *all* humans. But many of them.

I was a babe when I first found myself entranced by a dancing flame. I did not understand what it was, or what it could do. The bitter cold had been rattling my bones all day, and the flame offered warmth.

I stretched my hand out, hoping to bring its heat closer.

Touching it, of course, only led to pain. The fire ~~revenishly~~—ravenously devoured my skin. I cried, shaking my hand, but the flame refused to give up its meal. Until my mother doused it with water.

The burn on my palm had taken weeks to heal, and I gave fire a wide berth after that.

Until it became a part of me.

I never felt another burn. Instead, I incinerated others. Hundreds—nay, thousands had died by my hands over the years. Some deserved their painful demise. Most were innocent.

Am I remorseful? Of course. But it's a rather pointless emotion; it won't bring them back.

Perhaps you think me a monster. And perhaps I am. I suppose it doesn't matter. I am not ~~righting~~—*writing* this to receive absolution.

Someone once told me putting my thoughts on paper would—what is the saying? *Uncludder my mind.*

(That doesn't seem right. Uncludder? Or unclutter?)

If anyone is reading this, please bear in mind I only learned how to ~~right~~—write a few years ago.

And if putting these words to parchment helps to *uncludder* my mind...well, I would like to have a few moments of peace. Especially since I don't know how many moments I have left.

Perhaps I should start at the beginning.

I

HAIR TODAY, DYE TOMORROW

ADDIE

"Seriously, who wants to greet the end of the world scared shitless when you can be happy and shitfaced? Am I right?" I leaned against the pickup counter, fiddling with one of the coffee shop's cheap brown napkins. The mad morning rush had ended so it was quiet in the store. The only customers were me and a middle-aged man who'd set up a makeshift office on one of the corner tables.

My usual barista, a college kid named Sandy, rolled her eyes at me.

"True," she drizzled extra caramel syrup over my latte, "but, even with the whole Winchester beer plan, *Shaun of the Dead* still sucks."

I liked Sandy. The kid was cool. I mean, her electric purple hair was a little too much for her complexion—I'd have gone with lilac or mauve—and she had crapped on one of my favorite movies, but she had good taste. Mostly.

I waved my napkin at her. "Please. You just don't appreciate the humor."

"*Zombieland* is so much better," she said.

I pursed my lips. "Okay, that's a good one. But nothing beats Simon Pegg and Nick Frost fighting zombies to *Don't Stop Me Now*. It's a freaking classic."

"Two words." Sandy placed my latte on the counter in front of me. "Woody. Harrelson."

I shrugged and laughed. "Okay, yeah, he's pretty hilarious. I'll give ya that. Thanks!" I lifted the coffee cup and tapped the end against my forehead in a salute. "I'd never survive the AM rush without your go-go juice, Sands."

"It's almost noon...oh, and Addie!" Sandy called my name before I stepped out the door.

"Yeah?"

"That is a kick-ass dress." She flashed me a thumbs-up.

I grinned and smoothed a hand over the colorful patched pattern on my skirt. "Bonus points if you know what movie it's from."

She huffed. "Please. Don't insult me. It's Sally's dress from *Nightmare Before Christmas*. Aka..."

"The best holiday movie ever," we said in unison.

I grinned at her. "You're a good kid. Don't ever change!"

And then I ducked out into the frigid November air. Which only *felt* frigid because temps had been in the 70s yesterday and took a nosedive overnight. Pennsylvania weather was freaking bipolar.

Thank God my dress still looked badass when paired with leggings and boots. Otherwise, my thighs would've frozen by the time I got to my car.

I sipped my coffee as I drove away, letting the hot, sugary concoction warm my insides. I wasn't sure if the single shot of espresso did anything, or if I was getting a sugar rush from all the pumps of caramel. Either way, I was bright-eyed and bushy-tailed by the time I arrived at work.

Hair Today, Dye Tomorrow.

Awesome name for a hair salon, right? Not gonna lie, the name was the only reason I chose to work here. The place was a forty-minute drive from my apartment, and I'd gotten other offers from hair salons that would've been much closer. But who wanted to work at dull old *Pure Indulgence* when you had *Hair Today, Dye Tomorrow* as an option?

"Elsie!" I called, downing the last of my latte, as I walked into the salon and saw my first customer sitting in the waiting area. "Love that shirt on you!"

Her crisp blue blouse matched her eyes. "Thank you." A flush spread across her cheeks as she smoothed a hand over the shirt.

Elsie was a sweetheart. And she was old-style Hollywood gorgeous. At sixty-three, she looked way better than I did at thirty. She was trim and fit, her porcelain skin barely touched by age, and her wavy hair still full and healthy. Meanwhile, I was twice her size, had chubby cheeks, and looked like an overtired hobgoblin, even when I wore makeup.

I chucked the empty latte cup into the trash bin behind the register, grinning when my manager, April, shot me a dirty look from where she was shampooing a client's hair.

"Is that a Halloween costume you're wearing?" April hissed at me.

"Only if it's worn on Halloween." I winked at her as I strolled to my station. In my defense, this dress was too pretty to wear once a year.

April shook her head. "How old are you again?"

"You're only as old as you feel." I beamed before swiveling my chair around, motioning for Elsie to have a seat. "What can I do for you today, madam?"

"Well," Elsie sat slowly, "you remember that man in my aquatic class—I told you about him, didn't I?"

"Mr. Former Rugby Player? With the chocolate brown eyes…"

"Yes, that's the one! He—well…"

"He asked you out, didn't he?" I flashed her a smile.

She blushed again. "Yes, and, well, he is *younger* than me…"

"Age is just a number."

"…so I wondered if we could do something…oh, I don't know." She touched a hand to her hair. "Maybe a new color? Something different?"

"You got it." I placed the cape over her shoulders and pulled a hair color chart out of my drawer. "Hmm, so how 'bout the Medium Champagne?" I held the chart beside her face. "You could also do a Beeline Honey," I added. "But I'm not sure I'd go much darker than that."

Beneath the cape, Elsie twisted her hands.

"Do ya want me to pick?" I asked.

With an exhale, she nodded. "Am I being foolish?"

"Nah. It's first date jitters." I flipped through the color chart, comparing the shades to her complexion.

"First date…" she made a soft *huh* sound. "You know I was twenty years old when I had my last first date?"

The sad, faraway look in her eyes made my heart hurt; as though I was the one still grieving a deceased husband instead of her.

I'd never been married. Had no intentions of *ever* being married. But I still understood her pain and confusion. I'd been in that dark spot before. Many times.

I tapped her shoulder. "You know dating ain't that hard, right?"

She scoffed.

"Seriously. Start with a drink. An Old Fashioned will loosen you up."

She smiled. I knew her well enough by now to pick out her drink of choice.

"Have dinner," I continued. "Order whatever you want off the menu—don't be like those weirdos who only get *salads* because they're trying to impress their dates. I had a roommate who did that. She was always *starving* when she came home. Anyway...talk to the guy. Y'know? And if he seems dull, pretend to go to the bathroom and ditch him."

Elsie laughed. "Oh, Addie! That's awful! Please tell me you've never done that?"

I winked at her and glanced at the chart again. "Ooh, wait!" I'd just held a color next to her face that looked hella gorgeous. "I think we *will* go darker with your hair. What about Sparkling Amber?"

Her brow furrowed. "I'm not sure. What do you think?"

"This color, with your eyes..." I made the chef's kiss gesture. "You're gonna have this guy drooling all over himself."

She looked damn good when she left the salon. I'd cut and styled her newly dyed hair into a side-swept bob that accentuated her heart-shaped face. The darker color made her eyes pop. "You're gorgeous," I told her as she left. "Own it!"

My next customer, Scarlett, walked in a few minutes later.

"Addie, *darling!*" Scarlett strolled over to give me a spine-cracking hug.

"Hey, Scarlett." Oh boy, how many times had I told this woman to go easy on the hair straightening? Her brown locks were damaged AF.

I bit the inside of my cheek—hard—as I swiveled the chair around for her. I tended to blurt my thoughts out loud. And I didn't want to piss off one of my best tippers by saying her hair was sending me an SOS signal. "So," I said once the nasty thought had passed, "how's the hubby?"

"Oh, don't even get me *started.*" Scarlett leaned back in the chair with a disgruntled sound. "He wants to take up wood-working. He can barely use a steak knife without slicing a finger off, but he expects me to be okay with him using a *power saw?* Ugh." She gave a long, dramatic sigh.

A day in a hairstylist's life. Exciting stuff, huh?

But I freaking loved my job. I literally got paid to play with hair and gossip. Can you say *dream career?*

Still, after an eight-hour shift on my feet, I was beat. And the thought of going back to my apartment and cooking was...*meh.*

"I need pizza," I grumbled as I slid behind the wheel of my car. "With mushroom and olive toppings. Hmm. Definitely need pizza."

The best pizzeria in the area (and I'd tried all of them, multiple times) was a dumpy little place called *Doughy Delights.* The name was corny as hell and the place was nestled in the middle of a mostly abandoned strip mall, between an adult toy store and a beer distributor. Which, I mean, if a person was looking for a good time, they had the Unholy Trinity right there: pizza, booze, and sex. But a lot of people looked at the pizzeria, with its chipped siding and unfortunate location, and drove right by.

Thankfully, I never shied away from a restaurant. Because some of the yummiest places were the ugly little hole-in-the-wall shops.

I ordered the pizza before I started driving and was practi-cally tasting it when I parked my car at the strip mall, a few spaces down from the front door of the shop. It was dark out. The only lightbulb in the parking lot was flickering, as per usual. That light had never worked right.

An icy breeze smacked me across the face as I stepped out of my car. I drew my leather jacket tighter around myself as I dodged a massive pothole and skipped up the curb to *Doughy*

Delights' front door. Inside, it was stiflingly hot, thanks to the old-fashioned brick oven that dominated most of the space. The owner of the store, Bo, pulled my pie out of the oven as I walked in. My mouth watered.

"Hey, Addie!" He deposited my pizza into a box. "You're still stopping by on Saturday, right?"

I gave him a thumbs up. "You bet. Still nine AM?"

"Yup." Bo had a weathered face, and the skin around his eyes crinkled when he grinned. "But Morgan added Veronica to the list—the flower girl," he added when I wrinkled my nose in confusion.

"Oh," I waved my arm dismissively, "that won't be a problem. Kids are easier than adults. They're cool with whatever I suggest. But how are *you* holding up? Getting nervous? Father of the bride." I poked his arm as he placed the pizza box on the counter and rang me up.

"Not at all. I'm excited to get her out of my house." He worked hard to put a grumpy edge to his voice, but his lips curved in a playful smile.

His daughter, Morgan, was fresh out of college and getting ready to marry her high school sweetheart. And they had thrown me a little extra work. I was doing hair and makeup for the bridal party and had been invited to attend the wedding—including the reception. Which had an open bar. No way in *hell* I'd turn that down.

After paying for the pizza, I dropped a few bucks into the tip jar, as always. And, as always, Bo rolled his eyes and gave me a bashful grin. "You take care now, Addie." He waved and then turned when his phone rang.

I slipped out the door, clutching the warm pizza box close to my chest as a chill ripped up my spine. A *bad* chill. Like the tingly sensation I'd get while watching a horror movie.

I teetered on the curb, tempted to ask Bo to walk me to my

car. But that was stupid. There was nothing out there! Everything looked and sounded normal: traffic chugging along, an airplane zooming through the air, somebody arguing with a significant other in the shitty apartments above the strip mall...

Besides, my car was only fifteen feet away.

I stepped off the curb and booked it, trying to ignore the cold sweat dripping down my back.

"Oh, you stupid stone-aged piece of shit," I hissed as I pounded my thumb against the clicker and got zero response from my car. Which, okay, my car was old. Like, *a model not even made in the past two decades* old. So the clicker was hit or miss anymore. But it was still annoying when it crapped out.

I hissed out another curse as I propped the pizza box on the roof and shoved my key into the lock.

Above me, the light flickered. On. Off. On. Off.

I twisted the key, and glanced up, my blood running cold as the light went out and I caught my reflection in the window.

There I was: my blonde hair twisted into a braid, my purple eyes wide—yes, they were actually purple. A (*spectacular*) genetic defect.

Behind me stood a shadow. A human-shaped shadow.

I never saw their face. But the lock of their hair fluttering in the wind was so vibrantly red, it looked fake. Neon colored.

My heart hammered in my chest and my stomach gave a painful lurch. "Wh—"

I never got to finish my words.

A hand smashed into the back of my neck, shoving me forward. My forehead cracked against the hard glass of the window, and I dropped like a fucking stone.

2

A SNOWBALL'S CHANCE IN HELL

ADDIE

Oh Jesus *Christ!* My head hurt.

I groaned and flopped onto my side. The pain was nauseating. Like someone was squeezing my skull with an enormous clamp.

I'd overdone it with the alcohol again, hadn't I?

But I didn't remember going out for drinks. I didn't remember *anything*.

I grunted again. And then shuddered when someone else moaned in my ear. *Shit.* Did I bring someone home last night? Or, worse, did I go to someone else's place?

I pried my eyes open, one at a time, cringing as the sunlight drove white-hot needles of pain into my skull. I'd never drink again. Nope, nope, nope. I said this whenever I woke up hungover, but I meant it this time. I was too goddamn old for this.

And...the heck? Was I *outside?*

I blinked, staring at the cloudless blue sky above me.

What in actual *fuck* happened last night?

I racked my brain, trying to mentally retrace my steps.

Doughy Delights. Pizza. My head pinging off the car window.

Had I been abducted?

My stomach roiled when I moved, but I pushed myself into a sitting position anyway, swallowing rapidly. A high-pitched ringing sounded in my ears as my fuzzy vision took a few seconds to focus.

What in the heck??

This had to be the *deepest* pile of shit I'd ever gotten myself into.

I sat in the middle of a field, surrounded by towering pine trees. That alone would have been troubling, since I lived in a congested metro area, far away from wide-open spaces. But this field was also covered in bodies.

And I mean *covered.*

There had to be thousands of corpses. Some were missing limbs or heads, or...well, *everything.* Literally, there were random chunks of human scattered about—fingers, toes, gooey pieces of scalp, and...holy crap, that was an *eyeball!* Definitely an eyeball. And sitting right by my foot.

"Ew, ew, ew!" I squealed and tucked my knees up.

The grass beneath me was soaked with blood. The gently sloping hills of the field were like violent, crimson-stained waves. And, with my mind whirling at a hundred miles an hour, I swore those hills were moving, pushing the bodies closer.

Well, the hills weren't moving. But the body next to me was.

I screamed when a hand brushed against my arm. A very *small* hand. With teeny fingers and a delicate little wrist.

A fucking *kid.* Practically still a toddler.

Blood stained the boy's hair, and the front of his shirt,

thanks to the gaping cut on his forehead. A woman—presumably his mother—lay beside him.

Well, to be clear, her *body* lay beside him. Her head was M.I.A.

"Jesus," I hissed.

The kid whimpered, his fingers closing feebly around the sleeve of my jacket.

"Hey," I whispered to him, trying to keep the tremor out of my voice. "What happened? Actually, never mind...I..." I swallowed as I stared at the decapitated woman. "I'm gonna—"

The words died in my throat when the rolling sound of galloping hooves echoed behind me.

No.

No freaking way.

That had to be thunder, right? *Not* horses.

I glanced over my shoulder.

Fuck.

Those were horses.

A dozen of them, to be exact. All gigantic. All black. Even the *riders* wore shiny black armor. And, to add the cherry on top, some of them wore dark, spiked helmets.

The group drew to a walk as they approached a gentle hill to my right, facing away from me—thank *fuck*. Especially since the riders dismounted and started plucking bodies off that hillside. Some corpses got plopped over the back of the saddles. But most got tossed away while the riders made a sound of disgust.

I gulped down a ragged, wheezing breath. Seriously, what was going on here?

Beside me, the little boy cried. He stayed quiet. I had to give him that. But his low whine sounded like a scream as it reverberated across the field.

A rider spun around.

An *un*-helmeted rider.

Oh. Dear. Christ!

Terror lanced through my chest. The rider wasn't even *human!*

He was human-shaped, sure: two arms, two legs, and a head. But the similarities stopped there.

Pale gray skin stretched taut over his skull. And he was, literally, bone thin.

Well, okay, he wore armor, so I didn't actually know if he was bone thin. But his gaunt face, with those sunken cheeks and eyes, made him look...

Like Jack Skellington, my brain thought frantically.

Except Jack (despite being the best scarer in Halloween-town) had a friendly face. Because he was a character in a freaking kid's movie.

This rider's skeletal features made my blood run cold. Because he looked more like a creature in a gory B-horror movie.

He bellowed, his milk-white eyes rolling wildly in their sockets as he leapt back into the saddle.

Was he blind?

But then he looked right at me and bared his long, pointed teeth. The motherfucker could see just fine.

"Shit!" I didn't hesitate. Didn't think twice. I snatched the little boy under his armpits and hefted him off the ground. "Ah, fuck," I grunted. The kid was way heavier than he'd looked. Or I was just pathetically weak and out of shape.

Probably the latter.

"There are two alive!" The rider's warbled voice grated in my ears. He kicked his horse into a gallop.

I flung the kid over my shoulder, ignoring the rocket of pain that shot along my back, and *ran*.

On my best day, I wasn't exactly a track and field star. The last time I'd run had been for a P.E. test in high school. And I'd almost flunked.

Today? I was twelve years older, twenty-odd pounds heavier, and had a two-ton toddler slung over my shoulder. I moved at the Speed of Snail, tripping over bodies, slipping on blood-slicked grass, and cursing up a blue streak. My knees ached, and a painful stitch drove itself into my ribcage, making it damn near impossible to breathe. But I kept going.

And the hoof beats kept getting closer.

Into the tree line I went, gasping like a winded elephant. The kid whimpered as his wounded head smashed against my shoulder.

Into the tree line the horse followed, its rhythmic, bellowing snorts almost deafening. The rider's gleeful cackle made me shiver and kick it up another notch.

As if I could outrun a horse, right?

And then I heard hoofbeats coming from *in front of me*.

"Fucki—hey, hey!" I shouted, excitement bubbling in my stomach as a fine-boned bay horse crossed over my path. The animal was riderless but fully tacked: saddle, bridle, the whole nine.

The horse didn't stop when he saw me. Didn't slow down. Didn't even acknowledge my presence. But I got close enough to snatch one of the flailing reins.

The horse snorted, the whites of his eyes showing as he flattened his ears at me.

Normally, this would've scared me shitless. Horses were freaking *huge*. But right now? This stupid, skittish, too-big creature was my only salvation.

"Dude—c'mon. Stay still!" I held onto the rein for dear life. My shoulder popped as I lugged the two-ton toddler over the saddle.

Tha-thump, tha-thump, tha-thump, tha-thump.

Jack Skellington's black horse was right on top of us. And I didn't have a snowball's chance in hell at getting myself on the bay horse's back in time. The stirrups were too damn high. My legs were too damn short. And the horse wouldn't stop wriggling.

But the toddler? He had a shot.

"Hold on," I said to him as he clutched the pommel of the saddle.

Tha-thump, tha-thump, tha-thump, tha-thump.

"Go." I released the rein and shoved the bay horse's neck. "GO!"

The horse didn't need more encouragement. He flew into the trees while the toddler clung to the saddle.

Tha-thump-tha-thump-tha-thump —

"Agh, *fuck!*" I screamed as a hand fisted in my hair, lifting me clean off my feet. My body smashed against the black horse's rolling shoulder. "Let go!" A burning pain shot along my scalp.

The rider released my hair for a split second. But then his rough hand closed around the back of my neck. His long fingernails slashed into my skin, drawing blood.

My feet flailed, helplessly, several inches off the ground. *"Let go!"*

The rider had an iron grip. No matter how hard I thrashed and dug at his hands, I couldn't break free.

The forest whirled around me, trees rushing by in a blur as the horse galloped.

The rider pulled me up and up...

"So much flesh," he grumbled. "You'll be a fine meal."

"Excuse me?" Did I hear that right?

I'd definitely heard that right.

The rider dragged me past the horse's shoulder, clearly intending to sling me over the saddle. Like I was his prize.

Or, more accurately, his *dinner.*

I battered my legs against the horse's side, howled, curled my fingers into claws, and dug my nails into whatever flesh I could find. I probably looked like a damn gremlin. And when the rider reached for me with his other arm, I wailed and sank my teeth into his hand. His skin felt like a pumice sponge. Still soft, but also rough and gritty. The dark blood tasted like overcooked asparagus when it hit my throat.

"Bitch!" The rider drew his bleeding hand back and pummeled me across the face.

I nosedived into his crotch (*eech*) as the horse screeched and smashed into the ground. Its ass flew up in the air in a full somersault. The rider whizzed over his mount's neck.

And I went with him.

It felt like being launched on a roller coaster: my body zooming at a million miles an hour while my stomach stayed behind. Normally, I lived for that kind of thrill. But now...

I crashed to the ground with so much force, my bones rattled. The breath rushed out of my lungs. White spots exploded in front of my eyes. I couldn't move. Or breathe. Couldn't do anything but stare at the dark canopy of trees overhead.

The rider landed beside me, although he recovered much quicker. He rolled over, fisting his hand in my hair, holding me down. My scalp burned. I'd have bald spots when this was all over.

Assuming I survived.

A few feet away, the black horse squirmed on its back, all four legs straight up in the air. With a strained, hollow grunt, the animal righted itself and got to its feet. But the reins were tangled around its forelegs. The poor thing was stuck. Every time it took a step, it yanked on its own mouth.

The horse's harsh, almost panicked bellow filled the air.

The rider didn't seem to care.

He crawled on top of me, his hands groping my chest, nose buried into the side of my neck. He inhaled once. Twice.

"You creepy motherf—" I screamed, freeing a hand and ramming my thumb into his freaky white eyes. He reared back with a curse. I gritted my teeth and held on, digging my finger in. I wanted to make his eye go *splat*.

Whoosh.

A knife sailed through the air toward us, the blade glinting in the sunlight.

Thunk.

It hit home. In the back of the rider's head.

The hand fisted in my hair loosened as the rider's limp body flopped on top of me. His armor smacked against my boobs and...yeah. The girls were gonna have wicked bruises.

His body twitched as goopy midnight-blue blood trickled from his wound.

"Ew, ew, ew!" My breath rattled as I shoved him off me. Slowly, my heart running at a million miles an hour, I sat up. Slowly, arms and legs shaking, I pulled myself to my feet and found myself face-to-face with a man. A normal, red-blooded, *human* man.

My fucking *savior*.

And how did I repay him?

I doubled over and puked on his boots.

3
VARN

Where shall I start?

Scribing the harrowing events of the last few days would likely be enough to fill my bind of parchment. And I don't want to focus on the end of my life; I wish to compile its entirety, as accurately as I can recall it.

I had a name, once. Given to me by my mother when I entered this world. I don't remember it now. And I've been called many things throughout my life, so I doubt I'll ever recall it.

At the time of ~~righting~~—writing this, I am thirty years of age. Or perhaps twenty-nine? I'm uncertain of my age as I don't know when I was born.

It's odd, yes? Most humans know the year, if not the precise day, of their birth. In the olden times, it was customary to view the anniversary of one's birth as a celebration.

But I do not have this knowledge. And thus, I can only guess at my age; I have seen at least three decades on this earth, but I will not live long enough to see my fourth.

I spent the early years of my childhood in a ghastly place

called Detha, one of the many cities in Celestial-ruled Uchen. It is still controlled by Celestials. For all that I have achieved, I could not free my kin, and I never will.

Those fortunate to have never lived in a Celestial-ruled city will not understand the atrocities that occur behind those walls. It's better not to be born at all than to be born in a place such as Detha. Hence why my arrival was not an event to be celebrated.

In Detha, humans were treated as livestock.

No. I apologize, I've made an inaccurate statement.

The livestock were treated *far* better than the humans.

Detha produced food in abundance, but people still starved. The Celestials received our finest crops and cuts of meat, you see. Even though they did not *need* to eat our food, they enjoyed indulging themselves. The Wraiths, enforcers of Celestial law, were offered the second finest crops and meats. Humans were given whatever was left—hardly enough to feed a family, let alone a sprawling city.

The Wraiths of Detha governed with a heavy hand. Punishments were dealt frequently and swiftly for all manner of offenses. For example, sneezing too often could earn a human fifteen whiplashes. Coughing too loudly could result in the removal of a non-important limb—fingers, toes, ears, whatever the Wraith fancied. Failing to make The Offering, the daily basket of food humans prepared for the Celestials, was a death sentence. It didn't matter the reason. Even if a storm desimated—decimated a person's crops, or a plague struck their animals, The Offering was still expected. Leinceny —leniency was only given if the offender had something else to offer.

Another human, perhaps.

Wraiths savored the taste of human. And, although they were not spared the wrath of a Celestial when The Offering was scant, they happily endured the punishment if it allowed them to fill their bellies with human flesh.

I've been told it's our *souls* Wraiths truly crave, as they do not have one of their own. But, as they are incapable of extracting souls, they settle for flesh.

Varn, the odious Wraith who commanded the army, had an ~~instat—insatit~~...(I know how to spell this word, bear with me)...*insatiable*. Varn had an *insatiable* appetite for humans. He even had a favored method of cooking them: crisping their skin, while leaving their innards raw and moist. He also preferred his meals to still be alive when he consumed them. "Death makes the muscles too tough," I'd once heard him say. "But living muscle *melts* on the tongue."

I'm not certain how true that statement is, as I've never had the desire to test it. But I nearly became one of his meals.

I had only walked the earth for six (or five, or seven) years when Mama died. She succumbed to the cough, as did many others that winter. Papa had died of the same affliction two years prior. I don't remember him. Some days I struggle to recall Mama.

During the peak of the winter months, Varn holed himself up inside his house, his gaunt body propped before a roaring fire. He didn't much like the cold, you see. And he did not need to endure it when he had an army to do his bidding.

Varn's duty, his sole purpose for residing in Detha, was to ensure the Celestials were content. And the Celestials were easily contented, as long as they could engorge themselves on our food while simultaneously ignoring our very existence.

So Varn had a simple job: he ordered his soldiers to collect The Offering and keep us *motivated* to continue working.

His soldiers eagerly complied.

On the day Mama died, the Wraiths came to collect The Offering at dusk. They took me instead.

I was amongst five others—two of us were orphaned children, the other three had been Offered—brought to Varn's home that day. The Wraiths herded us into a spacious room where the ceiling seemed high enough to reach the heavens and the floor was made of a reflective material. I received quite a fright when I glanced down and saw my own ~~dishelved~~—disheveled, terror-stricken face staring back at me. I'd never seen my reflection before, and I was rather shocked at how monstrous I looked.

My surprised gasp did not go unnoticed.

"Quiet!" the Wraith beside me shouted. His whip lashed my arm.

I winced as blood pooled from the narrow fissure that formed in my dirt-caked skin and bit my tongue to stifle my cry.

The five of us stood beside a ~~behometh~~—behemoth fireplace while Varn sat at a golden table, his white eyes following our movements.

The first to be roasted was a man named Oisin. I knew him rather well. He and his family tended a herd of cattle near Mama's dwelling. Disease had taken most of his herd. The remaining cows produced little milk and were too thin to slaughter for meat. So he'd Offered himself. His sacrifice gave his family another day to either coax more milk from their cows or find something else to Offer.

I liked Oisin. He used to hum, claiming his cows were soothed by his voice and encouraged to give him more milk.

Now he shook silently, his face pale, eyes shimmering as the Wraiths stripped him of his clothing and strapped him to a spit. His wails reverberated off the high ceiling as his body hovered over the dancing flames. It took only moments for his skin to blister. The rancid odor turned my stomach to rot.

Oisin never ceased screaming. His voice had grown hoarse

when the Wraiths pulled his mottled body from the hearth and placed it on Varn's table. Oisin's cries only abated after Varn cut several long strips of meat from his abdomen.

I felt no fear as I watched this unfold. Or, perhaps I did and I don't remember, but I think I had accepted my fate. Death was a familiar friend in Detha.

"Next!" Varn shouted. He heaped several large hunks of skin, muscle, and fat onto a serving platter before passing the remnants of Oisin's body to his soldiers.

A Wraith grasped my shoulder, herding me toward the hearth.

"No, not that one! Too small." Varn spat food as he spoke. "There's no meat on those bones! Throw her on last." Crisped pieces of flesh dangled from his teeth when he smiled.

As it turned out, my slight, underdeveloped body saved my life.

A female Celestial plucked me out of the line as the Wraiths removed a keening woman from the fire; the third human to be placed on Varn's table.

"Don't be afraid." The Celestial's purring voice caused me to shiver. Her breath carried the scent of apples.

The Wraiths shouted in alarm. Varn, blood dribbling down his chin, stood. His golden chair made an awful shriek as it scraped against the floor.

"It's alright," the Celestial said. "Be at ease. There will be no punishment tonight for the meager Offering. But I am taking the girl with me."

It was uncomfortable, the way the Celestial pressed my back against her front and trailed her fingers over my shoulders. For the first time that night, I had an urge to scream.

But we flew away before I could open my mouth.

Of course, Celestials do not fly as birds do. Traveling with her was akin to...well, it's difficult to describe. I suppose it's akin to the hide-and-go-seek games children play. To be more specific: the part of the game where the seeker is blindfolded and spun until they're disoriented.

Once I had returned to solid ground, staring at glistering white walls, and crying because my stomach fluttered, the Celestial grasped my chin in her palms. "Drink," she commanded, pressing a glass vial to my lips. Radiant silver liquid swirled inside the container—her blood.

At the time, I did not know what it was. I merely balked at the scent: like a slab of cheese that had festered in the blistering summer sun.

I dug my teeth into my lips, keeping my mouth closed.

"Drink!" The Celestial pried my jaw open, ignoring my whimper of pain, and tipped the contents of the vial to the back of my throat.

I sputtered, prepared to spit the liquid out, but she clasped a hand over my mouth and pinched my nostrils, suffocating me. Forcing me to swallow.

The pain began immediately.

It felt as though every bone in my body were being broken, reset, and broken again. The sensation lasted for hours, *days*, with me screaming until I had no voice left. I clawed at my skin, digging my nails in so deep, I left welts. I vomited and fouled myself.

The Celestial stayed by my side, but her presence offered no comfort. She never spoke or sang lullabies to ease my torment, nor did she offer me a kind touch. She only shoved bits of food and water into my mouth a few times a day, keeping me alive, even as I pleaded for death.

When a second Celestial arrived, eyes alight with fury, I thought I'd been granted my wish.

Instead, I was taken again, forced to endure the dizzying way Celestials travel for the second time.

Black spots swarmed my vision as we landed. A deep, piercing sound filled my ears, making it impossible to hear anything else. The Celestial, a male this time, gently deposited me in a meadow. He said something, although I couldn't hear anything beyond the shrill noise in my ears. And then he left.

I finished the last dregs of my transformation alone.

Hours later, as the pain ebbed from my bones, I stared at a blue sky. It was still winter, and cold, and the grass had long since turned brown. But a promise of spring teased the air. The sun cast its warmth upon the earth. The breeze smelled of flowers—those that had bloomed early, perhaps hoping the warm days would stay.

I was all alone. Abandoned. And, as I would soon discover, I was no longer human.

4

CREEPIEST MOFO IN THE ANIMAL KINGDOM

ADDIE

"**O**h my God!" I spat the last bit of bile out of my mouth. Bleh. Lesson learned: spicy beef burritos (aka, my lunch) *burned like a bitch* on the way back up. "I am *so* sorry," I wiped the juicy chunks off my chin—*eck!* "That was disgusting. I did *not* mean to do that. But you...you, sir, are a savior and a fucking saint. And—" the words shriveled on my tongue once I got a good look at the man who'd rescued me.

The dude was small, with only a few inches of clearance over me. So he was five-foot-six (or five-seven if he stood on his tip-toes).

He placed a steadying hand on my shoulder (because I was swaying like an intoxicated moron). Which was nice of him, but the gesture gave me an eye-full of the shoulder holster he wore. And the sight almost made me puke again.

He was armed to the *fucking teeth*. Had to be at least a dozen knives strapped to his torso, if not more. Sheaths wrapped around both of his thighs, each holding hefty hunting blades. He also had two short and stubby swords strapped to his back. And the *clothes!* He really went the extra mile on this outfit: grungy leather breeches and a blood-stained gray shirt, cinched at the middle with a tooled leather belt.

What an *outlandish* getup.

A high-pitched, nervous laugh tore out of me.

The man said nothing. He took a knife out of his right thigh holster and used it to scrape my vomit off his knee-high boots.

"What is this? A *Lord of the Rings* cosplay?" My mind raced, struggling to find a rational explanation. But he didn't look like a *Lord of the Rings* character. More like a Viking. All he needed was the fur shawl.

Which still didn't make sense. Who dressed like this? Who walked around with that many knives? Guns I could've accepted. I wouldn't have *liked* to see guns, but at least they were somewhat normal.

And the rest of this guy's appearance completed the whole *Viking Viktor* vibe he had going on. His curly brown hair fell to his shoulder blades. He'd at least taken the effort to tie it back in a ponytail, but most of the sweat-slicked and frizzy strands had escaped the strap. His dark, wiry beard was slightly uneven, as though he occasionally chopped the ends off when it got too long, but didn't tend to it otherwise. A long, pink scar marred his left eye, turning that side of his face down into a permanent scowl. Which was a shame. Because he had gorgeous green eyes...

I squealed when the man abruptly spun around, plucked a teensy dagger from his chest holster, and hurtled it at another oncoming, black-armored rider. He stayed calm—like, *"oh, killing monsters? This is a normal Tuesday for me."* And he moved so fluidly, almost like a dancer.

As for me...

"Holy fucking shit!" I screeched when the (now riderless) black horse vroomed by us.

Viking Viktor chucked another knife, catching the animal in the throat. And the *gurgling* noise the horse made before it collapsed...

I clutched a hand to my stomach, fighting back a gag.

"Stay here," Viking Viktor said.

"W-wait—what?"

"Stay here." He sprinted in the direction I had just come from, heading straight for those...those...

What could I even *call* those riders? "Skeletons" didn't seem scary enough. And they weren't skeletons at all. They had skin. Not *normal* skin, but...

And the *blood*...

My stomach heaved itself into my throat as I remembered the overcooked asparagus flavor.

I inhaled slowly, and exhaled with a yelping, *"Gah!"* as a massive shape stumbled into my peripheral vision.

The black horse—the one I'd almost gotten carted off on—gimped its way through the trees. The reins were still wrapped around its forelegs, pinning its head down. It snorted, nostrils flaring, and made a low, pitiful whine.

It sounded like the awful meow a cat emitted before it hocked up a hairball.

Was that a normal noise for a horse?

Poor thing. It probably couldn't breathe properly with the way its head was cranked.

"Easy," I murmured as I stepped toward the horse. I didn't even sound like myself! My voice had gotten warbled. Like I was talking through a long pipe. "Easy."

It wasn't until I moved closer to the horse that I noticed the irregularities. Scales covered its body instead of fur. And it had bright red eyes. With slitted irises. *Cat eyes.* And the *teeth!*

"Jesus!" I sprang back when the horse snapped at me. It

didn't get far; only a few inches before it bellowed in pain, mouth gaping against the bit.

Two long, slightly curved fangs protruded from beneath its lips.

What the *fuck* was this thing?

The horse made the hairball hacking meow again as it strained against the reins. And no wonder they weren't breaking—they were *metal*. It looked like someone had strapped two bicycle chains to the horse's bit.

I sucked in a deep breath, wiping my sweaty palms against my dress. Okay, so this horse was the creepiest sonofabitch in the animal kingdom. Didn't change anything. It was still an innocent animal in pain.

If I could get the bridle off...

"Easy," I kept murmuring, hoping the horse couldn't detect the quiver in my voice. "Easy."

It watched me, its red eyes rolling, pointed teeth bared, but it stopped fighting against the restraint. Maybe it somehow knew I was there to help. I mean, its eyes seemed *too* intelligent. They roamed across my mid-section and focused for a long while on my hands, as though looking for a weapon.

Were horses smart enough to search for weapons?

"I can get that bridle unhooked for ya. Opposable thumbs, see?" I held out my hands and wiggled my thumbs. "They're handy in situations like this."

The horse gazed at my fingers again. It was unnerving as fuck. The animal was too *watchful*. Too human-like.

"It's okay," I said, taking a few more steps.

The horse cocked its head sideways, still studying me.

I raised my hands, brushing my fingers against the bridle.

With a squeal, the horse flattened its ears and whipped its head around.

"Whoa! Dude!" I threw myself backward. Just in the nick of

fucking time. A needle-sharp tooth brushed against the sleeve of my jacket. No skin broken—thank *God*—but that had been *way* too close.

"Y'know what?" I hissed as the horse writhed against the bit. "With an attitude like that, you don't deserve to be saved. Ever hear the expression *'don't bite the hand that feeds ya?'* Yeah, well, don't bite the hand that's trying to free ya either. Creepy-ass motherf—now that's not fair."

The horse lowered its head with a small whimper. It was so damn *pitiful.*

My heart clenched. "Are you trolling me right now?"

The horse whined again.

"You were two seconds from being freed before you went full Mr. Hyde—stop with that damn noise." I stepped forward. "I'll try again. But if you try to bite me again, I *will* leave you like this. No amount of crying will save you."

My fingers shook as I reached for the bridle. I didn't take my eyes off the horse. It kept its gaze trained on me. A stare down. And my opponent was eerily good at not blinking.

"I'm telling you..." I warned.

The horse's red eye rolled upward, gazing directly into mine.

I wrapped my fingers around the throat latch. "You got one shot. No do-overs. So don't blow it."

The horse flinched when I tugged at the buckle. Tensed. The tempo of its breathing changed, sounding like a racecar revving up for a trip around the track, but it kept still.

My fingers fumbled to undo the throat latch.

The horse's nostrils flared; its hooves shifted.

I had a few seconds before this animal detonated, and no clue which buckle had to come undone next.

"Fuck it." I snatched the top of the headpiece and yanked.

The horse threw its head back.

Somehow, it worked. It wasn't smooth (I accidentally wrenched one of the horse's ears), but it didn't seem to care. It spat the bit out. And once the bridle was off...

"Shit!" I dove to the ground as the horse let loose a growl that would've made Simba proud and bolted.

But this time, it wasn't trying to hurt me. It had just wanted me out of the way.

I sat there, mud seeping into the back of my dress as the horse steamrolled into the trees. The bridle clanged between its legs for a few strides before being kicked loose.

And then a *goddamn knife* hurtled toward the horse.

"Yo!" I yelled as the animal bellowed and skittered sideways, narrowly avoiding the oncoming blade.

Viking Viktor walked up to my side, a second knife clutched in his hand.

"What the hell is wrong with you?" I sprang up, karate chopping his wrist—

Okay, well, I didn't do a karate chop. I flailed my arms around like a whack-a-doodle and got a lucky shot. Still, it worked. He dropped the knife.

The horse disappeared.

Viking Viktor gave me a long, indecipherable look as he bent to retrieve his weapon. "Did it bite you?" he asked.

And, y'know what, for a weird Viking dude, *damn* if he didn't have a nice voice. Smoother than melted butter: a slow drawl with a slight accent that might've been Swedish. Or Norwegian? Or something else entirely. I sucked at guessing accents.

He sighed.

Wait. Shit, he'd asked me something, hadn't he? "What?"

"Did it bite you?" he repeated slowly.

"Ummmmm, it tried."

"Where?" He reached out, grasping my hand lightly.

"Whoa!" I flung backward. Why? Because, A.) he still held a knife and, B.) his calloused hands felt like steel wool scraping against my wrist. "The horse didn't *actually* get me—"

"You're sure?"

"—so what the heck was with the *V for Vendetta* act? Poor horse—"

"Answer the question. Are you sure it didn't bite you?"

"*Yes,*" I growled. "Why are you making such a big deal outta this?"

Viking Viktor stared at me, his eyes unnervingly calm, even as his fingers shuddered restlessly over his knife. "That was a venomous horse," he said.

Was he being serious?

"Their venom is a paralytic. One bite can leave you immobile for days. You'll be lucky to regain full use of your limbs afterward. So I hope, for your sake, you're telling the truth. Venom can sometimes be extracted from the wound, but only if it's done quickly. And you've wasted time arguing with me."

He said this so casually. Like he was talking about the weather.

Meanwhile, my head spun. Truthfully, I didn't think my head had *stopped* spinning since I woke up, but now it whirled around and around and around at a hundred miles an hour. Ready to fling right off the tracks. So, could I be blamed for what I blurted out next?

"What in ever loving *fuck* are you smoking?"

5
VIKING VIKTOR

Instead of answering my question, Viking Viktor walked into the tree line.

"We can't stay here," he called over his shoulder. "It's not safe."

"What do you—*hey!* Wait!" I sprinted after him, hissing when low-hanging branches whacked me in the face. Walking through the thick-ass underbrush was like trudging through quicksand. There were no paths or walkways to follow. Just bushes, tree stumps, roots, and random plants that may or may not have been poisonous—if I got poison ivy from this shithole place, I was going to be *pissed*.

And Viking Viktor moved way faster than me. Within seconds, I lost sight of him.

"Wait!" I barreled through another bush, sputtering as the evergreen thistles stabbed my tongue, and cried out when I collided face-first into something solid.

Viking Viktor's back.

To his credit, he'd at least stopped and waited. I mean, he

could've stopped out in the open, or called out to let me know where he was. But...small mercies, right?

And—*whew*, he stunk to high heaven. Like a sweaty gym bag that had been sitting in a hot car. Had he never heard of deodorant? Or soap?

"Please." I grabbed him when he started walking again. He had a cut on his forearm, above his wrist. The wound was red hot beneath my fingers, and it still seeped blood. But he didn't flinch when I touched it. He stopped and stared at me with those inscrutable eyes.

"Please," I whispered. "I'm, like, three seconds away from having a meltdown. I... where am I? How did I get here?"

He sighed. "This place is called Sakar."

Ummmmm...was that a real place?

"We're in Bafrus, one of our..." He trailed off, watching a drop of blood ooze from his wrist wound. "Bafrus *was* one of our countries."

Not helping...

"A Celestial sent you here."

Oh dear God...

"You're trapped here now, I'm afraid. As the rest of us are."

...this dude was definitely smoking something good.

"I'm sorry," he said, his voice flat. "The world you left behind was surely better than what you'll find here."

"What—"

"We need to keep moving." He tugged his arm out of my grasp. "There are too many Wraiths—"

"*W-wraiths?*"

"—and I need to get my soldiers to safety. If I can." He raised his gaze, staring at the snatches of azure blue sky poking out from between the trees. "If you want to come with me, you'll have to keep up."

He walked away again.

Chasing after him was stupid. This guy was, at the very least, a whack-a-doodle. At worst, he was a perverted serial killer. But...

The memory of the skeletal creature—on its *fucking poisonous horse*—sent a violent shudder up my spine, propelling me to stumble through the undergrowth after Viking Viktor.

He moved deftly through the woods, avoiding the vines, thorns, plants, bushes, and upturned roots. Meanwhile, I stepped over a teensy root and *thought* I cleared it with plenty of room. But nope. My toe rammed into the top and I stumbled forward with a strangled *oomph*, crumbling to my knees. Right in the mud, of course. Because finding a dry spot to fall was overrated.

Tears burned my eyes as I scraped the gunk off my dress. "So, Sakar's not in North America, right?" I asked Viking Viktor. "C-could it be in Europe? South America? Or...are there six or seven continents? I can never remember." My fingers itched for my phone. Lord Google would know the number of continents. Maybe it could even drop a pin on my current location...

My stomach made a fluttery *squitch-squatch*.

I couldn't remember where I'd left my phone.

Had I brought it into *Doughy Delights?* Probably not. I usually left it in the car's cupholder when I did quick food pickups. "Heh, that'll teach me, huh?" I swallowed. "I'll never leave my phone in the car again."

Viking Viktor said nothing.

"Is there an airport nearby?" I pressed. "Or, like, a boat dock—is that even what they're called? Boat docks? Boat ports?"

Silence.

My chest ached. "Seriously, if you'd let me borrow your phone—ten minutes, that's all I'm asking—I'll be outta your hair..."

Viking Viktor huffed. The end of his frizzy ponytail bounced as he ducked under a tree limb.

Rage bubbled inside my gut. "Oh, I'm sorry, am I *annoying* you?" I hissed a curse when that same tree branch whacked me across my temple. Apparently I didn't duck low enough. "Good," I rubbed at my stinging forehead, "you *deserve* to be annoyed, you stupid, fugly—what kinda game is this anyway, huh? Do you and your geek friends get your rocks off by dressing like warrior Vikings and medieval monsters and *kidnapping* people? Probably takes the sting out of the boring lives you guys run outta your moms' basements, right? I bet ya do the whole '*Man strong. Man rape woman*' thing too, huh? You get a power kick when you go full barbarian? You stupid sack of—"

Aaand, my mouth was off and running.

"I'm Addie, by the way," I hurtled at Viking Viktor's back after five (or ten...or fifteen) minutes of ranting. "Figured you should at least know my name before you pulled your pants down." I scraped sweat off the back of my neck—seriously, what happened to winter? It was like 90 degrees. *With* humidity!

Viking Viktor said nothing. He wouldn't even acknowledge my presence. So, when I saw another human being, I nearly jumped for joy.

The boy (he couldn't have been older than nineteen) leaned against a wide evergreen tree, one booted foot propped up against the trunk as he cleaned blood off his sword. He looked up as we approached.

The kid looked like he belonged on the cover of a YA novel. His golden-blond hair brushed against the tops of his shoulders and curled around his squared jaw. His eyes were the same vibrant shade of blue as the sky above us. He was tall and broad-shouldered. And he had dimples when he smiled.

"So that *was* a hybrid!" he exclaimed. He also wore a Viking cosplay outfit, but he didn't throw off the same *"I'm gonna pillage your town, rape your women, and eat your babies"* vibe Viking Viktor did.

Viking Viktor sighed and nodded.

"I told you!" The kid's beaming smile faded as I stumbled over a thick branch.

I'd automatically tried to return his smile, but I probably had the wild-eyed look of a slasher flick villain. Because seeing this boy—a handsome and otherwise normal-looking teenager, dressed in Viking clothes and holding a bloodstained sword...

The last tether holding my emotions at bay snapped. My vision blurred, and my lips wouldn't stop trembling. If this was a dream, I really, *really* wanted to wake up.

The kid stiffened and his gaze locked on my face. "But... she's...her..."

"I'm aware," Viking Viktor said brusquely.

The kid kept rambling. "And...an *adult?* Has an adult ever been—"

"We need to keep moving. Help her. Please." Viking Viktor waved his arm dismissively in my direction and disappeared into the trees.

"Not much of a talker, is he?" I grumbled. And then I flipped him off. Because...why not? I'd just been abducted. I was pissed. Flashing the finger wouldn't solve my problems, but it made me feel better. At least for a few seconds.

The kid stood beside me, still a little tense. But a bemused smile played across his lips as he watched my (immature) display. He bounced a few times on the balls of his feet, cast a nervous glance at the shrubbery Viking Viktor had vanished into, and said, "I'm Kaelan." He stretched his hand toward me.

Mud and blood had dried in cakey patches around his fingers, but I shook his hand anyway.

"Addie," I mumbled. "Hey, do you have a cell phone I could borrow? Your friend didn't. Or, he didn't want me to borrow it. But I'll be quick, I swear."

Kaelan's brow furrowed in confusion. His head tilted sideways.

My blood ran cold. "Oh, God. Please tell me you know what a cell phone is?"

"I'm sorry." And his blue eyes were downright doleful.

My insides bubbled with nerves. "How about a landline? A radio? Walkie-talkie?"

He gave me the same blank expression.

"Have you at least heard of America? The USA?" My pulse roared in my ears.

"These are things from your world?" he asked.

And either he was the greatest actor in the world—because his befuddlement seemed genuine—or...

My knees buckled as a violent tremor shot through my body. Sweat dripped down my back—a cold, clammy kinda sweat. My ears made a *whomp-whomp-whomp* noise.

I didn't even feel pain when my ass hit the ground. *Oh God. Ohgodohgodohgod.* I racked my fingers through my (now messy) braid. Did these people not know...*anything?*

"Easy." The boy, Kaelan, knelt beside me, his hands grasping my shoulders. Dried blood matted sections of his hair. *His* blood?

He had some cuts on his arms, and a large gash on his left thigh, but I didn't see any big wounds around his face or neck.

So was it someone else's blood?

That thought was somehow more disturbing.

"It's alright," Kaelan said. His words were soothing, but he kept staring at me like I had five heads.

I mean, it was warranted. I probably had mascara streaks on my cheeks and eyeliner smudges under my eyes. The droopy raccoon style didn't look good on anyone.

"It's alright," he murmured again.

I scrubbed a hand over my face. "It's *alright?*" I scoffed.

"You're not the first hybrid to arrive here."

"What?" My chest was ready to burst. And the forest twirled around me.

I grunted and pressed my brow against my knees. *Don't pass out. Don't—*

I whipped my head up with a yelp when fingers brushed against my right ear.

"Apologies." Kaelan drew his hand back and held it in front of him, palm open, as if to show me he was unarmed. "Only... you appear to have a barb stuck in your ear. It must be painful."

"A—what?" My hand flew to my ear. There was nothing there, except my—"Wait, do you mean this?" I traced my fingers over my barbell earring. Which was, indeed, a little silver arrow.

"Yes," Kaelan said.

"It's a piercing. Which hurt like a *bitch* when I had it done, but I've had it for years and it hasn't bothered me since."

His eyes widened. "You stabbed your ear *voluntarily?*"

"Oh, c'mon. You've never heard of piercings? I thought...I mean, it's a thing in a lot of cultures. Right?" I had a cottony feeling in my mouth. No matter how many times I swallowed, it wouldn't go away.

"And those markings on your arm..." Kaelan murmured.

I glanced at my right arm. At some point during my trek through the forest, I'd taken my jacket off and tied it around my waist. Which was disturbing because I didn't remember doing that...

Anyway, the fabric of my dress only covered my shoulder, leaving my full sleeve tattoo visible.

I was damn proud of this sleeve. It had taken me years to piece it all together, and it featured almost every nerdy, pop culture icon known to man: *The Goonies, Ghost Busters, The Iron Giant, Die Hard, Jaws,* and *The Nightmare Before Christmas*...to name a few. Multiple characters, from different decades and genres. I wasn't just a nerd; I was a badass nerd.

Kaelan tilted his head, still studying my arm.

"It's a tattoo," I said. "And yes, I did this to myself. *Voluntarily*. Paid hundreds of dollars to have people jab needles into my arm because I wanted to stare at this image for the rest of my life." Okay, well, that came out way harsher than I'd intended. I blew out a long breath. "Look, I'm—"

"Kaelan!" Viking Viktor's distant voice tore through the forest, cutting me off.

Kaelan sighed. "Can you walk?" he asked.

I nodded and allowed him to pull me to my feet. "I just wanted a fucking pizza," I whispered.

Kaelan held me steady when I swayed. "Pardon?"

"I had a pizza craving. That's the only reason I'm here. Because I stopped at *Doughy Delights* on my way home." A salty tear dribbled down my cheek. "And now my mushroom olive deluxe is getting cold on the roof of my car and—" I sucked in a breath that burned on the way down. Like a shot of whiskey. *Cheap* whiskey. "There are easier ways to get someone to start a diet, y'know?"

6

THE TOAD

LASS

T reached the forest as the sun dipped below the horizon and all traces of spring warmth vanished. The air turned bitterly cold. My clothes were still damp. Whether from the remnants of sweat, bile, or urine, I didn't know.

Above me, branches groaned and whined as the trees swayed in the wind. Animals yowled and slithered through the undergrowth.

My skin prickled as I wandered through the dense wood. A cold, heavy sensation settled into my gut, as though my bowels were cramping. Sweat dripped in a steady rhythm down my back, even as the frigid air cut through my tunic.

I'd never been outside in the dark before. Most humans in Detha weren't permitted to wander outside after sunset. As the Wraiths preferred to spend their evenings indoors (usually feasting on human flesh), only a scant number of guards patrolled our streets in the evenings. And they were less merciful than their daytime counterparts. 'Twas a death sentence for a human to be found outside their dwelling at night without just cause. And few causes were considered *"just"* in the eyes of the Wraiths.

So it was a peculiar thing, being outside at night. In the woods. Alone.

And, when secured in fear's iron grasp, the mind tends to ~~eaggerate~~—exaggerate. The hoot of an owl morphed into the braying shouts of a Wraith. The creaking of bushes became ~~ominious~~—ominous whispering.

I quickened my pace, desperate to find...something. A safe place to hide. A path out of the wretched wood. *Anything.*

The trees swayed again. Flutters of moonlight pierced the deep pools of blackness that had gathered beneath the trunks.

Rustle, rustle, went the branches.

I stopped, my belly suddenly feeling as though it were struggling to digest a rather large rock.

Rustle, rustle.

The noise seemed eerily similar to the flapping of wings.

Dim gleams of silver flitted across the dark ground before me. A scream rose in my throat, but I clasped a hand over my mouth before I vocalized it.

The pattern of moonlight was fractured. Feathered. As though filtering through a Celestial's wing.

I urged my weary legs into a run. I had no destination in mind, only the desire to put as much distance between myself and the Celestial as possible.

The vegetation thickened as I hurtled deeper into the wood. Thorns and twigs reached for me, their sharp edges digging into my skin, making me gasp. All the while, the branches above me continued to undulate and make that wretched *rustle, rustle* sound.

I only stopped when I emerged in a small clearing. The shadows were not so dark here. The moon provided more illumination. As I braced my hands on my knees and inhaled, my terror ebbed. The rational side of my brain emerged again.

Until the frog croaked.

A rather harmless noise. One that shouldn't have induced such heart-stopping terror in me. But it did. Why? Well, a person dying of the cough will develop a similar rasping sound.

Raaaph. Raaaphuh.

"Mama?" I bleated.

Raaaaphuh, croaked the frog.

"Mama!"

My feet slid against the grass as I galloped across the clearing. "Mama!"

It was foolish to hope. Mama was dead. I'd watched her demise unfold.

Her illness began gradually.

It started on the day of our first snowfall; always a ~~monumentous~~—momentous occasion. For the children, at least. I'm rather certain the adults felt nothing but fury as they stared at the white flakes. After all, they still had to complete their daily tasks, and the snow hampered their progress.

Mama was no exception.

We lived on a tomato field. The Celestials, of course, manipulated the soil; tricking it into thinking summer never faded—hence why tomatoes still grew, even as ice fell from the sky. The Celestials also gifted us with spools of mesh fabric to protect the plant life from the frigid air.

"'Tis material from the Celestial City, love," Mama had told me that morning as she unfurled the gleaming fabric and draped it over the vines.

I was ~~memorized~~—mesmerized as I ran my fingers over the silken-smooth mesh. But then the snow began swirling with renewed intensity and my focus turned to the layers of fluffy ice coating the ground. Such is the fickle mind of a young child.

Mama began coughing that day.

At first, it was a tickle that struck whenever Mama moved about in the winter air. She would clear her throat, cough a handful of times, and jest that she was developing an aversion to the cold. "Perhaps I'm turning into a Wraith," she said.

The thought was horrifying. I pictured a piece of Mama's soul escaping through her mouth each time she coughed. For how else did Wraiths lose their souls? "Mama!" I ran to her side, wrapping my arms around her midsection as tears burned my eyes.

"Hush, love." Mama stroked my hair. "I'm sorry...'twas only a comment made in bad humor. I have a touch of winter cough. Nothing more."

But the tickle worsened. Her coughs deepened. Mama's face grew paler and gaunter (is this a word? Gaunter?) as fever gripped her bones. Her lungs began emitting a wet, rattling noise when she breathed.

Soon, the cough took a firmer hold. Often, Mama would gag until she spat up a yellow substance she called *mucus*. Toward the end, she choked on blood.

In the final hour of her life, she staggered about our field, plucking tomatoes for The Offering.

I followed her, clutching our well-worn wicker basket, as she lurched between the rows of tomatoes, splattering blood on the Celestial's glistening mesh.

"You'll...be...alright...love." Each word was punctuated by either a wailing wheeze or a rumbling cough. She sluggishly plucked a tomato from the vine, inspected it with bleary eyes, and placed it in the basket. "We'll...finish...and...I need...sleep..."

Blood dribbled down her chin as she bent to retrieve another tomato.

"It's not ripe, Mama," I said. The tomato was green and dull. Not red and shiny as it should have been.

Mama swayed and placed the tomato in the basket. "Remember...love... sunset...don't...tarry..."

She could sense her life drawing to a close.

I could too. My fingers dug into the sharp edges of the basket while sweat pooled beneath my armpits. I began crying long before she collapsed.

And when she finally fell, after collecting only a handful of tomatoes, it was a traumatizing spectacle.

She vomited; spraying blood and bile over the vines, The Offering basket, me, and herself. Her chest made a strange *urk, urk, urk* noise as she struggled to breathe. Her pallid cheeks reddened; a vein pulsed at her temple.

I held her, sobs racking through my body as she suffocated, choking on her own bodily fluids. She toppled backward, bringing me down with her. I laid against her breast, screaming for help. The humans who lived nearby undoubtedly heard my calls, but no one came. The Wraiths, of course, offered no assistance. Why would they? Mama's death meant nothing to them. She was a human, indistinguishable from the rest, and entirely replaceable.

But the event tore my heart to pieces. I couldn't move afterward. My own lungs seemed to have been afflicted with disease as they struggled to bring air into my body. I laid there, curled against Mama's cooling corpse, while the sky above me darkened.

At sunset, the Wraiths came.

IN THE CLEARING, the frog croaked again. *Raaapuh.*

"Mama!" Tears streaked down my cheeks as I stumbled through the bushes. "Mama?"

It wasn't her. And I hadn't truly expected it to be. But when I saw that big, fat toad sitting at the edge of a small pond....

Raaapuh.

Rage gripped me. It chased the fear and the cold right out of my body. I'd never experienced such an emotion before, not even when the Wraiths grabbed my hair and tore me away from Mama's body. Not even as I watched those humans cooked over a fire.

But now...

The toad was a portly animal with bulging eyes. It didn't shy away when it saw me. It merely turned and leveled its gaze upon my face. Unafraid. Perhaps it was used to humans and had never been given a reason to fear them. Perhaps it thought me too young, too small, to do any harm.

The scream that burst from my mouth was raw and it clawed painfully at my throat. But I didn't care. I screamed and screamed and screamed. Because there was a hot, uncomfortable sensation curled inside my chest. Like a snake. Coiling and coiling.

My skin itched.

The toad blinked but still didn't move. *Raaapuh.*

"Shut up!" I yelled, clapping my hands over my ears. It drowned out the sounds of the toad, and the nervous twittering of the surrounding animals, but it didn't stop the memories. Over and over, I heard Mama coughing. Over and over, I saw her lifeless eyes staring up at me, her face covered in blood, her chest unnaturally still. I heard the harsh babble of Wraiths as they dragged me to Varn's home, their ~~skelatal~~—skeletal faces glowing through the darkness while they talked and laughed and jeered at me.

Over and over, I heard my own wails of pain as the Celestial's poisonous blood spread through my veins.

"Shut up! Shut up! Shut up!"

A hot, burning itch rippled across my skin. The snake-like sensation coiling inside me was poised, ready to strike.

The toad's bulging eyes were now fearful. Or, as fearful as a toad's eyes were capable of being. But his realization came too late. Before he leapt into the safety of his pond, I caught him.

"Shut up!"

The toad was cold and ~~slimey~~—slimy. I had no intention of hurting him. Truly. I'd only meant to give him a rough shake to quiet him. But it was too late for me as well.

Fire burst from my fingertips, consuming the toad.

I screamed again, this time in fear, and the animal slid from my burning fingertips.

He screeched and writhed as he hit the ground. Flames curled over his body, blistering his ~~slimey~~—slimy skin. I tried to put them out, but the fire remained wrapped around my fingers, and the more I touched him, the more he burned. In the end, I could do nothing but watch, helpless, as his body gradually stilled, and his cries tapered off.

The fire did not leave my fingertips.

It didn't hurt. Even as flame devoured my hands and

singed the sleeves of my tunic, my skin remained unscathed. But I couldn't extinguish it, and everything I touched burned.

"Help!" I flailed my hands through the air, sparks flying from my fingertips. "*Help!*"

But I was alone and too deep into the woods for my pleas to be answered.

7

PULLING NAMES OUT OF YOUR CHERRY-ANUS

ADDIE

Kaelan and I walked for another ten minutes. Maybe more. I was so focused on breathing and, y'know, not face-planting into the mud, I almost didn't notice the babble of voices filling the air. Not until someone bellowed, "Oi! Yer a right bastard. 'I need a headcount,' ye said. 'No one is allowed to leave,' ye said. And then ye and Kaelan disappear. That's two hundred and sixty-three now that ye've returned. It'll be two-sixty-four when Kaelan gets back."

Yikes. Someone was seriously P.O.'d.

We broke through the trees as the speaker shouted again, "Fitzroy, ye bloody moron. How many times did I tell ye to check that mare's shoe?" A woman stood between two towering oaks, her back toward us. She wore the same get-up as Viking Viktor and Kaelan (although her uniform came with a bow and arrows). Her red hair was twisted into a sloppy braid...

A lock of neon red hair had been the last thing I'd seen before my abduction.

My chest did a weird, fluttery thing. I didn't know if I was pissed, or hopeful, or both.

Was this my abductor?

But...no. This woman didn't fit the bill. Her wild curls were too carroty to match what I'd seen in my car window.

Drat.

As we moved toward her, I drew my eyes away from the back of her head and blinked in shock. She stood atop a gentle slope that led to a small clearing where *hundreds* of people were gathered (two-sixty-three, per her count). My jaw almost hit the ground.

This was like a full *convention* of Viking LARPers. They all wore the same type of clothing. They were all scruffy, dingy, and stinky (holy Christ, the stench was *awful*). And they all had weapons. Swords. Knives. Bows. Axes. Long pole thingys. And horses. Living, breathing, massive-shit-laying horses.

What the frick?

"Eh?" The woman whirled to face us. "What's that ye said?"

"Huh?" I gaped at her.

"That word ye—" The woman trailed off, her eyes narrowing as she scanned my face. She took a step back, freeing an arrow from its quiver.

Was she going to *shoot me?*

But she didn't grab her bow. She held the arrow in her hand and waved it in front of my face. "Oi, Kaelan! What's that?"

"A hybrid. I *think*." Kaelan's brow furrowed even as he gave me a small smile.

"My name's Addie," I said, but my mind got stuck on that word. *Hybrid.* That was the second (or third) time I'd heard the term. I hadn't thought much of it at first (too busy having panic attacks) but now... "You keep saying *hybrid*. Is that, like, the car?" I asked.

Kaelan shrugged, looking flummoxed.

The woman laughed and twirled her arrow through the air. "Car," she said, almost wistfully. "I haven't heard that word since I was a babe."

"So you know what a car is?" Hope surged in my chest.

"Only vaguely, I'm afraid," she said. "I remember me mam saying that word. She must've had one. They're horseless carriages, are they not?"

Pffft. My hope deflated. Like a balloon getting jabbed with a needle. Horseless carriages? Cars hadn't been called that in at least a *century*.

But she *knew* the word. So maybe she wasn't as coo-coo as the rest of them? "Hey, do you have a—" I started, but Viking Viktor (the heartless bastard) chose that moment to make a reappearance.

"Did Braxton ride back to the city?" he murmured as he strolled up the hill to the woman's side.

And, damn, this chick was *tall*. She easily had six inches of clearance over Viking Viktor.

The woman rolled her eyes. "Aye, he did."

"Didn't I say—" he started.

"Ye don't follow yer own fecking rules. Why should we?"

"Belanna," Viking Viktor stopped and pinched the bridge of his nose.

"Maeve isn' here," the woman, Belanna, kept twirling her arrow. She looked relaxed. Carefree. But her jaw ticked as she lifted her chin and glowered at Viking Viktor. "Likely the poor lass is dead, but Braxton needed the closure."

Viking Viktor's shoulders rose and fell with a heavy exhale. "Regardless, the city isn't safe—"

"And neither was the field. But ye went back there...*without* informing me, I'll add."

"The field?" I asked. "You mean the fucking *murder* scene back there? With the dead bodies and Skeletor things and—"

"As you can see," Viking Viktor cut me off, "there's a new arrival."

The tone of his voice was...flat. Impersonal. Dismissive. He talked about me like I was an old lamp he was getting ready to toss.

Belanna pursed her lips. "There hasn't been a new hybrid in years. What's yer power?" She turned to me.

"My—*what?*"

"Yer power," she repeated. "If yer a Healer, I might kneel and kiss yer feet. Marcel's also dead," she added to Viking Viktor.

He said nothing. Just dropped his gaze and hunched his shoulders.

"So if ye can heal, ye'll be everyone's favorite person." Belanna wagged her arrow in my face. "But other powers will be useful too. We're not in a position to refuse hybrids. So what's yer power? Are ye an Illuminator?"

"A Concealer?" Kaelan suggested.

Belanna's eyes lit up. "Yes! Dead handy, Concealers are."

My left eye twitched. "Concealer—like *makeup* concealer? I've got some of that in my bag. But, well, that's in my car. Along with my phone. And my car's not here..."

Belanna and Kaelan gave me blank stares.

Viking Viktor wasn't looking at me. His eyes never stayed still! He glanced at us, the soldiers at the bottom of the hill, the trees, the tops of his feet, back to us...

It was a wonder the dude didn't make himself dizzy.

Belanna frowned. "Surely ye have a power?"

"Oh my God." I dropped my head into my hands, digging

my fingers into my aching temple. "The hell kinda game are you guys playing here?"

Belanna turned to Viking Viktor. "Ye sure she's a hybrid?"

Viking Viktor tilted his head, surveying me speculatively. He'd started twisting his beard around his fingers. Something he did often, judging by those frayed ends. A nervous tic. "The Celestials sent her. I'm certain of that," he finally said.

"I saw the light too," Kaelan added.

"*Light?*" I asked. They ignored my comment. Surprise, surprise.

"But if she's powerless," Belanna tapped the tip of her arrow against her chin, "why is she here? What bloody sense does that make?"

Viking Viktor shrugged.

"Did they make a mistake?" Belanna asked.

Viking Viktor stared at me, still fiddling with his beard. "They never have before."

"Could she have a power she doesn' know about?"

"It's unlikely. But possible."

"You've got to be fucking kidding me." I raked my fingers through my hair, digging my nails into my scalp. "People don't have *superpowers*. I mean, unless you count being able to consume an entire large pizza as a superpower..."

"What is a pizza?" Kaelan asked. "You used that word earlier too."

"It's only the best invention since the goddamn wheel!" My voice sounded screechy. "And it's been around for, like, *centuries!* How do you not know what pizza is?"

"Poor lass." Belanna rested the arrow against her shoulder. "Yer looking unsteady. Best be careful ye don't fall."

I didn't even realize how much I was swaying until Viking Viktor reached for my arm, trying to stabilize me.

"No!" I flew backward and immediately regretted it when

the earth tilted sideways. I weebled. And wobbled...but I didn't fall down (har, har).

Viking Viktor started to say something (likely my name), but I cut him off. "*No!* I—" my breath hitched as a spasm clutched my chest. "Fuck, I think I'm having a heart attack." Black spots burst before my eyes as I doubled over, bracing my hands on my knees.

"Ye want water?" Belanna asked.

"No," I grunted.

"Ye want somethin' stronger?"

"Can I? Wait. No. Don't tempt me. I'm not desperate enough to take drinks from strangers. *Yet.* I'm—I'm freaking out here, okay? Like, where am I? Real answer this time. Don't pull a random word out of your ass and call it a country. Who are you people? Is this a cult? It's totally a cult. Right? That's why you've never seen cars, or cellphones, or *pizza. Jesus*...look, I won't tell anyone. You won't have the cops breaking up your pervy lifestyle. Scout's honor. I—*I just want to go home.*" I gasped as I finished because I'd spouted the words at warp speed without taking a breath in between. My vision blurred. I blinked rapidly and got the tears under control, but my breathing was still out of whack. With every inhale, my throat made a *hic-hic* noise. And it hurt.

Viking Viktor watched me, his nose slightly wrinkled, as though someone was holding a bag of cat shit beneath his nostrils and he was trying to block the smell. Or like he was thinking hard enough to make his brain melt. "I can't answer you," he said, "if you don't give me a chance to speak."

I straightened up, thrumming my hand against my too-tight chest. "Well, I'm done now. The floor's all yours." Until I got my breath back, at least.

"This place is called Sakar, as I've already mentioned."

Viking Viktor had such a *slow* drawl. Took him for-freaking-ever to get the words out.

I was gonna have a heart attack before he finished talking.

"More specifically," he continued, "we're in the country of Bafrus—and I assure you, none of these names were *'pulled out of my ass.'*"

Ooh, that smug, snarky bastard.

"Unfortunately, the capital city, Cynerik, has been overrun with Wraiths. The rest of Bafrus isn't fairing any better." Viking Viktor swallowed. "We're moving the survivors to Netheridge."

"N-Netheridge?" I stuttered.

"Our neighbor to the east," Belanna supplied.

At the same time, Viking Viktor said, "The largest country in Sakar."

My head was officially spinning. *Again.* "You guys are trolling me, right?" These names had to be made up. *Had* to be. I mean, *Bafrus?* Sounded way too close to Barf-us. *Netheridge?* Did a nine-year-old pick that one?

I turned, half expecting someone to jump out from behind the trees and shove a camera in my face. *Surprise! It's the new reality show! Chubby girl gets thrown into an epic sword-and-sorcery fantasy. Will she survive? Start streaming to find out!*

But there were no cameras. I couldn't even see power lines or any evidence of modern technology. There was just the sky, the trees, and the weird Viking people.

Kaelan stared at the ground as he dragged the toe of his boot through the dead leaves. Belanna had a sad smile on her face, and her gray eyes were amiable, but she said nothing.

"Cars," Viking Viktor droned, "cell phones and pizza are things from your world. They do not exist here." He continued twining his finger around the frazzled ends of his beard. "If I could send you home, I would. But a Celestial brought you here, and only a Celestial can bring you back. It's likely you'll never go home again." For a second, he almost looked sad. But then a shadow passed over his face. His mouth hardened as he dropped his hand away from his beard. "And I have *never* raped, nor thought about raping, a woman."

I blinked. "Wait, what?"

"It was one of the questions you asked earlier. Although I don't know how you expect a person to respond when you're never quiet."

Oh shit, had I actually asked that? *Out loud?*

I needed duct tape. Lots and lots of it.

"I'm—" I started.

Viking Viktor spun on his heel. "Kaelan, go saddle your horse. Belanna, make sure *she* stays quiet." He put his hands on his hips, examining the people at the bottom of the hill. "I'll be back." He jogged down the incline, his hair bouncing with each step.

Anger—hot, bubbling, almost painful rage—surged through my veins. It came out of nowhere. I suddenly wanted to grab the end of that ponytail and *rip it off.* "Fucking Viking asshat," I whispered. "I bet you *do* get off on scaring the shit outta women."

I hadn't meant for him to hear that, but the dude had ears like a hawk. He stopped dead, his shoulders bunching up again.

"Shit," I started. "Look, I'm sorry, I—"

"You'll stop calling me *Viking.*" Viking Viktor turned to face me again. "My name is Cheriour." He stepped forward, dropping his voice into little more than a whisper. "I understand this is new to you, but your boorish behavior stops now. Or I *will* leave you behind."

This time, when he walked away, I stayed silent. I didn't want to. I wanted to scream *("Cheriour? You definitely pulled that name out of your cherry-anus.").* I wanted to cry.

Instead, I silently clenched my hands into fists until my knuckles popped. This was nuts. Bona fide insane. Celestials? People with superpowers? Different worlds? A dude with a name that sounded like cherry-oar? This shit didn't happen. Not in real life. I mean, the teenage-kid-discovers-magic-land trope was present in almost every popular movie, TV show, book...*everything*. But no living person had ever actually discovered magic, or alternate realities, or fantasy worlds. And I was too freaking old to go on an *"adventure."*

My lungs tightened again.

*This isn't real. It's not real. There's a rational explanation—*there *has to be.*

And yet, everything *felt* real. Like the still-drying patches of mud and blood on my clothes. The sticky warmth of the breeze as it dried the sweat on the back of my neck. The heat of Kaelan's hand as he pressed it against my shoulder. "I'm sorry," he mumbled before he walked away. "No one ever wants to come here."

A sickening ball of dread festered inside my gut.

None of this, logically, could be real.

And yet, I couldn't convince myself it wasn't.

8

DROP-LANDED FROM A UFO

ADDIE

"**Y**ou worthless bitch! Why can't you keep your damn mouth shut?"

"Addie's a bright student. But, well, there've been issues. She argues with the other children, and she's constantly talking back to her teachers."

"Addie, sweetie, I wish we could find you a family. But with your record..."

"OMG. Addie, girl, I love you. But you get us in trouble every damn time we go out."

An array of foster parents, teachers, social workers, employers, and friends pranced before my mind's eye.

Okay...so I had a track record of being mouthy. But it wasn't *intentional.*

Kid me hadn't been able to control my verbal outbursts. At all. I vocalized *every* passing thought. Most of the time, I didn't even realize I was talking.

Adult me had more restraint. *Usually.* But in one afternoon (or evening, considering it had been nighttime when I went to get pizza) everything had come undone. Viking Viktor

—*Cheriour* had gotten blasted with a full stream of word vomit. And actual vomit as well. I didn't blame him for being pissed. But...

I wanted to go home! My lower lip trembled. I wanted my mushroom and olive pizza and a glass of wine (maybe the whole dang bottle). I wanted to sit on my squishy couch and binge-watch bad reality TV until my brain melted.

Sure, my life wasn't all sunshine and roses, but it was *my* life. And, in the blink of an eye, it had been taken away from me.

So, I was being a little (a lot) rude. And I definitely shouldn't have accused Cheriour of raping women. But how was I supposed to react? Did he expect me to be *happy*? *"OMG, this is so exciting! It's been a lifelong dream to trade in all the conveniences of modern America and come to Viking Land where monsters exist, and everything smells like horseshit. Best. Day. Evah!"*

Speaking of horseshit...

"Oh no," I mumbled as Cheriour strolled back up the hill, leading a small, brown horse.

I hoped to *God* he didn't expect me to ride that animal.

"Belanna." Cheriour rubbed at his temples. "Can you please help Darren get the wounded on horseback?"

I totally forgot Belanna was standing next to me, so I nearly jumped out of my skin when she spoke. "He complainin' again?" she asked.

"Always," Cheriour said.

"I'll go sort him out. Oi!" She shouted as she walked away. "Stop staring! Some of ye were new arrivals once. Ye didn't like to be stared at then, did ye? No. So mind yer manners!"

I blinked.

I hadn't even noticed a group of people were gawking at me. And it wasn't a *"hey, who's the new kid?"* kind of stare. They looked at me in absolute shock and horror, as though I'd drop-landed from a UFO.

At Belanna's shout, they dispersed, but a few of them still cast sidelong glances at me as they tacked their horses.

"We're leaving in ten minutes," Cheriour called as he came to a stop in front of me. The little horse halted too and blew out a long puff of air, its nostrils flaring. Its (adorable) ears swiveled back and forth.

"This is Sacrifice." Cheriour flipped the reins over the horse's head.

"That name sounds ominous as fuck," I muttered. And it didn't suit the little horse, who was *so* stinking cute. Especially with its facial marking: a crooked white stripe that ran between its eyes and tailed off on the right side of its nose. It looked like a drunk tried to draw a straight line down the horse's face.

"She's the quietest horse here," Cheriour continued. "Sacrifice won't shy or spook, but she is sensitive. Do *not* pull on the reins. Or kick her. There's no need to. She'll follow the group."

The horse lowered her head and batted her eyes. Almost as if to say: *don't listen to him. I'm an angel.* But then she pinned her ears and squealed because a horse walking at the *bottom of the hill* had pissed her off. What a *bitch.*

"No, no, nope." I waved my arms through the air and backed away. "You're crazy. *Crazy.* I can't ride a horse. I never even figured out how to ride a *bike* without training wheels. So I—I'll wait here and try to flag down the next airplane..." I retreated into the trees. "There's bound to be one at some point, right? And there are plenty of branches here. I can find an empty spot to spell *help...ooof.*"

A calloused hand snatched the scruff of my neck, dragging me back to Sacrifice's side. "If you stay here, you die," Cheriour said. "Give me your foot."

"That's a daring thing to say. How about I shove my foot up your—hey!"

Cheriour grasped my left leg and tossed me into the air. With another *"ooof,"* I landed belly-down over Sacrifice's back.

"Swing your leg over," Cheriour commanded.

I stared at the ground, which seemed dizzyingly far.

"Swing your leg over." Cheriour pressed his hands against my ass, pushing me upward.

"Hey! Hey!" With a grunt, I brought my right leg up, ramming my knee into Cheriour's chin.

He grunted.

"Oops," I said, my voice dripping with sarcasm.

Also, thank *fuck* I wore leggings under this dress. Otherwise, Grumpy Pants would have gotten an eyeful of my flowery underwear.

Once I was straddling Sacrifice and sitting upright, the dizziness only got worse. This was way too high. Sacrifice's back was way too narrow. Her mane was too snarled for me to get a good handhold.

"I want to get down," I said.

"You can't." Cheriour stroked Sacrifice's neck. "We'll be leaving in—why are you pulling on the reins?"

Sacrifice had moved her leg. Kinda.

Okay, she bobbed her head.

But I thought she was getting ready to bolt (spoiler alert: she wasn't) so I did a panic-snatch of the reins. Which she didn't appreciate. At all.

"Whoa, whoa!" I shouted as she flung her head up, ears lying flat against her skull. She felt like a coiled spring beneath me, ready to explode. My knees dug into the saddle, sending pain shooting down my joints. "I don't—seriously, I *cannot* ride a horse. This won't end well."

"Be still, Addie," Cheriour droned. "And let go of the reins."

"But—then how do I stop her?" I asked.

"You don't have to." Cheriour pried the reins out of my hands and twined them around Sacrifice's neck, wrapping the ends in a knot. Making it so I couldn't use them. "She knows her job. Let her do it. If you feel unsteady, hold on to the saddle."

My hands shook as I clutched the pommel of the saddle. My knuckles popped. But Sacrifice quieted almost immediately. She exhaled, lowered her head, and turned to level me with a haughty stare. "Bitch," I mumbled.

She seemed to think the same thing about me.

"Are you calm now?" Cheriour asked me.

"Not really."

"Well, I still need to get my horse saddled," he continued. "Stay here. Don't touch her reins." The bastard had the audacity to raise his finger at me. Like a teacher scolding a disobedient student.

"How 'bout you stop being a prick?" I grumbled under my breath. Although I was sure he heard me, he said nothing as he walked away.

My heart pounded. Like, *ready to burst out of my chest, Alien-style* kind of pounding. I couldn't breathe. Red blotches tinted the edges of my vision. Pressure built behind my eyeballs.

I focused on taking deep inhales as I stared at the crowd around me, really looking at them for the first time.

There were a *ton* of people. Two-sixty-four, according to Belanna (*five* with me added in). It hadn't seemed like a lot, but staring at them now, all clustered together with their horses...

My stomach curdled. These people looked like they'd climbed to the top of Mount Doom and took a detour through Oogie Boogie's casino on their way back down. So many were injured, and those injuries ranged from broken bones and head contusions to truly gruesome stuff. I mean...*shit*. One guy had a chunk of flesh missing from the side of his neck. As though something had taken a bite out of him.

I thought of the skeletal rider (a Wraith? Or some other awful monster?) who'd called me a *"meal"* and shuddered.

Another woman had lost her lower leg. The stump was wrapped in multiple layers of bandages, and already bleeding through. The woman screamed when a man put her on a horse. He got in the saddle behind her, holding her steady while she buried her pale, sweaty face in her hands and cursed.

Was she really going to ride like that? *Jesus.*

"Oi!" Belanna's voice carried over the crowd. Which was impressive, considering she was at the other end of the clearing. "Three minutes!" She stood beside a massive black stallion, holding him still as he pawed at the ground.

The flurry of activity increased.

Apparently horses required a lot of last-minute adjustments. Cinches had to be tightened and the saddle bags secured. Horseshoes had to be checked—one kid was using the blunt end of a *sword* to hammer a nail into his horse's hoof. The blade waved dangerously close to the kid's face.

I looked away. The last thing I wanted to see was that boy poking his own eye out.

As people mounted up, most horses ended up carrying two riders: one who was severely wounded and one who was slightly less injured.

These people weren't LARPers. They were real-life soldiers. Warriors. And they'd survived a battle that, judging by the field I'd woken up in, had been *savage.*

Did fights like that happen often around here? How many people had died? How many more would end up perishing from infection or blood loss? And *no one* wore helmets, so death from head trauma after falling off a horse was a real threat too.

That was likely the fate that awaited me.

I pictured myself nose-diving into the ground, my skull splitting on a rock, brains splattering...

I swallowed.

This place was hell. It had to be. Stinky, terrifying, hot-as-balls...*hell.*

My lungs tightened again. *Breathe! In. Out.*

Wait...

I watched as a man placed a little boy atop a gray horse. That pudgy kid, those chubby cheeks...*ho-ly shit!* It was the kid from the field! He was still *alive!*

For a second, my racing pulse slowed. Tears—this time *happy tears*—welled in my eyes.

"Away!" Belanna yelled as she swung onto her stallion and sprinted off.

With a sound like rumbling thunder, the rest of the soldiers nudged their horses into a gallop.

I had just enough time to see Cheriour leaping onto a broad chestnut horse, settling a wounded kid in the saddle in front of him, before my steed lurched down the hill.

"Whoa!" I yelled. "No, don't—whoa, easy! Go slow? Please?"

Sacrifice pricked her ears and chased after the rest of the horses, ignoring me. Her hooves ate up the ground. The wind whipped through my hair. The muscles along her back rolled and bunched as my ass smacked against the hard leather saddle.

I held her mane in a white-knuckled grip as we cantered behind the group of soldiers, weaving in and out of the trees. *I'm gonna die. Definitely gonna die.*

9

TERRICK

LASS

I scorched every blade of grass and destroyed several proud and beautiful trees. The plumes of smoke drove animals from their homes and sent them on a mad scurry to find safety.

"Help!" I screamed until my voice turned coarse. *"Please! Help!"* My fire-wrapped fingers trembled.

The ashy fragrance of smoldering wood and plant life filled the air. Some animals choked or sneezed as they darted through the vapors. It was only after a family of frogs hopped away from me, their eyes bulging, that it occurred to me I was standing near a pond.

"Water is fire's enemy, love," Mama had once said when she'd mended a burn on my palm.

I stepped into the pond, gasping when the cold water bit my skin and plunged my head beneath the surface. It hurt to open my eyes underwater, but I did it anyway, and I blew bubbles when I began crying in relief. The fire was gone!

But it returned once I attempted to step out of the water.

I dove under again. The fire left.

I emerged again. The icy wind lashed across my wet skin, seeming sharp enough to leave wounds.

The fire clung to my flesh, refusing to relinquish its hold.

The cold made my chest tight and sluggish. The water rocked my body, forcing me to shift my feet to maintain my balance...

I screamed when the soft bottom of the pond abruptly vanished, sending me plummeting deep into the water. My arms and legs flailed. Not in an organized fashion, as I didn't know how to swim. These were short, panicked movements, which only made me sink more quickly.

I glanced up, seeing the dim light of the moon shining at the surface. No matter how hard I fought to reach it, the water fought harder to push me down.

Black spots danced before my eyes as my lungs tightened. I reached a hand up, desperately trying to grasp onto something, *anything*, that would help pull me from the water.

I jolted in surprise when my fingers brushed against a soft, yet solid, object.

Another hand.

I was hallucinating, surely.

Fingers wrapped around my wrist. It was a big, powerful hand, and it pulled me to the surface.

The cold air seared my skin and slid like molten metal down my throat.

"It's alright," a voice said in my ear as an arm curled around my shoulder. "Lass...it's alright."

The fire did not return. Perhaps it had fled after being so close to death's embrace. Perhaps it found my waterlogged body a weak host. Regardless, I had vanquished the flame.

And I fainted before my savior carried me to shore.

THE FIRST THING I remembered upon waking was the pain. A band of pressure wrapped around my head. Every time I moved, it tightened. I was sure my skull would buckle. I'd seen enough people die from head injuries to know how horrific it looked. Blood would seep from every ~~orfice~~ orifice: my eyes, nostrils, ears, and mouth. My head would become misshapen, and my face would swell...

"Easy," a voice said as something cold and wet pressed against the back of my neck. A damp scrap of fabric. Oh, it was bliss! The water trickled over my heated skin, cooling me, and easing the pain.

"Try not to move, lass," the voice murmured again. A hand brushed against my shoulder. "This will pass."

And it did, although not immediately.

For several days I drifted in and out of consiousness—conciou—conciousness (I've never fully mastered the spelling of this word). I drifted in and out of *sleep* (I'll use a word I can spell correctly). The pain in my skull refused to abate. It spread, traveling down my neck, across my shoulders, and into my joints. Each time I woke, I cried out, unable to lift my head or open my eyes. And then the voice would speak again in its soft and soothing manner. The damp cloth would drape against the back of my neck, and I'd slip back to sleep.

"'Tis a fever, lass," the voice said on the fourth (or fifth, or perhaps sixth) time I'd awoken. "Rest. Do not fret."

When I next crawled out of the murky depths of sleep, my eyelids felt as heavy as stones. The dim light of the morning sun drove scalding needles into my head. Tears blurred my vision, and nausea clawed at my stomach, but I kept my eyes open.

A figure moved toward me, but I couldn't make out his features until he knelt on the ground beside me. It was a man —a *human* man.

"Easy," the man said when I tried to sit up. "Easy." He had a deep, rumbling voice.

It reminded me of a boy in Detha who had once lived a few dwellings away from Mama's. He'd been little more than a child, but his booming voice had sounded decades older. Conn, his name had been. He'd always been so gentle, so kind, especially to the younger children.

He'd died before he reached adulthood.

But the man who knelt before me now...

"You're so *old!*" I blurted.

In Detha, people seldom made it to adulthood. Those that did often didn't survive *long* into adulthood.

So it was quite a shock to see a man this old: his dark skin crinkled with age, his hair stark white.

The man chuckled. The wrinkles around his eyes deepened when he smiled. "I suppose I am, yes," he said. "To your eyes, I must seem ancient."

I watched his gnarled hands as he wrung water from a piece of fabric. "Who are you?" I asked.

"My name is Terrick." He pressed the cool cloth to the back of my neck. "And it's nice to see you awake. You were firmly in the fever's grip. I—you," he sighed. "Do you remember what happened? At the pond?"

I did. But I said nothing.

"Were you trying to start a fire, lass?"

I remained silent.

"You may have been too close to the bushes. That's why you lost control over it. But fortune was with you that night.

Had I not seen the smoke, I wouldn't have been able to save you."

So he didn't know. He thought I'd been trying to kindle wood. He hadn't seen the fire erupting from my skin.

I didn't know whether I was relieved or disappointed by this revelation.

"I can show you how to safely start a fire, if you'd like." Terrick pressed a hand to my shoulder. His palm was massive; he could have wrapped his fingers twice around the thickest part of my arm.

And it was only when he touched me that I realized how shaken I'd become.

The tremors ran along my spine, aggravating the ache in my skull. I whimpered and squeezed my eyes shut.

"It's alright," Terrick pulled the blanket tighter around me. I hadn't even realized he'd given me a blanket. He'd also given me fabric to pillow my head and had laid me in a small stone cave, where I was shielded from the worst of the elements. He'd taken care of me.

"What's your name, lass?" Terrick asked.

I opened my mouth to respond, but I couldn't remember.

No matter how many times I combed through my memories, I couldn't recall my name. Mama had hardly used it, preferring to call me *love* or *darling*.

But others had used my name, hadn't they?

Why couldn't I remember?

"It's alright." Terrick wrapped his warm fingers around my trembling knuckles. "Perhaps it will come to you later."

I shook harder. I didn't like this man; didn't like how big his hands were, how he seemed to tower over me, how solidly he was built. I was accustomed to the people of Detha, who'd often been little more than walking skeltons—skeletons. And I wanted...

"Mama," I whispered.

Terrick's weathered face drooped. "I don't know where your mother is," he whispered. "Do you remember where you saw her last?"

In our field, her lifeless eyes gazing at the sky. Her skin growing cold—not immediately, of course. But I'd sat by her side for hours, praying she'd wake up. "'Tis but a cough, darling," she'd told me when she first became ill. Her hands, even then, were icy as she stroked my cheeks. "I will not allow it to be stronger than me. Besides, I have you, don't I?" She smiled, although it was ~~tremorless~~ tremulous and didn't reach her eyes. "Your love will keep me alive."

But she hadn't been stronger than the cough. And my love was worthless because it hadn't stopped her from dying.

"Easy." Terrick's massive hands reached behind me, pulling me into a sitting position.

Tears slid down my cheeks.

"It's alright," Terrick's bear-like arms pulled me against him, pressing my face into the solid slope of his shoulder. "You're safe, lass," he murmured. "You're safe."

He held me as though I were made of glass and he feared I would shatter. But his kindness, his gentleness, and his soothing voice only strengthened my sobs.

I cried until my chest and stomach hurt. Until it seemed as though I had expended all the fluid in my body. I cried until my eyes were swollen and a sticky feeling coated my tongue. All the while, Terrick held me, his body warm, his arms encircling me. Protecting me.

10

THE NINJA TURTLES ARE INVOLVED?

I was certain of two things.

One: traveling on horseback sucked, and I was 100% not wearing the right bra for it. Plus, I had a teensy thorn stuck beneath my left boob, and it was driving me *insane!*

Two: I was in deep shit. With every hour that ticked by (and I swore time moved at The Speed of Snail to spite me), it got harder to hold on to my slim hope of finding a way home.

The landscape surrounding us was...well, *wild*. Almost completely untouched by humans. We traveled across muddy ground and overgrown sections of forest, often barreling through thick trees and bushes. There were no houses, roads, gates, fences, or *any* sign of civilization. There were only trees. More trees. Bushes. Grass. And the occasional steaming pile of horseshit.

I mostly traveled alone, flopping around on top of my horse (it was a wonder I hadn't broken the poor thing's back), shrieking whenever we went too fast or went down a steep hill. I probably (definitely) annoyed the crap out of everyone. The soldiers certainly kept a distance. And they whispered. A lot. Which grated my already raw nerves because I *knew* those low, babbling murmurs were about me. Especially since some soldiers would occasionally turn to give me long gawping stares.

Cheriour stayed several yards behind me. He said nothing, even when I tried to prod him into a conversation: "How are you not sweating your ass off wearing all that leather gear? Seriously, what's your secret? 'Cause I'm looking like a drowned rat over here."

I never got a response.

I was like the town leper no one wanted to go near. Which might've been a blessing in disguise. Because a noxious, stomach-churning smell kept wafting back toward me. And I didn't think the odor was coming from the horses...

Anyway, after *at least* six hours on the road from hell, Cheriour finally paid me a visit.

We'd slowed from a trot to a walk, giving the horses a breather as we navigated through another dense section of forest. More trees. Yay!

I never wanted to see another fucking tree again.

Sacrifice picked her way through the underbrush, her sides heaving beneath my legs. My *very* sore and cramped legs. Jesus. Muscles I didn't even know I had ached.

I glanced over as Cheriour drew his strapping chestnut stallion alongside Sacrifice. He made a weird *tsssk* sound when Sacrifice turned and flashed her teeth at his horse. She glowered at Cheriour, flicked her tail, but faced forward again.

"We'll be stopping soon," Cheriour said.

The boy riding with Cheriour grunted, as though responding. Which was impossible because the kid was out cold. His mouth gaped open as his head lolled back onto Cheriour's shoulder.

The kid wore the same Viking army uniform as the rest of

the soldiers. Although his was saturated with blood. Likely because his body had more holes in it than Swiss cheese.

The boy was *maybe* fourteen.

Anger frothed inside me. "Is that kid in your army?"

Silence.

"He is, isn't he? For fuck's sake, do you really force Teeny Boppers to fight?"

Cheriour tightened his grip on the boy's shoulder. "Don't comment on things you know nothing about."

I huffed out a sigh. "Then how 'bout you fill me in on some stuff? Because I'm flying blind. And, I'll be honest, I'm *not* a happy camper right now. My ass is numb. I've got underwire digging into my boob, and a thorn stuck somewhere in my bra. My head hurts. I want to go home. But you're telling me I *can't* and keep giving me half-assed answers for why I'm here. *'The Celestials sent you.'*" I failed miserably at mimicking his droning accent, but he didn't acknowledge it. "Well, *why?*" I pressed. "Who the fuck even *are* the Celestials? Why do they send people here? I just..." I sighed again, squeezing my eyes shut to stem the tears threatening to spill over. "Please," I added. "I know you explained some things earlier. And I swear I was listening, but *nothing* makes sense right now. Can you go into more detail? Or something? Help me out here. *Please.*"

I opened my eyes to see Cheriour staring off into the distance, totally not paying attention.

"Were you even listening?" I snapped.

"Of course," he said in a bored tone.

"Oh, you're a real—"

He whirled to face me again. "If you'd like an explanation, you'll need to let me speak."

I snapped my jaw shut, squashing the next thing I'd been about to say ("you're a real sack of shit").

Cheriour sighed and, when the boy in front of him groaned

again, he ran a hand over the kid's shoulder. It was a compassionate gesture. Almost tender. My heart clenched. Okay, so maybe the dude wasn't a *complete* sack of shit. Didn't mean I had to like him.

"I'm accustomed to giving this explanation to children." Cheriour leveled me with an unreadable stare. "They are easier to teach than adults."

"Why is everyone so shocked I'm an adult?" I grumbled.

"You don't act like one," Cheriour said softly. I almost didn't catch it. *Almost.*

I shot him a glare. His mouth twitched, but I couldn't tell if he was fighting a smile or warring with the desire to scream and smack me off the back of the horse.

Probably the latter.

"Har, har," I said. "What am I *supposed* to be? A toddler?"

"Yes. All the hybrids were children when they arrived here." Cheriour touched the kid's shoulder. "Liam was only three."

I swallowed as I stared at the unconscious kid. He'd been trapped in this hellhole since he was *three?*

"We once had thousands of hybrids in the army, each pulled from a different world or timeline," Cheriour continued.

"Pulled from different worlds *and* timelines?"

"Yes."

"But how is that possible? And they all have powers?"

"Celestials bring them here," Cheriour said. "A hybrid has the power of the Celestial who created them. In a limited capacity. Liam," he tapped the boy's shoulder again, "is an Illuminator. He creates light. But only for a few moments. It's useful when fighting or traveling in the dark."

"So what's your power?" I asked. "Being an ass—"

"I," Cheriour cut me off, "am not a hybrid. Not all of us are. In fact," he tilted his head toward the group in front of us, "hybrids only make up a quarter of my army now. Perhaps less. Most of them have died."

I stared at the soldiers as they chatted amicably to each other. A lump formed in my throat. "So, they arrived here as kids, and you trained them to become X-Men?"

"To become what?"

"It's...never mind." I glanced at the boy. The kid's head bumped against Cheriour's shoulder as the horses walked over the uneven terrain. "Do they get a choice? Can they say no?" *Can I say no?*

Cheriour's mouth thinned but he said nothing.

Welp, I had my answer.

"Why?" I asked. "Why would you put them through that? You ripped them away from their *families* so they could die in your stupid battles?"

"We don't take them."

"It doesn't matter. You still force them to *fight*."

"Again, you criticize something you don't understand."

I huffed and resisted (barely) the urge to flip him off.

"You're angry we train children to fight," Cheriour continued, "but you don't ask *why*."

"Okay. I'll ask now. Why?"

Cheriour's mouth twisted. "Your world has seen wars, I'm sure."

"There's always a war going on. According to the news, anyway."

"We are in the middle of a war here."

A shudder started at the base of my spine. "Yeah. With those—*Wraith* things, right? What *are* they, anyway? Demons? Zombies? The one who'd tried to nab me looked like Jack Skellington on steroids."

"The Wraiths," Cheriour said, ignoring my outburst, "are humans..."

"Are you shitting me? No, they aren't..."

"...without souls."

"I—*what?*"

"They are humans," he spoke more slowly, "who traded their souls."

"Traded them for *what?*"

"A painless existence. Wraiths are incapable of feeling emotion."

"All emotions? Or just things like fear and—"

"They have no soul," Cheriour repeated. "They feel *nothing.*"

"Why would someone do that to themselves?"

Cheriour stared straight ahead, his jaw ticking. "This world is not kind. Some prefer to live an empty existence. But the Wraiths are fodder; they are easy to kill. Celestials are not."

I blinked. "Aren't they the ones sending mutant kids to *your* army?"

"Yes."

"Then...I'm so confused." I knew I was nursing a concussion. But, man, this conversation had amped the headache up a few notches.

Cheriour's mouth did that twisting thing again. Like he was struggling to get the right words out. "There are *two* Celestial armies at war with each other."

"Oookay, so who are the good guys? If they're both Celestials..."

"It's...complicated." He sighed and tilted his head back, staring at the sky. A breeze trickled through, ruffling the frizzy strands of hair that had escaped his ponytail.

There was something about him just then. I didn't know what. Maybe it was his posture; the slumped, yet tense, stance of his shoulders. Or the tender way he held the wounded boy. Or the look on his face: a far-away, almost wistful expression.

Whatever it was, I felt like I was seeing him—*really* seeing him—for the first time.

He was not much older than me, but he looked ancient. Frail. Exhausted. As though he'd endured centuries of unending trauma.

So this time, when he talked, I kept my thoughts to myself.

"Celestial lore is present in nearly every culture," Cheriour said after a long stretch of silence. "I'm sure you've heard versions of it, yes?"

I nodded when he lowered his head and turned those toneless eyes toward me.

"This is because *Celestials* are present in every culture." He refocused his gaze on his soldiers. "They reign in the Celestial City, tasked with breathing life into humans, animals, insects, and vegetation. They are also responsible for the plagues, storms, and other disasters that destroy life. Whatever is needed to maintain balance." He paused. Pursed his lips. "Celestials are the Guardians of *all* Creation. And living things must eventually perish."

OMG. I had *so many* questions.

I sank my teeth into my tongue. Nope. I would *not* start running my mouth now. Not when he was finally talking.

Although, with his drawl, this conversation would take about a year.

My tongue ached as I dug my teeth in further.

Cheriour's gaze traveled endlessly over his soldiers. Tension rolled off him in waves, even as he continued in his unhurried cadence. "One Celestial, Ramiel, sought to use the power of the City for...other endeavors. He tried to declare himself King, even though the City has no solitary ruler."

There's one in every crowd.

Cheriour turned to me.

Fuck. "Did I say that out loud?"

"Some," his lips jerked, but he ignored my comment otherwise, "were eager to bow to Ramiel. Either they agreed with his philosophies or believed they would gain from his rule. The rest allied themselves with Raphael—"

"Ooh, the Ninja Turtles are involved?"

"—the most vocally opposed to Ramiel's ideals. This war began in the Celestial City. Had it remained there, catastrophe would've ensued. So Raphael lured Ramiel out of the city and trapped him here." Cheriour glanced at the heavens again. "Thus, humans were brought into the war. Ramiel began taking souls to create his Wraiths. Raphael," Cheriour's chest expanded as he inhaled, "created the hybrids, using them to help protect the rest of humanity. It worked. For a time." His jaw clenched. "Until an event forced Raphael to recall his soldiers to the City. There have been no new hybrids since. Liam was one of the last."

The metallic taste of blood filled my mouth as I wrenched my teeth out of my tongue. "The Ninja Turtle up and left? After he drop-kicked this fight to your doorstep? What a *jackass*. And this is the good guy?"

"It's not so simple," Cheriour said. "Raphael's priority was always to protect the Celestial City. If Ramiel were to succeed in his quest and regain access to the City..." He hesitated, furrowing his brow. Like he was constipated and straining to crap out the words. "This world won't be alone."

"The fuck does that mean?"

"Humans believe time to be a linear line." Cheriour's voice was now slower than a sloth creepy-crawling up a tree. "But it's vast. And complex. The past, present, and future exist simultaneously. Humans are too *limited* to see this. Celestials are not. Ramiel and his army are the exceptions. As long as they cannot return to the Celestial City, their powers are restricted. They cannot travel to different eras, nor can they seek refuge in another world. They are confined to Sakar and must live as humans do: experiencing time linearly."

"Well, that's *not* confusing. At all." I needed some Ibuprofen. At this rate, I'd need the whole freaking bottle to calm my raging headache. "Okay, so if Ramiel beats Ramiel—er, that's not right. Their names are *way* too similar. If he beats *Raphael,* what happens?"

"All of humanity will experience a fate similar to this." Cheriour gestured to his army. "Or worse. The life you knew before coming here, your home, will cease to exist."

I swallowed, picturing a Celestial—although what did they even look like? Fat little angelic cherubs? Big monsters like the Witch-King of Angmar?

I envisioned the Witch-King (with wings) smashing into cars, destroying our tallest buildings, gnawing, breaking, hacking, burning...

Okay, I'd officially seen *The Lord of the Rings* too many times.

My stomach soured.

Was a scenario like that even possible? Couldn't be. That stuff only happened in movies. Right?

Then again, traveling to a different world (or timeline, or wherever the heck I was) shouldn't have been possible either.

"So," I cleared my throat when my voice cracked, "you guys —the humans. And hybrids, I guess. You're fighting—"

"To live," Cheriour said. "Nothing more."

"But if you win the war—"

"We can't." Cheriour's posture changed, going ramrod straight. "Only Raphael and his army can claim that victory. We can win battles. If we do, we're granted another day to live. If we lose, we die."

My stomach did a nervous twist. "So why am I here?" Because this was the important question, wasn't it? Definitely the most selfish one. But it had been churning in my head since I woke up in that field.

Why was I here?

Cheriour shifted in the saddle and stared at me, his eyes cool, even as his jaw tightened. "You are..." he started, but then he stopped. Took a deep breath. "You—" he paused, his brow crumpling. "I'm not certain. But I suppose you're here to die. Along with the rest of us."

II

STALKED BY A GODDAMN HORSE

ADDIE

After dropping that massive bomb (*"I suppose you're here to die."* Seriously???) Cheriour exited stage right. "I need to speak with Belanna," he said, cutting off the slew of questions ready to erupt from my mouth.

He cantered to the front of the group, leaving me alone while my head reeled.

I tightened my fingers around Sacrifice's mane, glancing at the now-dark sky. What I wouldn't give to see a plane. Or a satellite. Something normal. Rational. Something that gave me hope.

There were just the stars. And the waning moon. Which looked *exactly* the same as back home. Just brighter, without the city lights and pollution stealing their thunder.

What a freaking disappointment. The least this crappy world could've done was give me something fun to look at. Like a neon green moon, or a row of alien planets peeking out from behind the stars.

"Whoa!" I yelled when my *noble steed* slammed on the

brakes, flinging me onto her neck. "What—oh, shit, are we stopping?"

There was a wall of halted horses and riders in front of us.

"Thank God," I mumbled. My ass had taken a beating today.

Belanna's booming voice drifted back from the front of the group: "We'll stop here. Four hours only."

Four hours? That was it? Well, I wasn't gonna waste any of those precious two hundred and forty minutes by staying in the saddle.

I swung my leg over but my muscles were rubbery and sore, and it was a long drop. My feet smashed to the ground, my knees buckled, and I landed on my butt with a pained *"ooof."*

A few soldiers chuckled. Not a cruel *"haha you suck"* kind of laugh. They seemed genuinely amused. Perhaps a little sympathetic. In response, I grinned and pushed myself back to my feet, brushing mud and dead leaves off my ass. "Oops. And I haven't even started drinking!"

That got a few more laughs.

"Are you alright?" The blond-haired boy, Kaelan, walked toward me, leading his chunky gray horse.

"Other than my poor dress getting ruined, I'm good." I spun around. "How bad does the back look? Do you think it's salvageable?"

He tilted his head as a chuckle tumbled out of him. "There is quite a bit of mud, I'm sorry to say."

"Damn." I scrubbed at my butt more rigorously, but most of the dirt had already settled into the fabric. "Seems silly to be worried about a dress, huh?" I huffed. The kid probably thought I'd lost my marbles. Or maybe he thought I'd never had them to begin with. (Sometimes I questioned that myself). "I mean, you guys fight monsters and are holding this world together with duct tape, and I'm worried about a $25 dress. It's pretty damn stupid, right?"

Kaelan's eyes were kind as he surveyed me. "The dress is from your home. There's no shame in being attached to it."

I sighed, my fingers curling around the edge of the skirt. There was a hole by my left hip. Probably from when the Wraith had nabbed me earlier. "It's not just that, it's..." I had this feeling in my throat; like I'd gulped down too much food.

The first time I saw *The Nightmare Before Christmas,* I'd been six. And on enough meds to take down a horse. After what happened to my parents...I had issues. Like night terrors, explosive anger, excessive word vomiting, and anxiety out the wazoo.

My first foster mother, Freda, took me in, even though she already had two foster kids. She used to say she liked *'my spark.'* But I was a major problem. I threw daily temper tantrums and sometimes scared the other kids. Rather than beating me into obedience like...well, some of the others, Freda seemed to understand why I lashed out. And she made it her mission to help me reach a better headspace.

On a muggy October afternoon, six months after I arrived at her house, she'd popped the *Nightmare Before Christmas* on the TV and watched it with me. While also letting me eat a big-ass bowl of cookie dough ice cream for dinner. The other kids had been at after-school events, so I'd had Freda all to myself.

It'd been the best day ever. At least for kid me. It was the first time I'd fully relaxed in over a year.

And Freda loved *The Nightmare Before Christmas.* She watched it non-stop in October, November, and December. She hummed *This is Halloween* whenever she cleaned. Her favorite cardigan featured Jack Skellington, Zero, and Oogie Boogie. And a red-suited Jack perched atop our Christmas tree every year.

Her obsession eventually became mine.

God, I had loved her.

But the people we loved the most usually didn't stick around.

"It must hold a special place in your heart," Kaelan said. His soft voice made me jump.

"It does." I smoothed my hands over the grime-coated dress, blinking back tears. "So," I cleared my throat, "what's with the pit stop? I *want* to take a breather. Trust me. But if it's only four hours, why bother? We'll get to wherever we're going a lot faster if we keep moving. Right?"

"The horses need rest. So you'll need to take Sacrifice's saddle off. I'll help!" he beamed at me, grasped Sacrifice's bit, and led her to a cluster of trees. "Cheriour said you've never untacked a horse before." He secured the animals to a low-hanging tree limb, keeping a sizable distance between Sacrifice and his horse.

My arms ached just looking at the clunky leather saddle. And the half dozen or so saddle bags. "I've gotta take that all off?"

"It's not so bad," Kaelan chuckled. "I'll show you. Once we're done, make sure you rest too," he continued. "Niall is still a several days' ride from here."

"Sev—you mean *hours*, right? Several *hours*?"

"Days," he repeated.

Exhaustion hit my bones like a battering ram. *Days?* One afternoon of bumping around the woods on horseback had been brutal enough. I had to do this for *days?*

And there was another problem, which presented itself after Kaelan helped me heft the two-ton saddle off Sacrifice's back.

"Aw crap," I groaned as a twinge shot through my bladder.

"I'm gonna guess there're no toilets out here, right? Porta potties? Anything?"

Kaelan's blank look was all the answer I needed.

Wonderful. *Great.* I'd always wanted to take a piss out in the woods while surrounded by hundreds of strangers.

I hated this fucking place.

SLEEPING WAS out of the question.

On a good night, it would've taken me an hour to drift off. At least. Shutting my brain down was a slow process.

This was *not* a good night.

I laid on the hard ground. Roots, rocks, and twigs dug into my back. My body hurt. I needed my ultra-plush mattress. And my body pillow. And my air purifier. A TV wouldn't have hurt either; some background noise to drown out my misery.

Instead, I listened to the horses snorting, shuffling, and sloppily gulping up grass, while also surrounded by a cacophony of humans snoring, grunting, and farting. (Aka, the worst white noise sounds ever).

And few people had some serious stomach issues. Because, *phew,* there was a toxic cloud hanging over this camp.

Tears stung my eyes as I stared at the starry sky.

Fatigue made my body ache, but my mind kept swirling, going over the *what-ifs.*

What if I'd gone home after work? Or had gotten a craving for Chinese food instead of pizza? What if I had asked Bo to walk me to my car? Or if I'd parked in a different spot?

What if I'd done just one thing differently? Could I have avoided this whole nightmare?

Those kinds of questions could drive a person mad.

I wiped at my wet cheeks but stopped as a new sound drifted toward me. A noise that sounded like a cat's hairball-hacking meow.

Mowow.

Didn't the venomous horse make a noise like that?

Mowow.

I sat bolt upright.

The guy sleeping on my right side grunted, burped, and rolled over. No one else stirred.

Ice ran through my veins. Should I scream?

A twig snapped.

Were we about to be under attack?

Mowow.

Or was I hallucinating?

Why was no one else moving? These were ultra-powered Viking soldiers! Shouldn't they have been trained to sleep light and listen for signs of danger? Instead, they were all snoring away. Useless lumps.

Mowow. Snort.

A massive shape lumbered through the trees. A horse. Definitely. It was saddled, but riderless. *And* bridle-less.

The horse I'd set free?

The animal snorted again, its red eyes glowing eerily in the dark. A long, pointed tongue slithered between its lips as it watched me. Longingly. Hungrily.

"You've gotta be shitting me." I scrambled away, grunting when my back collided against a tree trunk.

The horse's ears pricked. It took a step forward. Two.

Whoosh!

An arrow hurtled through the trees. The horse keened, flashed its creepy-ass fangs, and pivoted, avoiding the blow.

Whoosh!

Another arrow went flying. And then another.

The horse bolted. The stirrups clanged against its sides as it weaved through the trees.

"Ye alright?" Belanna knelt beside me, resting a palm on my shoulder.

"Jesus!" I clasped a hand over my heart as it went *whomp-whomp-whomp* at record speeds. Heart attack. That was *definitely* gonna be in my near future.

The guy on my right grumbled again. He lifted his head to stare at me blearily before he flopped down and carried on sleeping.

"Ye alright?" Belanna asked again.

"No," I mumbled. "No, I'm not *alright*. But I'm alive, so I guess that's something." My heart wasn't slowing down. It *hurt* as it hammered against my breastbone. "That—that horse..."

"It's following yer scent."

"What?"

"Cheriour told me ye freed a Púca—a very foolish thing to do. Monstrous creatures, Púcas are."

"*Pooka?*"

"Aye. And ye got quite close to that one. It learned yer scent. I saw it following us earlier, but the damn buggard is too fast. And too smart. I can't get a clear shot. Anyway—" she thumped my shoulder again.

I winced. Belanna's *friendly* smacks were hard enough to bruise.

"—if ye see it again, and I'm sure ye will, kill it."

"Kill it?"

"Aye."

"With what? The power of my mind?"

"Ye haven't got a weapon?" Belanna's brow furrowed.

"Oh...sure. Yeah. Y'know, I totally forgot about the machete

I have stashed in my bra." I tapped my palm against my forehead. "Silly me."

A smile flashed across Belanna's face. "Here." She reached into her leather vest and pulled out a piddly knife.

I took it from her. The blade was barely longer than the palm of my hand. "Thanks, but what am I supposed to do with this? Poke the horse in the eye?"

"If ye can. It's a small target, to be sure, but it'd bring the beast down. Ach, don't worry," she ruffled my hair. "I'll be watching out for it too. But it's always best to be prepared."

With that, she gave me another bone-rattling thwap on the shoulder and walked away.

CHERIOUR WAS the worst travel companion ever. Dear *Lord!* The dude didn't respond to *anything* I said. And, the next morning, I really tried to get a conversation going.

"Do they make cushy seat covers for these saddles? Because my butt is *killing* me."

"Okay, but Ibuprofen is like the miracle drug, y'know? I wish you guys had some."

"Is a horse supposed to shit so much? Or does Sacrifice have an irritable bowel?"

Like, c'mon, those were all decent conversation starters.

"You guys ever heard of vitamins? And how vitamin deficiencies mess with your body?" I said this as I choked on an ultra-dry cracker. Kaelan had called it *hardtack* when he'd shoved it in my hand earlier. It'd been the only item on the menu for breakfast.

Well, there'd also been a mystery-meat jerky that looked

like dried tar. But who knew what kinda havoc that would wreak on my stomach?

"Bleh." I sprayed a bunch of still-dried crumbs when I talked. Most of it ended up in Sacrifice's mane. "Oops," I chuckled when she flattened her ears. "Sorry! Anyway, there's no nutritional value in this. None. Not that I care about food being healthy. But it should at least taste good, y'know?"

Cheriour said nothing.

When I looked over my shoulder at him, he had this odd, mouth-puckered look. Like he was trying not to laugh.

Or trying to hold in a frustrated yell.

We'd been riding for hours. Judging by the sun, at least. It'd still been dark when we hit the road, and now the sun sat high in the sky.

"Fuck, it's hot!" Sweat trickled down my back. "You know it was almost winter when I left home—"

A gurgling noise sounded behind me. I turned as Liam, the boy riding with Cheriour, started choking. And then vomiting.

In three calm movements, Cheriour halted his horse, dismounted, and laid the boy on the ground.

"Is he—" I started.

"Eimear!" Cheriour called to a woman on a pudgy brown horse riding a few feet in front of us. "Tell Belanna to stop."

The woman nodded and cantered away.

"Hunter, Timothy!"

Two middle-aged men turned when Cheriour called their names.

"Check the wounded." Cheriour kept his head down, stroking Liam's back as the boy spat up mouthfuls of blood. "Pull the ones who aren't faring well. Leave the ones that are."

"Aye." One man nodded.

"And tell Cathal we'll need more yarrow and calendula."

The two men rode off as the rest of the army halted.

"You," Cheriour waved a hand in my direction, "can dismount. Don't untack, but loosen her girth."

"Uhh," I started

"Kaelan!" he called.

"I'm coming!" Kaelan had already dismounted. His blond hair bounced over his shoulders as he jogged toward us, leading his disgruntled horse. "Braxton said you read his mind," Kaelan said to Cheriour. "Elijah and Jane are ill too—"

"They've all gone too long without healing." Cheriour's mouth was set in a hard line. "I'll need your help in a moment. For now..." he gave me another dismissive wave. Like he was saying, *please get the annoying bitch out of my hair.*

Kaelan nodded. "There's a stream nearby. We'll get the horses watered."

"Take mine as well." Cheriour held out his horse's reins.

"Of course." Kaelan grabbed the rein and led his two horses into the trees, motioning for me to follow.

I slid to the ground, squealing when pain rocketed from the balls of my feet. "Goddamn. Does this ever get easier?"

Behind me, Liam retched again. I turned, tugging on Sacrifice's reins, moving her closer to Cheriour. "Do you need—"

"Take care of your horse, Addie." Cheriour tugged at Liam's shirt, inspecting the seeping wounds underneath.

"But I—"

"Take care of your horse." There was no anger in Cheriour's voice, but his tone left no room for argument. He'd given me an order. And he was used to having his orders obeyed.

It felt like a rock had plopped into my stomach.

Blood glistened on Liam's chin. He made strangled *huck, huck* sounds when he breathed. The kid was literally *dying.*

But it wasn't like we could roll up to the nearest urgent care and ask for help.

"Addie!" Kaelan said. "The stream is over here."

Sweat slicked my palms as I led Sacrifice deeper into the woods, following the sound of Kaelan's voice. She walked docilely beside me, her head bobbing next to my shoulder. Until—

"Whoa!" I squealed when she flung herself backward, nearly ripping my arm out of its socket. "What gives—aw, fuck."

A dark shadow slithered through the trees on my left side. A distinctly *horse-shaped* shadow.

Sacrifice gave a nervous, wet snort, spraying boogers all over my arm. I didn't care. Because the shadow had pivoted to face me, its red eyes flashing through the trees.

The goddamn Púca.

"Shit." My nails dug into my palms as I held onto the reins for dear life. Sacrifice kept going backward, shaking her head, desperately trying to get the bridle off.

The Púca flicked its ears toward me.

"Kaelan!" I screeched. "It's—the—*help!*"

But by the time he circled back to get me, the Púca was gone.

I was officially being stalked. By a goddamn horse.

Fuck my luck.

12

MUTINY

LASS

Terrick, as it turned out, was...

"A hybrid," he said.

"There's no such thing," I sniffed. The boy from Detha, Conn, had told us stories about them. Hybrids. Humans given Celestial powers. But Conn was *always* telling stories. Mama used to say he had ears sharper than a two-edged sword.

"That boy misses *nothing*," she would groan whenever I'd repeat one of his tales. "Don't mind what he says, love. He ~~eggaerates~~ exaggerates."

"And yet, I *am* a hybrid." Terrick winked and plucked a stone off the ground. "Watch." He stretched his arm out, cupping the stone in the palm of his hand. It was a small rock, caked with dirt.

And then it vanished.

I gasped, reaching for his hand.

The stone was still there. I felt its jagged edges when I traced my fingers along Terrick's palm, but I could not *see* it.

"I'm a Concealer." Terrick fluttered his fingers, and the rock reappeared.

I took the stone from him, pressing it against my nose to inspect every crevice and flake of dirt on its surface. "You've tricked me. Somehow," I accused.

Terrick laughed. "I have not. It's my ability. To Conceal; to make objects, or people, seem like they've vanished, even when they're still in front of us. Here..." He grasped my hand and pressed it to the ground.

My fingers disappeared before my very eyes. They were still there, of course, but they'd adapted the same color and stringy texture as the brown grass. When I shifted my hand to grasp the stone, my skin changed again, this time appearing as gray and coarse as the rock.

I touched my other finger to the back of my Concealed hand. My skin remained smooth and pliant, despite looking jagged and rigid.

All the while, Terrick kept a light hold on my wrist. His fingers grew cold and sweat-slick as I poked, prodded, and marveled at my Concealed flesh. Once he let go, my hand returned to its normal shape and color.

I stared at him, excitement simmering in my chest. "Can you Conceal the bush next? Or the tree?" I pointed to a thin pine.

Terrick laughed, even as he wiped a trickle of sweat from his brow. "No, lass. My abilities are not so powerful. And not nearly as ostentatious as what other hybrids can do. Especially the Illuminators! They are quite a marvel to behold. Aiden is an Illuminator—he is my neighbor. Well, it has been a few years since I left Swindon, so I *hope* he is still my neighbor."

I swallowed. This wasn't the first time Terrick had mentioned this place. *Swindon.* He'd been journeying there when he found me.

"You're recovering your strength quickly now. And you've kept your meals down for the second day." Terrick's palm rested upon my shoulder.

I had, indeed, successfully consumed three small meals of berries and dried meats, after days of fighting with a ~~rebelus~~ ═rebellious stomach that had rejected everything I ate. This was a good thing, Terrick kept telling me. It meant the last of the fever had left my body.

But now my stomach began churning again.

"I'd imagine you'll be well enough to travel in a few days," Terrick continued. "You'll *adore* Swindon, lass. There are no Wraiths there..."

A Wraith-free city.

Conn had spoken of this notion before. Only once. And his words had come with dire consequences.

"THERE ARE Celestials on our side. Not many, mind. But enough. And humans once fought beside 'em, they did." Conn's hands flew through the air as he recited his tale. It was dusk, and adults often sent small children away from their dwellings while The Offering was prepared. Conn was always eager to keep us entertained. He'd seen us gathered in the alleyway between the rows of dwellings and had sat on the cold, muddy ground beside us. As Conn was only a few years away from adulthood, he looked abnormally long and gangly as he hunched in that dark alley with us young ones.

"'Twas a land not far from here. The humans there said, 'we don't want to serve the Celestials.'" Conn swiped a hand through his gnarled brown hair as he continued. He was too exuberant to be still. "And the Celestials—the good 'uns—they said 'help us win and you'll get your wish.' So the humans—they weren't much for fighting, mind—they made their own weapons and stood beside the Celestials. 'Tis said Ramiel 'imself was there..."

A few children squealed in fright. I stayed silent, only because my heart seemed to have taken residence in my throat.

It was a name we knew well. Ramiel. The Conqueror. The Celestial we all feared the most.

"Ah, but 'e did not have a mind to attack the humans," Conn chuckled at our terrified faces. "'Twas his brethren he wished to fight. So the Celestials fought each other, and the humans fought the Wraiths—ah yes," he whispered when another murmur of fear traveled around the group. "They fought *Wraiths*. They were brave souls, them humans. Many lives were lost. But the humans won. And they was given the freedom they asked for. Never again will Wraiths haunt those lands. Never again will humans go hungry while Celestials feast on their crops. They are *free*." He became breathless, his dark eyes glistening with excitement. And, naturally, he'd gotten the children tittering (this is a word, is it not?) with ~~exhileration~~—*exhilaration* as well.

We loved Conn's stories.

But such tales were not permitted in Detha.

Two days later, Conn was whipped until his back was torn and bloodied.

Open wounds became angry wounds if not tended properly, Mama always said. Angry wounds led to fever.

Conn's wounds became angry.

The last time I saw him, he staggered through the alleyway where the children gathered at dusk. His normally sun-kissed face was whiter than a fresh sheet of snow. Sweat dripped from his brow, despite the winter's chill. His fever-bright eyes were focused on something in the distance. He did not stop. We called out to him, but he ignored us.

Death visited him that night.

A week later, a group of boys—Conn's friends—mutinied.

Ice coated the ground that morning. I slid on it as I stepped outside our dwelling.

"Careful, love." Mama grasped my arm as a wet cough bubbled inside her.

Above us sat a heavy, gray sky. Something cold slithered inside my gut, although it was not caused by the dull, early morning light.

Dread. Mama had always called that sensation *dread.*

She seemed to feel it too. Her fingers trembled around my arm.

"Mama—" I started.

"Hush," she hissed.

The boys emerged from the alley, armed with sharp slabs of wood. A few had strapped pieces of tree bark to their torsos, an attempt to mimic the Wraiths' armor.

Mama's breath shuddered as the boys crossed the street, gathering by Conn's dwelling.

Other families emerged from their dwellings. Some returned indoors when they caught sight of the boys. Most carried on with their chores but cast worried glances at the cluster.

A few brightened at the prospect of a mutiny.

"Ah," a rosy-cheeked woman exclaimed. She placed her hands on her hips, surveying the boys. "And you'll think you'll kill Wraiths with them stakes, eh?"

One boy, the tallest in the group, clutched onto his shard of wood so tightly, his knuckles whitened. "No. But we'll all be dyin' soon anyway, so why not try? It's what Conn would've wanted."

The rosy-cheeked woman nodded grimly. "Agreed." She returned to her dwelling but re-emerged a moment later wielding a broad piece of firewood. "And I'll be joinin' ya. I'm getting too bloody old to be making bread for those ungrateful sods. These hands aren't what they used to be, but they've got some strength left."

Others joined. Soon the group of mutineers boasted almost two dozen members.

Mama's hand never stopped trembling. She did not move to begin her chores. Nor did she join the mutineers. She simply stood still, her lips drawn into a tight line. "Inside," she whispered to me.

Her head whipped to the side when Wraiths marched down the street. Their black armor glinted in the gray light.

The mutineers, now trembling, brandished their wooden weapons. "We'll not be workin' today," the tallest boy yelled.

"You tell the Celestials they can make their own bloody bread," the rosy-cheeked woman spat.

"We work this land," a broad man said. "We tend the animals. This is *our* city."

"Inside. Now!" Mama shoved me through the door, ignoring my protests.

"Mama!" The inside of our dwelling was dark and quiet. The slippery sensation inside me grew, threatening to crawl up my throat. I dug my nails into the closed door, wanting, *needing,* to be back outside with Mama.

"Stay there, love." Mama's voice quivered. "Don't come out. No matter what you hear."

I never asked why Mama remained outside. Likely she feared she would be seen as a mutineer if she failed to begin her chores, but she wished to shield me from the bloodshed. I saw it anyway.

Through the narrow wooden slats of our door, I watched as the group of mutineers attacked.

The humans were ill-equipped and too weak to battle the Wraiths. The minutes-long ordeal turned into a ~~massacer~~ —massacre.

Afterward, half of the ~~rebelus~~—rebellious humans were taken alive, and screaming, to Varn's house. The rest were left to die on the street.

We were not permitted to tend their wounds, give them water, or ease their suffering. Instead, the Wraiths gathered us in a half circle around the mangled bodies and forced us to watch as they gasped their final breaths.

But that was not the last time I saw the mutineers.

The rosy-cheeked woman found me on the day Mama died.

Her skin had turned gray, her cheeks hollow. Her white eyes roamed apathetically (this is spelled correctly, is it not?) over me as I cowered by Mama's body. She was a mere shadow of the woman she'd once been. But I recognized her voice as she cited my crime: failing to prepare The Offering.

The woman ignored my frightened wails and shrill pleas as she took me to Varn. There was no compassion or sorrow left in her. How could there be? She no longer had a soul.

She'd been amongst the group taken to Varn's house on the day of the mutiny. And they had turned her into the very thing she'd sought to destroy: a Wraith.

Some fates were far worse than death.

"Lass?"

I startled as Terrick clasped a weathered hand to my shoulder. "You've gone pale."

I turned away, tears burning my eyes.

"We can wait if you'd like," he said. "I've plenty of food and supplies still. Winter is leaving us. We need not go to Swindon right away. We can wait until you're ready."

I wouldn't *ever* be ready.

I'd seen what happened when humans tried to break free of Wraiths, and I didn't want to know what atrocities awaited me at Swindon.

13
LOST MARBLES

ADDIE

I'd lost my marbles.

It'd taken three days, but the marbles were definitely gone.

Because when I'd left the sloped meadow to use the little girl's room (aka, the thickest cluster of trees I could find) the ground had been covered in grass. Lush, green grass.

Now it was covered in yellow and white flowers.

"For you." A man plucked a yellow flower from the ground and handed it to me as I walked by. "It's nearly the same color as your hair." He winked.

I ogled him, my brain still stuck on *where the heck did these flowers come from?* The dude was cute: tall, with dark hair and eyes, and a well-trimmed beard. But he was doing a great Captain Jack Sparrow impression. Sweat beaded on his brow as he swayed. His fingers quivered around the flower.

"Captain Sparrow?" The man's nose crinkled in confusion.

"Er...never mind. That was meant to be a private thought. But my mouth doesn't always get the memo. And thanks." I took the little plant from him, tracing my fingers over the velvety petals. "Not to be rude, but where—eek!" I grabbed his shoulder when he wobbled. "Yo, I think you're flagged."

"Eh?"

"How much have you had to drink?"

"I don't drink when I'm working."

"*Working?*"

"Yes."

I pressed a hand to my temple, although it did jack-squat to ease my near-constant headache.

The man chuckled. "Would you like to see? How about a flower to match your eyes?" He grinned and rooted through the leather fanny pack around his waist. "Ah! I knew I had one in here."

I squinted at the teeny object clutched between his forefinger and thumb. "Is that a seed?"

"Sure is." He knelt, digging a shallow hole in the ground.

"You know we're leaving soon, right?"

"Hmmm." He popped the seed into the hole and scooped the dirt back in place.

"There's no way you're gonna remember where you planted that."

The man pressed his hand to the soil. "It will only take a moment." As he spoke, a green leaf sprang out of the dirt.

"Gah!" My heart was off to the races again.

A bulbous, pulsating...*thing* emerged next. It looked like a freaking alien egg!

"No, no, *nope.*" I waved my arms and backed away. "The past few days have been batty enough. If a tentacled creature busts outta that thing...well, buddy, you won't have to worry about the alien killing ya. I'll make sure I wring your neck first."

The man chuckled. "It won't harm you."

"Like hell!" The undulating egg was several inches tall and still growing.

I took another step back, letting out a strangled, *"shit,"* when the egg burst open. No monsters sprang out (halle-freak-ing-lujah). Instead, short, vibrant purple petals curled toward me. A sweet scent filled the air.

"It's—that's—you—that's a hycinth!" I gasped.

"Hyacinth," the man corrected.

"Close enough. But—how—you—aw, hell, I should've stayed away from the food. And water. Now I'm freaking hallu-cinating..."

The man carefully extracted the flower and straightened, handing it to me. "Take it," he laughed. "I assure you, it's real."

And it smelled *awesome*. Sweet and spicy, like expensive-as-shit perfume. I buried my nose into the petals and inhaled.

"You're not hallucinating," the man said. A trickle of sweat ran down his cheek. "Although I remember thinking the same thing when I arrived here. This world often seems like a bad dream."

Ding! The lightbulb went on inside my head. "You're a *hybrid*, aren't you?"

"Yes. I am a Gardner."

"Holy shit! You guys really have magical powers?"

"I wouldn't call it magic..."

"That's so cool!" I stared at the flowers. "You can wave your hand and bring plants to life?"

"Not quite." He patted his fanny pack. "I must have a seed. And I don't relish forcing vegetation to grow so quickly—it's quite traumatic for some of them. Not the hyacinth, though. You needn't worry. That's a rather hardy flower."

"The process looks kinda traumatic for you too," I muttered as he see-sawed on his feet. "You need to sit?"

"No. I'm alright. And I still need to grow more yarrow and calendula. For the wounded," he added.

"Ah. Well...give me a shout. Or something. Y'know, if you feel like you're gonna black out. I can't do much to help, but I'll make sure you don't whack your head on the way down."

"I know my limitations." He grinned and held out his hand. "My name's Cathal—"

"Hey! Wait...Cheriour was talking about you the other day! It's nice to put a face with the name. I'm Addie, by the way." I clasped my fingers around his.

Cathal didn't pass out that day. But the poor guy was puking his guts up fifteen minutes later.

"'*I know my limitations,*'" I mimicked him. "Yeah right." I stroked his back, wincing on his behalf as he heaved and spasmed.

SO HYBRIDS WERE REAL. And Cathal wasn't the only one.

Like, Belanna? She could speak to animals.

On day six of our awful road trip, she trotted back to talk to Cheriour. She mumbled nonsense about how the birds were monitoring the Wraiths, but there was a cluster of sparrows she hadn't heard from yet and she was concerned.

What a load of crock.

Belanna whipped her head around to flash me a boastful smile. "Ye don't believe me, eh?"

Because *of course* I'd blurted my judgmental thought out loud. Stress had stolen whatever control I'd once had over my mouth. "I mean," I looked between Belanna and Cheriour, "you're making it sound like the birds are *speaking* to you."

"Aye." She raised her eyebrows. "'Twas the power I was given."

"T-talking to birds?"

"All animals," Belanna said. "But 'tis not as simple as talking, mind."

As she spoke, a twittering brown sparrow flew down from the trees. It landed on my shoulder, fluffed its wings, gave my earlobe a soft nip, and flew away.

Belanna looked smug as shit.

"Did you—" I stared at the bird's retreating form. "That was a coincidence, right? You did *not* tell it to do that. No way."

"I did."

"How? You didn't even say anything!"

"I don't need to speak. They understand me."

I swallowed and then thought of the horse-shaped shadow I'd seen—yet again—in the trees that morning. "If you talk—"

"I don't *talk*—"

"Whatever. If you *communicate* with animals, what about those venomous horses?"

"Ah, the Púcas. Unfortunately, they're not normal creatures. Rather like hybrids themselves, they are. I can't communicate with them. But I *can* communicate with that mare." She pointed at Sacrifice. "Braxton—he's me brother, by the way—he chose a good horse for ye, didn't he?"

"If you say so." As we spoke, my "good horse" swung her ass to the side and tried to kick Cheriour's mount.

"Ach, she may be a little testy with the other animals..."

"*A little?*"

"...but she knows her job. And she's not fussed about having an inexperienced rider. In fact, she thinks ye have a sturdy seat in the saddle—"

"My ass begs to differ..."

"—but she finds yer voice grating. Anyway, Cheriour, I also

108

wanted to tell ye there's water ahead we'll need to be crossin' soon. Ye don't need to worry," Belanna told me. "Sacrifice loves playin' in the water. Ye," she wagged her finger at Cheriour, "may have some issues. Yer fellow's not fond of gettin' his feet wet." With that, she hummed a cheery tune and rode away.

"She's a few cards short of a full deck, isn't she?" I asked Cheriour. "Has that power scrambled her brain?"

He didn't answer. No surprise.

And the water Belanna mentioned? Yeah, it was a freaking mile-wide river.

The gunky-brown water roared along at the bottom of the bank. Had to be going ten miles an hour. At least. And with those violent white caps...

I gasped when the first horse strolled into the river. Oh *hell* naw. What if the current whisked these poor animals away? Could horses swim? And this one had two men on its back: one lucid and one severely wounded. What chance did they have if the horse went under?

But the angrily swirling water didn't even reach the horse's chest. The animal and its passengers reached the other side safely.

More horses walked forward. Some nonchalantly strolled through the water. Others got skittish and took the crossing at a run.

And then it was my turn.

"Don't dump me," I pleaded as Sacrifice plodded down the bank. "Don't—*eeek!*"

She lunged forward with a squeal, splashing the water with her forelegs as she plunged her nose beneath the surface.

"I told ye she likes playin'!" Belanna said as her giant black horse charged up the hill on the other side, shaking water off his legs.

Sacrifice kept her head down, blowing bubbles as she

plowed through the river. And it wasn't until we reached the other side that I realized Cheriour was no longer beside me.

He stood at the bank, trying to coax his horse to step into the river. But the animal had planted his feet, refusing to budge. Cheriour, to his credit, didn't seem flustered or angry. He dismounted and stroked the horse's neck, his mouth moving endlessly as he spoke into his mount's ear.

Figured. Getting Cheriour to talk to me was like pulling teeth, but he had no problem blathering to a freaking animal.

Cheriour turned his horse around and sent him butt-first into the water. It worked. But as soon as the horse's feet hit the stream, he lost his shit.

"Back. You're alright," Cheriour repeated in his monotone voice while the horse did a series of stiff-legged pogo hops that sent plumes of water into the air. By the time they finished crossing, Cheriour was *drenched.*

I laughed. "Sorry." I clapped a hand over my mouth when he angled his head toward me. "I'm not laughing at you...no, actually, I kinda am. But I'm more laughing at *him.* I've never seen a horse do that before!"

Cheriour's boots made a *squish-squish* sound when he walked. "He's still green," he murmured, stroking the horse's neck.

"Green?" I asked.

Cheriour shoved his sopping ponytail over his shoulder and flicked the reins over the horse's head. The horse stood with his legs braced, eyes wide, as big drops of water fell from his chestnut fur.

"I dunno what you're looking at," I pressed, "but he's not *green.* He's more like an auburn."

"Green," Cheriour said, not even reacting to my sarcastic quip, "means young. Inexperienced." He gave the horse an affectionate bop on the nose and moved toward his saddle.

His *empty* saddle.

No more Liam.

And, y'know, maybe I was a softie, but a pang shot through my chest when Cheriour's shoulders slumped.

"You might wanna dry your pants," I said.

"What?"

"Your pants," I repeated. "They're soaked. They're not gonna dry right in the saddle. You'll end up with a wicked rash down where the sun don't shine. And no one's gonna help smear ointment on your ass."

That got a reaction! Cheriour's shoulders jerked as he pinched the bridge of his nose. From this angle, it almost looked like he was praying: *Lord, give me strength to deal with this cuckoo-crazy bitch.*

But he wasn't staring at his saddle anymore. So...mission accomplished. Kind of?

Liam had passed away that morning. And I knew my bad jokes couldn't heal the pain of losing such a young kid. I just wanted to lessen the ache. At least for a little while.

The problem?

Liam wasn't the only one to die.

Within four hours of leaving the river, three more people perished. The total body count for the entire road trip was now over a dozen.

The soldiers were dropping like flies.

I leaned against the rough bark of a tree, watching as Cheriour and Belanna dug a shallow grave. I hadn't meant to watch this.

But I'd wandered a little too far trying to find a quiet spot to go number two.

Look, I wasn't *ashamed* of the natural bodily function, but I still liked to do it in peace. Y'know?

And now that I was here...

Well, it felt morbid as frick to watch the burial, but it also felt wrong to leave.

The three corpses were stacked in a neat pile beside the gaping hole. They were still clothed, although the other soldiers had stripped the bodies of their weapons, boots, belts, leather vests...anything useful.

I'd seen similar sights in movies, but there was a *distinct* difference between fake bodies on a screen and corpses in real life. For one, I didn't know dead flesh turned purple and gray, almost like bad bruising. In the movies, they'd just looked pale. The stench of decay burnt my nostrils, even though I stood several feet away. It was suffocating. Nauseating. And *unnatural* to see a human so still, their limbs stiff, their eyes blank.

My gut lurched.

I rested my head against the tree, closing my eyes and breathing shallowly as the world tilted sideways.

"Are ye alright?" A voice asked.

"No," I mumbled.

The sound of a cork being popped filled my ears, and a leather flask was pressed into my quaking hands. "Here," the voice insisted.

Please be alcohol. I took a sip.

Bleh. It was water.

"Thanks." I opened my eyes and came face-to-face with Belanna—

No.

This was her brother.

Her *twin.* The two were identical: same carroty hair, same

gray eyes, same tall and broad-shouldered build. The only differences? He had a beard. And she had boobs.

"Brandon? Right? Or, no, that's not it..." I squinted and pointed at him. Normally I was good at remembering names, but I'd had a lot of them thrown at me recently. And this dude must've been hiding somewhere because I hadn't seen him before.

He flashed me a smile. "*Braxton*," he held out a hand, giving my arm a vigorous shake. "And I haven't been hiding anywhere. Ye really do that, eh? Talk without realizing it?"

"Guilty. Sorry."

"Nothin' ye need to be apologizin' for." He had a booming laugh, but the mirth didn't reach his eyes.

Belanna had said he was looking for someone at Bafrus. Someone who'd died.

I gnawed on my lower lip, *before* my mouth betrayed me again, and raised the flask in a half-salute. "Thanks for this. But you'll be my best friend forever if you've got something stronger."

This time, his chuckle was more genuine. "Ah, so it's the good stuff yer looking for." He took the flask back. "I'll let ye know if I find any, but most have run out."

"Damn it."

"My sentiments as well." Braxton popped the cork back in and re-attached the flask to his belt. "Ye've handled yer arrival here very well. When Belanna and I arrived, she cried every night for two years. She'll never admit to that, of course." He winked.

"And you guys were kids?"

"Aye. Must be near thirty years ago now." He rubbed the back of his neck. "It's hard to recall sometimes."

Thirty years?

OMG. I was definitely gonna die here.

Braxton turned suddenly and I tilted my head up as Cheriour stepped beside me. He leaned against the tree trunk, crossed his arms over his chest, and fixed me with that impassive stare.

I almost thought he was going to say something. Maybe ask if I was okay.

But...nope. He turned to Braxton. "We're a few hours away from Lamex. Belanna still hasn't been able to confirm the condition of the village. Have you had any luck?"

"No. Even our most reliable birds have vanished."

Belanna and Braxton didn't just look identical; they shared the same power.

Cheriour frowned, tapping two mud-caked fingers against his beard. "She was sure it was Elion," he said.

"Aye. So am I."

"He knows we still have Speakers in the army."

"Certainly seems that way."

Cheriour sighed. "Alright, Braxton, can you help with..." he trailed off, pointing a thumb over his shoulder.

Braxton slumped, but he nodded.

"You," Cheriour said to me. "Come with me. We have to talk."

14

ZOMBIE SKIN

ADDIE

Because he was Cheriour, we couldn't just find a quiet spot to chit-chat. Oh no. *"We need to talk,"* really meant: *"first you're going to help me bandage some of the wounded and get them on horses. And I must work in* total *silence. I'm a man, after all, and can't multitask for shit. When we're done, it's time to skedaddle. Once we're on the road again, we'll talk."*

Anyway, an hour (or two) later, after the army had cleared the thickest part of the forest, Cheriour finally spoke. "We're going to pass through a town called Lamex. It's the first town in Netheridge's borders."

There was a part of me—a tiny, but still hopeful part—that got a jolt of excitement. A *town*. It would be the first sign of civilization I'd seen in a week.

"We believe it has been infected," Cheriour said, derailing my train of thought.

"What?"

"We aren't certain. But Elion has been killing birds."

"Wait...infected? Elion? You can't drop these bombs and

expect me to follow what you're saying. Use your words. Elaborate a little."

"I will," Cheriour's lips jerked, "if you give me a moment."

"Ah. Okay, sorry. You..." I sank my teeth into my lip. *You talk too fucking slow!* Those words had been on the tip of my tongue before I bit them back...*literally.* "I'm super impatient. Y'know?" I amended.

Cheriour gave me one of his vacant stares. "Several days ago," he said, "one of Belanna's birds saw Elion near Lamex. But the birds she's sent to verify the sighting have failed to return."

"And Elion is...?"

"A Celestial. Most call him the Plague Bringer."

"Plague Bringer? Are we talking about a *bad head cold* or *The Black Death*?"

Cheriour dipped his chin to his chest. "His illness is cruel. The infected never survive."

A cold, despairing feeling curdled in my gut.

"There is no cure," he continued. "You must understand that. *There is no cure.*"

The darkness in my stomach deepened. Like a black hole had opened, swallowing me from the inside. "Why are you telling me this?"

"Because," he paused when his horse stumbled over a dip in the ground, "if what we fear is true—"

"Are we still going to Lamex?"

"Yes—"

"Hang on, there's a town full of sick people, and you're gonna march your army through without masks, or hazmat suits or-or *anything?* Are you trying to make sure the disease spreads to everyone else?" I didn't have *'succumbing to mystery plague'* on my *'Ways to Die in Viking Land'* Bingo card. But here we were, riding toward impending doom.

Where was my venomous horse stalker when I needed it? I'd rather take my chances with the animal than the plague.

"It doesn't spread that way," Cheriour said. "A person will only fall ill if they've been in direct contact with Elion. And he doesn't linger once he's infected a town. So, yes, we will ride through Lamex." He ran his fingers through his snarled beard. "It won't be a pleasant sight. And you won't agree with what we'll need to do. But you'll keep your mouth shut. Or," his throat bobbed, "I'll do what I must to ensure your silence."

My head snapped back. This was a total one-eighty for him. Sure, he'd told me to be quiet before, but he'd never *threatened* me.

Cheriour tugged at the end of his beard. *Hard.* "I wouldn't ask my soldiers to enter this town if I had another choice. It will be traumatic for everyone. Your thoughtless way of speaking may make it worse."

My insides squirmed. "I-I don't say things to hurt people."

Cheriour twisted in the saddle to stare at me. "I know," his voice gentled. "But you *do* speak without thinking. And careless words can cut deeper than a blade."

I didn't say anything to that. I couldn't.

Shame, desperation, and hopelessness washed over me like a mammoth tidal wave. Choking me. Mashing against my body, dragging me further and further beneath the surface.

I wanted to stop.

But I couldn't.

So I tightened my hold on Sacrifice's mane and stared straight ahead. My hands shook. And every step we took felt ominous.

WHEN WE FIRST ARRIVED AT the minacious town, it seemed innocent.

Lamex looked like a European village: narrow cobblestone streets twisted around small, Tudor-style houses. Instead of driveways and yards, each house had a livestock pen where goats, horses, and cows stood beneath the hot afternoon sun, munching on leftover scraps of straw.

It was silent for a few minutes. Almost peaceful. The town was quiet, quaint, and inviting. A gentle breeze wafted through the air, drying the sweat on the back of my neck. But the wind also carried a smell—practically whacked me across the face with it.

I rammed my knuckles into my mouth, choking back a gag at the awful stench. It was like I'd stuck my head into a New York City sewer and taken a big whiff.

Actually, it stunk *worse* than the sewer.

The odor was a rancid combination of urine, feces, puke, and decay. And I wasn't the only one affected by it. One of the first riders into the village, a gray-bearded man, pinched his nostrils shut. A few others sputtered and choked and used the crooks of their elbows to cover their noses. Even Cheriour looked a little green in the gills.

But the soldiers continued forward, navigating the tapered streets, while the stench hovered like a heavy cloud over us.

My sweat-slick fingers tightened around Sacrifice's mane as we approached the first cluster of houses. Bodies were stacked beside every building. There were adults, children, and even *infants*. Tears welled in my eyes.

What *was* this? What virus caused skin to rot away? Some bodies had almost none left to cover their tendons and bones. And the sparse bits of flesh remaining were alarming shades of red, gray, and blackish-brown. *Zombie skin.* Except zombies weren't usually lying in puddles of bloody vomit, with diarrhea crusted on the seat of their pants.

The sights got more horrific as we went farther into the town. Because some people were still alive.

Those who still breathed did so mechanically. Their blood-shot, glassy eyes stared unblinkingly at us. Blood and pus oozed from their rotted flesh. They staggered about, ignoring the army traveling through their streets.

I passed a small house where a young woman strung laundry on the line outside her front door. Her skin had decomposed; her hands and arms had almost no flesh left. She left blood streaks on her sheets but didn't seem to notice them. Or maybe she didn't give a shit. Because, not two seconds later, she doubled over and puked black goo into her wicker basket of linens. Then she reached in, shook the bile off the sheets, and hung them on the line.

I clapped my hand over my mouth as my stomach made a sticky *squitch-squatch* sound. Sacrifice halted, her ears swiveling. Like radar, picking up on my unstable emotions.

And, at first, I thought the blond-haired soldier was there to help. He was off his horse and walking from house to house. I waved at him. "Yo!" A sour tang coated the back of my throat —like freaking artichoke hearts (I hated those things). "Hey, she needs help!" I pointed to the woman, who stood a few feet away from him.

He turned. Slowly. His skin vibrated with barely contained tremors.

"You got any water on—*the fuck?*" I screeched.

The soldier approached the sick woman with his sword raised over his head.

"Wait!"

But the man swung his weapon down. The blade whistled. There was a sickening *thwap* as it sliced through the woman's neck.

The woman's body remained standing, even as her head flopped into the wicker basket. Her torso hit the ground a few seconds later with a strange, contorted spasm.

Holy. Fucking. *Shit!*

My jaw opened with an audible *pop.*

Blood splashed across the woman's sheets. It had sprayed the man's face too. He spat out a mouthful and wiped his sleeve over his beard.

Ice whooshed through my veins. There was nothing, *nothing*, that could've prepared me to see a person—an innocent, sick, unarmed woman—murdered in cold blood.

"You—oh, you bastard." My hands shook as I fumbled through my saddle bags, looking for something, *anything*, to chuck at the man's fugly, murderous face.

Where the frick had I put Belanna's knife?

But then the man turned.

And, okay, he was *not* the cold-blooded killer type. His eyes were red and teary as he swiped blood off his sword with quivering fingers. "It had to be done, didn't it?" he sniffled. "She wasn't going to last much longer, was she?"

I froze.

It had to be done.

This was why Cheriour had pulled me aside to give a warning. *"There is no cure."* He knew this was going to happen—he probably gave the order.

Careless words can cut deeper than a blade.

I sank my teeth into my tongue, fighting the angry, hurt,

and confused words that were gurgling inside me. The blond man, with his pale and tear-stricken face, didn't need me bitching at him. He needed a freaking hug.

I started to dismount to do just that, but then the other woman showed up.

She staggered onto the street, vomiting gooey black bile as she walked. Her eyes roamed over the house, resting for a brief second on the headless woman (her sister? Friend? Lover?) but her face showed no emotion. I didn't know if she recognized the woman or not. Even when she glanced at me, her glazed eyes were empty. There was no shock, fear, anger...*nothing.*

Zombie eyes.

The woman looked no older than twenty. She was still a girl. A kid.

The blond man sagged when he saw her.

"Don't!" My voice was a shrill whisper.

He ignored me, raising his sword again.

"It's alright, Garvin," came Cheriour's drawl. He walked behind the woman; his blood-soaked knife already outstretched. "You and Addie can go to the square," he continued, jerking his head in the direction he'd come from. "I'll take care of her."

Garvin let out a shuddering breath. "Thank you," he mumbled before he booked it down the street, his boots slapping against the cobblestone.

I kept still, too stunned to ask Sacrifice to move.

Cheriour grasped the woman's shoulders. She didn't react. Just continued to pan her dead eyes around the houses.

"Don't," I squawked. I had a strange bubbling sensation in my chest: unsure if I wanted to cry, scream, or hurl. Or do a combo of all three.

Cheriour paused, his knife poised over the woman's throat. "I understand," he said.

"What?"

"Wanting to spare her. I understand. But it's wrong."

"She-she's... *fuck*, she's not even old enough to drink!" Which, since he wasn't from 21st century America, meant nothing to him. "She's practically still a kid," I added.

"Yes, she is." Cheriour's hold on the woman's shoulder tightened when she choked on more black bile. "But can you justify leaving her in this condition?"

The woman's discolored skin was peeling away in big chunks; the yellowed bone of her right arm protruded through a thin, mottled layer of muscle. Her lungs rattled wetly with every inhale. She vomited almost non-stop. The poor thing had to be in *excruciating* pain.

"We can't heal her," Cheriour said. "She'll continue to deteriorate."

"But haven't you—did you at least *try* to find a cure?" It felt like a massive rock was sitting in my stomach.

"We have. Many times. The result is always the same. This disease kills them slowly. I'd rather end their suffering quickly." He turned the woman toward him and tilted her head back, baring her throat. She didn't protest. Not even when he lifted his blade. She stared at the heavens, her eyes unfocused, her mouth hanging slack. Dried blood and puke caked her chin.

Cheriour smoothed his hand over her brow, murmuring an apology before he slit her throat.

I squeezed my eyes shut. I was cold all over and shivering, even as the sun baked my skin.

The woman died silently. Almost peacefully.

Cheriour picked her up and laid her next to the decapitated woman.

So they *had* known each other. Or maybe he was guessing. But the look on his face as he stood up...

It lasted barely a second before he sucked in a breath and wiped his expression clean. But it'd been long enough for me to glimpse the pure *anguish* that writhed at his insides.

"I'm sorry," I mumbled as Cheriour walked over to pat Sacrifice's nose.

He said nothing, but a ghost of a smile touched his mouth. Not a cheery grin. Definitely not. More of a *"thank you for not being a crazy bitch and acknowledging my pain"* kind of smile.

"Go to the square," he murmured, "and wait there until I return. We'll be finished soon."

He walked away before I could say anything else.

15

SWINDON

 LASS

Terrick and I emerged from the forest on a late-summer afternoon.

I'd spent much of the morning ailing with an aching belly, so Terrick carried me through the last leg of our journey. I clutched at his neck with slick, trembling hands, and buried my face into his shoulder. Terrick always smelled like pine needles. The scent had become a comfort.

"There now, lass," he murmured as we approached the town called Swindon. "I'm putting you down."

"No!" I clung to him.

"Yes. You're perfectly capable of walking." He bent, depositing my feet onto the ground. "Now...open your eyes, lass." His rough, gnarled hand touched my cheek.

"I can't. They're stuck." I raised my chin.

Terrick tapped my shoulder. "Don't lie."

I drew back when he grasped my hand. "I won't go!"

"We're already here."

"I hate Wraiths! *Hate* them! I want to go back to the woods."

"There are no Wraiths in Swindon."

"*Don't lie,*" I repeated his earlier statement.

"Lass." Laughter warmed Terrick's voice. "I'll strike a bargain with you. If you open your eyes and see a Wraith, we'll return to the woods. If you cannot find one, then you'll accompany me into Swindon. Does that sound fair?"

It did, but I said nothing.

I pried my eyelids apart and angled my head toward the village. I expected to see ramshackled (is this a word?) dwellings and armored Wraiths.

Instead, rows upon rows of houses lined the village streets. Some buildings were as big as Varn's home. Most were bigger. Humans walked to and fro—and they were unlike any humans I'd ever seen. They were so very *large*. And robust. Layers of fat and muscle covered their bones. They wore hole-less clothes.

(This doesn't seem right. Whole-less? Holeless? Not holey?)

Well, in Detha, our threadbare clothing had provided little warmth or protection. And, when the fabric wore through, there often wasn't any spare cloth to patch the holes. But in Swindon, the humans wore thick cloth; their tunics and breeches unmarred by tears. And *boots!* Only a dozen humans in Detha had possessed a pair of boots. Everyone had a pair in Swindon!

"Have you found a Wraith?" Terrick asked.

My eyes roamed over every building, human, and animal I could find. There were no Wraiths.

Still, I said nothing—I never did like admitting when I was wrong—as I followed Terrick into the town.

"That's the shoemaker." Terrick pointed to a small, triangular building with a wooden sign in the shape of a boot hanging over the front door. "We can go there in the morning to have shoes made for you. And here—" Terrick nodded toward a small, paunchy building. "Millie, the seamstress, will make you proper clothing. She's the only one in the village with *colored* fabrics. You could have a green tunic if you wish. Or *blue.*

"And Carragh..." Terrick's voice lowered as we passed a portly old woman selling bread from a wooden stand. I looked at him and found his cheeks tinged pink. "She is the finest bread maker in Swindon. Perhaps in all of Sakar." A smile stretched across his lips. Despite his praise, he barely spared her steaming loaves of bread a glance. Instead, he kept his eyes focused on her, only drawing his gaze back to me once we turned a corner. "What do you think so far, lass?"

Truthfully, I was stunned. And my neck ached. This lively, noisy, *wondrous* place had me twisting in every direction, trying to absorb all the new sights, sounds, and smells. I wished I had more than two eyes. Or that I could turn my head all the way around. Like an owl.

The scent of cooked meat drifted through the air as we passed the market. My stomach gave a hungry grumble.

Terrick chuckled. "There will be food at the inn, lass," he assured me.

"In?"

"Yes. A tavern. Temporary housing," he amended when I furrowed my brow. "My home is likely unlivable at the moment. It's been years since I've...well, we'll be far more comfortable at the inn."

As we moved toward the heart of the town, the other humans began to notice us. Slowly, at first. A few odd glances here and there. The occasional raised eyebrow. Many of them recognized Terrick. They called out to him. He waved cheerily back. Sometimes they made jests at his expense.

"Oi, Terrick," a man said, "where did you find that wee little thing?"

"A child? At your age?" another man asked with a hearty chuckle. "My, my Terrick. I've misjudged you."

"I have always been full of surprises, Jethro," Terrick laughed, even as he gave my arm a gentle squeeze.

"Ah, such a sweet lass," a stooped, toothless woman said when we passed by her. She pinched my cheek and laid her hand on Terrick's arm. "It's good to see you again, Terrick. You look happy."

We walked. And we walked. And we walked. The streets seemed never-ending, the people too numerous to count. They were boisterous; full of life and joy. They ate and drank freely. Laughed loudly. Some played music. Some sang.

In Detha, they would have all been whipped for causing such a ruckus.

In Swindon, it seemed there were no such rules. But still my eyes roamed, endlessly shifting through the masses of humans.

"Have you seen a Wraith, Lass?" Terrick asked as we passed a tavern. Screeching music drifted through the doors while scores of men and women slurred and sang in horribly off-key tones.

Heat spread through my chest. Embarrassment. "No." It pained me to admit defeat.

Terrick's weathered face wrinkled as he smiled.

Terrick rented a room for a month at *The Black Bull Inn*; so named because of the innkeeper's bull. The ~~behometh~~—behemoth creature was prime breeding stock with his lusty, rippling muscles and shining black fur. He seemed terrifying;

almost too large to be a real animal. But he was as mild as a kitten. And I adored him. I spent many a morning perched on the top railing of his pen, sharing my porridge. I ate a spoonful, fed him a spoonful, and so on until my bowl emptied. Afterward, I traced my fingers around the swirl of hair on the bull's brow while he leaned his massive head against my lap, utterly content.

The innkeeper, Lorcan, was the bull's human counterpart: a thickly muscled man with a scarred face and a kind heart. He called me *cailín álainn*—or *pretty girl.*

"Ah, *cailín álainn!*" he greeted me in the mornings. "I've added some berries for you." He winked as he handed me the bowl of porridge. "But let's keep that secret between us, shall we? I don't want my other patrons to be jealous. And be sure Noro doesn't take more than his share."

Noro, of course, being the black bull.

At first, Noro consumed most of the berries. Truthfully, I was stricken with terror at the thought of eating the fruits; a delicacy I'd never been permitted to indulge in. Surely it would have been more beneficial for the delectable little treats to go to Lorcan's prized bull?

But Lorcan added a handful of the sweet fruit to my porridge every morning and, eventually, the temptation became too great. I ate one. Two. They were ~~equistite~~ (that's certainly not the correct spelling. ~~Eqsuite?~~ *Exquisite?):* bitter, yet sweeter than even Mama's finest tomatoes. And, well, Noro seemed content with the porridge, so I kept the berries for ~~myself.~~

Those first days were simple. Quiet. Terrick woke at dawn and went to complete the renovations to his dwelling.

"It's fallen into disrepair," he told me. "But it's nothing I can't fix. You'll love it there, lass. Our lodgings are above the shop. Although not quite as big as what we have here at the inn," he gestured to the spacious room we were renting, "it will be all ours. There's even a livery barn. Perhaps I'll find a bull for you to keep there." He smiled when I gasped in excitement.

While Terrick was away, I played with Noro or helped Lorcan clean the tables in the tavern. Or, sometimes, I rested in our rented room, curled against the windowsill, watching the busy village life below. I was usually sad on those days. Sad that Mama, Conn, and all the people from Detha would never know a vibrant life such as this.

But the sad days became fewer as the weeks passed. 'Tis the ~~resilency~~ resiliency of a child, I suppose. I'd been too young to hold on to dark emotions. Too young to dwell on the past when my future looked so bright.

And when Terrick deemed his dwelling livable again, I was given an important task: to help him reopen his shop.

His *book* shop.

It's a rather silly notion. Terrick earned coin by selling parchment bound in scraps of leather. He called them fiction books. Meaning that, while the stories seemed real, and sometimes frightening, they weren't. There was nothing historical or factual about them. They were the product of someone's imagination.

As I said, it's a silly notion. Why would someone wish to waste ink and parchment on a *lie*?

But, in Swindon, the townspeople adored Terrick's fiction books. They celebrated when he reopened his shop.

"Ten years, Terrick," one woman cried. "You've made me wait *ten years* to discover what happened to the boy wizard!"

"Apologies, Róise," Terrick bowed his head as he handed the woman a broad tome. "But after...well, the time away has done me good." He turned to where I was dusting his fiction books and gave me a playful wink.

There was darkness in Terrick's past, although I never

asked him about it. At the time, I hadn't noticed it, even though the evidence was there.

For instance, a great armoire occupied much of the wall space in our dwelling. I passed it every day. Sometimes I amused myself by tracing my fingers over the intricately designed flowers carved into the wood, or marveling at the gowns inside. And I never questioned why Terrick possessed an armoire full of lady's clothes.

Terrick gifted me with trinkets when we moved into his dwelling. Toys, he'd called them. Wooden figurines of horses, and other objects. ~~Frivoulous~~ frivolous things, clearly made for small hands. Like mine. They were already old and well-used when I received them. I lovingly played with them every day but never asked where they came from.

During those early months at Swindon, I busied myself with my ~~indulgances~~ indulgences: eating until my stomach felt as though it would burst. Proudly polishing my new boots and telling another girl that I had the *finest* boots in town. She, of course, maintained her boots were finer, while her brother was convinced *he* possessed the superior boots. Our shoes were identical (quite like the girl and her brother). They'd been crafted at the same shop, likely with the same strip of cowhide. But we did rather enjoy teasing each other.

Terrick, sadly, couldn't find a bull, but he brought goats into the livery barn. Wee bastards. They ate everything: my food, my clothes, Terrick's fiction books. One even tried to gnaw on the toe of my precious boots.

I *adored* the little buggards.

They were warm, and soft, and had tolerant dispositions. They didn't care if I sang while I cleaned their pens—I was, and still am, a wretched singer. I'm certain the dulcet tones of my voice damaged their hearing. They didn't bite or kick when I played with them, which often involved me hanging onto their necks, fiddling with their ears, and kissing their noses. And they stood patiently while Terrick taught me how to coax milk from their udders.

I still remember the day Terrick gave me my first cup of the creamy liquid.

"It's good for you," Terrick laughed as I savored the thick concoction. "Some people believe it helps children grow."

"Helps them how?" I asked.

"It makes your bones strong."

"How?"

Terrick smiled. "It coats them, like armor, and protects them from injury while you grow."

"Ah." And, considering I was the smallest, and thinnest child in my age group, I diligently drank the goat's milk every morning. Sadly, Terrick was wrong in his belief. I grew. All children do. But I remain, to this day, smaller than most.

All in all, we lived in that splendid town for over six years. The Golden Days, as I've always called them. Where happiness reigned and darkness seemed like a distant memory.

Of course, it was not us who decided to leave Swindon.

We were chased out of the town.

16

STANKY CULTURE SHOCK

ADDIE

A somber cloud hovered over us as we left Lamex.

The people in front of me rode silently, all traces of conversation gone. Even Cheriour looked like a ghost, his face pale as his eyes roamed the landscape. But to be honest, I tried not to look over my shoulder at him too often. Because every time I did, I saw the dark gray smoke billowing into the sky behind him. Smoke that came from the hundreds, perhaps thousands, of plague-infested corpses. And their houses.

Incinerating the bodies made sense. But the whole town seemed excessive. At first. Until Braxton made a doleful remark as we left: "We don't have enough people to be fillin' those houses. And I'd rather see it burn to the ground than have Wraiths settle here."

There weren't enough people.

Back home, shitty developers built dozens of new buildings every day because we had no shortage of people *needing* a home. The question was whether they could *afford* one.

Here, hundreds of buildings had been destroyed. Because

you couldn't sell houses when most of your potential buyers were dead.

What a depressing fucking thought.

The soldiers did, thankfully, corral the livestock before we torched the town. Listening to animals being burned alive would've been the last straw for me.

We now had horses to spare. Some of them pulled rickety wooden carts filled with sheep, goats, chickens, pigs...Old MacDonald's entire farm. Excluding cows. They were too big to put in the carts and too slow to follow the horses, so they were left in the fields. *Away* from the inferno. But Belanna made an exception for one obese bull—seriously, his flubber jiggled as he waddled along—because he was *"prime breeding stock."*

All-in-all, it was a slow procession away from the town. A funeral march.

Even when we'd put the village behind us, my hands wouldn't stop shaking.

If *I* was struggling this much, how were the rest of them fairing? What about Cheriour? He'd likely given the orders. And he'd also taken the grim task of walking up and down the streets with a torch. How the heck was he holding himself together?

I leaned back in the saddle, muttering *"whoa"* to Sacrifice. I still couldn't be trusted with reins, but she listened to voice commands. She slowed, allowing Cheriour's horse to catch up.

Cheriour was the picture of tranquility. Like a smooth sheet of ice over a body of water. But I was getting the impression that scary, slithering monsters hid beneath that ice. Monsters that undoubtedly wreaked havoc on his insides.

I stretched a hand out, touching his arm (and nearly tumbling out of the saddle).

He didn't move. Didn't look at me.

"I'm—" I started.

"We'll arrive at Niall by nightfall," he cut me off. "Its ruler, Quinn, has been unpredictable of late. Please mind your words with him." He shrugged my hand away and left me alone at the back of the group.

Well...that could've gone better, huh?

Mowow.

The distant sound had me whipping around so fast, my neck cracked. My horse stalker's black body slithered through the trees behind me. But then it paused, poked its nose out of the foliage, and turned toward the village.

The Púca looked at me again. And looked back at the village.

With one last hungry stare in my direction, the animal turned and strolled toward the village with its ears pricked, tail swishing.

The scent of death had been more tantalizing than my rank and sweaty booty.

"Good," I mumbled. "I hope you burn to the ground with the rest of the town, you creepy sonuvabitch."

THE REST of the day passed in a blur. Not to say it went *fast;* every minute seemed like a decade. But I couldn't remember much about that afternoon. Shock did goofy things to a person.

My brain only came back to life when we emerged from the woods, and I saw lights twinkling against the night sky before us.

"Niall," Cheriour said when he noticed me gaping at the sight. He'd resumed riding alongside me at some point in the afternoon. Although he gave me a wider berth, probably terrified I'd reach out and rub my cooties all over him again.

"That's the city?" I asked. The lights brightened as we drew closer. Like a beam of hope at the end of a long tunnel.

Did they have electricity? If they did...

Ah, crap. Never mind. I should've learned my lesson: *don't get your hopes up.*

It hadn't been the city glowing in the dark. It was a colossal wall. And the "lights" came from the dozens of sconces hanging from the top section, each holding a flame-lit torch.

My heart dropped to my toes.

This disappointment cut the deepest. Maybe because it was the end of the road. And the last ounce of hope I'd been clinging to had been thoroughly, painfully squashed.

Tears blurred my vision. The life I'd known was *truly* gone. Kaput. I'd never see home again.

As for my new life...

I blew out a breath as our group halted outside the two massive wooden doors in the center of the wall. Those doors had to be fifteen feet high, at least. Opening them took ten buff men, five at each door, shoving with all their might.

Christ. Sure, it wouldn't be easy for Wraiths to bust into this city. But what happened if the people inside needed to get out, and ASAP? Did they have fire drills here? Probably not.

A tired cheer rose from my road trip crew when the gates came to a shuddering halt. Deafening noise rumbled from the city inhabitants as the soldiers darted through the entrance. Some people called out to loved ones and friends. Understandable. But then others made an almighty fuss when they saw the livestock carts. Because apparently claiming animals was a free-for-all around here.

"That pig there—no, the one with the black spots. I'll take him!" a woman yelled.

Welp. Guess the black spotted pig was gonna be bacon. Or pork chops.

"I'd like the gray goat!" a man bellowed.

Interesting. What, exactly, did people do with goats? Eat them? Milk them? Fuc—

Nope. I wouldn't go down that rabbit hole.

But that guy sounded *very* excited.

"Good gracious, what a beaut!" another woman laughed when the fat bull waddled into the city.

I wrinkled my nose. A beaut? Really? That was one of the fugliest animals I'd ever seen.

Beside me, Cheriour huffed.

My inner monologue must've turned into an outer monologue. "Sorry," I mumbled. "I swear I'm not normally *this* obnoxious."

He kept his gaze fixed on the soldiers shuffling through the entrance. And he said nothing as more ruckus rose from the streets.

Of course, being stuck at the back meant I only got to *hear* this commotion. I didn't see much of it until all the other soldiers had filtered into the city—Cheriour and Belanna being the only two exceptions. They walked in on either side of me. Like two bodyguards.

Was it comforting to have guards? Or terrifying? Cheriour's face gave nothing away. But Belanna's normally vibrant smile had vanished.

Okay, terrifying. Definitely.

"This Quinn guy's gonna be that bad?" I asked.

They didn't answer.

So, to distract myself from my suddenly icky-feeling stomach, I glanced around.

Niall was the Viking Land version of Philadelphia: a sprawling city that wasn't *quite* big enough to compete with the scope of a place like NYC. Tall columns of row homes twisted around the cobblestone streets. There were no livestock pens here; too many buildings stacked on top of each other and not enough space on the claustrophobia-inducing roads to allow that. A car would've gotten stuck trying to drive through. The horses barely fit. Sometimes people had to flatten themselves against nearby walls to avoid being run over by the animals.

So where did the livestock live? In people's homes, apparently. Probably not *all* of them—no way that tubby bull would fit through any of the narrow doorways. There had to be fields or barns somewhere. But the woman who bought the black-and-white pig led the walking slab of bacon right into her house.

These city people were...*different.* At least compared to what I was used to.

They all wore similar garb: leather breeches, boots, and shirts. Simple. Working outfits. Some women spruced it up a bit and wore knee or ankle-length dresses over their breeches. The clothes were grimy. The people even dirtier.

Hygiene? These people hardly knew her.

It was a culture shock, to be sure. A *stanky* culture shock.

But everything also seemed...*familiar.* Because these people, despite their grunge, were normal.

Nearby, a man leaned against the side of his house, smoking from a long pipe. Kids ran by us, laughing, while their parents barked at them to *"stop causing a ruckus"* or to *"get your wee arse in bed before it gets a smack."* A young couple were having a domestic spat because one of them had *"left ruddy, muddy boots on the fucking table again!"* And one street had a little barbecue going on. People were sprawled on the ground or perched on wooden crates. They sizzled skewers of meat over a fire and chugged beer from wooden mugs.

Food, a grill, and alcohol: a perfect recipe for a good time.

And being surrounded by all this lively chatter lifted my spirits. It almost felt like I was back home.

Almost.

"Oi! Welcome back!" A woman called to us as she dumped a chamber pot out her front door.

Yup. A whole bucket of urine going right onto the street. Yum.

The woman had a kind face and a big, brown-toothed smile. She waved cheerily until her eyes caught mine. Then she stopped dead, her hand flying to her mouth. Her face changed color faster than a traffic light, going from red, to white, to green in three seconds.

Aw shit. Had I been saying my judgy thoughts out loud? *Again?*

"We'll explain later, Deborah," Cheriour said to her.

"But—" she protested.

"Later." Cheriour's voice was firm.

The woman nodded, gave me another wide-eyed glance, and darted back into her home.

If she had been the only person to react that way, I would've figured she was the town Looney Tune.

But she wasn't.

More people gave me weird, dazed looks. One man started to walk over to me with his hand outstretched. Cheriour nudged his horse closer to Sacrifice's side, blocking the man from getting to me.

"Okay, what the heck is going on?" I asked.

No answer.

"Have I been word vomiting? Or do I have bird shit in my hair? Why is everyone staring? Or...oh, is it the tats?" I looked at my sleeve tattoo. "Or the dress?"

Silence.

My skin prickled. The tats and dress might've explained *some* of the confused stares. But not Deborah's odd reaction.

So...what the heck was going on?

We trekked for a few more minutes, with people gawking at me the whole way, before we reached the castle.

Yes. It was a bona fide freaking *castle*. Not a big one. Maybe six stories tall, although it had four towers that probably reached seven stories. It was only slightly larger than the wall that surrounded the city. And it wasn't much wider than a sports stadium.

In terms of structure, I'd seen better. This one got two stars out of ten in my book.

But the rest of it? Fifteen stars out of ten. Easily.

Because what set this castle apart and had me almost breaking my neck trying to see it from every angle, were the walls. They were white. And I wasn't talking about a dingy, creamy color. Or a sterile *psychiatric ward* kinda white. Naw. This building *popped* against the night sky. Like it was illuminated. It seemed fake: too pristine, too vibrant, too bright. It hurt my eyes to stare at it.

"Wow!" I blurted. "How d'you get the building to shine? You got LEDs embedded into the wall? No. That can't be it. You guys don't have electricity, right? Or do you? Hmm. Did you use reflective paint—hey! Ouch!"

Cheriour had grasped my arm. Tightly.

"I'm not trying to be rude; I'm just saying—"

"Hush." With a jerky movement, Cheriour pointed to the front of the castle.

A man with short, sandy-colored hair and a graying beard strolled down the luminous front steps.

"Quinn," Cheriour said, his voice quiet...*too* quiet. The kind of voice you'd use to placate someone before they did something stupid. I knew it well; it'd been used on me plenty of times.

The man, Quinn, lifted his head as he came to the bottom of the steps. I had a split second to take in the structure of his face—his chiseled jaw, the dark shadows that ringed his sky-blue eyes, and his high cheekbones—before he cursed. In one swift move, he plucked a blade from his belt and chucked it at my head.

17

HEADLESS ADDIE

I screamed.

Cheriour yanked my head down.

The knife whipped through my hair. It brushed against my scalp but didn't get close enough to draw blood. Thank *God.*

I let out a raspy breath as Cheriour's fingers tightened against the top of my head, keeping my chin pressed to my chest. My pulse thundered in my ears. I'd been *centimeters* away from being a freaking corpse!

"What is this?" Quinn hissed. Like a snake—a slithering, murderous *snake.*

"Quinn, calm yourself," Cheriour said.

I flinched when I heard Quinn stomping toward me.

"Be still, Addie," Cheriour whispered, forcing my head down even further.

"*Calm myself?*" Quinn's haughty voice was way too close.

"*What the fricking frick?*" my muscles coiled, screaming at me to run. But I couldn't. Cheriour had me pinned down with an iron grip. And my *noble steed* wouldn't move. I dug my heels into her side. She grunted, her shoulders twitching, but didn't budge.

Freaking Belanna. She'd told Sacrifice to stay put, hadn't she?

But I kept squirming and nudging Sacrifice to move. Until Cheriour murmured a warning and dug his fingers into my scalp.

Quinn's boots thudded across the ground again. "Release her."

"No," Cheriour said.

"Cheriour..."

"No. Not until you're willing to listen."

A shiver rippled along my spine. Okay, so if I survived this exchange, I owed Cheriour the biggest *thank-you* gift of all time. I needed to bake him a big-ass cake, or wash his underwear, or *something*.

"Quinn, yer being silly," Belanna said.

"*Release her,*" Quinn snarled. "I want to see her eyes."

"You've already seen them," Cheriour said.

My *eyes?* Sure, their funky color had garnered attention before. But usually, I'd get a few compliments from older women or flirty guys. No one had ever tried to *murder* me.

Quinn took four steps. Paused. Took five more steps. Paused. "I *knew* this would happen."

"It's not as you think, Quinn. She," Cheriour's fingers jerked against my skull, "is not from this world. I saw her arrive."

"Aye, as did Kaelan," Belanna added.

Quinn scoffed. "You seem to forget Ramiel knows your weakness, Cheriour. And he would not hesitate to exploit it."

I winced when Cheriour's nails raked into my scalp. It seemed like a reflex. As though he wanted to make a fist but couldn't because he was holding my head. "He hasn't." His voice was eerily quiet. He reminded me of Anthony Hopkins (*"hellooo Clariccee"*). "This woman may be insufferable—"

"Yo!" I gasped.

Cheriour's hold tightened. "—but there was no guile in her eyes. She knew nothing of this world. Nor our war."

"And you've never trusted the wrong person before." The sarcasm in Quinn's voice was thick enough to cut with a knife.

Cheriour didn't miss a beat. "I've spent the last week studying her. She's useless."

"Ye should have seen her face when I gave her a knife," Belanna chortled. "The lass was terrified of it."

"She will likely not survive long in this world," Cheriour said. "So, if you still wish to kill her, I'll not stop you—"

"*Excuse me?*" I grumbled. So much for him being my big freaking hero. I definitely wouldn't wash his underwear now.

"Hush," Cheriour said to me before continuing, "but you *will* spill innocent blood if you take her life."

"I'd rather not take the chance." A loud *ziiing* punctuated Quinn's words.

Aw *crap*. That sounded like a sword being drawn!

Quinn moved closer. And I was a sitting duck.

I wriggled my head, grunting when Cheriour's unyielding grip tore a few strands of my hair out. "Let me go!" I gasped. "At least give me a chance to run!"

"Quinn," Cheriour said.

Quinn's footsteps stilled. "You said you would not stop me..."

"I won't." Cheriour's fingers spasmed. When he spoke, his drawl was even more pronounced. "But ask this of yourself: even if your suspicions are true, would she want this?"

"Who *she?* Me?" I grumbled. "No. I sure as fuck don't want this!"

"*Be still,*" Cheriour hissed.

"Am I not allowed to defend myself?" I asked.

"No."

"Okay, but I'm really freaking out here." Understatement. My lungs were locking up. "And my neck's starting to hurt." Also an understatement. Sharp needles of pain shot through my shoulders.

Cheriour let out a low *"hmmm"* and released me.

My neck made a deep grinding sound as I stretched my head back, working out the fresh kinks.

Quinn stood a foot away, *glaring* at me. Like he thought I'd pissed in his Cheerios or something. "Why don't you take a fucking picture?" I asked. "It'll last longer."

Even in the darkness, I saw his cheeks redden. His fingers flexed around his stubby sword.

Belanna laughed, diverting Quinn's attention away from me. "You find this funny?" he asked her.

"Aye, I do." She chuckled again. "And if yer done throwing yer tantrum, I've got soldiers that still need tending to."

"I'm aware." Quinn pointed at the castle. "They're already inside."

"Perfect. So why don't ye stop belly-achin' and get to healing? Hmm?"

Quinn sighed. "Belanna..."

"Ach, I know. *'This isn't yer country. I give the orders, not ye.'*" Her accent was too heavy to mock Quinn's voice. "But ye've not given any orders. Yer just traumatizing the woman."

"Her eyes—" Quinn began.

"Are you seriously hung up on the color of my eyes?" I blurted. "They're purple. Big deal. If they creep you out, too bad. I can't change them. Move the fuck on."

"Watch your tongue—" Quinn started.

My chest burned. "I'll watch my tongue when you stop

throwing knives at people." Why the heck were my hands shaking?

Cheriour made a muffled sound and tilted his head back, staring at the heavens. Another *Lord, give me strength* pose. Belanna stared between me and Quinn, her eyes bright with excitement. She looked ready to grab a bag of popcorn and settle in to watch the fight.

"You—" Quinn started.

"Quinn," Cheriour interjected.

Quinn's face had gone white. His lips curled over his teeth. But he didn't seem as angry as...*scared.* "I want her gone," he spat. "Innocent or not, she can't stay."

"Casting her out would be as good as killing her," Cheriour said.

"I don't care."

"I do. If you are to kill her, do so quickly. I won't doom a human to suffer."

Quinn started pacing again. But he stopped when he noticed the soldiers perched at the top of the castle steps. They watched us, as though unsure whether they should come down and risk Quinn's wrath. And behind us, a few towns-people had wandered away from their houses to listen to our conversation.

Our impasse was becoming a spectacle. Which worked in my favor.

With short, jerky motions, Quinn rammed his sword back into its sheath, his eyes darting around the houses. "She can stay in the city."

"I'd rather her stay in the castle. She's too unfamiliar with our world," Cheriour said.

"There are no open rooms in the castle."

"There's one."

Quinn's mouth opened and closed. Opened and closed. He

looked like a fish gasping for water. "I'm *not* putting her in that room."

"It's a waste to keep it vacant." Each word Cheriour spoke was quiet. Carefully measured.

"She could stay with me," Belanna offered. "I'll be stayin' close to the castle."

"I don't want her in the city." Cheriour turned to her. "And you need to get Cynerik's soldiers settled."

Belanna shrugged. "But if she stays with me, I can get her trained for ye."

Cheriour almost cracked a smile. *Almost.* "You threw your last trainee off a cliff."

"Aye. Well, Elliot had a fear of heights. He doesn' anymore...."

"*Jesus.* You killed someone?" I gaped at her.

"No, he's alive," Belanna chirped. "Only broke two bones."

Only. That was a ringing endorsement. *Come train with me. You'll only break a bone or two.*

Also...

"Wait, training? Like sword-and-shield-fight *training*?" It had taken a minute to sink in. But now that it had... "Oh no. *Hell* no. Absolutely not. I'm not a sword-wielding kinda person. I'm...uh...cleaning! A cleaning person." I sure as shit was not. My idea of *cleaning* was putting the dirty dishes *in* the dishwasher instead of leaving them in the sink. But a little white lie never hurt anyone. "I can clean this castle for you...like a scullery maid? Is that the term?"

"You should know how to defend yourself," Cheriour said.

"Am I to understand," Quinn closed his eyes, "that she *truly* doesn't know how to fight?"

"Can you stop talking about me like I'm not standing right here?"

"She doesn't," Cheriour said.

"I told ye she was afraid of the knife. She's powerless too," Belanna added.

Quinn opened his eyes and leveled me with a long, condemnatory stare.

My skin itched. Like an, *I'm having an allergic reaction to something* kind of burning. Beneath me, Sacrifice shifted and shook her head, likely sensing my agitation. I kicked my feet out of the stirrups, desperate to get out of the saddle. Cheriour's hand dropped to my wrist, his work-roughened hand shackling me.

"Then she's a liability," Quinn said after a long beat.

"Agreed." Cheriour tapped his thumb against my wrist. "But she should be given a chance."

Given a chance? A chance to do what? Prove to these lunatics I was worthy of *living*?

Quinn pursed his lips. "Fine. But we won't waste our time on a lost cause. One month. If she doesn't progress by the end of the month, you *will* escort her from the city. Or kill her, if that's what you prefer."

"That seems fair," Cheriour said.

The fuck was he smoking? No, it *didn't* seem fair.

"Bull—" I hissed when Cheriour's hold tightened. It didn't hurt. But if he held me any tighter, there would be pain.

"She can stay in that room." Quinn's nose wrinkled, as though disgusted by the very idea. "*With* a guard. You may be foolish enough to trust her, but I am not."

"Didn't you just call me a lost cause? What do you think I'd do—"

"Hush," Cheriour muttered to me before he nodded at Quinn. "Understood."

"Fine." Quinn's eyes, when he turned them toward me, were brimming with hate. And terror. And anger.

The itchy sensation kept creepy-crawling across my skin. "What is—*ouch!*"

Cheriour squeezed my wrist, sending a quick shot of pain up my arm.

Quinn's lips thinned. For a second, I thought he would march over and gut me with his sword. But he turned away with a grunt. "Cheriour, take her to her room. I'll find someone to guard it once I finish tending the injured. Belanna, you can help me. Where is Marcel?"

"Dead," Cheriour said.

Quinn dropped his head into his hands with an aggravated noise. "You...*get rid of her.* I'll be needing your help as well."

With that, he darted up the steps, barking orders at the soldiers standing by the castle doors.

Cheriour turned, leaning close to my ear to keep the curious gawkers from overhearing his words. "I told you to mind your words with Quinn."

"Okay, well, I wasn't expecting the jackass to throw a knife at my head! And the way he talked to me..."

"Stop...*quiet...*" Cheriour shook my arm.

Er, no. He wasn't shaking my arm. I was doing that all on my own. My entire body trembled. A sickly sensation settled in my stomach. I could still feel that knife whipping through my hair. If Cheriour had been a half a second later pulling me out of the way, or if that knife had gone a centimeter lower...*bam.* Headless Addie.

Cheriour's fingers loosened. His thumb rested against the inside of my wrist. Could he feel my jackrabbiting pulse? Probably. "I'll show you to your room." His fingers rubbed a soft, slow circle over my skin. "Rest tonight. You'll be safe."

Yeah...safe.

For now.

18

THE INCIDENT

LASS

Humans are flawed creatures. We are more intelligent than other beasts of the earth; capable of great kindness, empathy, and creativity. Yet many of us are ruled by the same base emotions that drive a boar to attack, or a hound to hunt. For all our advancements and so-called intelligence, we are little better than animals.

My first experience with cruelty—*human* cruelty—came after we'd lived in Swindon for over six years.

THE...*INCIDENT* occurred on a tranquil winter evening.

The market had begun to close for the night, but Terrick had sent me to retrieve a loaf of bread to have with supper. He had an insatiable appetite for bread.

And for the bread maker.

"Ach, you're a lucky girl," Carragh told me as she handed

me her last loaf. "I was about to give this to the pigs. It won't be much good tomorrow—likely'll be harder than a rock. You and Terrick best eat it tonight."

"We will." I tucked the bread under my arm and handed her a coin.

She waved my hand away. "No, child. I'll not be takin' payment for stale bread."

"If you do not take it now, Terrick will bring it later." I smiled at the hopeful expression that crossed her face.

I may have been young, but I was not foolish. Carragh and Terrick enjoyed each other's company.

"Keep your coin." Carragh fought to keep from smiling.

"As you wish." I turned and walked back through the market, jiggling the coin in my hand. Many of the vendors had retired for the evening. Indeed, when I turned a corner, I found the street deserted, and the booths emptied.

Except one. The dressmaker, Darcie.

I liked Darcie. She was kind, and never without a smile. She hadn't even gotten angry when my buck, Ned, had escaped his pen the year before and gleefully explored the market, consuming everything in his path. Including one of Darcie's fine gowns.

Darcie had merely laughed as I'd wrestled the cloth from Ned's tightly clamped jaw. She'd also refused Terrick's payment, claiming the entertainment she'd received watching me corral my wayward goat had been fair compensation for the gown.

Normally, Darcie would have packed her fabrics away before sunset. But, that night, they still hung from the booth, flapping in the breeze.

The sight was unusual, but not a cause for concern. Until I heard the cry. It was muffled and quiet, but unmistakably afraid. Most children might have run away from the noise;

perhaps to fetch an adult. It's what I should've done. Instead, I foolishly ran *toward* the sound, batting the fluttering dresses away as I peered over the booth.

Darcie lay face-down on the ground. She'd been stripped of her clothing.

A man crouched over her. I recognized him, but only vaguely. Grady, I believe his name was. He was a market vendor as well, but one Terrick had rarely visited.

Grady was still clothed but had pulled his trousers to his knees. His reddened face was contorted in what looked to be pain. One gnarled hand clasped over Darcie's mouth, the other yanked on a fistful of her hair.

At the time, I didn't fully comprehend what I was seeing. I was too young. I'd never seen humans copulating before. But I still knew something was wrong.

I backed away, a cold sensation writhing along my spine. The loaf of bread slipped from my numb fingers, landing on the booth with a loud thud.

Darcie whipped her head up.

A steady stream of blood ran from her nose. Grady had struck her. Likely several times. Bruises marred her throat and shoulders. Her wild, terrified eyes found mine.

She tried to speak—perhaps to ask for help. But with Grady's palm stuffed between her lips, all that came out was a stifled gag.

Raaaphuh.

My skin prickled.

Before me, Darcie roiled in pain against the ground. But, in my memories, I saw Mama collapsing in the tomato field. I saw that great big toad, with his bulging eyes.

My blood coursed like fire through my veins. My palms itched.

I wanted to help Darcie. But my emotions whirled in a

dizzying frenzy and my body seemed to have turned to stone. I couldn't move toward her. Nor could I step away.

Raaaphuh, came Darcie's muffled plea.

"Stop," I whispered, clasping my hands over my ears. It dulled the noise but did nothing to ease the raging itch spreading across my skin.

Grady drew back. "Oi!" he bellowed.

Darcie tried to yell. *Haapufh!*

"Stop! Stop!" I closed my eyes and screamed.

I don't remember what happened next. Perhaps my brain rid itself of the traumatic memory. I'm told that is possible; the human brain is quite fascinating.

Regardless, the next thing I knew, I stood before the smoldering market booth, staring in horror at the two bodies on the ground. Both Grady and Darcie were unrecognizable—their flesh turned mottled shades of black and red. Their faces were swollen and puffy, teeth bared as though in agony.

They weren't breathing.

"No, no, no," I whispered.

Flames danced over my fingertips.

Another scream filled the air, but this one was not from Darcie.

Darcie would never scream again.

Instead, Carragh stood a short distance away. One hand covered her mouth, the other was outstretched, her trembling finger pointing at me. "You-you...*what have you done?*"

I stared at her, a chill gripping my body despite the fire that frolicked over my skin. The scent of charred flesh filled my nostrils.

More people spilled onto the street.

"A hybrid?" Some questioned as they studied me.

"Impossible," others scoffed. "No hybrid has that ability."

"That's Seruf's power. Mark my words."

~~Constornation~~—Consternation filled their eyes as they circled me. Some faces I recognized. Lorcan, for example. The innkeeper who'd once put berries in my porridge.

"Help," I whimpered. "Help!"

The fire would not abate. It traveled along my arms. The sleeves of my fine green tunic were reduced to ash.

My skin remained unblemished.

"Help me!" I whirled in panic. Embers floated from my body. They looked like stars against the night sky.

"She'll burn the market down!" A man said.

Tears filled my eyes when people began drawing weapons.

"Please!" I gasped.

Lorcan stepped forward.

"Please *help me!*" I staggered to his side.

He whispered, "I'm sorry, *cailín álainn,*" before he struck my head with the blunt end of a knife.

I awoke back in Terrick's dwelling.

"Lass." He knelt beside my bed, pressing a damp cloth to my brow.

"Don't touch me!" I sprang up, staring at my fingers.

But the fire was gone.

"It's alright, lass," Terrick whispered. His gnarled hands shook as he wrapped them around my knuckles. "Lorcan said the flames disappeared once you were ~~unconcious~~—unconscious. It's alright. Oh, lass..."

A long wail burst from my throat. It *hurt*, as though Lorcan had speared his knife through my chest.

Terrick pulled me into a tight embrace, rocking me slowly back and forth as I howled and quivered. He dried my tears, pressed cool cloths to my neck, and guarded me when I slipped into an uneasy slumber.

It was a night that would haunt me for the rest of my life.

Even to this day, I see Darcie and Grady when I close my eyes. I smell their burnt flesh in my dreams.

They were the first humans to be destroyed by my wretched power.

But they would not be the last.

TERRICK MUST HAVE BEEN TERROR-STRICKEN. I was a hybrid that shouldn't have existed. One with the same power as the Firestarter Celestial: Seruf, Ramiel's trusted companion.

And I had no control over my ability. I was volatile. Dangerous. Had Terrick decided to abandon me, he would have been justified in doing so. I was not his kin. I was merely a girl he'd found in the woods.

But he stayed by my side, assuring me I was not to blame for what had happened.

Meanwhile, the people of Swindon, the kind-hearted folk we'd lived alongside for six years, turned on us.

Accusations swirled around the village:

"You never said she was a hybrid, Terrick!"

"Is she *truly* a hybrid? I've never heard of one with such a destructive ability."

"She couldn't control it."

"She killed two people!"

"How do we know Seruf didn't create her? Has she, perhaps, been Seruf's spy all along?"

"She'll kill again. Mark my words."

Terrick tried to plead my innocence. "The lass stumbled across a traumatic event. And, for a child to see such a thing...

but it doesn't mean she *can't* control her powers. You know her! She's a good lass. She won't hurt anyone else."

His words fell upon deaf ears.

The townspeople, long frightened by the Celestials' wrath, would never trust me.

People stopped visiting his shop. They kept a distance when we walked through the streets. Eventually, vendors found excuses to withhold their merchandise from Terrick.

"I've got no eggs today, Terrick. The hens are old—don't produce as much as they used to." The rather rotund man wouldn't even look at us.

"Ah, yes, but I'm afraid the last pig is already spoken for. Perhaps if you'd arrived sooner?" The pig keeper rubbed a hand against the back of her neck and turned away.

The most hurtful betrayal was Lorcan's. When Terrick and I approached the inn, hoping for a hot meal, Lorcan waved a knife at me. "I'll not have you coming near this place anymore, girl," he said.

Girl.

I was *cailín álainn* no more,

And Swindon no longer welcomed me.

It still could've been a safe haven for Terrick. All he had to do was rid himself of me. But he didn't.

"I'll never leave you, Lass," he told me on one of the many nights I cried myself to sleep. He pressed his lips to my brow, holding me close while sobs wracked my body. "You are not evil. Nor are you a monster. The townspeople are frightened. They've seen too many horrors in their lives. Do not listen to them."

So, we prepared to leave our home.

And what the townspeople never knew, or perhaps never understood, was that they could never fear or hate me as much as I feared and hated myself.

19

GASOLINE WHISKEY

ADDIE

Cheriour kept looking at me, probably stunned I'd gone a solid five minutes without saying a single word. A new record for me.

Shock was an absolute *bitch*.

My body moved on autopilot as we entered the castle's big-ass foyer. The barren room was the size of a cathedral. Minus all the stuff that made cathedrals cool. It boasted no furniture, decorations...*nothing*. Instead, wounded soldiers sprawled across the ground. We maneuvered around them to get to the stairs.

I should've felt something as I stepped over semi-conscious bodies. Anguish. Disgust. Fear. *Something*. But I was too numb to process those hard-hitting emotions.

"Right," Quinn's voice drifted toward me. "I'll mend Ben, Ruben, and—" he cut himself off with a harsh sigh as he took an armful of bandages from the man walking beside him. "Paige may need to go first. She won't last much longer with that inflammation." He knelt beside a woman with a badly distended leg.

At that moment, a strained and hollow curse rose from beneath my feet.

I'd stomped on a guy. And the poor bastard had a very obviously displaced collarbone. "Shit, sorry!" I hissed, stumbling away from him.

He grumbled, choked, and blacked out. And that funky-shaped collarbone? It was honestly the least of his worries. He also had a big ole hole in his stomach.

I expected my gut to twist at the sight. It didn't.

"Ten minutes, Cheriour," came Quinn's conceited voice. He gave me one long, hard glare before he lowered his head and peeled bandages away from the woman's festering leg.

Cheriour said nothing as he grasped my arm and guided me toward the main stairway.

We passed an armory on the right side of the steps. The door sat ajar, giving me a chance to peek into the cavernous room that was packed, from floor to ceiling, with hundreds, maybe *thousands,* of pointy objects. Swords. Bows. Arrows. Axes. Things that would make die-hard LARPers go nuts.

And then Cheriour and I went up. And up...and up. Had to be ten, maybe eleven floors. On a coiled stairway barely wide enough to fit two people. It was dark too. No windows. No lights. Just the white stone walls, which were not nearly as luminescent on the inside as they'd been on the outside. I banged my elbows at least a dozen times. Cheriour, however, sidled through with no issues.

After getting off the dizzying stairway, we walked down a narrow hall lined with closed doors on either side. The place was pretty damn desolate. Lotta stone. Still no windows. It was like a prison. And the air was hot and stagnant. Sweat poured down my back as my lungs struggled to get oxygen into my body.

"This is your room. Eighth door. On the right side." Cheriour shoved the aforementioned door open.

The room was as sparsely decorated as the rest of the castle. It had a bed, a desk, a fireplace, a few wooden buckets, and...that was it.

Oh, and two postcard-sized windows. Both covered with wood shutters.

The place smelled musty. Stale.

"Is it just me, or is the air kinda thin up here?" I wheezed, leaning against the doorway as white spots danced before my eyes.

"You may want to open the shutters." Cheriour snatched a tinder box off the desk and moved toward the bed...and the candle that sat on the headboard.

My mouth was suddenly drier than the damn Sahara.

"Until you've earned Quinn's trust, you will be confined to this room." Cheriour lit a match. *Woosh.* A cheery little flame now bounced above the candle, so very close to those dingy, unmade bedsheets...

A low ringing sound filled my ears. I shivered, even as beads of sweat slid down my cheeks.

"You'll be assigned guards." Cheriour moved around the room, lighting another candle over the desk. "Be mindful of your mouth around them..."

His words melted into gibberish as my brain soared far, far away.

The flash of memory came on abruptly—it always did. Hot, dry air rushing over my skin as flames sashayed closer to me. Smoke filling my lungs; the taste of sulfur on my tongue. The odor of pork chops oozing into my room.

And, above all else, the raw, pained scream of my mother...

My ass hit the ground with a *pphhlapp*. The back of my

head cracked against the door frame. Didn't feel the pain though—was too busy, y'know, trying to *breathe*.

Cheriour spun around. "Addie?"

"Put them out!" I gasped.

"Wha—"

"Put them out!" I yelled. God, the *stench*.

"What is wrong?"

I wrung my hands together. "Put them out...I...I don't—I don't like fire."

Cheriour's eyebrows shot up—the first time he'd seemed shocked at something I said. "You don't like fire?" he repeated slowly.

"No. Not while inside. Do you know how quick fire spreads? Okay, yeah, the walls are stone. But those sheets would go *poof* in minutes. *Minutes.* And it's not easy to get out of a burning building. People *think* it is until...and flesh burns are..." My eyes burned as tears threatened to fall. "Put them out. Please."

To his credit, Cheriour didn't argue. He licked his fingers and doused the candles.

Of course, without them, there was zero light. The room was dark. Dreary. Creepy AF.

"I'll take it you don't want me to start a fire?" Cheriour drawled, gesturing to the empty hearth.

"Fuck no." I pressed my head against my knees, still fighting for oxygen, and screamed when his hand touched my shoulders.

"Be still." Cheriour knelt beside me. He didn't do or say anything else. He just stayed there, one hand resting on my arm, the heat from his palm seeping into my skin. I listened to the steady cadence of his breathing and tried to force my lungs to follow the same rhythm. At first, it was like trying to inhale underwater. But it got easier. It always did. And, once I'd stopped straining for air, everything else re-stabilized. I was still shaking and dripping in a cold sweat. But my head cleared.

"Thanks," I mumbled.

Cheriour drew away and stood, holding out a hand to help me to my feet.

"Guess this is another thing to report to Quinn." I slapped my clammy palm into his. "'*The useless bitch has meltdowns over a fucking candle.*'"

Cheriour hauled me off the floor. "This room has been vacant for several months—"

I sniffled. "Is that supposed to, like, justify me losing my shit?" I had a lovely tear/snot combo streaming down my face. And my knees wobbled so hard, I had to brace my hand on the wall to keep my balance.

Cheriour moved around the room again, throwing the window shutters open. "Give it a few moments and the air won't seem as thin in here. Tomorrow I'll find clothes for you."

"Hmm..." This wasn't the first time I'd been offered clothes. Belanna had tried to give me a dead woman's shirt and pants the other day. "Can't I—"

"The garments you wear are impractical," Cheriour said. "You will need new clothes."

I looked down at my dress. It was grimy but had held up surprisingly well. My leggings? Not so much. They looked more like fishnets now. That was what I got for buying the cheap pack at Walmart.

"Meals are served in the kitchen at dawn, midday, and dusk," Cheriour continued. "But tomorrow evening there will be a gathering at supper to discuss recent events. I expect you to be—"

A bug scurried across the floor, right in front of my foot. Some kinda fat beetle: "Fuck!" I squealed, jumping backward and slamming my shoulder against the door frame.

"It's an insect," Cheriour said dryly. "It won't hurt you."

"I hate bugs." And, considering the filthy state of the room, the bed was probably chock full of creepy crawlies. No way I was sleeping there tonight.

"They'll not bother you." He paused, running a hand over his snarled ponytail. "If you wish to clean yourself..."

My ears perked up at that. "You guys have a shower?"

"There is a communal bathing room on the first floor you may use."

Communal bathing room? "That sounds disgusting."

"Then don't use it. Now, I am needed downstairs. Do you need anything before I leave?"

"Actually..." My brain made an almost audible *whir-whir* sound as it got back online. "I have two questions."

He sighed but waved his arm for me to continue.

"Who did this room belong to? Quinn was pretty damn adamant he didn't want me staying here..."

"The room belonged to Lasair. The former ruler of Netheridge."

"Former? As in—"

"She's gone," Cheriour said flatly.

"Ah." OMG. The death rate here was through *the freaking roof!*

"And your other question?" Cheriour pressed.

"Well...what happened earlier..." *Why* could I still feel that knife slicing through my hair? I swallowed as goosebumps raced along the back of my neck. "Quinn tried to *kill* me. Because...he saw my eyes? Did I hear that right?"

It took Cheriour a bit to respond. He pursed his lips. Frowned. Tugged at the ends of his beard.

"Don't strain yourself," I said.

My comment rolled right off his shoulders. "I'm sure you're aware your eye color isn't common," he said.

"No shit, Sherlock."

"But we know of another with the same abnormality."

"*Interesting.* There's a fellow purple-eyed mutant here? Who?"

Cheriour gestured to the room. "Lasair."

"Yer scared, aren't ye?" Belanna chuckled.

I glanced at the wooden cup she'd plopped on the desk in front of me and grimaced at the odor. It was alcohol. And normally I would've downed it without a second thought. But this smelled like *rubbing* alcohol—something likely to leave me on my hands and knees puking over a toilet.

Er...well, puking over a *bucket*. The Viking version of a toilet.

I lifted the cup, swishing the liquid around as Belanna hoisted herself onto the edge of the desk. "Ye *are* scared!" she raised her eyebrows in a challenge.

"Of drinking? Never. Of sucking down mystery substances? Absolutely. That's how you end up drugged."

Belanna chuckled. "'Tis whiskey."

I took another whiff. "*Phew.* That is *not* whiskey."

"'Tis!"

"Okay, let me rephrase: it's not *good* whiskey. This is some bottom-shelf shit that'll burn a hole in my esophagus." The scent alone had singed my nose hairs.

Belanna's smile widened. "Ye can't handle strong liquor?"

"Of course I can. As long as it's not shit."

"Prove it." She reached for her own cup and raised it toward mine.

"Prove what? That your whiskey's shit?"

"That'll be the best whiskey ye'll be finding here..."

"Well, that's depressing. *If* true..."

"So if ye're wanting a drink, this is it." She flashed a smug smile.

I lifted my chin. "On three?" I'd regret this. Big time. But never let it be said that Addie Collins turned down a drink.

"Aye."

"Fine. One. Two."

"Three!" Belanna declared.

I shot the whiskey to the back of my throat and swallowed. And I usually relished the burn that accompanied strong drinks. But this one left a foul, almost acidic tang on the back of my tongue. I had to fight to keep it down.

Belanna knocked back her drink, gave me a self-congratulatory smile, and poured herself another from the flask she kept tucked in her vest.

I slapped my hand over my cup when she leaned across the desk. "Nope. I'm good. One shot before noon is a good way to start the day." I belched. "Two usually means you've got a problem."

"Ach, two isn't even enough to start me day with a clear head."

"And you don't think you have a problem?" I raised an eyebrow.

"Oh, aye, I know I have a problem." She tapped her forehead. "Being a Speaker is me problem. But nothin' will be fixin' that. So I drink." She didn't even wince when she guzzled the second shot. "And nothin' will be curing yer woes either. So ye might as well have another." She waved her empty cup in my face.

"*Hell* no. And I do *not* think that's whiskey. It's like gasoline."

Belanna laughed. "Don't ye be making excuses because ye couldn't handle it." She poured herself another glass, this time taking slow, languid sips. Savoring the fiery petrol flavor.

I rolled my eyes. "Take it easy there, Calamity Jane. And aren't you supposed to be...watching me? Or something?"

"Aye, I am. I'm watching ye choke on yer liquor."

"Har, har. I don't think this is the *'guarding'* that asshat—"

"Eh?"

"Quinn. I don't think this is the *guarding* he had in mind. Y'know, he sent this bitch up last night—"

"Ye mean Rhona?"

"That her name? She didn't introduce herself. Just barged in here, barking that she'd put a knife in my back if I tried to run. Then she stood at the door and gave me the creeper stare. I swear she didn't blink all night. The bitch is like a weird *Terminator* cyborg...I didn't get *any* sleep. Also, do you wanna know how many dead rats I had to throw out the window? Five! And I don't even know how many *live* rats are still in this room."

That was, literally, how I'd spent the night. Cleaning. As best I could, anyway. Squashing bugs. Chucking dead rodents outside. Fighting the urge to taunt the woman who never peeled her eyes away from my ass.

I had a nice ass. Didn't mean I wanted a creepo Viking woman eye-humping it all night.

"Rhona talks tough," Belanna chuckled. "She's harmless though."

"Harmless? She was *armed*!"

"And she'd never use those weapons on a human. Nah. If ye had run, she'd have caused a ruckus to get Quinn's attention, but she wouldn' have harmed ye. Now Quinn..." she grimaced.

"He'd *gladly* put that knife in my back," I scoffed. It'd been at least eight hours since our rocky introduction. And I still got goosebumps thinking about that knife and the damage it could've done.

Outside, a series of deep, booming laughs drifted into my room. I stood, mainly to hide my sudden jitteriness, and walked to my little porthole (aka, window). I couldn't see much at first. The window was too small. The ledges on the castle wall were too wide. And the early morning sun was right in my eyes. But if I stood on my tiptoes, and angled out slightly, I saw a stretch of green lawn, where a cluster of men and women huddled together, each holding a long, wooden pole.

The booming chuckle had come from Kaelan, who was doubled over, his wooden stick braced in front of him. And, standing next to him, was Cheriour.

"Cheriour organizes the mornin' trainin' here," Belanna said as she leaned against the second window, a few feet away from me.

"*Training?* Everyone just got back last night!"

"Oh, aye. We try not to take lengthy breaks. A dull soldier is a dead soldier."

Well, that sounded ominous.

"Cheriour's an excellent teacher," Belanna continued as Cheriour thumped a still-chuckling Kaelan on the shoulder before turning to the rest of the group. It looked like he was giving instructions, but I was too far away, and couldn't hear much over Kaelan's braying. "He'll get ye sorted in no time," Belanna said. "Watch."

With Kaelan's laughing fit now done, the session officially began.

And I was *not* prepared for Cheriour's moves. *Holy Moly!* He looked like a dancer. Every swing of his stick was fluid and precise. When he struck someone, he got their ankles, wrists, or behind their knees. Small targets. But effective, given the reactions of the other soldiers, who either buckled or dropped their sticks when hit. And Cheriour rarely missed. His nimble feet soared over the ground as he pivoted around his opponents. He turned on a dime. During one part of the session, a woman tried to sneak up behind him. Cheriour whirled and had his pole up to defend himself before she'd even raised hers. The motion was effortless for him. Elegant. If he slapped on some spandex and pointe shoes, he could've joined The New York City Ballet Company.

In comparison, the other soldiers training with him looked like clumsy bulls barreling across the field.

My heart made a stuttering *thimp-thump* in my chest. Nothing to do with fear this time.

Until...

It was the *thwack* heard around the world. Cheriour's stick caught an onrushing man in the jaw. Specs of blood flew into the air, looking like big-ole raindrops. The man crumbled, clutching at his broken face.

"Ach, see, Garvin got sloppy," Belanna tutted. "Moved before he had his feet under him."

The training session kept going, even with Garvin kneeling on the ground.

"Are...he...*shit,*" I hissed when a woman barreled into Garvin's side, swinging her stick to ward off Cheriour's attack. "They've got a man down. Doesn't he need an ice pack? Something? Shouldn't they at least be stopping?"

"He'll get himself moving. Once his vision straightens again," Belanna laughed.

My heart rolled over inside my chest this time very much a terror response. Garvin got trampled four...*five* times. "That's barbaric," I hissed. "And you call Cheriour an *excellent* trainer?"

"Aye. See, Garvin's getting to his feet. No harm done."

No harm done. Sure. The guy only had a broken jaw and a half dozen bruises on his body.

Belanna winked at me. "We'll see if he's learned his lesson. Always make sure yer feet are under ye, Addie. Very important."

Dear freaking God.

I was *so* screwed.

20

FECKING BRIGHT EYES

ADDIE

"Stop fidgeting." Cheriour tapped my hand as I tugged at my shirt.

I dropped my arm with a sigh and continued following him down the twisting stairway. "These clothes are so freaking uncomfortable," I grumbled. The wool was as coarse as sandpaper. And my skin was super dry. Because, y'know, bathing in a wooden barrel with grimy water and ammonia-scented soap hadn't exactly been *replenishing*.

"Yer lucky," Belanna had said when she'd led me to the bathing room. "The water is fresh."

"Fresh" my ass. That mucky bath probably gave me a staph infection.

I rubbed at my collarbone.

"Stop," Cheriour said.

"How 'bout you focus on walking? Don't worry about what I'm doing," I snapped.

As soon as he turned around, I scratched the itch rippling across my rib cage.

I also shouldn't have tried to wash my clothes. Lesson #2 of the day. Right behind: *don't hop naked into germ-infested water.*

As soon as I'd started scrubbing dirt off my clothes, everything came apart at the seams. *Literally.* My leggings morphed into crotchless pants. Panties? *Pfft,* gone. I'd refused to put my dress in the water—the only smart decision I'd made. Although, surprisingly, my bra had fared okay. Thank *fuck,* because bras weren't a thing here, and my girls were way too boisterous to leave hanging loose.

So I couldn't *argue* when Belanna handed me the sandpaper outfit. It was either wear it or go nude.

I probably would've been more comfortable in the nude.

At least the new getup didn't *look* terrible. The plain black shirt was...well, a *shirt.* The sleeves were a little too long and it was snug around the bust, but it worked. The brown pants weren't made for someone with a booty, so I'd had to leave the top laces undone, but they fit okay otherwise. The boots came a little over my knee and stunk to high heaven, but they molded to my foot like a glove.

Small mercies. I mean, the clothes could've been uncomfortable as hell *and* fuglier than a burlap sack.

Cheriour turned to face me again as I reached a hand over my shoulder, trying to get an itch on my back.

"Scratching will make it worse." His lips twitched.

"Shut up," I grumbled.

As we drew closer to the second floor, a cacophony of voices rose to greet us. Barbs of nervous anticipation shot through my chest, but I swallowed them and kept my chin high as we descended the stairs and turned the corner into the dining hall.

It was jam-packed. People stood shoulder to shoulder. Or *sat* shoulder to shoulder, if they'd been lucky enough to nab a stool from one of the four long tables. And the room was massive; twice the size of most cafeterias. So for it to seem claustrophobic with this crowd...

"The entire city is here," Cheriour said, no doubt catching my slack-jawed expression.

My eyes roamed over the sea of people, and I got a jolt of excitement when I realized most were holding wooden beer mugs. "Oooh, is this open bar? What kinda beer do y'have on tap?" The beer *had* to be better than the whiskey. Even the cheap-ass beers from back home were drinkable.

Cheriour simply motioned for me to follow him into the room, weaving in and out through the tight spaces between people.

"I swear I won't get shitfaced! Although, I *am* a happy drunk—oh crap! Sorry!" I exclaimed when I trod on someone's foot.

The guy smiled. He was an older man with bushy gray eyebrows and a friendly face. "'Tis no—"

He cut himself off, eyes widening, as he turned to face me.

"We'll explain later, Jael." Cheriour ushered me away.

"Is...wait...was that about my eyes?" I asked. "*Again?*"

Cheriour said nothing. But, as we parted the ocean of humanity, dozens of others twisted around, stood on their tiptoes, or craned their necks to stare at me.

"Is anyone else gonna try to *kill* me because of my eyes?" I whispered. "Should I be on high alert right now?"

"No," he grunted.

"You sure?"

"Yes." Cheriour found a somewhat quiet corner to shove me into. It was still crowded. But I recognized most of the people who stood around us. Like Kaelan. And Belanna and Braxton.

"I'd not fuss much, Addie." Belanna sidled over, clapping

her hand against my shoulder. "Yer eyes are so fecking bright, people can't help but notice.

I rolled my *fecking bright* eyes at her.

"But the stares will stop soon enough." She shrugged. "My soldiers didn't gawp at ye on the ride over, did they?"

Kaelan, who leaned against the wall next to Belanna, huffed out a laugh. "They were too scared." He glanced over Belanna's head and stage whispered: *"She threatened to gouge their eyes out."*

"Staring is quite rude." She smacked my shoulder again. My knees almost buckled beneath the force of her impact. "And ye had enough to be worryin' about."

"Please tell me you were just messing with them," I said. "You wouldn't *actually* have mutilated their eyes. Right?"

"Aye. She would've," Braxton chuckled.

At the same time, Belanna scoffed, "If ye make a statement with no intention of following through, 'tis nothing but an empty threat. And they'll know it." She said this in a sing-song voice. "Ach, there's Quinn."

Holy moly. She was a *lun-a-tic*. Fully certifiable. "The heck is wrong with y—" I started. But then Cheriour tapped my arm and I realized, too late, that silence had fallen upon the rest of the room.

And I was a loud talker.

Oops.

Belanna, Braxton, and Kaelan snorted. A few other people laughed too. Most spun around, gawking at me, only turning away when Cheriour shook his head or made quiet sounds of disapproval.

Across the room, Quinn stood on a table, elevated over the crowd. He looked no less miserable today. He had his arms crossed over his chest and a wretched pout on his mouth. Although, thankfully, he ignored my outburst. "I'm sure you've all heard about Bafrus" His blue eyes swept the room. He waited until he had everyone's attention before he continued. "It has, indeed, fallen."

A low murmur wafted through the hall. Beside me, Belanna's laughter died. She went rigid; her face pale.

"Belanna and Braxton evacuated most of Cynerik," Quinn continued. "But were unable to reach the rest of the towns. At this time, we are asking everyone here to stay within the borders of Netheridge. And we may need to discuss evacuating the towns close to Bafrus' border." He glanced at Cheriour, who nodded slowly.

"Now," Quinn folded his hands together, twisting his fingers and cracking his knuckles. "We have also lost Lamex this week to Elion's plague."

Tension rolled into the room like a gigantic black cloud.

My gut churned as I thought of the sick woman vomiting into her laundry basket.

"We've searched extensively," Quinn continued, "but haven't seen Elion within Netheridge's borders since. That doesn't mean he's not here. Elion has been taking birds. The Speakers," he turned his gaze to Belanna and Braxton, "can't track his whereabouts. Therefore, I am doubling the guards around the city. I've sent word notifying the other towns in Netheridge to do the same."

The tension cloud thickened. Like the air on a humid summer day. Before a thunderstorm exploded. Goosebumps prickled along my arms and back.

"If Elion is seen," Cheriour added, "remember to aim for his wings. I know you've all been told this before. But many soldiers at Bafrus forgot their training. And died." His hand went to his beard, twisting the edges. "So I'll reiterate: injuring a Celestial's wings will immobilize them. Temporarily. They'll not be hindered by any other attack."

A shudder ripped up my spine. The Celestials actually had wings? And mauling those appendages only *temporarily* incapacitated them? What killed the bastards?

"Nothing," Cheriour said, keeping his voice low so only I could hear it.

"What?"

"The Celestials. Injuring their wings will slow them down. But they *can't* be killed. Not by humans."

"But what if you...I dunno, hacked their head off?"

"The Celestial would reattach it," Cheriour said calmly. "And kill the offending human."

"Oookay. What about the hybrids?"

"They are still human. And their powers are useless against a Celestial."

This kept getting better and better, didn't it?

I turned back to Quinn. He rattled off information about crops, and the new livestock brought in from Lamex, but I couldn't absorb anything he said. My mind was still stuck on the unkillable Celestials.

"Lastly," Quinn called after several minutes. "I'm sure most of you have noticed we have a new arrival."

My thoughts came to a screeching halt.

"Cheriour tells me he found her outside Cynerik. Yes," he added when a few people made noises of disbelief, "I'm aware of how long it's been since we've seen a new arrival." Quinn never took his eyes off mine. And I didn't look away. That would've given him way too much satisfaction.

"Perhaps her appearance is a good omen," Quinn continued, his voice flat. He couldn't even pretend to buy the shit he was pedaling. "In the meantime, she'll start training with me in the morning."

With *him???*

I looked at Cheriour. But he said nothing. He didn't even meet my gaze.

"I'll ask that everyone give her space," Quinn continued. "Show her the same courtesy you've given to new arrivals in the past."

His words sounded fine. Almost considerate. But there was so much *hatred* in his stare. Kindness was the last thing on his mind.

And this dude wanted *to train* me?

"I thought *you* were the combat instructor?" I hissed at Cheriour.

Cheriour turned those toneless eyes toward me. "Quinn wishes to oversee your training."

Quinn, now finished with his speech, hopped down from the table and left the room.

Around us, dozens of trays were being carted through the doors at the other end of the hall, each piled high with meats, cheeses, and—well, I didn't know what the rest of the stuff was. Mystery substances.

But whatever appetite I might've had was long gone.

I'd been *dreading* joining Cheriour's training crew. I would've preferred to scrub the germ-infested tubs every day for the rest of my life than do one day of fight club. But I trusted Cheriour. He'd be a brutal teacher, yes. *Ooooh* yes. But he'd also be fair.

I didn't trust Quinn. At all. He'd probably slit my throat and tell everyone I tripped and impaled myself on a sword (a scenario that had a high likelihood of actually happening). I didn't want him within twenty feet of me with a weapon.

"Quinn is prideful. Not mean-spirited," Cheriour said.

Because *of course* I'd been talking again. "You sure about that?" I thought of the blade whizzing through my hair.

Instead of answering me, Cheriour turned away with a

soft-spoken, "I'm sure you're hungry," and beckoned for me to follow him to one of the food-laden tables.

"Distracting me with food," I mumbled as I walked behind him. "You're starting to know me a little *too* well. This would normally work. But I've tasted the food around here and—yo!"

Cheriour flopped a strip of meat into my hands.

"Did you stick your fingers in the food? That's *gross*...hey now..." I held the meat to my nose. "This smells pretty good." And the taste wasn't half bad either. It was steak. Not *good* steak. More like the cheap, thin-sliced stuff you'd get at a *meh* steak sandwich place. But it was like a top-dollar filet mignon compared to the hardtack I'd been choking down the past week.

"Good choice, sir," I said. "What else is decent to eat around here?"

He inclined his head before he moved toward the table. And I swore—couldn't be sure, with the background noise— but I *swore* he breathed a chuckle.

21

DARFIELD

T errick cried as we packed; the first time I'd ever seen tears in his normally jovial eyes.

"We'll take only what we need, lass. Nothing more," he said as he plucked a wooden doll off the shelf. He traced his fingers over the doll's face and smoothed his thumb over its braids. His lip trembled.

"Dorothy is good at drying tears," I said. I'd christened the doll with that name after Terrick and I began reading the fictional adventures of Dorothy and her dog. An exciting tale I would, sadly, never finish.

Terrick blinked and returned Dorothy to the shelf. "As much as she would doubtless enjoy the journey," he tapped his thumb against Dorothy's shoulder, "I'm afraid she isn't an essential item."

"You're sad," I murmured.

"No." He wiped his moist cheeks. "The dust is bothering my eyes." His smile was strained. "You'll never fit those clothes in your saddle bag if you fold them like that," he chuckled as he surveyed my haphazardly piled garments. "Here, lass, we'll fold them together."

His grief was palpable, even as he tried to hide it from me.

And, at the time, I hadn't understood the brevity of the situation. I didn't learn of Terrick's past until many years later.

HE'D BEEN a soldier in his youth and had helped to liberate Sakar from Ramiel's rule. While in the army, he met Lucy.

When the first war ended, and Sakar was declared free, Terrick and Lucy moved to Swindon.

As Terrick opened his fiction book shop, Lucy became a wood crafter. She designed each item of furniture in Terrick's dwelling, including the flowered armoire. After she bore Terrick a daughter, Lucy also used her skills for toy making.

The little Dorothy doll had been Lucy's creation. Their daughter had adored the doll. As had I.

Terrick had many years of happiness with his family. In that regard, he was luckier than most. But I've found happiness lowers one's pain tolerance. If one is not used to a life of anguish, they'll find themselves unable to bear the burden when tragedy strikes.

Terrick's daughter was nearing adulthood when she accompanied her mother into the forest to collect wood. It was mid-summer, and the day promised to be sunny and arid. Lucy harnessed their old horse to a cart and told Terrick she'd return before nightfall.

She did not return.

Terrick found Lucy, their daughter, and the horse the next morning. All three were drained of blood. Their murderer, a

wild Púca, still stood nearby. The creature had been long abandoned by its masters and nursing a crippling injury to its left
forehoof. Perhaps Lucy and her daughter had been inattentive,
thinking themselves safe while close to Swindon's borders, and
had been easy prey. Perhaps hunger had lent the Púca speed
and drove it to ignore the pain as it hunted its meal. Regardless, the creature went to its grave with a full belly.

And Terrick lost his family.

But their shadows clung to the dark corners of his
dwelling.

Haunted by the echoes of those old memories, and unable
to cope with his grief, Terrick left Swindon. He spent a decade
journeying across the land, collecting new books and teaching
children to read. But no matter how far he traveled, or how
long he stayed away, he'd always been able to call Swindon
home. The memories of his family remained preserved in his
dwelling, ready to welcome him when his grieving eased. And
it had, for a time. I think he found some measure of happiness
again when he brought me into his home.

Until I forced him to leave it again. Permanently.

And, although I didn't fully grasp what he was losing, I
knew his sadness was my doing. Guilt rested upon my shoulders; heavier than any milkmaid's yolk.

This was my fault.

And I've never forgiven myself for it.

Terrick's face seemed to age another decade as he strapped
our meager possessions to the saddles. He had found a livery
willing to sell him two beasts: a wide-chested bay stallion and

a small speckled gray pony. I think, perhaps, the livery owner was grateful we were using his animals to leave Swindon.

Terrick spared his home a parting glance before he turned to me, forcing a smile. "There, lass, didn't I tell you we'd fit all your clothes if we folded them properly? Come now, let's get you in the saddle..."

The townspeople watched as we departed on that balmy, wintry morning. Some held weapons and regarded me with mistrust and hostility as I followed Terrick through the winding streets. Words swirled through the air.

"That's not a hybrid. Mark my words."

"Seruf sent her. I'm certain of it."

"Why are we allowing it to live?"

"Well, I'll not be killin' it and riskin' Seruf's wrath."

Sobs racked through me. They spoke about me as though I were an object they'd taken an aversion to. As though I wasn't *human*.

"It's alright, lass." Terrick drew his horse alongside mine and reached over, grasping my shoulder.

I shied away from his touch. He pulled his arm back with a sigh.

Glares and whispers followed us into the forest.

"Pay no mind to what they've said," Terrick told me once we were well clear of Swindon's borders.

I sniffled and wiped my tears with the back of my hand.

"Fear is an ugly thing, lass. It often makes people say what they do not mean. You are not a monster. You are a hybrid. One...*gifted* with an unusual power."

Gifted?

I thought of Darcie and Grady's scorched bodies. "It's not a gift," I snarled.

"You may not see it as one now—"

"I *killed* Darcie." The words burned my throat.

"I know, lass. You lost control—"

"Then how can you call what I have a *gift?*" The wiry gray strands of my pony's mane blurred as moisture filled my eyes. The pony flicked his ears back, no doubt sensing my distress.

"You could do great things with your power." Terrick's voice remained steady, even as his eyes brightened with unshed tears. "You only need to learn how to control it. I can show you how, lass. We'll learn together."

Terrick's faith in me never wavered.

I only wish it had been rewarded.

DARFIELD WAS A SPRAWLING CITY.

A towering castle stood on the shoreline, overlooking a violent sea. The city streets were overcrowded: there were houses stacked on top of each other, rows upon rows of shops, and people clustered so closely together, they bumped elbows as they walked. And the sheer breadth of merchandise available was awe-inspiring.

In Swindon, we'd had one shoemaker. Darfield had thirteen. There were also fabric stores on every street in Darfield, some selling cloth in dazzling shades of reds and yellows.

I gaped at the red gown that hung in a shop window. "How did they *do* that?" I asked.

Terrick smiled. "I'm not certain. But it's quite beautiful, isn't it? And look here, lass! This one nearly matches your eyes!"

The tunic in question boasted a swirl of soft reds and blues. I pressed my nose to the glass, my eyes combing over the brilliant garment, studying every detail. The material was unlike any I'd ever seen, more resembling the calm ripples in a pool of water than the normal weaves and pulls of fabric.

Terrick squeezed my shoulder. "Ah, lass. When we have more coin, perhaps I'll buy it for you." There was a note of worry in his voice. He'd had precious little savings when we left Swindon. But that had been several months ago, and our supply had dwindled since.

It was silly for me to covet something so needlessly expensive. But I'd never wanted anything as badly as I wanted that tunic.

Still, I reluctantly pulled myself away from it and followed Terrick through the town.

The stench of ale and the sweet aromas of smoked meat hovered in the air as we passed no less than a dozen taverns. Music seeped from pub doors. And many of those establishments were open well into the wee hours of the morning.

Darfield, I quickly learned, was a city that never slept.

But, for all its grandeur, it lacked Swindon's kindness.

In Swindon, a man with few coins could rent a room at an inn, so long as he agreed to supplement the cost with work. Darfield permitted no such exceptions. And, with our funds in dire ~~straights~~ straits, we couldn't find lodging.

We spent the first week sleeping in the stalls with our horses. In the mornings we'd wash in the water troughs, shake the straw out of our clothes, and Terrick would leave to search for employment.

"Would you like to join me?" Terrick asked each day.

And, each morning, I responded the same: "You only talk about boring things all day."

To which he would chuckle and pat the top of my head. "Well, please stay close to the stables. Darfield is a large city, lass. You can't roam as freely here as you could at Swindon."

He was incorrect in that statement.

There was *more* freedom in Darfield. The people were so consumed in their own frenzied lives, they didn't spare me a glance as I journeyed through the city. It was a relief to move about without feeling angry leers and hearing whispered accusations.

Often, I went to stare at the tunic. It had gone unsold, likely because of the exorbitant price. One hundred coins, enough to feed and house a family for a month. But the garment was utterly resplendent. There were golden ~~tassles~~ tassels on the laces. It shimmered in the sunlight. And the fabric's color changed with the position of the sun, appearing raspberry pink in the morning light, deep plum in the evenings, or on sunless days, and orchid in the afternoon.

I was ~~mesmorized~~ mesmerized. It didn't matter the tunic was made for an adult and would have been an ill fit for me. I still envisioned myself wearing it. In my imaginings, I'd stroll through the streets, the majestic material sparkling. People would notice me, undoubtedly, but for the *right* reasons. Instead of whispering about how dangerous I was, they'd murmur about how wonderful I looked...

On one warm and sunny afternoon, I became so distracted staring at the tunic, I didn't notice the boy sprinting around the corner. Not until he crashed into me.

I grunted as I fell, my shoulder colliding with the stone street. The boy landed on top of me in a heap, his gangly legs and arms entangled with mine. "Apologies," he groaned.

A few people stopped and stared but did not move to assist us. Most were too absorbed in their own worries to notice what had happened.

It took a moment for the boy to right himself—his legs were far too long for his body—and then he bent down, extending a hand toward me.

"Have you been blinded? Or are you merely daft?" I asked,

refusing his offer of help and rising on my own. "Did you not see me standing here?"

"Yes," the boy's hand dropped to his side. "I did. But I thought *you* saw *me*. I called out—" he glanced over his shoulder and, without warning, snatched my arm.

"What are you—" I began.

"Laugh." He flattened his back against the wall of the shop and spun me around until I faced him.

"What?"

"Laugh," he hissed as he crouched, ducking his head beneath mine. "Pretend I've told you a joke."

I glared at him as a throbbing pulse beat through my bruised shoulder. "I doubt I'd find any joke of yours amusing."

"Please." Sweat beaded on his brow. He was breathing heavily and his eyes—the most gorgeous blue eyes I'd ever seen—were wide.

Perhaps it was those eyes that swayed me. They were every bit as ~~mesmorizing~~—mesmerizing as the tunic. I did as he asked, although I found it quite difficult to force a sound of glee.

"*That's* your laugh?" The boy gave me a baffled look. "You sound like a braying donkey."

I scoffed. "Perhaps if you had an ounce of charm..."

"I've more than an ounce..."

"...or wit..."

"...I also have that..."

"...you'd hear a genuine laugh. But, at the moment, I'm annoyed. So I can either continue braying or..."

The boy dropped his gaze, giving my arm a frantic squeeze. "Continue laughing. *Please.*"

As I carried on with my strained guffaw, three armored men ran past us. Soldiers. One of them grunted, "I'm sure the wee bastard went this way."

"He'll stay in the alleys," another said. "Easier for him to hide. If we turn here, we may be able to catch the blighter before he reaches the border."

My forced laugh died as the soldiers turned down another street. "Are they looking for you?" I asked the boy.

He grinned and straightened. "Looking, yes. Finding, no. Not if I can help it."

I stared at him with narrowed eyes. "Why are they hunting you?"

"I left my post."

"Why?"

"Because I don't want to be in the army." He shrugged.

"Perhaps you should have considered that before you joined."

"I didn't join. Or, rather, I didn't *choose* to." The boy cleared his throat and ran a hand through his walnut-brown hair. "Humans have the freedom to choose their profession. Hybrids don't."

"You're a hybrid?" I scoffed. This smug, lazy boy was so very much unlike Terrick, the only other hybrid I knew.

"I am. One of many. The army won't even miss me."

"If that were true, they wouldn't be searching for you."

"Well, they may miss my *ability*. Certainly not me. I am *not* a skilled fighter." He waggled his fingers in front of my face, as though offering his raw and blistered palm as evidence to his claim.

I'd gotten sores like that before too. When I first began mucking the goat pens, my hands had been ravaged by the coarse pitchfork handle. Terrick rubbed a salve on the lesions each evening, assuring me my skin would harden and I'd stop getting sores. He'd been right.

This boy clearly hadn't learned that lesson. "Perhaps if you spent more time training and less time fleeing, you would not have such blisters," I said.

"I've no wish to train. These are musician's hands, you see. I'm developing ~~callises~~ callouses in the wrong places. Soon I'll have difficulty playing the harp."

"The harp?" I asked. At the time, I couldn't picture what it was. In Swindon, some of the townspeople used flutes to carry a tune, but none possessed an instrument as grand as a harp.

"Have you never heard a harp being played?" the boy gasped.

I shook my head.

"Pity. An absolute pity. It produces such a *wondrous* sound—"

"Surely not if *you're* playing it."

"*I*," the boy stuck out his chest proudly, "am the finest harpist in Darfield. Ask anyone. You must come with me sometime. You'll find yourself in love with—oh no," he groaned.

The soldiers had turned back onto the street and were staring at us.

"Drat." The boy straightened and gave me another beaming smile. "Luckily for me, I'm faster than them." He squeezed my arm. "You've beautiful eyes. Has anyone ever told you that?"

And, with that, he sprinted away, the soldiers pursuing him.

22

MR. SHIT BRICK

ADDIE

I hated mornings. *Especially* mornings that started at the ass-crack of dawn, after I'd spent the night sleeping at a desk (to avoid the icky bed). I had a knot in my neck the size of a tennis ball and a numb left ass cheek. I was *not* bright-eyed, bushy-tailed, or ready to seize the day by the horns.

But I *tried* to be friendly.

"So what's for breakfast?" I asked my new guard (a scrawny guy with a salt-and-pepper beard) cheerily when he barged into my room.

"If you wanted to eat, you should have woken up an hour ago," he said.

I pursed my lips. "Rhona didn't tell me that." Miss *Stick-Up-Her-Butt* had resumed her spot at the door yesterday and stared at me. *All. Freaking. Night.*

The man shrugged. "Not my problem. Here..." he chucked a sword at me, probably expecting me to catch it. But he *clearly* didn't know me.

I ducked away with a squeal. The weapon clattered to my

feet, mashing my toes. "Yo! Ouch!" I winced. "I'm already up! I didn't need the extra wake-up call!"

The man grunted. "Pick up the sword. Quinn is expecting you."

I stared at the long blade as my stomach gave a nervous churn. This was a real sword. Like, steel blade, pointed tip...*REAL*. "He's not gonna train me with actual weapons? Is he?" Fuck. Quinn *was* trying to kill me!

"The blade is dull," the man said.

Dull. Yeah. Sure. I picked the sword off the ground. And, because I was me, I tapped my pointer finger against the blade. To test it. I drew back with a pained hiss as the edge sliced my skin. Blood oozed from the new cut. *Dull my fucking ass.* This sucker was sharp! And *heavy*. Weren't swords supposed to be light and swishy? This one was like a cinderblock.

And I had to haul it with me down all ten flights of stairs. Clanging it against the walls. Whacking it on the steps. Tripping over it. I got a strenuous workout before the exercise had even started.

We didn't go out the front entrance. Instead, we hung a hard right at the bottom of the stairs and slipped through a narrow door to a small, square courtyard.

On another occasion, this would've been a picturesque spot to sit with a cup of coffee. The four castle towers curled around the (overgrown) grass yard like a glistening privacy fence. An oak tree stood in the center, the branches swaying in the slow, sticky breeze.

It was peaceful. Quiet. Cool...*ish*. I mean, the humidity was still through the roof, but the sun hadn't crept over the tops of the towers yet.

Unfortunately, the peace was interrupted as soon as I saw Quinn standing beneath the tree, glowering at me. His sword rested tip-down in the ground; his hands cupped over the hilt.

"You're late," he snapped.

Ooooh boy. This was how it was gonna be, huh? And I'd been about to say: *"good morning."* Because I thought if I gave him a thousand-watt smile and did a little ass-kissing, we could start over. On the *right* foot this time.

Wrong.

"I came down as soon as your lackey collected me," I said. "You shoulda sent him ten minutes earlier if you wanted me here sooner."

Quinn's face reddened. "I expect you here before sunrise each morning—"

"That's not specifying a time—"

"Then I'll specify it. If the sun is already over the horizon, you're late. And I won't tolerate tardiness. I have too many other tasks to attend to."

"So why not have someone else train me?" I grumbled. *Anyone* else. I might've even let Belanna shove me off a cliff.

Quinn pursed his lips but didn't answer.

Great. This was going *splendidly* so far.

"So, uh," I started, desperate to break the tense silence. "Do your swords have names?"

"What?"

"Like, in *The Lord of the Rings,* they named their swords. Sting, Narsil—"

"Why would we name an inanimate object?"

"I dunno. To give it power, or something? I thought that was a thing." Those fantasy movies had lied! What a shock...*not.*

"It's not."

"Oookay. Well, where do we begin?" I *so* wasn't in the mood to put up with this shit brick.

And I definitely, 100%, did not want to deal with him *swinging a sword at my freaking head!*

There was no warning. None. Quinn stood there, looking P.O.'d at my every breath. And then he *lunged*, whipping his blade around.

I screeched and ducked out of the way. "Yo!" I yelled. "What the fuck?"

"You weren't paying attention!" he said.

"We were talking! Or, at least, I was *trying* to have a pleasant conversation before you—gah!" I didn't move quick enough this time. His sword barreled into my left shoulder. And thank fuck the blade was somewhat dull. As it was, the blow hurt like a motherf'er. A deep, numbing pain shot down my arm, making my fingers tingle.

He would've taken my arm off with a sharp blade.

"Still not paying attention." Quinn raised his sword again.

"Just-just—*give me a second!*" Goddamn, my shoulder really, *really* hurt! "Some warning would be nice too!"

"The Wraiths will not warn you before they attack. Why should I?"

Whoosh!

His sword smacked against my right thigh. My knee buckled, and I cried out, the numbing pain now rocketing up my sciatic nerve.

Quinn wasted no time. "If you lose focus on the battlefield..."

Thwack!

Air rushed out of my lungs as the next blow bounced off my rib cage.

"You die," Quinn finished.

Thump!

The last hit went to my gut, leaving me doubled over, choking and wheezing.

How on earth was I supposed to avoid him? He moved faster than QuickSilver; darting around me and landing blows before I got my feet moving. "You're a lunatic!" I gasped, pressing a hand to my ribs. Everything hurt! And, yeah, I was a total pansy with pain. But still...

This wasn't training. Training would've required him to teach me how to defend myself. He'd taken an opportunity to pummel me, knowing I wouldn't be able to hit him back.

"Don't—" Quinn growled and turned away, ripping a hand through his hair. "Don't *look* at me like that! You have a weapon. *Use it.*" He pivoted to face me again. The dim sunlight glinted off the edge of his blade as he raised it.

I hadn't even caught my breath, and he was ready to start another round of *Whack-an-Addie?* Fuck my life.

I curled my hands around the hilt of my sword. *Use it.* Yeah, okay. I wanted to *skewer* the bastard. Like a pig on a stick.

I pounced, winging the sword through the air like a baseball bat.

Quinn sidestepped out of the way.

"Ooof!" The force of my overly enthusiastic swing almost sent me to the ground, where I would've belly-flopped on my sword. Huh. That would've been a shitty way to go. *Addie Collins: spun herself dizzy and impaled herself on her own weapon.*

I backed away from him, laughing—because my adrenaline was pumping and making me woozy—and my heel caught a rock, hidden beneath the tall grass.

Tiiiimmmbbbeeerrr.

The back of my head hit the ground with a whipping *crack!* A blinding burst of pain exploded behind my eyeballs, and black spots blossomed across my vision.

With a low curse, Quinn chucked his sword aside and knelt beside me, his gaze cold as he watched me gasp, groan, and scrub at my eyes. I winced when his fingers pressed against my face, very Vulcan-Mind-Meld style.

I blinked once, twice. The black spots vanished. The pain

receded. It felt more like an *I've been staring at a computer too long* headache rather than a *what the hell did I drink last night?* kind of throbbing.

I reached for the back of my head when Quinn pulled away. I had some blood in my hair, but it was already dry and sticky. There was a small lump on my scalp, the size of a mosquito bite. And it kept shrinking, even as I prodded it. "Huh. So you're a healer hybrid? I'd say thanks for nixing my concussion. But *you're* the reason I whacked my head."

"You tripped," Quinn said.

"Yeah. Because you were *attacking me,* and I was trying to get you to stop."

Quinn's lip curled. He stared at me like I was a fat ole slug he'd smashed beneath his boot. "Get up. And pick up your sword; we're not done yet."

Rapunzel, Rapunzel, let down your hair.

Ha! If only it were that simple to escape my prison—er, *bedroom.*

I sighed as the humid breeze trickled through my little porthole and pressed my face against the coarse stone of the windowsill. This had become my favorite spot. Most days, the window was the only thing keeping me *somewhat* sane. And, when I'd gotten tired of standing on my tiptoes to look outside, I'd shoved the desk over, stacked the chair on top of it, and *voila,* I had a window seat.

Or a *throne,* as I liked to call it. Because it looked like a lopsided royal seat.

My guards gave me funny looks whenever they saw me

perched up on my makeshift throne. Did I care? Hell no. I needed the fresh air. Needed to be surrounded by the sounds of city life below.

I couldn't see it from here, but there was a tavern nearby. Things got rowdy there. And I could always count on the dulcet tones of someone drunk singing to drift into my room at two a.m.

I loved it. Listening to someone butcher a sea shanty reminded me of my own drunken expeditions. It reminded me of home.

Many of the soldiers from the castle migrated to the tavern after sunset—including Mr. Shit Brick himself.

Oh, yes. Quinn seemed to have a wee bit of a drinking problem. He snuck out behind the rest of the soldiers and staggered back well after they'd all returned. No wonder he was such a ray of sunshine in the mornings; he was *always* hungover.

Not that I blamed him. I wished I had the option to drink myself into oblivion every night. This world was a *nightmare*. And the two weeks I'd spent trapped in this shithole room had been pure hell.

Fourteen full days.

They'd seemed like a freaking eternity.

My month *shape up or pack up* mandate? Still a thing. So my original statement was inaccurate: I'd been trapped in this room for two weeks, the only exception being the one hour a day I spent being Quinn's punching bag.

And, boy, did I feel like a used-and-abused piece of sparring equipment. My skin had turned almost the same shade as my eyes (the apparent source of Quinn's wrath). I was *covered* in bruises. A heavy layer of gooey, seeping blisters coated my palms. They stung when I sweated. Throbbed whenever I tried to hold something. And ached the rest of the time. The big toenail on my left foot had turned black and was about ready to fall off, the result of me dropping my weapon on my toes. *Repeatedly.* Pretty sure I had a couple of broken toes too.

I was a hot mess.

But thank God Quinn always Mind-Melded the concussions away. He didn't dare let a head injury leave me dazed—that might've dulled some of the pain.

I pressed my forehead against the windowsill, watching as the sun rose over the trees in the distance. If only I could be like Rapunzel. And have magical glowing hair long enough to double as a rope. I'd use it to climb to freedom and—

And...what?

Assuming Quinn's lackeys didn't hunt me down, and I got out of the city, where would I go? To the woods? I'd be dead in a week. Or less.

It was a fate I'd be facing soon enough, anyway. Once Quinn booted me out of Niall.

I jolted when my bedroom door swung open.

Judging by the soft *thumping* to my right, the sudden movement had scared my guard too. And, well, she wasn't exactly *friendly,* but I kind of liked this guard. She was about my age and had a fun laugh...when she wasn't stuck babysitting me, of course. But I'd seen her staggering back to the castle after a night in the bar many times. And she had the most *gorgeous* complexion. Clearest skin I'd ever seen. Paired with her chocolate-colored hair...hmm. If I'd been at my workstation at the salon, I could've had this woman ready to dazzle on the red carpet in less than an hour.

I missed my job. So freaking much.

"Are you listening?"

I blinked because—*holy shit*—Cheriour was standing right in front of me.

The hell had he come from?

Maybe Quinn hadn't fully magicked away my last concussion. Either that or I was sleep-deprived. Probably the latter, since I still hadn't gotten the nerve to use the ick bed.

"Not really," I grumbled. "And unless you've come here to tell me you've got a one-way plane ticket for me to go home, I don't care."

He sighed but didn't rise to the bait. "Quinn has ended your training sessions."

"Oh good. So he's kicking me out early?" It was an effort to keep the tremor out of my voice.

"No. With the news of certain events, Quinn needs to focus his attention elsewhere."

"'Certain events?'"

"Yes."

"Care to elaborate on what that means?"

"No."

"Okay then." I shrugged.

"I train with a group in the mornings. But, based on what I've seen of your sessions with Quinn—"

"Oh, you mean the hour a day he spends beating the snot outta me?"

"—you aren't ready to join my group," Cheriour continued. "Therefore, I will give you a private session this afternoon."

"Cool. So are you gonna teach? Or use it as an excuse to batter me around?"

Cheriour propped a hand on his hip. "Quinn...is fighting his own demons. And is too proud to admit his judgment is skewed. I'm sorry." He said this on a long, tired sigh. And I wondered, maybe foolishly, if he'd spent the last two weeks arguing against Quinn on my behalf. Because he looked almost as exhausted as I felt. "You'll not receive the same treatment from me," Cheriour said. "But if you're not willing to learn, I won't waste my time."

Relief crashed into me so hard, I almost slid right off my throne. I could've hugged him then. My savior. And a fucking saint.

Instead, I gave him a thumbs-up...

And watched his brow furrow. "Is that meant to be a crude gesture?"

"This?" I wiggled my thumb. "Nah. This means 'you got it.' Now *this*," I flipped my middle finger up, "is a crude gesture."

Cheriour huffed and turned to my guard. "You can bring her down at mid-day."

"Is lunch included?" I asked.

Cheriour didn't respond as he ducked out of the room.

"Guess not."

23

LOVE TAP

ADDIE

"**S**eriously," I insisted, "a pair of scissors, that's all I need. You wanna know how good it'll feel to have that hair off your neck?"

My chocolate-haired guard grunted noncommittally but kept walking, her heavy, matted braid bouncing with each step.

Outside we went, where the afternoon sun was searing hot and the air was thick enough to cut with a knife. I was already sweating—no surprise there.

"You would look *amazing*," I said to my guard's back. "I'd give you a side-swept cut—very easy to take care of. Just wash and go."

She grunted again.

"Or we can stay with the longer style. But I think you'd love a short bob if you gave it a chance," I pressed.

That remark didn't even earn me a grumble.

Instead of taking me to the courtyard, the woman led me around the side of the castle. The sun-burnt grass crinkled beneath my boots as we walked.

Cheriour sat cross-legged in the field between the castle and a small lake. A long wooden pole lay draped across his legs, and he used a knife to whittle bits off the end.

"Thank you, Lottie," he mumbled to my guard, although he didn't pull his gaze away from the pole. "You don't need to stay."

With a curt nod, Lottie turned and marched back to the castle. Probably (definitely) happy to be rid of me.

"Her name's Lottie?" I asked. "That's cute! I'm trying to talk her into letting me cut her hair. She's not having it. But I'm persistent. We'll get there."

Cheriour said nothing. Just kept chopping on the pole.

"You could be my next makeover," I said. "You've got pretty coarse hair..." *Understatement.* His thick hair curled in every direction, even though he'd tried to tame it back into a pony-tail. There was literally a frizz halo around his head. "But I could get some of the bulk out—"

"Take this." Cheriour thrust the wooden pole into my hands. I scrambled to catch it but only held onto it for a brief second before he shook his head and snatched it away.

"What'd you do that for?" I huffed.

"It's too long." He shaved another inch off the end and handed it to me again. Only to take it away again.

The third time was, apparently, the charm.

"Good," he said gruffly as I leaned the top of the stick against my shoulder.

"You're sure?" The pole was almost as tall as me. "Still seems pretty big."

"It's meant to be."

"Oookay. I mean, I don't know much about this fighting stuff, but I've never seen a five-foot sword—"

"It's not a sword."

"Well, *duh*. But it's a dummy sword, right? Er, a practice sword?" I corrected when he gave me a blank stare.

"No."

"Okay, but..." I trailed off, my mouth suddenly Sahara dry again. "Oh no. Uh-uh."

Cheriour had heaved himself to his feet and was brushing grass off the seat of his pants with his left hand. His right hand, however, held another wooden pole.

My muscles ached, reminding me I was already covered in bruises. I couldn't take any more hits. Uh-uh.

I grasped my pole in both hands. It was awkward. Too long. Too unbalanced. When I held it in front of me, it wobbled. Although maybe that was because my hands were shaking...

Cheriour sighed and opened his fingers, letting his stick clatter to the ground. "There. It's gone. Now, will you stop backing away from me?"

"What? Shit." I hadn't even realized I was moving. I forced my feet to be still, but I kept a white-knuckled grip around my pole.

Goddamn. Two weeks was apparently all it took to develop PTSD.

Cheriour crossed one arm over his chest, and rested his other elbow against it, leaning his chin into his palm. His eyes were narrowed. Deliberating. Analyzing.

"These are not swords," he said. "Or *dummy* swords. I'm training you to use a polearm."

"A...what?"

"Pole. Arm," he repeated slowly.

"Like a spear?"

"A spear is a type of polearm, yes. They're easier than swords."

I stared at my stick. It seemed way too long. Too cumbersome. I'd end up tripping over it. "Can't I use a knife?"

Cheriour's left eyebrow rose. "You had a knife. And didn't want to use it."

"Well, that was different. I was...I dunno. Still thinking I'd find some way to go back home." I dug my nails into the pole. "But if I'm stuck here, and I *have* to fight, wouldn't I be better off using a small weapon? Something I can jab and stab with?"

He stepped closer to me, ignoring the way my hands panic-spasmed around my stick. Closer. Closer. Until his nose was only an inch from mine.

He had some *seriously* gorgeous eyes.

And surprisingly pleasant-smelling breath. Not minty fresh. More tea-scented...

"A Wraith will *not* smell pleasant," Cheriour said.

"Aw crap. Did I say that out loud?"

"And you'll need to be this close to one to kill it with a knife," he continued. His warm, green tea breath tickled my cheeks. "Are you willing to do that?"

My stomach churned. I knew what the Wraiths stunk like. Knew how freaky their milky-white eyes looked up close. "Nope," I said.

"Then we'll continue with the polearm." Cheriour stepped away.

"Is there *any* other alternative? I really don't think I'm coordinated enough to use this. What about a bow?"

"A bow requires strength and precision," Cheriour said. "You have neither. Nor do you have the time to learn. Polearms are easier."

"Or I could...*not* fight? Seriously, I don't mind being the castle cleaning lady..."

"You don't have that option." Cheriour bent to retrieve his stick but paused. "If I pick this up, will you remain calm?"

"As long as you don't start swinging it," I said. But a little shudder still raced up my spine once Cheriour had a weapon in his hands again.

He didn't use it to hit me. Thank Christ.

Instead, for fifteen minutes, he demonstrated how to hold a polearm and told me to mimic his stances.

It was—*le gasp*—an actual training session! I was *learning* something.

Unfortunately, the stick was still awkward as fuck, even when I mastered the basic hold.

I didn't care what Cheriour said; a knife would've been easier.

"Now," Cheriour shifted his stick in his hands and moved toward me, "I'm going to do an overhand strike—"

My stomach dropped to my toes.

"Stop backing away," Cheriour said. "I won't *hit* you—"

"Like hell," I said. He already had his stick raised.

"I want you to block me. *Listen*, Addie. Focus. If I bring my weapon down, you'll need to bring yours up. It's simple."

Simple. Yeah. Sure. My blistered palms ached as I gripped my stick.

Cheriour dropped into a lunge. Getting power from those hindquarters to make his blow more painful.

Oh God, Oh God!

He sprang up, his pole swinging down.

"Agh!" I squealed and squeezed my eyes shut as I threw my arms (and the pole) up to protect my face.

Thawp.

The two slabs of wood connected with enough force to send vibrations up and down my arm.

I opened one eye, my mind racing to assess the damage. No broken bones. No pain.

Because I'd blocked him.

"Holy shit!" I squeaked. "I did it!"

Cheriour drew away. "I wouldn't celebrate yet—"

"Oh, come on! Cut me some slack—"

"—especially since you closed your eyes. Don't do that again."

I pursed my lips. "I mean, that's more of a reflex..."

"Then learn to ignore it. Closing your eyes leaves you vulnerable. Now, I'll do three strikes: upper hand, right side, underhand." Cheriour demonstrated the moves, his pole swishing through the air. "In that order."

"Okay..." *Damn.* Once had been hard enough. Now he wanted me to do this *three times*?

"Focus," Cheriour said. "And move your feet. If I step toward you..."

He lunged forward, bringing the pole down.

I scrambled back, bringing my stick up.

"Good." Cheriour nodded. "But keep your eyes open."

"They are—" I cut myself off with a squeal when his pole rapped against my right shoulder. It didn't hurt—he'd barely given me a love tap—but my heart still kicked into overdrive.

"Not good," Cheriour tutted. "You closed your eyes. And lost concentration because you were arguing. Let's try again."

Beneath the hot afternoon sun, my life became a blur of movement. Block. Dodge. Duck. Sidestep. Repeat.

I'd never exercised so much in my *life.*

By the end of the almost two-hour session, I was dripping with sweat, and *sincerely* wishing I still had my cotton panties. Swamp ass with wool fabric? *Eek.*

I pushed my sticky hair off my forehead, flapping the collar of my shirt to fan myself as Cheriour collected the stick from my shaking hands.

"That wasn't awful," he said.

I pouted. "Not awful? I did everything you asked!"

A ghost of a smile touched his lips. "You did. Hence why it was 'not awful.'"

"Jeeze. What the heck do I have to do to get a 'halfway decent?'"

"Train harder."

Train harder. Okay, sure. That'd get me through the next two weeks. But what happened after that? Quinn wanted me trained for a *reason*, and it wasn't so I could get toned arms and a chiseled six-pack. "What's the point?" I asked.

"The point?" Cheriour held both poles in one hand, swinging them idly. He wasn't even breathing heavy.

"I mean—" I fanned my face, but it didn't do jack squat against the sweat trickling down my chin. "Look, I don't want to be a Debbie Downer here, but let's be real: I ain't a kid anymore. And there's a hard limit on how many new tricks an old dog can learn. I'm not gonna be a good fighter. Ever. And I'm sure you've got way better shit to do, so why waste time training me? What is the point?"

Cheriour scrutinized me for a long while. He let the poles rest against his side as he raised his other hand. He looked like he wanted to reach out and touch my shoulder. Which had my stomach twisting itself into a pretzel. In a *good* way. Nervous anticipation. But then, after a very obvious pause, he ran his fingers through his hair.

And why, why, *why* did that gesture leave me disappointed?

"Living is the point," he mumbled. "I've seen enough death. I want to see you live. And I'll do what I can to help you survive here."

My heart did a weird stutter step. *Damn.*

Cheriour was walking proof that judging a book by its cover was a shit move. On our first introduction, I'd accused him of raping women because he looked like a Viking. And now

I felt like absolute crap about that. Because under that burly appearance: the snarled beard, the frizzy hair, the face that never cracked a full smile—under all *that*, there was a truly compassionate human being.

And a good-looking one too. Just a shame his face was buried beneath so much wild hair. "Can I ask you something?" I blurted.

Cheriour's shoulders heaved. "What?"

"Can I cut your hair? A *full* cut."

His eyebrows rose. "Excuse me?"

"Look, I'm a hair stylist, so I know what I'm doing. And I wouldn't go crazy; you have such pretty curls; it'd be a shame to chop them off. But they're so weighed down right now. If I gave you a proper trim, those curls would *pop*."

He tilted his head toward the sky in his now-familiar *Lord give me strength* pose and walked away.

"Is that a yes?" I called after him.

His shoulders twitched, but he didn't respond.

"I'm definitely gonna get my fingers in his hair someday," I muttered, tingling with excitement at the very thought.

24

THE BLUE-EYED BOY

LASS

Terrick was suffering.

He tried to hide his sadness, but he was often slow to rise in the mornings. He laid awake late into the night, staring at the ceiling of the livery barn. Sometimes he cried, always stifling the sounds, trying not to wake me. I was, however unfortunately, a light sleeper.

Guilt ate at me. It was as though a great beast had taken residence inside my belly and was *delighting* in clawing and devouring my insides. My ability, my curse, had not only taken two lives, but it was also causing someone I loved great misery.

I wanted to bring Terrick joy. So I ventured into the crowded market, clutching onto two of the five coins we possessed, searching for something that would make him smile.

"Fish! Fresh fish! Two coins a piece!"

"Oi! What you mean it's too expensive? Think ye could make it better?"

"The price is four coins. Not three. Now get out of 'ere. I don't want to be seeing you again until ye can pay what I ask."

A swirl of voices surrounded me. Sellers shouting prices. People arguing. Haggling. This market was far larger and louder than the one in Swindon. It was overwhelming.

As was the merchandise being offered. In addition to food and clothing, one could purchase all manner of useless items. One woman, for instance, had an array of glimmering ~~jewles~~— jewels laid out at her booth. The colorful stones were threaded with bits of string and were meant to be worn around a person's wrist, ankle, or neck. And, indeed, several women walked amongst the crowd sporting ringlets of ~~jewles~~—jewels around their throats.

A waste of coin, to be sure. The *jewels* served no purpose and looked rather cumbersome to wear. But, as one girl exclaimed to her mother, *"they're beautiful!"*

Another merchant sold plates and cups made with decorative glass. They, at least, were functional as well as beautiful, although I wondered how practical they were. Surely glass would break easily? The standard wood and metal seemed to be the sturdier options, and there were merchants aplenty selling those as well.

As I said, the market was overwhelming.

And entirely unwelcoming.

I wandered along the streets, surveying the wares for sale at each booth, my fingers curled around my coins, which were proving to be insufficient. The prices were exorbitant.

I'd almost given up hope when I passed the cheese seller.

I paused, gaping. The remarkable cheese on display was soft and creamy, more of a liquid than a solid food.

A man and a woman stood by the booth, speaking with the vendor.

"'Tis a spread," the vendor, a gray-haired woman, said. "I make it meself, I do. Ye put it on bread, ye see?" She pulled a knife from her apron, cut a slice of bread from one of the loaves on her stand, and dipped the edge of the knife into the cheese. The creamy substance clung to the blade. "And then ye spread it." She dragged the knife over the bread, smearing cheese across the surface.

It felt as though my bottom jaw had become disconnected from the top. I couldn't stop staring. The cheese resembled a fluffy cloud as it sat atop the bread. And I wondered what it would taste like. Was it bitter, as most cheeses were? Or sweet, like milk?

The man took the first bite. "Hmm!" he exclaimed as crumbs dribbled down the front of his tunic. "Beda, this is *excellent!*"

The vendor, Beda, drew herself up proudly. "Aye, I told ye. Ye've never tasted cheese like this before, have ye? Ye—oi!"

I flinched as she whipped her head around to look at me. I'd been so ~~mesmorized~~ mesmerized by the cheese, I hadn't realized I was moving closer to her booth.

"Away with ye, child." Beda waved her arms.

"But—" I stretched my hand out, prepared to give her my coins.

"Away!" Beda squawked.

"This is hardly a way to speak to a customer—"

"If ye wish to make a purchase, come back with yer mother," Beda snapped.

"I have no mother."

"Yer father, then. Now go. Away! I have real customers to tend to." Beda marched toward me, her bony, gnarled hands flailing through the air.

Anger flared inside me. "Anyone with coin is a *real customer.*" I waved one of my coins in front of her face.

Her eyes followed the movement, but she didn't relax her stance.

"You Wicked Witch," I muttered as I closed my fist around the coin and turned away.

It was a term I'd learned from the stories Terrick had read to me in Swindon.

"What is a Wicked Witch?" I'd asked him.

"An unkind person, lass," he'd told me. "One who delights in tormenting others."

Beda's brow furrowed. She knew I'd insulted her but had likely never heard the phrase before. "Away with ye," she snapped again. "If I catch ye here again, yer knuckles'll be bleedin.'" She clutched her knife and turned to apologize to her *real customers*.

"Children," she huffed. "There's a group of 'em that are always causing me grief. Sticking their fingers in me cheese..."

My eyes and cheeks burned as I walked away. I was so angry, so disappointed, and so preoccupied with listening to her talk, that it took me a moment to notice the itch in my palms. I rubbed them against each other to alleviate the prickling, and my stomach turned to rot.

My two silver coins had melted.

I stopped, staring at my hands, which had grown hot enough to liquefy silver. There were no flames yet. But the itching beneath my skin grew.

Panic swelled inside me. I couldn't stay here! People brushed against my arms as they navigated the congested market. I would hurt someone!

My breath escaped in ragged gasps as I staggered off the street, going behind a line of booths and stumbling into the stone wall of a nearby building. I clutched a hand to my chest, willing the itch to subside...

And then I heard the sound.

It was a sharp noise, bordering on shrill. Melodic. Haunting. Music, clearly, but unlike any I had ever heard before. It caused a strange stirring in my chest; a tingling sensation one normally feels before they're about to laugh. Or, perhaps, cry.

The itch eased. The tight, dreadful sensation in my stomach quieted, as though the emotive melody had swept it away.

I turned, desperate to find the source of the music.

And I saw him through the half-open door of a tavern. He sat beside a large wooden sculpture, his fingers dancing over the strings stretched through the center of the instrument. His head was bowed, and his hair obscured much of his face, but I knew it was him. The blue-eyed boy.

He was every bit as talented as he'd claimed to be.

The sounds he produced from that wooden sculpture—the *harp*, as he'd called it—were hypnotizing. Both hopeful and heartbreaking. Upbeat and sorrowful. I never knew a simple tune could induce two polarizing emotions at once.

I was not the only one entranced. Indeed, there were several people inside the tavern watching him intently, their drinks and meals forgotten. A few others had paused their market perusal to listen as well.

The boy didn't seem to notice he'd garnered an audience. Or, perhaps, he didn't care. He kept his head down, his eyes closed, as his fingers plucked at the delicate strings. Each chord produced a distinct note, some shriller than others. Under an inexperienced hand, the instrument may have sounded grating. But, beneath the boy's nimble fingers, it was...

~~Magikal~~ Magical.

Another word from Terrick's fiction books: something extraordinary. Otherworldly.

Magical.

I didn't know how long I stood there. A few minutes, at least. The market life swirled around me, but I paid it no heed.

I was unable to tear my eyes away from the blue-eyed boy who produced such wondrous music.

"There he is. The impudent child..." A harsh voice drifted over my head.

Two men, both clad in leather armor and wearing swords at their belts, walked past me.

Soldiers.

My belly clenched.

They were heading toward the tavern. And the blue-eyed boy.

I've no wish to train. The boy once said. Now I understood why. For his hands, capable of creating such captivating, ~~melodius~~ melodious sounds, were surely ill-equipped to hold a weapon.

I did not pause to consider my actions. I merely threw myself forward, colliding with the backside of one of the soldiers, and loosed an agonized wail.

The soldiers turned.

A few people stopped and stared. Most importantly, the boy ceased playing. He watched me through the open tavern door, his eyes wide.

"Are you alright?" The young soldier who knelt beside me had a patchy beard and a kind face.

My eyes watered. 'Twas not me summoning fake tears—I do not have such a talent. I'd wrenched my right knee and was genuinely in pain.

The soldier reached for me, likely to place a hand on my shoulder.

But I thought of the melted coins in my palm and drew back, further twisting my aching knee.

"Child?" The soldier prompted.

Through my blurred vision, I saw the blue-eyed boy

scramble away from the harp, sprinting to the back of the tavern.

I only needed to keep the soldiers' attention on me a moment longer.

"She was," I sniffled, "cruel to me."

The soldier's brow furrowed. "Who?"

"T-the woman w-with the c-cheese."

"That'd be Beda." The other soldier sighed. Age lines creased his brow, and his dark brown hair had begun to gray. "Stealin', were ya?" he asked me.

"No," I said.

He scoffed. "And what other cause would she have to—Oi! The wee bastard's gone. *Again.* Leave the child be, Connor. If she was stealin', old Beda will have taught her a lesson."

With a somewhat reluctant sigh, the young soldier, Connor, stood and followed his companion into the tavern.

I'd given the blue-eyed boy a chance to escape. Mere seconds, but I hoped it was enough.

My knee throbbed. I returned to my feet with a wince and limped to the other side of the street. A few people stared but did not offer to help. Nearby vendors guarded their wares and peered at me with heedful eyes.

Each step was agony. I made it only a short distance before I stopped, leaning against a wall that divided a bakery and fabrics shop. The ache did not subside, and my knee had developed a rapidly beating pulse.

"Have you hurt yourself?"

I flinched when a voice sounded beside my left ear.

The blue-eyed boy leaned against the wall next to me, a smug smile stretched across his lips.

A strange, quivering emotion gripped my insides. "Are you daft?" I asked. "Those soldiers were just here!"

"And now they're two blocks away, likely thinking they'll

catch me at the next tavern. Although they *would* have caught me at this one, had you not started squealing like a pig."

"I did not *squeal!*"

The boy's grin widened. "You've quite the flair for dramatics, eh? But I saw the way you landed. It's the right knee you injured, yes?" He stretched a hand toward me.

I sidled sideways, evading his touch.

His smile faded. "I'll not harm you," he said.

But I may harm you. The thought passed through my mind, though I dared not say it out loud.

He reached for me again.

I moved again.

He frowned. "Do you fear me?"

"Of course not."

"Then why do you cower?"

"I don't." I raised my chin defiantly. This time, when he reached for me, I forced myself to be still. I didn't breathe, terrified any miniscule movement would send the fire spiraling out of control.

The boy brushed his fingers against my forehead. His hands, despite the clusters of blisters, were tender. Kind.

The touch lasted only a second.

I exhaled, trying not to seem pleased when he put a distance between us again. And it was only after relief seeped into my muscles that I realized my knee was no longer aching.

"You're a Healer!" I gasped. Terrick had told me of the Healers—the most coveted hybrids in all of Sakar.

The boy waggled his fingers. "I am...*unfortunately*." He huffed and swiped a lock of hair out of his eyes. "Now, tell me, did the sobbing only begin *after* you injured your knee? Or were you weeping for joy upon hearing my music?"

"Weeping for joy?" I scoffed. Of course, his melodies had

brought me close to tears, but I thought it best not to inflate his ego further.

"Don't worry, you aren't the only girl in Darfield to find herself overwhelmed while watching me play." He grinned.

The boy *reeked* of arrogance. But there was gentleness in him too.

He was aggravating.

And yet, I laughed. Something I hadn't done for many months. Not since the *incident*. "Perhaps I was *weeping*," I giggled, "because your ham-handed playing made my ears bleed. Have you considered that?"

The boy chuckled and leaned toward me, a devious glint in his eye. "I don't believe you would've been so quick to intervene on my behalf if you found my playing *'ham-handed.'*" His eyes twinkled. "Your pig-squealing was intentional, was it not? To warn me?"

Again, I raised my chin, reluctant to admit the truth. "I had to do something to drown out your wretched playing."

He threw his head back with a guffaw. "Either way, you've given me time I wouldn't have otherwise had to myself. And I think I'll use it to help you." He winked. "I heard you had a run-in with Beda. Mad old woman. Convinced children are creatures sent by Ramiel to destroy her merchandise. I," he thumped his hand against his scrawny chest, "can get the creamy cheese you seek. But I'll not be doing it for free, mind."

"And why not? I helped you without expecting repayment."

"Ah, so you're admitting to helping me!" His eyes glimmered.

"Well," I cleared my suddenly parched throat, "did you not say my pig-squealing gave you time to escape?"

"It did. But then you insulted me, so the good deed has soured a bit. Hence why I'm still willing to help you, but at a cost. If I succeed," he pursed his lips, "you shall come watch me play again, *without* the sarcastic banter. Tomorrow night, at Elton's tavern."

"And if you fail?" I raised my eyebrow.

"Then you, dear lady, shall still come watch me play, but you may make all the delightful sarcastic quips you'd like." He held out his hand. "Have we a deal?"

I laughed again and almost placed my palm in his without a second thought. But a glint of silver, caught between my index and middle finger, drew my eye. The last remnants of my precious coins, melted into a crevice.

I hesitated, drawing my hand back. "I don't have any coin to offer her. Or you." I curled my fingers into a fist, hoping he wouldn't see the flecks of silver.

The boy watched me, the expression in his eyes softening.

"It's...Ter...my father," I said. "He's been searching for employment..."

"There's no need to explain," the boy's voice gentled. And then his lips curled upward once again. "It'll only sweeten the deal. If I should succeed in securing your creamy cheese, *free of charge,* you shall come with me tomorrow night and," he dropped his voice to a whisper, "you'll tell me about this power you're trying to conceal."

I drew back as though he'd slapped me. "How dare—"

"Your secret would be safe with me," he added hastily. "I'll not speak of it to anyone. Certainly not the *army*." He shuddered. "You're too spirited. The army is so...dull. It would be a crime to see them extinguish your *spark.*"

My heart fluttered. A bead of sweat dripped down my back. He knew. He *had* to. Why else would he have chosen those last few words?

But the boy only maintained a patient smile, waiting for me to respond.

If he didn't know about my curse, would he treat me more harshly once he discovered what I could do?

Or would he still wish to be my friend?

I swallowed and placed my other hand in his.

He would learn the truth eventually. Perhaps it would be best if I told him first.

"You have yourself a deal," I said. My mouth felt odd—too dry. And my tongue seemed to have grown to twice its size.

The boy barked out a laugh and, to my very great surprise, kissed my knuckles.

It was an odd sensation, having a boy's lips pressed against my skin. Odd, but not unpleasant. His mouth was warm and soft. His breath tickled.

A storm of conflicting emotions filled my chest. But, before I could berate the boy for his forwardness, or properly analyze why his kiss made my innards quiver, he whirled away, heading to Beda's stand.

I did not follow. One encounter with the old woman had been quite enough. So I waited, watching the endless wave of people moving through the streets. The moments passed tediously. After a while, I moved away from the wall, thinking the boy had failed and didn't want to bruise his pride by admitting defeat.

At that moment, he emerged from the opposite direction. He was panting, his face red and gleaming with sweat.

"Did you lose your way?" I asked.

He shook his head. "Soldiers." He glanced over his shoulder. "Drat. I can't stay." He pressed a square package, wrapped in leaves, into my hand. "Tomorrow night," he rasped. "Meet me here. I'll walk with you to the tavern." His eyes were alight with excitement, even as he sprinted away.

THE CHEESE WAS UTTERLY *DELIGHTFUL*. Sweeter than milk.

"Lass," Terrick groaned in bliss. "Where did you *get* this?" He licked the creamy cheese off his fingers—we hadn't any bread to spread the cheese onto, so we'd simply dipped our fingers into the box.

"A friend," I said. I couldn't keep the smile off my face as I thought of the blue-eyed boy.

"A friend?" Terrick repeated, his face glowing with joy. "You've made a friend already? That's *wonderful*, lass! Hmm..." he took another bite. "Please tell your friend they're welcome to gift us with this cheese anytime they're feeling charitable."

"He didn't gift it," I mumbled. "He merely helped me to buy the cheese. I took two of our coins." My face heated. "I'm sorry."

Terrick's smile did not wane. "Well, your friend certainly helped you spend those coins wisely. This is a *delicacy*. And there's enough here to last a few days." He patted my knee. "Thank you, lass. This was a treat."

I went to sleep that night with a full belly. As I curled into my bed of straw, listening to my pony shuffle about, I imagined what a friendship with the blue-eyed boy might look like; what adventures we could experience together.

But, as my waking thought melted into a dream, the images changed. I saw the blue-eyed boy screaming in terror and agony as his skin blistered. I saw myself standing before him, flames dancing over my fingers. The people of Darfield clustered around me, crying out in fear—

"Lass!"

Flames greeted me when I opened my eyes. They were consuming the stable.

The horses screeched in panic as embers fell from the burning ceiling. Smoke swirled; Terrick choked on it as he leaned over me. "Lass!" He touched my arm and cried out when his hand burnt.

Fire rippled across my skin. My clothes had disintegrated, as had my straw bed. And the fire continued to spread, and spread, and spread....

"I'm sorry, lass," Terrick coughed and sputtered. He raised a knife over his head, his eyes watering. "I'm sorry." He drove the handle into my temple, rendering me ~~unconcious~~ —unconscious.

I WASN'T BLAMED for the fire.

A stableboy had left a candle in the hayloft. According to the rumors, at least. I'm certain Terrick was the source of that falsity. But no one questioned it. Flames and straw were a deadly mixture, after all. And, with people from the neighboring houses and shops working together to extinguish the flames and rescue those trapped inside, no human or equine lives were lost.

It should have been a relief.

But it wasn't.

I'd nearly killed again. And that night began the longest and most miserable stretch of my life.

25

BUG GUTS

ADDIE

The plus side of having my new teacher? I got to leave my prison every morning and join The Breakfast Club (my name for the group, not theirs).

The downside? Well...

I stared at the goop in my bowl. "Is this bug guts?"

Braxton slid onto the bench beside me, already partially finished with his bowl of bug guts. "Id's porddridge," he mumbled around a mouthful.

"Ah, porridge. Of course. How could I have mistaken it for anything else?" I'd never seen porridge look so gray. And slimy. And the way it jiggled when I moved the bowl...

Blech.

"It won't kill you," Kaelan laughed as he sat across from me.

"That's debatable." I glowered at my bowl. "I miss bacon. *Why* can't we have bacon and eggs for breakfast?"

"There'd never be enough," a raven-haired woman named Moira answered. She sat diagonally from me and was happily slurping up the porridge.

"Eggs are used for other things, ain't they?" the blond-haired man, Garvin, added. He wasn't asking for clarification. He tacked a question to the end of *every* sentence: *"Yes, the sky is blue, ain't it?" "My name is Garvin, ain't it?"*

"Seems an awful waste to eat eggs by themselves," Belanna said. "The chickens work hard to make them, ye know."

I rolled my eyes. "Jeeze. I didn't know eggs were such a hot commodity."

"I'm sure the chickens from yer world can't lay more than one egg a day," Belanna said.

"Probably not. But most of our chickens are raised in a lab and pumped full of steroids, so maybe they can. I dunno."

Five sets of eyes stared at me in shock. And revulsion.

I shrugged. "There are a lot of free-range chickens too. I think. Look, the vegan lifestyle's not for me. I tried it. And, I'll have you know, I can make a wicked mushroom and spinach omelet."

"What's an omelet?" Kaelan asked.

"What's an—oh my *GOD*, you poor deprived child." I poked at my goopy porridge. "Although maybe it's a *good* thing you've never had an omelet. You'd never be able to go back to eating this crap..."

This was The Breakfast Club.

And if my life were a movie, this would've been the training montage section. Music would have been blaring (preferably 80s pop) as I worked with the group and got stronger and faster. Eventually, I'd reach some pinnacle (like darting up the steps to Philadelphia's Art Museum) and, *voila:* fully trained soldier.

If only it were that easy.

Instead, I endured hours of long, grueling training sessions that displayed how much I sucked at life. I wasn't getting better. Sometimes I swore I was getting worse. And my clock was a tickin'—only five days left. Five days to either shape up or ship out.

My stomach churned.

Well, my appetite was definitely out the window now.

"Are we sending soldiers to Jabbart?" Moira's voice pulled me out of my thoughts.

"No," Braxton said. "Maddox is sending them."

"But Sanadrin is farther." Moira's brow furrowed.

"Aye, but they have twice the riders we do." Braxton tended to wave his spoon (or whatever he had in his hand) when he spoke. I was used to having my arm sprayed with bits of his food. "And," he added, flinging a glob of porridge onto my wrist, "there's an element of surprise. Seruf won' be expecting the riders to come from Sanadrin, will she?" He tapped the spoon against his temple and smirked.

"Seruf?" I asked.

"The Firestarter," Belanna supplied before she jumped into the conversation. "And have ye seen Gerty with a bow? If Seruf's there, and unexpectin' of the riders coming from that direction, Gerty'll get her."

The most frustrating thing about being in a new world? Trying to figure out who's-who and what's-what. It was like building a thousand-piece jigsaw puzzle while someone handed you one piece at a time.

But I'd gotten the outer edges assembled.

This place, Sakar, had four countries. Possibly five—they sometimes mentioned a place called Vatra, but they'd all clam up whenever I asked about it. So Vatra was either enemy territory or a country they'd lost. Like Bafrus, which they also didn't talk about much.

Sanadrin was the capital city of Victarion (and I'd laughed

for a solid five minutes after hearing that name), our closest neighbor. Maddox was the leader there.

Jabbart was a city in a country called Marach. Two days ago, we'd received news it was under attack. That bombshell had come during breakfast. And, while everyone had looked horrified, Belanna had gone pasty white and bolted out of the room.

"Is she okay?" I'd asked.

Garvin had nodded, his mouth drawn into a thin line. "Reminds her of what happened at Cynerik, don't it?"

Braxton had sighed and plopped his slice of bread onto the table. "We didn' get warning."

Belanna had managed to put up the façade of her normal cheery self when she arrived at the training session. Braxton had remained glum and distant.

"Have ye heard about Muirin?" Garvin's whisper pulled me back to the present.

"Aye," Braxton said.

Belanna sniffed. "I've heard rumors. No animal has provided confirmation. Don't be getting yer hopes up."

"Yes, but—"

"I'd rather we *not* discuss unproven speculation."

All six of us jumped when Cheriour spoke.

He sat at the end of the table, silently eating his bug guts. The dude was like a Ninja; he never made a freaking sound. I hadn't even known he was there.

Cheriour pushed himself away from the table, picking up his empty bowl. "The sun is almost up," he said. "I know the recent news has been grim, but it has not affected the time of my training."

"Ach, the sun's barely awake!" Belanna said.

At the same time, Braxton declared, "We're not late yet."

He waved his spoon, splattering a blob of porridge over my face. "Sorry," he chuckled, reaching over to help me wipe the food away.

Cheriour sighed and walked out of the room.

"You know," I said to Braxton as I licked porridge off my lips, "your saliva does not make this shit taste any better."

"'*Shite?*'" he remarked. "This is a treat!"

"Hmm. Well, how 'bout you finish mine? Then you'll get an *extra* special treat."

Braxton grinned and snatched my still-full bowl of bug guts, downing it in two big gulps.

Yech.

Outside, the sun peered over the horizon. The sky was pink. Cloudless. And it was already hot as balls.

I was drenched in sweat by the end of our warmup, and the salty moisture *burned* as it seeped into the still-raw blisters on my palms. Supposedly, the sores would turn to calluses one day. Or so Cheriour said. It seemed like a load of crock. I got fresh sores at the end of every session. How was the skin supposed to harden when I kept ripping it open?

"Addie!"

My head snapped up when Cheriour barked my name. "Present," I mumbled.

"You're with Kaelan," he said.

I flashed Cheriour a thumbs up. I'd rotated through training partners a few times, but Kaelan was my favorite. He was a sweetheart and was content to go at my pace.

"Belanna—*no.*" Cheriour shook his head when Belanna sidled to Garvin's side.

Belanna and Garvin were *extremely* competitive. They'd probably kill one another if they had actual weapons.

"Belanna, I want you with Braxton—"

"I'm to be stuck with me own brother?" Belanna groaned.

Braxton grinned and tugged on the end of Belanna's braid.

"You both need work with the sword." Cheriour had the ultra-patient kindergarten teacher voice down pat. "Moira and Garvin, you both need practice with the bow."

"Ha! See, Garvin, it's not just me who thinks yer horrible." Belanna smirked.

Garvin wrinkled his nose and rolled his eyes.

"Addie and Kaelan will continue to train with the polearms," Cheriour droned.

No surprise there. I'd only used one other weapon: the bow.

It looked so much easier than flinging the freaking polearm around. Draw the string back and shoot, right? So I'd *nagged* Cheriour until he let me try it.

Ha.

That string had felt like it was attached to a brick house. I'd whacked my boob on the release (gave it a nice shiner too). And the arrow had gone so far off course, I'd almost hit Garvin. Who'd been standing on my right side, nowhere near the target.

Yeah, I was sticking with the polearm.

"Alright," I turned to Kaelan and wrapped my aching hands around my stick. "Ready to rumble?"

His mouth twitched. "You say the oddest things."

"Addie!" Cheriour called. "You and Kaelan will go for two-minute intervals. Two *full* minutes. If you stop early, you'll start over."

"How are you gonna know if I stop early? You don't have a stopwatch."

He ignored me. "Kaelan, don't give her instructions today. I want her to watch and anticipate. If you say anything, you'll start over."

Kaelan nodded.

"Beginning now," Cheriour shouted.

"Gah!" I barely got my arm up to block Kaelan's overhand swing. "Crap!" I stumbled back, swinging my pole around to stop him from whacking me in the ribs.

Cheriour's voice became white noise as he shouted instructions and critiques: "Garvin, breathe out. Elbow up, Moira. Belanna, stop showing off. Kaelan, pick up the pace."

Pick up the pace???

Swing. Thwack. Swing. Thwack. My arms burned with the effort. It had to have been two minutes already, right?

But Cheriour was still watching me, so probably not.

Swing. Thwack. I gritted my teeth. *Focus.* Kaelan sidestepped and I moved with him, blocking his next strike. He gave me an encouraging smile before he brought his pole up, nearly catching me under the chin. *"Shit."* I snapped my head back to avoid the hit.

And, in that half second, a movement caught my eye.

Quinn stepped onto the field.

Kaelan lunged again. I flew back, never taking my eyes off Quinn, and—

Crack!

I cried out as my left ankle rolled. A piercing and tingly pain rocketed up my calf.

Kaelan grabbed me when my leg buckled. "Are you—"

"Kaelan and Addie, start over!" Cheriour said.

I cursed under my breath. My ankle throbbed, and I wasn't even bearing my full weight on it.

"Start over!" Cheriour called again.

"She's—" Kaelan began.

Cheriour strode across the field toward us. "It doesn't matter. Start over."

"I can't," I gasped. "I need to sit—"

"No, you don't." Cheriour now stood only a few feet away. "*Start over.*"

Kaelan, to his credit, looked a little upset as he released my arm and stepped back, raising his weapon again.

I gasped—goddamn, my ankle *hurt*! Like someone had driven a red-hot needle through my bone.

Kaelan's pole rapped against my arms. The impact was light, but it still sent me spiraling sideways.

He reached for me again.

"Uh-uh." Cheriour pushed Kaelan's arm out of the way.

I crashed to the ground in a crumbled heap, my stick smacking me across the face.

"Addie," Cheriour said. "Get up."

"I can't." Every time I moved my leg, the fire throbbing in my bones grew hotter. Angrier.

"Ignore it."

"Screw you," I ground out. "I think I broke my ankle."

"Because you got distracted. Whining won't make it better." Cheriour knelt, putting his face level with mine. When he spoke again, his voice was a soft murmur. "I'm not doing this to be cruel. When you're injured in battle, succumbing to pain is a death sentence. Get up. Ignore the discomfort. Start again."

He stood, never pulling his gaze away from my face.

I wiggled my toes and bit back a cry when a fresh jolt of pain bulleted up my ankle. Warrior Princess, I was not.

"I'll give you thirty seconds," Cheriour said. "You can either compose yourself, or you can prepare to leave the city." He turned his back to me, focusing on the others as they completed their exercises.

Quinn still stared, likely waiting for me to throw in the towel. I swore his smug gaze was going to burn a hole in my forehead.

I didn't want to get up. Or fight.

But I also didn't want to let Cheriour down. He'd stuck his neck out for me. Multiple times. Giving up now would be a shitty way to repay him.

Slowly, wincing the whole time, I got to my feet. My ankle was about as sturdy as a toothpick. I clenched my jaw until it popped. *Two minutes.* I could do this.

"Go ahead," I said to Kaelan as I braced myself.

We started again.

Kaelan shifted to the right, the left, forward, left, sideways —pretty much every direction except backward. Every time he moved, I had to move, and each step was *agony*.

I'd partnered with Kaelan enough times to learn his little tells. He tilted his upper body before he stepped. So if he went to the right, he'd lean his shoulders that way first. If I noticed it in time, if I moved fast enough, I could beat him to the spot.

"Motherfu—" I skittered to the left, countering the step Kaelan had been about to take.

He paused and tilted his shoulders forward.

I did a short bunny hop, wobbling on my weak, searing ankle, and forced him to stumble back.

He stopped again and lifted the tip of his pole over his head; like a lumberjack, getting ready to split wood.

I threw my hands (and my pole) up to protect my face.

Swish. Clank.

The end of his stick clashed with the edge of mine.

As my right arm went down, absorbing the force, my left arm swung up, smashing my pole into Kaelan's temple. And it was a *hard* hit. A dull (and squishy) *thunk* pierced the air. Kaelan's head snapped sideways. He blinked, looking dazed.

"*Eeeeek!*" The pole slipped from my fingers as I clapped a hand over my mouth. "I am *so* sorry!" I reached for him and combed my fingers through his hair. "Are you bleeding?" He wasn't, *thank God*, but he'd have a lump. "Can you see okay? How many fingers am I holding up?" I flashed two fingers in front of his face but tore them away before he could realistically count them. "What are concussion symptoms again? Headache, puking...and fainting? Do you feel like you're gonna puke or faint? Because—why are you smiling?"

Kaelan had this big, shit-eating grin on his face. "It wasn't quite two minutes," he said, "but that seems to be a good stopping point. Do you agree, Cheriour?"

I whipped my head around. Cheriour still stood a few feet away, but he'd turned to face us again.

"I agree." Cheriour twisted his fingers around his beard. "That was *almost* adequate, Addie."

Considering his critiques were either *"awful"* or *"not entirely awful,"* an *"almost adequate"* was like winning a gold medal at the Olympics.

"I don't get it," I blurted. "I nearly knocked him out..."

"You anticipated his movements, and reacted accordingly. That was all I wanted you to learn today."

"Um, well...are you *sure* you're okay?" I tapped Kaelan's shoulder. "Can you remember what you ate for breakfast?"

"Bug guts," Kaelan chuckled.

"Har, har."

"Addie, take a breath," Cheriour said, although he wasn't looking at me anymore. His eyes roamed over the others as they completed their exercises. "I'll talk to Quinn about mending your ankle. Do you need healing, Kaelan?"

"I'm fine." Kaelan rubbed at his temple. "I'm alright, Addie. Honest."

And he seemed to be telling the truth. His eyes were clear. He wasn't wobbling or slurring his words.

I should have been relieved.

I'd done something right. For once. And I hadn't hurt Kaelan. All was good.

But...

Across the field, Quinn tilted his head, leveling me with an indecipherable look. It wasn't mean, or smug, or disappointed...or *anything*. Just a long, blank stare. But it left me feeling cold.

26

MUSTARD MILL

ADDIE

" I 'm sorry...*what?*" I gaped at Cheriour as he leaned against my bedroom doorway.

"You're coming with us," he repeated calmly, even as his right fist twitched against his thigh.

"Coming with you?"

"Yes."

"To-to fight the monsters—"

"Wraiths."

"—attacking Sinadrin?" It felt like someone had stuffed a wad of cotton down my gullet.

"*Sanadrin,*" Cheriour corrected. "But yes. You are to ride with us. When you return, Quinn will allow you to stay, and he'll remove all restrictions." He glanced at the sallow-faced man who was acting as my guard for the day.

"*If* I return," I said. "*If*—as in, what's the likelihood of me dying? Fifty percent? Seventy? One hundred?" I raked my fingers through my hair as fear bubbled inside my chest. "What the fuck? Seriously! *What. The. Fuck?* I got one lucky shot during yesterday's training, and you lunatics think I'm ready to fight at Helm's Deep?"

"I don't—"

"You know what—no. Don't say anything." I paced, shaking my hands, pulling at my hair, doing anything, *anything* to ward off the terror that sizzled through my veins. "I've gone along with all this shit so far," I hissed. "With your stupid training, and dirty bacteria baths, and shit food. And I've *tried* to limit my complaining. I really have. But now you want me to—no. Nope. *Hell* no."

"Addie—"

"No! I'm not going with you."

"Addie." His voice dropped. A warning. One I blew right past.

"Fuck you!" I cried. My brain kept flashing between different images: the Wraith who had wanted to mow down on me when I first arrived. The field I'd woken up in, and the sheer number of corpses. And battles I'd seen in movies and TV— that scene in *Braveheart* where William Wallace took an arrow to the chest was hitting differently now.

Cheriour grabbed my arm to stop my pacing. His grip was gentle but unyielding. I tried to jerk away. He held fast. *"Let go!"* My voice sounded funny. High pitched. Wobbly.

"Be still, Addie. Listen to me," he hissed when I tried to pull away again. "An attack is imminent. And many of Sanadrin's soldiers are still assisting Jabbart. We *must* help them. If Sanadrin falls, the rest of Victarion will follow."

My throat constricted. Spasmed. What could I even say to that? *"I'm sorry this world is falling apart. But...I can't help you! Why am I getting dragged into this?"*

Which was (apparently) exactly what I said out loud.

"I *wouldn't* drag you into this battle. If I had the choice."

Cheriour's nose wrinkled. "You are too inexperienced. But Quinn has ordered you to ride with us. I can't disobey him."

"Quinn's a goddamn psychopath!" I spat.

"Stop." Cheriour's voice was quiet, but stern.

"No!" I squirmed, even as my shoulder gave a painful *pop* against his hold.

"Be still, Addie," his drawl morphed into a slur. "I *will* do what I can to keep you safe. I promise."

"And *why* would you risk your ass for me?"

"*Be still.* Breathe." His fingers tightened around my arm. Not harshly. More like he was anchoring me. Keeping me upright.

Huk-hic-huk. My lungs made weird clicking/wheezing noises. The room dipped and swayed, while my stomach sloshed and splashed. Like a ship on the high seas.

"Breathe." Cheriour gave a long, audible exhale, as though demonstrating how to breathe.

I followed the steady rise and fall of his chest, blowing out choppy puffs of air, and inhaling short mouthfuls until the room stopped swaying. And my lungs stopped making those strange sounds.

"This isn't fucking fair." I wiped tears off my cheeks. "If the Celestials wanted me dead, why didn't they...I dunno, grab a gun and pop my brains out? *Bam.* Over and done with. *Why* did they send me here?"

Cheriour was quiet for a long moment. His thumb trailed along my arm, as though apologizing for holding me so tightly, and he let his hand slide away.

And I almost, *almost,* pulled his hand back. Because his palm had been gloriously warm against my clammy skin. His touch had made me steadier.

Instead, I wrapped my arms around myself and willed the

woozy, sea-sick sensation to go away. I would *not* puke on his boots again.

"You're right. This isn't fair." Cheriour focused his gaze on the door. "For you. Or for anyone."

For *anyone.*

A stark reminder that a lot of people could die. It wasn't just my pathetic ass on the line here.

"I'm sorry," I mumbled. "For, y'know, the meltdown. That was selfish, huh?" My stomach rose into my throat. "But I'm a total wimp. I *can't* fight. And," I blotted more tears off my cheeks, "this place is *awful.* Everyone who lives here suffers. And it's getting to me. Y'know?"

"It upsets me too." He lowered his head, his shoulders constricting with tension.

I ran a hand over my teary/snotty face as a humorless laugh puffed out of me. "You're trying to keep an entire country from disappearing off the face of the earth. And I'm over here being a self-centered, whiny bitch. I'm sorry. Really. I don't mean to make things harder for you—"

"There's nothing to apologize for." Cheriour didn't even spare me a glance as he jerked his chin to the door. "Come with me."

And I had no strength left to protest.

My feet felt like anvils as I followed him out into the hallway. "Bye," I said glumly to my guard, who didn't respond. Not a surprise. Most of the guards ignored me. Probably because I annoyed the crap out of them.

Normally, at this time of day, people would be making a beeline to the kitchen for breakfast. There would be talk. And laughter. And gossip. Typical early mornings on a job. But the atmosphere today was different. The castle halls were crowded, but no one spoke or looked at each other. My sniffles sounded like gunshots in the quiet, tense air.

I kept my head down, scrubbing my knuckles against my eyes. The tears slowed but wouldn't stop. Not until several minutes later, when Cheriour pushed open a door that led to—

"Is this your *bedroom*?" I blurted.

Cheriour inclined his head and stepped inside.

This small room was little bigger than a college dorm. And Cheriour was an absolute *slob*, which made the space seem claustrophobic. Sheets hung off the paper-thin mattress, which was pressed beneath the sill of a teeny window on the far wall. A mountain of trash sat perched atop the ramshackled desk in the corner. Clothes, mismatched pairs of boots, papers, and a *shit-ton* of pointy weapons littered the floor.

The dude slept with an entire armory at his disposal and enough trash to fill three dumpsters. He couldn't even *walk* without stepping on stuff.

I used the toe of my boot to push a lump of dirty clothes out of the way. "You ever heard of a fun activity called *'washing your stanky underwear?'* Because this is..." the flickering light caught my eye. A short candle rested on the windowsill, its gyrating flame only inches from a stack of papers.

One strong breeze and *poof,* those papers would start smokin'.

Cheriour turned when I stopped and followed my gaze to the candle. "Ah," he grunted. "Why do you fear fire?" He stumbled over a pair of shoes as he went to extinguish the candle.

The tight sensation in my chest loosened a bit once the flame was out. I blew out a breath. "My parents died in a housefire."

He gave me a long, studying look before he plucked a weapon off the bed. "How old were you?"

"Five," I said. "You know, it's funny. I can't even really remember what they looked like. But..." I trailed off as a phantom sound filled my ears.

"Addie! Addie...Don't...do you hear me? Don't.... no matter what..."

I closed my eyes.

"But?" Cheriour prompted.

"Sometimes I still hear my mom screaming."

"I'm sorry," he said.

I opened my eyes, started to respond, and completely lost my train of thought when I glimpsed the monstrosity of a weapon in his hands. "What is *that?*"

He held the weapon toward me. "It's yours."

My brows shot up. "You're joking, right?" The weapon was a big axe on a stick. Actually, it was worse. An axe only had a single blade. This sucker had a blade on one side, a meat mallet on the other, and a spear in the middle. Oh, and the other end of the stick had a point on it too. There were way too many sharp edges.

"It's a poleaxe," Cheriour said.

"That's nice. Since you named it, you can keep it."

"It's similar to what you've been training with—"

"No, it's not. My stick was longer and didn't have all the pointy bits. "

A spasm tugged at Cheriour's lips. "The pointy bits will help keep you safe," he said. "As for the size..." he tugged at the handle with both hands. With a dull *click*, the little foot-long axe transformed into a five-foot polearm.

"It's *retractable?*" I blinked.

"Yes. I thought you'd find it easier to carry. Especially on horseback."

This time, when he handed it to me, I took it. The mechanism was almost the same as a selfie stick or other similar equipment. It was easy to use; I extended and retracted it twice. And it wasn't nearly as heavy as it looked. It weighed more than my wooden pole, but not by much. "Did *you* make this?" I asked. "This is a custom weapon, not something you pulled off a shelf."

Instead of answering, Cheriour turned away. "Harnessing it to your back would be best. You'd only have to reach over your shoulder—"

"Being careful not to impale my arm—"

"—to draw it. I should have a scabbard in here..." he surveyed his pigsty of a bedroom. "Somewhere." He bent and rooted through the (seemingly endless) piles of clothes.

"I'm surprised you can find anything in here," I chuckled. "It looks like you set a bomb off."

He said nothing, but the backs of his ears reddened.

I fought back a grin. "What are you looking for, exactly?"

"A scabbard," he grunted.

"No idea what that is."

"A leather strap."

"Ah." I wandered over to his bed and peered around, trying not to touch his sheets because...when was the last time he'd washed them? If he'd *ever* washed them. *Yeck.*

A warm breeze whistled through the window, ruffling the pile of papers on the sill. He had a stone on top, to keep them from blowing away, but I still got a good eye-full of the front page.

"Wait—hang on," I reached over and scooted the paper out from under the rock. "This is Monschau! Germany!" The picture was a black-and-white sketch of Tudor-style buildings lining a canal. Which could have been the homes here, in Sakar, but a few of the buildings in the drawing were definitely restaurants. People sat outside at round tables, the plates in front of them stacked high with food. And the mountains and ruins in the background were a dead giveaway. "It *is!* I mean— you don't understand, I *drained* my bank account to go back-packing through Europe after high school. Worked my way through almost every country in the EU until...well, that's a story for another time." I waved my arm to shoo the memory away. "And Monschau—I stayed there for a month. *Best place ever!* Absolutely loved it. I'd recognize it anywhere. But..." I stared at the picture again, and then glanced at Cheriour.

He stood motionless on the other side of the room, the leather strap dangling from his fingers.

"How the *hell* do you have a picture like this?" I asked. "And it's a *sketch!* Did you draw this? How would you even know about this town? Have you been there? Did you—"

"We need to go," Cheriour grunted.

"But—hey!" I yelped when he strode across the room and tossed the leather strap over my head.

"So what was your favorite part about Monschau?" I asked. No response.

"Did you go to the mustard mill?"

Silence.

"How 'bout one of their Christmas markets?"

Cheriour quietly adjusted the leather around my torso.

"Are we gonna pretend I didn't see—"

"*Focus,* Addie. I'll only show you how to do this once." Cheriour popped my poleaxe into the holster, demonstrating how to secure it.

The harnessing rig was cool. There were two straps: one slung across my chest diagonally, the other clipped around my waist. The axe part sat at my hip with all the pointy ends safely concealed in leather. Thank *fuck.*

Unfortunately, the other end, which rested against my left shoulder, was *not* covered. I saw the tip out of the corner of my eye.

"Stop worrying about it," Cheriour said.

"I didn't even say anything. I don't think. Did I?"

"You didn't have to. The end is not as sharp as it looks, and it's angled away from your face. Now—*focus*—when you withdraw the poleaxe, you'll need to release this clip first." He tapped on the leather pouch covering the axe head. "Understood?"

"Yes, but—"

"I doubt you'll be foolish enough to slice your hand on the blades," he added, correctly interpreting what I'd been about to say.

I wasn't so sure. And I *hated* how tight this thing was. Like a damn corset.

I tugged at the straps. "It's kinda uncomfortable."

"It's fitted correctly. The leather will soften as it wears in."

I pulled the straps a little harder. *Stretch, motherfuckers!* "Sooo, you've got a seriously creative mind. A regular genius. Between this," I let the straps go, shimming my shoulders a bit to work the stiffness out of the leather. "And your *spot-on* depiction of a German city in the 21st century." I waved the paper under his nose, grinning when he snatched it out of my hands. "You drew that picture, don't try to deny it."

He sighed as he put the drawing back under the rock.

"I mean, it's *stunning*. But you *are* gonna have to tell me how you knew about Monschau—"

"Sacrifice will be saddled with the rest of your supplies." Cheriour interrupted. He moved around the room, plucking knives from the floor, under the bed, behind the desk (it seemed he left things wherever they fell) and strapping them to the holster he wore on his chest.

"Supplies? How long—"

"Two days," he responded. "To reach Sanadrin."

"Two days? Are we going to make it in time to help them?"

He clipped the last knife into place but said nothing.

27

LOST YEARS

LASS

T should pause my tale here to make something clear.

This part of my life was rather *unkind*. Almost cruel. But I do not, nor will I *ever*, blame Terrick.

He could not teach me to control a volatile ability he didn't understand. If he'd sought help, Darfield's soldiers would have taken me away. I likely would have been forced to join the army. But Terrick feared a worse fate and did not want to see me tortured.

Moving to another city would have only provided a temporary reprieve. As long as the cursed fire ran through my veins, Terrick and I would not have been accepted anywhere.

So Terrick did what he could to ensure I had a home, and I was safe, even if it came with a cost.

Terrick was a kind man with a big heart. Cruelty had never been his intention. He simply didn't know what else to do.

My descent into misery started simply enough.

"This tonic will help you sleep," Terrick told me.

We were staying in yet another livery stable, our horses tied a few feet away from us. My little speckled pony had a burn mark on his left flank. I hadn't been able to stop staring at it.

It had been a full day since my fire ravaged the stables.

"I don't want to sleep," I mumbled.

"You must, lass," Terrick coaxed. "The tonic will keep the dreams away. You won't hurt anyone else. I promise."

And it *did* keep the dreams away. For a while.

Months passed.

Terrick found employment at a tannery. I hated him working there. It demanded too much from his age-ravaged body. But we needed the coin.

His new position also came with lodging: a small room on the top of the shop.

When we moved into our new dwelling, Terrick wrapped me in a threadbare blanket and kept his arm around my shoulders as we climbed the stairs. "My child," he'd said to our new landlord. "She's quite ill."

In hindsight, I should have questioned his motives. I was perfectly healthy. If our landlord had spared me more than a passing glance, he would have seen that. But, at the time, I'd closed my eyes, wishing I could disappear.

And I did. Terrick was, after all, a gifted Concealer. Even when he did not use his power.

I SPENT four years in Darfield, trapped in that small, ~~claustrofobic~~ claustrophobic room above the tannery, barred from the outside world.

That hadn't been Terrick's intention. He'd meant my situation to be temporary while he searched for a solution to my ever-growing power.

"Perhaps it is linked to your emotions," he said one afternoon. "Your power seems to be at its strongest in the presence of fear or anger. If I can teach you to school your emotions...I once had several books that discussed this very topic." A hint of sadness crept into his voice.

I turned away, burying my face in my sleeve to hide my tears.

Terrick was correct, but it is not an easy thing to control one's emotions. The more one tries to restrain them, the harder they fight. The more one restricts them, the faster they gallop out of control.

As the tonic lost its ~~eficacy~~ efficacy, the dreams returned. My brain delighted in tormenting me with horrific images while I slept, and it gave my hated power ample opportunity to seize control.

Terrick became adept at recognizing the signs, and always woke me before my fire damaged the building. But, in doing so, he wounded himself. Burns marred his palms and arms.

Every time I stared at his mottled skin, my stomach turned to rot. My panic grew. It's an awful thing when you fear yourself. There's no way to escape. No relief from the constant churning of anxiety in your gut, or the horrifying images that run unbridled through your mind.

I'd never been so terrified. Even on that day in Detha, as I'd waited to be cooked, I did not experience the same intensity of terror that I felt during my time in Darfield.

Terrick tried to help. He gave me meditation exercises to "purge my mind of negative thoughts." He also taught me a stretching exercise he called *yoga*, which was meant to calm my mind.

They didn't work.

As my fear grew, and my power became more temperamental, Terrick turned to the tonic, increasing its potency.

When I drank the tonic, my mind became blessedly blank. My emotions numbed. Sleep came easily, and I slumbered deeply, never dreaming. But wakefulness became more and more difficult. Even when I was awake, I was rarely alert. A permanent cloud seemed to hover over my eyes. My brain sometimes struggled to form coherent thoughts. The days, weeks, months, and years passed in a blur.

Once, I remembered being startled by the snow falling outside because my last clear-headed memory had been of summer. The seasons had changed, twice, without me noticing.

I never left the room.

Terrick maintained the lie that I was his ailing daughter and was too sick to leave bed. No one questioned him.

He spent his days laboring at the tannery. At night he returned, damp and dingy and smelling of alkaline and ash. If I was awake, he'd eat his supper with me, often telling me the stories he'd learned from his fiction books. I'm sad to say I don't remember any of them.

On my clear-headed days, I noted how quickly he was

aging; his skin sagged more and more, and his hair turned whiter and whiter. Sometimes, he stared at me with tears in his eyes and desperation etched into his face. He hated what he was doing to me. He would try to make up for it, using his spare coins to buy me things: wooden dolls, cheeses in a variety of flavors, hair pins, or ~~jewles~~—jewels. At one point, he procured the beautiful tunic I'd once spent so many hours admiring. Surely, he had saved his coin for months to afford such an exorbitant gift.

And I couldn't summon the energy to wear it. Truthfully, I don't recall when I received it. I simply noticed it one day, hanging in the armoire, its dazzling color muted in our poorly lit room.

The last years of my childhood slipped away. I spent my days sitting by the window, dully watching the world change.

Often, I saw the blue-eyed boy, always dressed in military leathers, as he visited the shops on our street. It seemed he'd given up his quest to leave the army. He'd grown into his too-long limbs, although his frame remained thin and somewhat gangly. His smug smile faded, replaced by a grim expression that aged him beyond his years. It made me sad.

I wanted to hear his music again.

If I went down to him, would he play the harp for me? Would his smile return? Would he accept my apology for not upholding my end of the wager?

I wanted to speak with him. Desperately. But I never did.

As I began the path toward adulthood, my power grew with me. The tonic lost its ~~effacy~~—efficacy again and my dreams returned with renewed vigor.

Every night I woke screaming, fire erupting from my fingertips.

Every night, Terrick rendered me ~~unconcious~~—unconscious, usually by wrapping his arm around my shoulders and applying pressure to the sides of my neck. It caused a momentary flash of panic as my airways were restricted, but then I slid into darkness. And the fire retreated.

It was a barbaric system. But it worked.

For a time.

Terrick was old. And those four years were as unkind to him as they were to me. Between the guilt that weighed on him and the strain of his tannery duties, his days on earth were rapidly ending.

It happened on an autumn eve.

I'd been having a clear-headed day. Enough to notice the blue-eyed boy, fully into adulthood now, walking with a woman on his arm. He smiled again. Maybe not as vibrantly as he had a few years prior, but he smiled. A hot, dark feeling coiled in my chest. Jealousy. I hated that girl, with her shimmering black hair; *hated* that she'd been the one to bring the light back into his eyes. In another world, it would have been *me* clutching onto his arm as he strolled through the streets. It would have been my voice making him smile and laugh.

I cried when the boy left my sight. Although I made sure my tears were dry when Terrick returned that evening.

Terrick moved slowly, pausing on every third step up to our room. When he walked through the door, he was winded. His face was pale, and a blue vein pulsed at his temple.

"Ah, lass," he gasped as he heaved himself into the nearest chair. "Give me a moment to catch my breath, and then we shall eat. I've thought of a good story to share with you; one of my favorites from childhood."

He never caught his breath.

Even as I spooned broth into his bowl, he wheezed. His hands shook.

"Perhaps the day fatigued me more than I thought," he said when I asked if he was ill. Speaking brought on a violent coughing fit that left him red-faced and teary-eyed.

I placed a hand on his shoulder. There was a chill on his skin, and it wouldn't go away, no matter how many times I tried to create friction to warm him.

"I'm sorry, lass," he whispered. "The story will have to wait for another night."

I helped him to his bed. Afterward, when the cloud seeped across my vision again, and the energy left my body, I curled onto my mattress, asleep before my head hit the pillow.

I didn't take the tonic.

And the dreams returned.

I was back in Swindon, listening to Darcie scream. The acrid smell of burnt flesh rose to my nostrils, churning my stomach. Flames danced across my fingertips, growing, and growing, and growing until Darcie was consumed in the blaze.

"Stop! Please!" She cried.

I stared at my trembling fingers. No matter what I did, no matter how hard I tried to will it away, the fire kept growing. "I-I can't!"

"Please..."

"Go away," I moaned at the inferno. "Please, go *away*. I don't want this!"

"Please, love."

I gasped. It was no longer Darcie speaking.

It was Mama, now trapped in the swirling fire.

"Mama!" I screamed. "Mama, something's wrong—a Celestial did something to me. But I *don't want this*! Tell me how to stop it!"

She stared at me, her flesh blackening, and bubbling tears seeping from her eyes. *"It's your fault I'm dead, love,"* she rasped.

The flames grew. "I didn't—"

"You didn't kill me, but you might as well have. I could have left Detha and gone to Sakar. If only I hadn't been cursed with another mouth to feed."

A sickening pain speared my chest. "Mama—"

She coughed. Blood dribbled down her chin. *"I should have Offered you to the Wraiths when you were born."*

I awoke with a blood-curdling screech, which morphed into a cry of panic.

Flames engulfed the room. They roared across the ceiling and along the walls, disintegrating everything in their path. The smoke was thick; I could hardly see past the tip of my nose.

"Terrick!" I screamed.

Dimly, I heard shouts coming from outside.

"The tannery!"

"Water! Fetch water!"

"Terrick!" I dropped to the floor in a crumbled heap and crawled. *"Terrick!"*

And then I found him, lying face down on the ground, a mere three steps away from my bed. *"Terrick!"* It took all my strength to turn him over.

His eyes were open but glassy and unfocused. "Terrick!" I shook him, tugged on his arms, screamed into his ears—I did whatever I could think of to rouse him. He remained still and lifeless.

He'd died trying to wake me from my nightmare.

And, while I understand now that his demise was not my doing—his heart was failing long before that torturous night —at the time, only one thought possessed my mind: *I killed him.*

I wanted to die too. For what was the point of living? The fire had taken *everything* from me. As long as it held me in its wicked clutches, it would continue to steal everything I loved and cared for.

I sobbed as I curled beside Terrick's body. I pressed my face into his chest as the flames roared around us, consuming the building. And I pleaded for the fire to take me.

The fire, of course, would not harm me. It couldn't.

28

DEATH BEFORE LUNCH

On the road again. Joy.

Reunited with my not-so-noble steed, who tried to kick every horse who came within a twelve-foot radius of her rear end. Double joy.

Riding out in a fucking monsoon. *Triple joy.* With cherries on top.

It started raining an hour after we left Niall. And it didn't just drizzle. Nope. This was the kind of rain that caused mass flooding. Because it came down too hard and too fast and the ground was going *WTF??*

And y'know what didn't mix? Wet (wool) clothes and a leather saddle. *Ho-ly hell.* I got some major rug burns on my ass.

But I wasn't alone in my misery.

Cheriour looked grumpy as fuck with his hair plastered to his forehead and his clothes and boots squishing every time he shifted in the saddle. Kaelan wrapped a shirt around his head to create a makeshift hood. It kept his eyes dry, but most of the water shot down the back of his shirt instead. Moira's long-legged bay stallion kept losing his shoes in the muck. "There's *nothing* I can do," she snapped when, after the third time, Cheriour berated her for holding the group up. "He's never had great hooves. And the mud's pulling his shoes right off." She stomped on the spongy ground to emphasize her point.

Only two people seemed okay with our situation. Belanna rode at the very front of the group, one hand perched on her hip while she merrily swung her legs against her horse's sides. Braxton was a few rows back and spent most of the trip screech-singing some upbeat tunes.

The whack-a-doodle blood ran thick in that family.

It was a slow trek. By mid-afternoon, the ground had turned treacherous. As in, *use caution, or you'll wipe out.* I learned that lesson the hard way.

We were cantering through the woods. Sacrifice had already been struggling with the ground, doing a lot of tripping and grunting. As we rounded a corner, we passed a stopped horse and his black-bearded rider. "Wee lad's kicked himself," the black-bearded man grunted as he lifted his horse's foreleg.

The horse turned his head toward Sacrifice. Almost as if to say, *hello.*

And Sacrifice, the little bitch, saw his friendly gesture as a threat and decided he needed to be eliminated. ASAP. Her little ears flattened, and her hind end swung around in a massive kick.

"Whoa!"

Me and the man screamed in unison. His horse squealed and leapt into the air. Sacrifice's back legs slid out from under her. She groaned. I yelled. The ground rose to meet me and...

Splat.

My shoulder smashed into the mud. Thankfully, it was a soft landing. And Sacrifice got her feet under her before she crashed on top of me. But man, oh man, if I didn't almost crap my pants.

"Easy lassie," the black-bearded man called as Sacrifice snorted and darted sideways. She gave me a wide-eyed look, as though shocked to find me off her back.

"You alright?" The man asked me.

I gave him a thumbs up. "I'm good. No broken bones." *I think.* I wriggled around a bit before I stood up. Just to be sure. Nope. Nothing broken. But my whole left side was *coated* in a thick layer of goop.

"You," I waggled my finger at Sacrifice as I snatched her reins, "really need to turn your bitch mode off."

She pricked her ears and gave me an affectionate head-butt.

"Uh-uh, it's too late to butter me up. You almost got me killed." But I patted her forehead before I clambered back into the saddle. Because she *was* pretty damn cute.

An hour later, after several more horses slipped, we had to concede defeat. And slowing to a walk meant sacrificing a night of sleep. We stopped for only two hours, mostly to re-shoe the horses, check them for injuries, and to give them a breather.

The monsoon ended when the sun rose the next morning and *poofed* the storm clouds away. A crystal-clear sky stretched overhead.

But the day turned hot and muggy and, with the water-saturated ground, it became a bug's paradise. Flies buzzed incessantly around the horses, biting their ears, legs, and the undersides of their bellies. Even picking up the pace didn't help. The little bastards flew as fast as a horse cantered.

Sacrifice's tail swished and swashed as she fought a losing battle against the bugs. Gnats formed a halo around my face. They flew in my eyes, tried to go up my nose, and droned in my ears. *Nothing* deterred them. They didn't give two shits if you swatted at them. And killing them? Ha. That was about as good as slapping a sugar-coated sign on your back that said *bug murderer.* Once you killed one, thousands more came out of nowhere to exact revenge.

When the sun set and we made camp for the night, no one got much rest. Because the skeeters (aka, mosquitos) were awake and ready to party. And ooh boy, they feasted well on my flesh.

"Fricking skeeters," I grumbled as I swatted the one on my thigh. Fucker had sucked blood right through the fabric of my pants.

"Here." Cheriour knelt next to the tree I was sitting against and held out a bouquet of purple flowers.

I pursed my lips. "Aww, that's so sweet. What's the occasion?"

His hair was almost sticking straight up (humidity and coarse hair didn't mix well), which gave him a bit of a Gene Wilder as Willy Wonka look. Especially when he shook his head and said, "What?"

"You're handing me flowers," I chuckled. "See, back home, guys give girls flowers for special occasions. So, what's the special occasion? Surviving my first horseback road trip in a monsoon?"

Cheriour maintained his stony expression. "It's lavender. It'll help repel the bugs."

"Ah." I plucked a handful of flowers from his hand. "*Lavender.* Y'know, I used lavender-scented stuff all the time back home, but this smells *way* better. Guess that's what happens when it's *au naturel.* Hmm." I *loved* lavender. Such a crisp and clean scent, a sharp contrast to the B.O. cloud that always hung over the army. "Thanks!"

"I didn't grow it," Cheriour said as he walked away. "Cathal did. You can thank him."

Did the lavender trick work? Kinda-sorta. It kept some bugs away. Not all of them. The freaking skeeters were relentless.

When we departed again in the morning, I had bites all over my arms, legs, neck, and even one on my cheek. And rug burns on my ass from the wet saddle. I was a miserable old hag. But, hey, at least I smelled like lavender. So I *tried* to cling to that bit of positivity. Until...

"Belanna, I need you to keep the pace steady," Cheriour said when he mounted his horse. "We're close to Sanadrin."

"Close?" I asked Cheriour as Belanna cantered to the front of the group. "H-how close?"

"With luck, we'll arrive before noon," Cheriour said.

With luck. Sure. Because dying before lunchtime would be *extremely* lucky, right?

And, of course, time always added a little pep to its step when you were dreading something. The morning slid away. The afternoon sun baked the still-boggy ground. Sweat dripped down my back, making the bug bites itchier.

I had a fluttery feeling in my chest. And in my stomach. I kinda wanted to puke, but I'd barely eaten the past few days, so I had nothing to upchuck.

"How many times do you think a heart can beat during a person's lifetime?" I swatted a fat, green bug off Sacrifice's neck. "There's gotta be a limit, right? That's why some people just drop dead. Heart ticked its last tock."

Cheriour rode beside me, his eyes roaming as he tried to ignore my babbling.

"Because if there's a limit, I might max mine out before we get there." I heard my booming pulse, even above the rolling thunder of cantering horses.

"We've nearly arrived," Cheriour said. "If you feel you're going to expire, do it now. While I still have time to unsaddle Sacrifice."

"*What?*"

"There's no need for her to endure the horrors of battle if her rider has died."

"So, if I dropped dead, right here and now, you'd unsaddle the horse and...what would you do with me?" My voice sounded high-pitched and wheezy.

Cheriour shrugged. "The vultures will dispose of your corpse."

"*You'd leave me lying there?*"

He shrugged again.

"What if I wasn't all the way dead? What if I was unconscious?"

"Vultures aren't finicky."

"So much for being my mighty protector," I grumbled.

Cheriour's mouth twisted. Sometimes he looked like he was so, *so* close to grinning. But then he'd wipe all expression off his face. Like a robot hitting the reset button.

I hated when he did that. I hated that I couldn't read his emotions. Because a part of me got a little giddy at the thought of him finding my cheeseball quips amusing.

Or maybe fear was making me giddy. It was definitely making me sweat worse than a priest on a playground.

(Fear also made my humor wildly inappropriate.)

My sticky hands trembled around the reins. Sacrifice shook her head, her teeth grinding against the bit.

"Calm yourself, Addie," Cheriour said.

"Calm myself," I scoffed. "That's a good one. We're about to get freaking *massacred!* But if I ride to my death *calmly,* everything'll be peachy keen, right?"

Cheriour made a choking sound that *100%* sounded like a repressed laugh.

Be still my freaking heart!

But a sudden wave of shouting rose from the army, and all hints of Cheriour's laughter faded.

"...arrived!"

"...several hundred..."

"Sanadrin...outnumbered..."

Everyone was screaming at once. The words were jumbled, but it didn't take a rocket scientist to figure out what was going on. The Wraiths had arrived. There were hundreds of them. We were outnumbered.

My mouth was so dry, I couldn't even muster up enough spit to swallow.

Next to me, Cheriour said something, but he sounded like the teacher from Charlie Brown. Like, I *heard* him, but the words were gibberish. *"Wah wah woh wah wah."*

White spots flashed in front of my eyes. My chest got painfully tight.

The still-wet grass whizzed beneath Sacrifice's churning hooves as she carried me closer and closer to the battle.

I shivered.

How could my skin be ice cold when I had sweat pouring off me?

"Addie!" Cheriour said. "Calm yourself..."

A noise rumbled through the air. An awful, gut-wrenching sound.

Screams.

And, I mean, everyone's heard screams before. Shit, I'd gotten plenty of earfuls whenever I went to an amusement park or haunted house. But this was different. Because hearing people shriek when they were kinda scared but knew they weren't in any real danger was totally different than hearing the outright *wails* of the dying.

My shivers intensified.

It wasn't *one* person dying. There had to be *hundreds*. And the yells, the cries, the anguished bellows, and pleas for help only grew louder as we zoomed along the grassy field.

"Addie!" Cheriour reached over and rapped his knuckles against my shoulder. "Draw your weapon."

I looked at him, vaguely wondering why he had so many flies buzzing around his face.

"Your poleaxe," he said. "Take it out. Have it ready."

More and more flies swirled around him.

I didn't move.

"Addie!" He whacked my shoulder again.

I blinked.

The flies around his face disappeared.

Or...there hadn't been any flies, had there? Just black vision spots. Because my system was on red alert, and my brain had its finger on the restart button.

"Addie." Cheriour shoved his horse over, smashing into Sacrifice's side. She tensed but didn't kick out this time. "Look at me." Cheriour gave my arm a hard shake.

I blinked again. Even if I wanted to talk, I couldn't. My tongue had rooted to the roof of my mouth.

"Focus, Addie," Cheriour said. "Draw your weapon. *Now.* We're approaching from the east."

As he spoke, clusters of riders broke away from the group and made a hard left.

Cheriour reached down, grasped Sacrifice's bit, and pulled us to the right.

"We need to keep them away from the castle gates," he continued. "If we succeed...."

My tongue stung when I ripped it free. "Let me guess:

they'll run away with their tales tucked between their legs? No plan B, C, or D for them. They'll take one shot at getting into the castle. If it fails, they'll pack up and go home." No idea where this anger had come from, but I was seeing red. Probably because I was, *literally*, being ponied to my doom. "You know that kinda shit only happens in movies, right?"

"Addie..."

"Bad guys don't *give up* because the good guys threw them off their game."

"Stop talking," Cheriour said through clenched teeth, "and *listen* to me. Sanadrin's riders are returning. Belanna says they'll be here within an hour. *If* we can keep the Wraiths away from Sanadrin, we'll soon have reinforcement."

A shaky breath rattled out of my lungs. "*If*," I said. "*If* we can hold them off? You don't sound too positive."

"It will be difficult," he said.

"Well," my throat clicked when I swallowed, "thanks for sugarcoating that. I feel *soooo* much better now. *Not.*"

29

CREEPY DOUCHENOZZLE

U p the hill we went, the horses huffing and puffing as they struggled with the steep incline. I snatched Sacrifice's mane to keep my upper body forward while gravity did its darndest to shove me the other way.

And then we reached the top.

Fuck. I should've let gravity do its job.

A sloping, rocky field stretched before us. It was *covered* in jagged stones. Looked like a freaking death trap.

At the end of the field, shadowed by the towering mountains that surrounded it, stood a hulking black fortress. The kinda place you'd expect Sauron to bunk in. The sprawling building was almost the size of a high-rise. Its windowless walls were made of black stone with sharp, dagger-like tips. And the way it crouched over the rows of houses at its feet; like a massive dragon hovering over its latest kill...

A chill raced up my spine as Sacrifice began the descent.

Oh God. Ohgodohgodohgod.

Sacrifice swerved around large boulders. Her hooves smacked against rough patches of ground. Occasionally she grunted and her head bobbed, as though the footing hurt her, but she didn't slow down.

My knuckles popped as I grasped my poleaxe in one hand and a fistful of her mane in the other. And my eyes burned as I stared, unblinkingly, at the battle below.

It was a blur of color and sound. People screamed. Sunlight glinted off metal weapons. Riderless horses tore around in panic. The Wraiths sat astride their black beasts, cutting people down as they steamrolled across the land. And the dogs...

Hold up. Those *weren't* dogs. They were tall, gangly creatures. Completely furless, the ridges of their spines visible through the mottled skin stretched across their backs. Their white, fleshless skulls blazed in the sun, even as their dark, hollow eye sockets absorbed light. And their fucking teeth had to be *at least* a foot long.

I watched, petrified, as one of the hellish dogs ripped into a man's leg. It tore the limb *clean out of its socket*. The man fell, bawling, while the dog munched on his dismembered thigh.

"Hellhounds," Cheriour said as another dog tore a man's head off his shoulders.

"Excuse me?" I gasped. "Hell. As in the *place*? Where damned souls and crooked politicians go? Are those dogs from—"

"Aim for their stomachs. Or throats." Cheriour swung his horse around a boulder. "Be mindful of their teeth."

He made it sound so easy, didn't he?

"The Wraiths need to be separated from their Púcas." He pulled a knife from his chest holster. "They'll be slower then. Easier to kill. But you remember the Púcas?"

They're venomous. I nodded, although my head felt weird. Numb. And my ears kept buzzing.

"I'll watch over you. As much as I can. But *keep moving*," Cheriour said. "If you're idle in battle, you'll die."

And, with those final words of comfort, we plunged head-first into the fray.

Sacrifice barreled into a dog—*hellhound*—without hesitation. The creature gave a startled yelp as her hooves pounded against its blotched skin. The impact nearly sent me flying head-first over her neck.

Why, *why* didn't saddles come with seatbelts?

A knife hurtled over my shoulder, stopping another oncoming hellhound in its tracks.

Beside me, Cheriour drew a short sword from his scabbard and began skewering everything in sight. Hellhounds? Stab. Grounded Wraiths? Double stab. He was so damn *fast*, flinging himself from one side of his horse to the other, never losing his balance.

As for me? Ha. Sacrifice did all the work. She mowed down two more hellhounds and one Wraith before I remembered I was, y'know, *holding a weapon*.

But then I almost lost the damn thing when a hellhound leapt toward me, teeth bared, red foam bubbling from its mouth.

"Holy, motherfucking—" I screamed, thrusting my poleaxe toward the animal. The tip sank into its shoulder with a *squelch*. "*Bastard!*"

The hellhound snarled, its teeth snapping less than an inch from my arm. It pulled itself free of my weapon, spraying blood over Sacrifice's shoulder, and lunged for me again.

"Gah!" I barely got my poleaxe up in time. "Why didn't you die? You creepy motherfucker—ew, ew, *ew!*" The spearhead sank into the hellhound's throat. Blood squirted over my face. The creature died with a rasping cough and started to fall, taking my poleaxe with it.

"Shit!" I jerked my arm back, but the poleaxe was lodged in the hellhound's jugular. *"Shit, shit!"* The hound fell. But my poleaxe stuck. I dragged the corpse across the field, flopping and splatting it over the stones. And my weapon *still wouldn't come loose.* Jesus. Did hellhounds have superglue on their insides?

"Addie!"

Cheriour's warning bellow came a few seconds too late.

As I wrestled with my poleaxe, a second hellhound barrel-rammed into my other side. And I nose-dived right out of the saddle, crashing on top of the dead hellhound and whacking my chin on the poleaxe handle. The hound's blood got *everywhere*: on my clothes, my skin, even in my mouth. I spat, gagged, and rolled off the corpse.

A few feet away, Sacrifice squealed as the second hellhound clambered into the saddle I'd vacated. She hopped and bucked, but the dog dug its paws into her shoulders and sank its teeth into her neck.

"No!" I screamed, wrenching at my poleaxe until it came free with a wet pop. *"Get off of her!"* I ran to her side, swinging my poleaxe over my head. The first strike was a swing and a miss. But the second was a home run, slicing through the hellhound's throat.

As the hound died, it snarled and savagely bit the poleaxe handle. Thank *fuck* I had a long weapon. Because if those massive fangs had snapped around my arm, I would've been picking the disembodied limb off the ground.

But the hound only managed to put two small punctures in the handle before it slid lifelessly out of the saddle.

"Sacrifice!" I called. Blood streamed from the gaping wounds on Sacrifice's neck. But before I could snatch the reins, she ducked sideways, galloping headlong into the battle.

Without me.

"Fuck." I clutched my poleaxe and spun around. I couldn't see a single human—

Well, not true. There were plenty of bodies on the ground. So, to amend my original statement, I couldn't see a single *living* human. Just the hellhounds. And the Wraiths. And those awful, red-eyed Púcas.

"Addie!" Cheriour's voice sounded like it was miles away. "Hold on!"

From an even further distance, I heard Belanna screaming, "They're at the gates! We need to drive them back—oi, I didn't say for *us* to go back! Forward, ye bloody fecking cowards!"

Other shouts drifted over to me. Commands. Cries for help. Agonized warbles. But I couldn't see anyone.

It was like I'd been transported out of this world and into a place where humans didn't exist.

"Keep moving!" Cheriour called.

I blinked. Oh, fucking *hell*. I had four hounds encircling me. Like sharks, swimming around their prey.

Ready or not, it was Go Time.

A hellhound jumped at me. I shuffled back and raised my poleaxe, shielding my face. The animal's teeth scraped against the handle. With a grunt, I shoved my weight into its chest, sending it sprawling onto its side. The hound growled and sprang into the air, getting ready to pounce on my shoulders—

Thwack.

The head of my poleaxe sliced its belly. A hit that was 100% pure luck. But I claimed the victory anyway.

"Take that, ya creepy douchenozzle," I hissed as the hellhound crumbled.

The other hounds hunched down, snarled, and prepared to dogpile (har, har) on top of me.

I swung my axe at one and sliced its chest, stabbed a second, and...

Whoosh! Thunk.

Thank *Christ* for Cheriour and his knives. Because that final hound had been at my back, preparing to take my head off. I never would've pivoted in time to protect myself. But Cheriour's knife now protruded between the ridges of the hound's spine and the creature was so busy howling in pain, it had forgotten about me.

I'd survived the first few minutes of this battle. *Barely.* But I was still breathing. I had to keep this going. Had to keep moving. Had to...

"Addie!"

Cheriour's voice cracked. I glimpsed him, still on his horse, several yards away. Fighting (literally) to get to me. Beneath the blood already slopped across his cheeks, his face had gone white.

Hoofbeats echoed behind me.

I turned, digging my sweaty fingers into the handle of my poleaxe, and saw the Púca. It was too close and moving too fast. The Wraith riding it had its arm outstretched, clawed fingers reaching toward me.

I froze.

There wasn't enough time, wasn't enough space, for me to do *anything*. This was it. The end.

With a bellowing roar, the Púca slammed on the brakes. Mud sprayed from beneath its hooves. Its hindquarters sank and, when the Wraith yelled and kicked, the horse flung itself up into a full-fledged backflip and landed with an earth-rumbling *thud* on top of its rider.

The Púca's legs flailed through the air for a second before it flipped itself back over.

The Wraith lay on the ground. Not dead but stunned.

"What the—" I started.

With another roar, the Púca planted its front hooves on the

Wraith's face and heaved itself to its feet. There was a hollow *crunch* as the Wraith's helmet (and skull) buckled beneath the weight.

"—hell was that about?" I finished.

The Púca swiveled its head toward me, ears pricked. A pointed tongue slithered between its fangs.

"Oooh, *fuck*." How the heck was I supposed to kill a *horse?* A hound had been one thing—they were about the size of German Shepherds. Not small, but also not massive. But Púcas? They were freaking *huge!* And fast, and strong, and with those poisonous fangs...

The Púca flattened its ears and lunged.

I screamed and flung the poleaxe in front of my face, closing my eyes, waiting for the impact.

It never came.

The Púca ran past me, its eyes fixated on another Wraith.

And another Púca.

It sounded like a firework exploding off its base when the two beasts collided. And the fight was *vicious.* Both Púcas rose onto their hind legs, teeth flashing. They flailed their front hooves through the air, like boxers jabbing at each other.

The Wraith riding the second Púca flopped out of the saddle. Bad news for me because as soon as the rider got to his —sorry, *her* feet (this rider was a curvy woman), she charged.

The two Púcas roared as their front hooves crashed back to the ground.

The rider winged her sword through the air.

"Shit!" I dove for the ground and barely, *barely,* avoided being decapitated. And I screamed again when a set of dinner-plate-sized hooves brushed dangerously close to my left pinkie.

One of the Púcas had its fangs buried in the other's neck. I couldn't tell which horse was which; they looked *exactly* the same.

With a grunt, I rolled myself onto my back, raising my poleaxe as the Wraith brought her sword down. There was a *ziiing* when the blade scraped against the shaft of my weapon. The blisters on my palms screamed and my arms struggled to absorb the impact.

Again, she tried to stab me. Again, I managed to block her in time. She moved so damn fast, I couldn't sort my hands out quick enough to get a hit in. Not while lying on my back.

I cursed as her third blow almost took out my right eye. If I'd been a half second slower getting my arms up...

Mowow.

A colossal black shadow passed overhead. The Púca. It jumped over me, landing inches away from my legs, and bull-dozed into the Wraith.

I sat up, shaking from head to toe, as the Púca dug its fangs into the Wraith's shoulder. The other Púca lay on the ground behind me, legs twitching, blood pouring from the gaping wound under its cheek.

I turned back around as the female Wraith hit the ground, her body going rigid. Her milk-white eyes rolled in their sockets, and she made this strange gurgle/gasp sound. She was still alive, but she didn't move.

The venom.

So this was what happened when you got bit by a Púca.

The Púca snorted, spraying boogers and blood over the Wraith's body, and cocked its head toward me.

"Umm," I scrambled to my feet, "you don't wanna eat me. Honestly. I maintained a steady junk-food diet until about a month ago. My blood's *super* sugary. Bad for your teeth, y'know?"

The Púca licked its lips and took a step, *two*, in my direction.

"Well, yeah, I guess sweet blood would taste pretty darn good. It's not *real* sugar, though," I added. "We Americans love chemicals. And we put fake shit in *everything*. It'll upset your stomach—" I bit off with a squeal as the horse reached my side and pressed its muzzle to my shoulder.

But instead of biting me, it sniffed noisily, fanning its metallic-scented breath across my face. I held my chest still, praying the Púca wasn't searching for a good artery to drink from.

The Púca backed away, lowering its head. And the way it looked at me, with its intelligent red eye meandering over my face...

Its *eerily* intelligent eye.

"Wait," I squinted. "I *know* you."

Crazy, right? The horse looked identical to all the other Púcas. But now I was 100% certain this was the Púca who'd done the backflip a few minutes ago.

And I was 99% sure this was the Púca I'd freed when I first arrived in Sakar. The one who'd stalked me.

"Well," I murmured, "I guess we're even now, huh? A life for a life, right?"

In response, the horse bellowed, ears flattening, and bolted away.

Although that might've had less to do with what I'd said, and more to do with the knife Cheriour had chucked.

"Why do you *insist* on tempting the Púcas?" he asked as he came to a halt beside me. He was horseless now and had a big ole slash wound across his back.

"I-it killed its rider," I said.

"They've been known to do that."

"But—"

Cheriour snatched my arm, yanking me out of the way of a galloping hellhound. "Did the Púca bite you?" he asked as he swiftly killed the dog.

"No."

"You're sure?"

"Positive! I-I think..." Oh, it would sound *stupid* if I said it out loud. *I think the poisonous horse killed its rider, and another Púca* and *another Wraith because it was protecting me.*

"Addie. You need to *focus*." Cheriour pulled me behind him and hurled a knife at another hellhound. And then he shouted, "Ethan!"

A gray-bearded man staggered into us, wiping his bloodied hair out of his eyes.

Wait.

That was his *skin*. The dude had been scalped. *Almost.* It wasn't a very clean job, considering he now had a flap of skin dangling over his face.

"Head to the castle," Cheriour said.

"But—" Ethan started.

"You're not fit to fight," Cheriour's voice was quiet but firm.

Ethan swayed, his face ashen. The gooey chunk of scalp flopped over his eyes. He'd never make it to the castle. The building was a mile away. At least. This guy would be lucky if he made it ten feet without fainting.

"I'll go with you," I said. "To the castle. I'll make sure you get there in one piece. This is something I can do," I added when Cheriour looked at me. "I'm a shit fighter, but I've got the defense thing down. Kinda. I can help him. Be a human shield, y'know?"

Cheriour nodded. "Maddox is—" he stopped, plucked a teensy knife out of his chest holster, and flung it across the field. There was a hollow *urgh* as the blade hit a Wraith's chest.

"Maddox is a Healer. He'll be waiting at the castle. Bring as many wounded to him as you can. But move *quickly*." He threw another knife.

He was so stinking casual about this. *"Oh yes, I can have a full conversation while killing monsters. And you thought I couldn't multitask..."*

"Addie!"

I flinched when Cheriour yelled. "Yeah, okay," I said. "Get the wounded to the castle. Got it." I stared at the array of bodies zigzagging across the ground. There were so many...

"I'll watch your back." Cheriour's voice softened. Just a smidge. But then a Wraith sprinted toward us, and Cheriour shouted again. "Go! Addie, don't stand there. *Go!*"

30

MONSTER

LASS

I remembered falling.

As the floor of our room collapsed, Terrick and I tumbled down, and down, and down. The impact rattled every bone in my body and left me screaming in agony, but I never loosened my grip on Terrick. The building crumbled around us. Wood splintered. Leather burned. The tannery owner and his family were trapped inside. The stench of their singed flesh hovered like a cloud in the air.

In my arms, Terrick melted. His eyes frothed and disintegrated. His skin blistered, blackened, and turned to ash. I held onto him, even when all I had left were charred pieces of bone.

In the end, the city people found me, unclothed but unharmed, hovering over the skeleton of the only father figure I had ever known.

Voices rang out.

"Is that Terrick's child?"

"Can't be. Didn't he say she was too weak to leave bed?"

"Been dying for years as I 'eard it."

I crouched lower, wishing they would go away.

They encircled me, stepping over the wreckage. They weren't fearful, but they didn't have a reason to be. Terrick had kept me and my curse well-concealed during our time in Darfield.

"Are you alright?" A hand touched my bare shoulder.

I backed away with a scream. The fire had dwindled to a mere flicker at my fingertips, but the itch beneath my skin remained.

"How did you escape?" A man asked.

Nausea coiled in my belly. A sob suffocated me, even as my eyes remained dry. But my numb fingers maintained their iron-clad grip on Terrick's corpse.

"Come away, child." More hands touched my shoulders, guiding me away from Terrick.

"No," I rasped.

"There's nothing to fear. You're safe now."

Safe? I'd never be *safe* again. Not when the thing I feared most was myself.

"Your father's gone, child. I'm sorry."

They wouldn't *stop*.

The itch beneath my skin grew.

Hands touched mine, prying my fingers from Terrick's skeleton. Someone else patted my shoulder. Yet another person combed their fingers through my hair.

"Don't *touch me!*" The scream exploded from my throat, accompanied by a rush of fire spreading along my arms and torso.

Those attempting to comfort me were the first to die. Their pained cries rang into the night air as they burned.

Run.

I stared at the ~~massacer~~ massacre before me, my chest painfully tight.

Not all perished. Some had wisely stood out of the

flame's reach. They ran, likely to spread the news of the tannery's destruction. And I heard the word they all whispered.

Monster.

Another term I'd learned from Terrick's fiction books. This one had two meanings: a strange and horrible creature, or a human capable of great wickedness.

I was both.

Monster.

My stomach heaved. I must have vomited—the sticky taste of bile coated my tongue—but I didn't remember. A fog crept across my brain, distorting my thoughts. My body moved stiffly and on its own accord, as though another entity had taken control of my limbs.

As I stood to flee, I noticed something shiny rippling in the cold autumn wind.

The tunic.

It lay draped over the crumbled wooden beams of the building. It was whole. Unburnt. Its colors dazzled even through the smoky haze. I staggered to it. Shards of wood, stone, and glass cut into my bare feet, but I felt no pain.

How had the tunic survived?

It had been hanging in the armoire when the fire started and should have burned with the rest of our belongings.

My flame-wrapped fingers stretched out. The fabric was cool to the touch, unbothered by my fire.

I peeled the tunic away from the wooden beam and slipped it over my head. It was, as I'd once suspected, made for an adult, and for someone with a much larger frame than mine. The sleeves cascaded beyond my fingertips, the hem brushed against my shins, and I had to re-wrap the laces—an arduous task with my hands so unsteady—to close the front over my chest.

The tunic did not disintegrate, even as the fire continued to twirl over my skin.

I staggered through the city streets, my bloodied feet slipping on the stone. People screamed when I passed them. I wrapped my arms around my chest, shivering. When the fire left me several minutes later, I missed it. A wretched curse it may have been, but it had provided some measure of protection against the cold.

I wandered, hardly aware of which direction I traveled in. And I heard more shouting; cries that a Celestial had attacked Darfield.

"The tannery...did you see what it did to the tannery?"

"It looks like a *child!*"

"Can Celestials change their form?"

My vision blurred. I sulked in the shadows, slipping into narrow alleys whenever I saw people approaching. They were hunting me now. I had to leave.

And yet, the thought of fleeing made my chest hurt.

My time at Darfield had certainly not been kind. The years had produced few good memories. But I'd had a home in this city. I'd had someone who loved me and had tried to do what was best for me. That was gone now. I was barely into adulthood (only seventeen if my estimates are correct) and I was alone.

My options were bleak. The humans' hatred for Wraiths and Celestials ran deep. If I stayed, I'd undoubtedly be tortured to a slow, ~~excrutiating~~ excruciating death. Which should have frightened me, but it didn't. I didn't care what they did to me.

I worried what *I* would do to *them.*

Seven soldiers rushed by my alleyway. They didn't notice me; their eyes focused on the plume of smoke rising from where the tannery had once been. I waited, holding my breath.

When the sound of their footsteps faded, I emerged from the shadows—

And gasped as rough hands encircled my arms.

The fingers tightened, spinning me around, bringing me face-to-face with my captor.

The blue-eyed boy.

But a boy no longer.

I knew he'd grown but witnessing the changes from my bedroom window wasn't as shocking as observing them up close. He was taller than I remembered; the tip of my head only reached his chest. Bands of muscle corded around his arms. A thick coat of dark whiskers obscured much of his face. But his brilliant eyes were the same, even as they regarded me with apprehension.

"So it's you," he said, still grasping my arms. "The girl with the flair for dramatics."

I gaped at him, unable to speak.

"I waited for you," he murmured. "But I never saw you again. I did not believe you the type to dishonor a fairly won wager, so I thought something had happened and perhaps you'd left the city."

My breathing turned ragged.

"Yet you've been here all this time?" There was no malice in his eyes. Only confusion.

I was locked away, I wanted to say. *Locked away so I couldn't hurt anyone.* But the words wouldn't form.

The boy's brow furrowed. "What happened to you? Where are the sarcastic quips that once rested on your tongue?"

"Where is the careless smile that once brightened your face?"

I didn't realize I'd spoken out loud until the boy sighed, his hold on my arms softening. "Long gone," he said. "The army extinguishes a person's spirit. And I am, first and foremost, a

soldier in Darfield's army." His voice sounded flat. Dull. "We've
—*I've* been ordered to detain you. Dúnlang will question you.
He's a Shield, you understand. Your power may not work on
him. In fact, he's counting on its ~~ineffacy~~ inefficacy against
his ability." His frown deepened. "You've killed innocent
people tonight."

It hurt to meet his gaze; especially since he understood the
full gravity of what I'd done.

"They say you're evil," the boy said.

I am. Tears burned my eyes.

"I don't believe that."

My head snapped up.

He laid his hand on my shoulder, his touch gentle. "An evil
creature," he whispered, "would not show such remorse." He
used his thumb to wipe a tear from my cheek. It was a tender
gesture, and it only made me cry harder.

His touch terrified me. I wanted him to leave. To run.
Before my fire consumed him too.

I also yearned to lean into his hand; to feel the scrape of his
work-roughened fingers against my skin.

"You are Terrick's daughter?" the boy asked. "His *supposedly*
ill child?"

I nodded.

"How long have you had your ability?"

I stared at my bare feet, saying nothing.

"Those were melted coins in your hand that day in the
market, were they not? No," he smiled at my bemused look, "I
have not forgotten. At the time, I thought you were an Illuminator; they've been known to generate enough heat to melt a
coin. I didn't know..." he inhaled. "You can't control your
power, can you?"

I stayed silent.

"Were you *ever* able to control it?"

Again, I did not speak.

The boy sighed again. "I'm sorry," he said. "Drat it all. Did —the things I said—did I frighten you away when I spoke of the army? Is that why you and Terrick never sought help? Dúnlang is a pompous blaggard, and I would not wish you to meet him. But Ellard, the Celestial—*no,* he's not like The Conqueror," the boy added when I made a strangled sound. "Ellard helps protect Sakar. He's fair. And kind. He would've helped you. *I* would have helped you."

A tremor coursed through me. I didn't know what hurt more. That the boy still remembered me, even after four years. Or that help had been so close. I'd only had to go down to him, as I'd yearned to do countless times while I was confined above the tannery.

Shouts reverberated off the buildings.

I flinched. The boy drew in a long breath. "It's too late now," he said. "Ellard has been away for several months, and Dúnlang will not allow you to live." Sadness crept into his eyes as he dropped his hand and wrapped his fingers around my knuckles. "Come with me."

I wrenched my hand away.

The boy's eyes softened. The laugh that escaped him was thin. Nervous. "Allow me to clarify...come with me so I can show you a safe way out of the city. I've no wish to take you to Dúnlang."

"No? He's your commanding officer."

"Indeed."

"Yet you would defy his orders to help me escape?"

"Yes."

I glowered at him. "Why?"

The boy lowered his head and winked. "Defying an order is more entertaining than obeying it. And I still like your spark."

His mouth curled into a smile. "I don't want to see Dúnlang extinguish it."

Trusting him was foolish. He might have led me right to his commander. Or, worse yet, I might've loosed my power on him. But the flame no longer pressed against my skin. And I did not care if the boy brought me to my doom. I only wished this night-marish evening to end. So I threaded my fingers through his—his hand was wondrously warm—and allowed him to lead me away.

He followed the same pattern as I had: lingering in the shadows, hiding whenever footsteps approached. After several tense moments, we reached the edge of the city, where a narrow river trickled behind the rows of houses.

The blue-eyed boy stepped up to the water's edge.

I stopped, my heels digging into the damp grass and soft soil. I remembered all too well the terror of drowning, the pain as I inhaled water, filling my lungs until they seemed ready to burst.

"It's alright," the boy said.

"I-I can't..."

"Swim?"

I nodded.

"You don't have to." He let go of my hand and stepped into the stream. The water lapped at his ankles. "It's shallow here and won't deepen until you've reached the river. You'll know when you've arrived; the water swirls in reverse. That is your destination." He glanced at me, as though to make sure I was listening. "Follow this to the river and then walk along the bank. It's a seven-day journey, by foot, to Vaporia. You will find food and supplies there, but I don't recommend you linger. Dúnlang will send soldiers to search for you. Continue following the river until it tapers off in Wyncook Forest. From there, it's but a few days' journey to Niall. You'll be safe there.

And Niall is easily recognizable—the Celestials built the fortress. It is a *resplendent* sight to behold." His eyes shone with excitement as he reminisced. "Ah, sometimes I wish I could be as eloquent with my words as I once was with my music."

As I once was. "Do you still play?" I asked.

The boy, who'd begun walking out of the water, glanced at me. "Pardon?"

"The harp. The last we'd met, you wanted to leave the army—"

"Because I was a musician, not a soldier." His playful smile returned. "Yes, that was quite a while ago, wasn't it? I haven't played the harp in..." His lips pursed. "Must be near two years now." He waggled his fingers. "They became warrior's hands after all."

A heavy feeling settled into my gut. He'd lost the one thing he'd been so passionate about.

But there was no time for us to mourn the death of childhood dreams. The soldiers still searched for me, and their bellows drew closer as they reached the outskirts of the city.

The boy's smile faded. "Go now," he hissed. "And make haste. I'll try to draw their attention elsewhere, but I can't guarantee they won't search the stream."

He wrapped his arms around my waist, lifting me off the ground and depositing me into the water. I grimaced when the cold liquid sloshed against my raw and still-bleeding feet.

"Here." The boy touched his fingers against my forehead, healing my injuries. "There aren't many stones beneath the water. Once you've reached the river, you can bind stalks of grass to slip over your feet. It will help."

I nodded. But, as I turned, the boy grasped my hand again.

"You never told me your name," he said. His fingers twitched against mine. "I looked for you. Many times. I questioned everyone in the market. But without a name, I had little chance of finding you."

"I have no name," I whispered.

His head tilted sideways. "Surely, you must."

"Terrick," the name tasted like ash on my tongue, "called me lass."

"Lass," the boy repeated. His thumb rubbed my knuckles. "I hope we meet again, Lass."

"And will you tell me your name? Or is this to be a one-sided acquaintance?"

"There's your delightful sarcasm!" he laughed. "Quinn Byrne, at your service." He dipped his head into a small, silly bow.

But the bout of playfulness was short-lived.

"Who's there?" a man shouted. "Oi! There are voices over here!"

"Go," the boy whispered. "Be safe, Lass." He turned and sprinted toward the city.

Quinn.

I repeated the name in my head as I trudged through the stream. I didn't want to forget it.

True to Quinn's word, the water never rose above my waist, and its current was gentle. Slow. Easy to navigate. It was frigid, though. A chill seeped into my bones that wouldn't abate, even as the sun rose, bathing the earth in its light and warmth. I continued moving, dragging my heavy feet through the muddy bottom of the water, fighting back the urge to stop, to cry, to wallow in my misery. Quinn had taken a great risk to see me safely from the city. I vowed to reach the river if only to honor the sacrifice he'd made for me.

It was evening again when I found the reverse-swirling current. The waters here were higher, reaching my chest, and more violent. I could go no further.

I climbed up the riverbank, grunting as my hands and feet struggled to find traction on the slick grass. And then I sat there, shivering, as I watched the savagely churning waters.

I wished Quinn had fled with me. Perhaps a few years ago, he would have been eager to escape. We could have run away together, perhaps finding a place where he could practice his music. And I...

Oh, but it was an absurd notion. If Quinn had accompanied me, perhaps he would have found his freedom, but fate would not have been as kind to me. No matter where I went, I carried my power with me. And I'd only ever be seen as a monster.

As darkness descended upon the earth once more, I stood and gave myself another moment to lament everything I'd lost before I walked away.

31

BUCKETS OF BLOOD

ADDIE

"It's alright," I grunted when a woman leaned into my shoulder. "You're fine...gonna be right as rain soon."

That was the baldest-faced lie I'd ever told. Thankfully, the woman was too disoriented to call me out on it.

I grasped my poleaxe, using it to support my weight as I staggered across the rocky terrain. The woman flopped against my shoulder, moaning. Around us, the fight was still going strong. Stacks of dead and wounded crisscrossed over the ground. And carting someone who could barely walk through this mayhem was a *nightmare*.

The woman whimpered as I yanked her to the side, narrowly avoiding a dive-bombing bird.

"Sorry, Addie!" Belanna shouted from across the field. "Another one's coming on yer left..."

The bird *whooshed* past my left shoulder, talons outstretched, as it made a beeline for a Wraith. I ducked out of the way, cursing when I mashed my right knee against a boulder. "Motherfu—"

The woman whimpered again.

"Fuck, sorry," I hissed. "Bumpy road, y'know? But you're okay. You're going to be fine..."

She'd be a seriously lucky duck if she survived. Because the only thing keeping her innards from becoming out-ards was the strip of fabric I'd wrapped around her abdomen. Fabric I'd torn off a dead guy's shirt. *Super* hygienic, right?

"You're okay," I kept saying. "Don't get me wrong, you're totally gonna scar, but stomach scars are badass. I've got one from an ovarian cyst I had removed a few years ago..."

I didn't know if my rambling helped these people or annoyed the shit out of them, but I kept at it anyway. If I were in her shoes, and my guts were being held together by a dead man's cloth, I'd want someone to talk to me. Take my mind off the pain. Reassure me things were alright, even if they weren't.

"See?" I puffed as we stumbled through the last group of soldiers blocking us from the city walls. "We made it! Easy peasy."

The woman sagged, her eyes rolling into the back of her head.

"I'll take her from here!" A man rushed to my side, lifting the woman off my shoulder. Maddox. The Healer. And a scary-looking mofo with his six foot five frame and linebacker shoulders. But he seemed as mild as a kitten. He moved slowly, spoke softly, and didn't even carry a weapon. Because he said he "*didn't trust himself with sharp objects.*"

Same, bro. *Same.*

"Her stomach..." I started.

"Yes, I see it," Maddox said. "It shouldn't be too complicated to mend. Especially as you've done a wonderful job with the bandaging. Thank you, Addie." He turned, pushing the wooden door open with his shoulder, and brought the woman inside the city.

I dashed back into the fray.

"Fucking *Christ!*" I nearly jumped out of my skin when someone snatched the back of my neck. *A Wraith.* It had to be. This was it. The end of the line...

"Hold on, Addie," a voice said in my ear.

My knees buckled. "Moira! Damnit, don't *do* that! I'm already—"

Moira dug her fingers into my neck as a curved knife whistled through the air. It was too close and coming too fast.

I screamed.

And the knife came to an abrupt stop less than an inch from my face, as though it had hit a wall. It hovered for a moment, the blade making a tinny *ziiing* before it flopped to the ground.

By some miracle, I hadn't shit myself today. *Yet* (I checked, just to be sure). "Holy cow," I clasped a hand to my chest as my pulse roared.

Moira dropped her hand away from my neck.

"Did you—that's your power, isn't it? You're—I didn't know you were a *hybrid!*" I turned to face her.

She smiled, although she looked pale. Shaky.

"Thanks!" Why did my voice sound super screechy? "I owe you. Big time."

"Keep your eyes open, Addie." Moira bumped her knuckles against my shoulder and dove sideways, driving her sword into a hellhound's gut.

Out of the corner of my eye, I spotted Cheriour wrenching knives out of dead Wraiths. He didn't look at me. I didn't look at him. It was the system we'd worked out. We stayed within eyesight of each other. He jumped in and saved me whenever I was in deep shit (assuming Moira didn't beat him to it). But we never acknowledged each other. We just did our jobs.

My rubbery legs ached as I ran across the field, occasionally kneeling to check on fallen soldiers. I'd been doing this for at least an hour. And I still wanted to scream every time I knelt beside a dead body. *Especially* a body I recognized. Like the flirty guy who once grew an entire hyacinth because it matched my eyes.

Cathal.

His poor body was ravaged by multiple punctures and fractures. Sweat still coated his brow and soaked his hair. He hadn't been dead long. Probably only a few minutes.

If I'd been a little faster, could I have gotten him off the field in time?

A bitter tang filled my mouth as I touched the top of Cathal's head. "I'm—Christ, this isn't fucking fair. You were a cool dude. I'm so freaking sorry."

And then I left him. Alone. To be trampled by the other soldiers, Wraiths, hellhounds, and Púcas. Because he was gone, and I couldn't help him.

I almost cried in relief when I found someone I *could* help.

"Alright, buddy," I said to a grizzly, brown-bearded man. "Whatya say we get the hell out of Dodge, hmm?"

He stared at me, his eyes slightly glazed. His *entire* right arm had been ripped off. Shoulder and all. He'd lost buckets of blood.

I spun, looking for the nearest dead body. A woman lay spread eagle a few inches from me...

Well, her *body* was there. No idea where her head was.

"Sorry," I whispered as I yanked her shirt off. She hadn't been wearing a bra or any binding underneath, so her girls were on full display. "OMG, I'm *so* sorry." I hoisted her onto her side, using her arm to cover her chest. Didn't matter that she was dead, and long past caring about her privates hanging out. It didn't seem right to leave her exposed.

I crawled back to the man and began wrapping. Wasn't

easy, especially since my fingers kept slipping into the gaping hole where his shoulder should have been (*gag*). But he didn't flinch, cry, or curse. He stared straight ahead. Beneath the tangles of beard and hair, his face was white as a sheet.

"Alrighty." I scooted to his other side, flinging his only arm over my shoulders. "Alley-oop. *Uggh*, c'mon, dude." I poked his ribs when he flopped his full weight on me. "I ain't a pack mule." My knees knocked together. "And you're not a lightweight. Stand up!" I braced the end of my poleaxe against the ground. I sucked ass at using the thing as a weapon, but it made a handy walking stick.

The man groggily, laboriously, pulled his feet beneath him.

"There ya go—uh-uh, come on," I grunted when he went limp again. "I can't carry you. It's not far though, I promise. A big tough guy like you can hold it together for a few more minutes, right?"

We tottered along. "That's it," I huffed. "One foot in front of the other. There's a song for that. We have a Christmas movie back home...y'know what Christmas is? Ah, never mind, probably not."

I was so busy rambling, it took me a second to notice the change in the air. A rolling echo of thunder rumbled the ground. I couldn't turn my head, not with the man's arm plopped over my shoulder, but my heart somersaulted as the people around me shouted. *Not* the same agonized yells that had been my soundtrack for the last hour. These were joyful sounds. Cheers.

Maddox came out of the city to greet me, a wide smile stretched across his face.

"I missed something, didn't I?" I winced and rubbed my shoulder when Maddox took the bearded man from me.

"Our riders returned," he said, still smiling.

I whirled around.

Sure enough, a mass of horses and riders circled the remaining Wraiths and hounds. And there were a *ton* of them (humans, not Wraiths). It made the army from Niall seem puny in comparison.

The Wraiths were outnumbered now. And they abandoned ship, scrambling to get back up the hill.

"It's over?" I gasped.

"Not yet." Maddox shifted the bearded man more securely over his shoulder and nudged the door open. "But it will be soon, I expect."

My knees sagged.

This nightmare was almost over. I was still alive. Whoo-hoo! Time for shots.

Right?

But I didn't feel relief. Or happiness. Or *anything*.

I stared at the bodies littered over the rocky field. The mounds of dead and dying.

How many people wouldn't get to drink tonight? Or eat another meal? Or see their loved ones again? I'd ridden along-side most of these people. We'd commiserated about the shitty weather and slippery ground together. Had slept as a group beneath the clusters of angry storm clouds. Had risen this morning and faced the blood-red sunrise...*together*. And a good chunk of them hadn't lived to see the sunset.

It was hollow, the feeling that spread inside of me. Empty.

Tears burned my eyes as I walked amongst the bodies, hoping, *praying*, I'd find someone still alive. But these were dead, most mangled beyond recognition.

Most. Not all.

I stopped, my fingers trembling around my poleaxe.

Moira stared up at me. Blood coated the front of her shirt and seeped lazily from the two puncture wounds on the side of her neck.

A riderless Púca stood a few feet away, its tail swishing as it smacked its blood-soaked lips. But this was not the Púca who'd saved me earlier.

That Púca had an intuitive gaze. Very human-like.

This one had dull eyes. Dumb. Hungry. Red drool dripped from its mouth as it surveyed me.

And then it pounced.

"Fuck!" I squeaked, whanging my poleaxe through the air.

The tip sliced into the crest of the Púca's neck. The animal howled and threw itself backward.

My back muscles screamed when I yanked my weapon free and braced it in front of me again.

The wound on its neck was deep. Ugly. Not enough to kill the S.O.B. though. "C'mon, you sack of shit!" I snarled.

With a low whimper, the Púca backed up a few more steps. It cast me one last reproachful glance before it turned and trotted away.

I stood for a moment, waiting. The Púca would be back. I was sure of it. The fugly bastard was probably giving itself more room to gather momentum.

But it trotted right up the hill. Away from me.

I turned, making sure the coast was clear of all other venomous horses before I dropped to Moira's side.

"Please, please, *please* don't be dead," I whispered.

Her eyes sluggishly followed my movements. Breath rattled her lungs.

Halle-freaking-lujah! "That's a helluva hickey you've got there." My laugh sounded high-pitched. Strained. "I'd ask if the kinky bastard showed you a good time, but I think I already know the answer."

Moira blinked slowly.

"Let's get you out of here. And then you and I can have a nice long talk about love bites." I reached under her armpits, heaved, and let out a frustrated *"urrggh"* when she didn't budge. "Heh." I wiped at the sweat on my brow. "This is why weaklings shouldn't fight in battles. My arms are gassed." And my muscles *were* aching, but that wasn't the problem.

Moira was rigid. Stiffer than a plank. I couldn't bend her or shift her weight, so I had zero chance of getting her off the ground.

"Okay." I patted her shoulder as her eyes rolled back toward me. "Okay, plan B," I detracted my poleaxe and shoved it into my holster, "I'm gonna have to drag you. It'll mess your back up, but I'll get you to the castle. Don't worry." I squatted, grasped her inflexible arms, and heaved.

She moved an inch. *Maybe* two.

"Addie." Cheriour stood beside me, wiping blood out of his eyes.

"OMG, perfect timing!" I panted. "Can you get her legs for me?"

Cheriour knelt and touched the top of Moira's head. "She's gone."

"No. The Púca bit her. And she's gone all stiff...but she's still alive!"

"She's not."

"She is! Look at her eyes!" I glanced down. And my stomach dropped to my toes.

Moira's eyes had rolled into the back of her head. They weren't moving anymore. I held a hand in front of her mouth, hoping I'd feel her breathing. I didn't.

"But you said the Púca venom's a paralytic! Not a death sentence." I hissed.

"It is," Cheriour murmured. "But the Púca took too much blood."

My stomach heaved itself into my throat as I touched Moira's cheek. Her very *cold* cheek.

Not twenty minutes ago, Moira had saved me from decapitation.

Now she was gone.

I stood, clapping a hand over my mouth. My palm stunk. Like sweat. And blood.

"Addie..." Cheriour rose to his feet.

I turned away, blinking back tears as I muttered a scathing, *"Fuck this fucking shithole place!"*

And then I stomped off, heading further into the battlefield, praying I'd find at least one person still alive.

32

MISFIT TOYS

ADDIE

"Y ou ever been so tired you forget how to do basic things? Like, how to walk and talk? Or what day it is? How old you are? Or," I grunted as my fingers fumbled over the strip of cloth I was trying to tie, "how to do a simple knot? Because I'm there." The fabric fell out of my hands. "Goddamn it."

Maddox's chuckle echoed in the cavernous dining hall...or whatever this room was. Looked like a dining hall to me, with candle-laden chandeliers running the length of the room. It only needed a few long tables to complete the picture. Instead, people sprawled across the bare floor. Some had blankets. Most didn't. Some were lucid. Most weren't. Some quietly stared at the flickering candlelight. Most cried, whimpered, grunted, or wailed.

The *wounded ward* was not a fun place.

Sure, Maddox had the Vulcan Mind Meld healing ability. The problem? He was one man. And trying to heal all the wounded had almost landed him in the sickbed alongside them. After an hour, he'd started swaying on his feet, his nose bleeding. But he kept going...until he vomited into a bag of fresh bandages. *Then* he conceded defeat.

So the new rule: those in immediate danger of dying received healing. The rest got the best healthcare Viking Land had to offer: a few poorly trained nurses (including me), gritty gasoline-scented alcohol (used to both rinse wounds *and* numb the pain), bandages that were kinda-sorta clean (and smelled moldy), and a cushy spot on the stone floor.

I mean, seriously, why would anyone ever want to go to a regular hospital when they had this five-star service?

The man I was bandaging grunted when I accidentally scraped my nail against the festering hole in his thigh. See? Top-quality care. I didn't even have gloves because...why would I? Sticking my bare, blistered hands right into a wound was way more sanitary.

Being able to think and see straight? Overrated. Sleep deprivation was the way to go. I was only helping people with serious injuries—missing limbs, compound fractures, and lacerations, to name a few. I didn't need to be alert, right?

Oh, and my patience? That flew out the window hours ago.

"For fuck's sake." The fabric slipped through my fingers again.

"Here."

My head whipped up when Cheriour knelt beside me, pushing my hands out of the way. "Thank you for helping, Addie. But I'll finish bandaging him."

I didn't argue. Mostly because my muscles were goop, my heart seemed heavier than an anvil, and my brain had turned to mush (aka, I was *exhausted*). I sighed, drew my knees into my chest, and watched him work.

He had a steady hand; almost unnaturally quiet. His movements were fluid, his fingers nimble. He didn't fumble to tie knots or fidget with the bandages. Half the time he wasn't even looking at what he was doing, his eyes too busy roaming around the hall. But he never faltered.

Wasn't that him, though? Quiet. Nimble. Self-assured.

Protective.

Cheriour stared at Maddox, his lips pursed as the other man weeble-wobbled across the room. Cheriour didn't stop working, but tension rippled over his shoulders. He shifted, ready to spring to his feet. But Maddox kept himself upright and moved to his next patient.

Cheriour exhaled but kept his eyes roving, as though afraid to let anyone out of his sight. His tension never ebbed.

He reminded me of Atlas; the titan sentenced to carry the world on his shoulders.

My anvil-weighted heart did a weird spasm, pummeling the inside of my chest.

I wanted to give Cheriour a hug. Or a massage. Those taut shoulders probably had some *massive* knots. But I didn't know if he liked hugs. Maybe he had a personal space bubble he didn't want crossed. Or maybe he was a snuggle bug. I had no idea.

I'd spent most of the last month with the guy, and I knew almost *nothing* about him.

Did he have a favorite food? Favorite story? A favorite color? What had his life been like before he became the army leader? Was he born here? Or ripped away from his home? Did he have a family? A girlfriend? Boyfriend? What made him smile? Or laugh? And what did his laugh sound like?

"If you wanted to know those things," Cheriour finished tying the bandage and raised an eyebrow at me, "you could've asked."

I blinked. "Aw fuck, was I talking out loud again?"

He hummed and laid the unconscious man's head on a makeshift pillow.

"How much did I say?"

"You asked me a dozen questions. Do you truly not realize when you're speaking?"

I shrugged. "Not always. When I was younger, they said it was stress or PTSD. Something like that. They said with time and therapy, I'd outgrow it. I kinda did, but not really. Not all the way. And it's worse when I'm upset. Or tired. Or both."

Cheriour leaned back on his haunches and stared at me for a few beats. Long enough to make my skin prickle and my stomach squirm. "What happened to you?" he asked when he resumed his ADHD room scanning. "When you were a child?"

"Depends on who you ask, I guess. I've had a lot of people say the house fire...y'know, the one my parents died in. Well, some people swore that fire melted a part of my brain." I laughed, even as an acidic tang coated my tongue.

"I'd like a serious answer."

"Oh, I'm *dead* serious. Shit, my one foster mother, Mira, tried to have a lobotomy done on me. It's an outdated treatment for mental illness," I added when his forehead scrunched. "Doctors would induce brain damage and turn people into vegetables. Made them 'easier to handle.' It's not *legal* anymore because it's so fucked-up. But if Mira could've found a way, she would've had it done on me. She was a crazy old cu—"

"You haven't answered my question," Cheriour interrupted softly.

"Ummm, yes I did. Kinda. But *you* didn't answer any of *my* questions," I pointed out. "You gotta give before you can take, buddy."

"Cheese."

"What?"

"My favorite food. Cheese."

"Interesting. I can get behind that; cheese is awesome. But," I narrowed my eyes, "you picked the easiest question."

His lips twitched. "A question is a question. I answered one. Now it's your turn."

"You're getting off on a technicality. But, whatever...after my parents died, I spent the rest of my childhood bumping between orphanages and foster homes. And then I aged out of the system. I've been on my own ever since."

Cheriour was silent for a while. "There's more to it than that," he finally said.

"Sure there is. But why should I give a more in-depth response when all you said was '*cheese?*'"

"Lavender," he said. "My favorite color. You said your parents died in a fire. Were you harmed?"

"Wow. You're sticking with the easy answers, aren't ya? Is it only the *color* lavender you like? Or the scent too? Because I *love* the scent."

He said nothing. Just watched the room, waiting for me to respond.

I rolled my eyes. "*Fine.* But your next answer better have more than one fucking word. And no. I wasn't hurt. Not sure how I got out—the firefighters said I must've jumped out a window. If I did, I don't remember. I escaped without a burn, scrape, or bruise. But my parents..." I ground my teeth together as the phantom cries filled my ears. "You ever hear someone burn to death?"

"I have," Cheriour said.

"So you know how awful it is. Imagine being five years old and freaking *terrified* because you don't understand what's going on, and your mom and dad are *screaming.*" A big, fat, salty tear dribbled into my mouth. *Pleh.* I sputtered, sniffled, and scrubbed at my (very damp) cheeks with both hands. No shits given that I smeared blood and poultice all over my face. "This is why I have issues. *Childhood trauma.*"

"You endured the death of your parents," Cheriour asked gently, "and then went to a caretaker who wished to torture you?"

"Well," my voice still sounded too thick. Too raw. I cleared my throat. "I didn't have any other blood relatives. Or, at least, not any good ones. Pretty sure I had a grandmother with dementia and an aunt who'd been locked up for drug use and prostitution. But no one else. So I went to live with the other misfit toys. And all the kids at the orphanage got fed the same bullshit line: '*this is only for a little while. We'll find you a family.*' Except...it's expensive for people to adopt. Those that can afford it usually want *babies*, not snot-nosed little kids with attitude problems. Heh. *Snot-nosed.*" I wiped at my teary cheeks and runny nose. "That's me! Anyway, the orphanage couldn't keep all of us, so we got sent to temporary families. And it's a messed-up system. Most of my foster parents only took me in because they wanted that sweet government paycheck. Once I became too much of a problem, they gave me the boot."

Cheriour's eyes were now stuck on my face, burning a hole in my cheek. Figured. The one time I *wanted* him to look away, he gave me his undivided attention.

"I'll be fair," I waved a hand in front of my face, trying to dry my eyes, "they weren't all like that. Some genuinely wanted to help. But..." I trailed off as I thought of Freda. My first foster mother, with her weathered face and kind smile. The cute button bun she'd twist her hair into. Her gnarled hands mixing food in a big glass bowl, while I stood beside her, ready to add the butter as soon as she gave me the green light.

The problem with thinking of Freda? Images of her alive

were soured by the memory of her body sprawled across the living room floor.

"Bottom line," I said, "I never stayed anywhere for more than a year. I scraped my way through high school. And then I was on my own. Government said, *'Happy 18th Birthday! Now get off your lazy ass and get a job.'* So, yeah." Sweat pooled in my palms as I dug my trembling fingers into my thighs. "That's my origin story. Happy now?"

Cheriour still stared at me, although not as intensely as before. Mainly because Maddox was on the move again and had grabbed some of my spotlight.

I blew out a long, shaky breath and pressed a hand over my eyes. A sharp pain throbbed behind my temple. Like someone had driven an ice pick into my brain (trying to lobotomize me. Har, har.). And I was sure Maddox had heard my little outburst. Which was embarrassing because I hadn't meant to say all that out loud. Word vomit. It came up in full chunks tonight.

"My family's gone as well."

Cheriour's voice was so quiet, so soft, I almost didn't hear him.

I jerked my hand down to find him staring off into the distance, his eyes restless again.

"Some perished in battle. But most..." His left hand rested against his knee, and his fingers flexed as he spoke. "Most fled. They found they couldn't, *wouldn't*, face the horrors of this war. So they left. I don't know where they are now. But I am certain I'll never see them again."

I didn't know what to say to that. Other than, "I'm sorry." But that never made anything better, did it? *It sucks you lost everyone. I can't do a damn thing to bring them back. But, y'know, sorry.*

I *was* sorry, though. Genuinely. Because I knew what that hurt felt like.

Silence filled the room after my half-assed apology, broken only by the occasional grunt or cry from one of the wounded. Or my sniffling.

"You should sleep, Addie," Cheriour murmured.

He looked so damn small, sitting in the middle of that yawning room, with his wild hair twisted into a man-bun and his eyes shadowed and forlorn.

"How old were you?" I asked. "When your family left?"

His fingers flexed again. "Old enough."

"What does that mean? Old enough for *what?*"

"To have seen it coming." His jaw ticked. "I vowed to give my life fighting this war. I thought they'd do the same. But the signs were always there. Their hesitance. The way they spoke of preserving what they had for as long as they could. They stayed when we still had a chance of surviving. And they fled when that hope died."

"Do you ever wish you'd gone with them?"

"No." And there was *zero* hesitation in his voice. "I have no grandeur notions of victory. But fleeing isn't the answer. It won't save us. And I won't abandon them." He jerked his head toward the wounded soldiers.

I stared at the hordes of semi-conscious people. There were hundreds of them. *Hundreds.* And with one magical healer and a slew of shitty medical practices, a lot of them would die.

Wasn't that the theme here? These people fought tooth and nail every day, and they lost. Because they were stuck in a war they had no chance of winning.

Who *wouldn't* grab their possessions and make for the hills if it offered a chance of something better?

If Cheriour had gone with his family, he might've spent his

days in relative peace, rather than yo-yo-ing from one grueling battle to the next.

Maybe a peaceful Cheriour would have smiled more easily. And laughed.

My heart did the funny spasm thing again. And my fingers itched, suddenly restless. I reached out, pressing my hand against his.

He jolted but then stilled, allowing our joined hands to rest against his knee.

I curled my fingers around his knuckles—whew, he had some *rough* hands. Dozens of little, jagged scars speckled his skin. "You're braver than me." I rubbed my thumb over a big scar on the outside of his wrist. "For staying. If I had the chance, I'd be flying away like a bat out of hell. I'm too much of a coward to stay."

Cheriour's fingers tensed and relaxed. Tensed and relaxed. "You have many faults, Addie. But cowardice is not one of them."

I laughed. "Have you met me? I'm the *definition* of a spine-less chicken."

"I have. Met you." With his face only inches from mine, I saw flecks of silver in his green eyes. Saw the way his throat muscles convulsed as he gulped. "And I don't think you would run so easily," he said.

My stomach tightened when he turned his hand over, touching the tips of his fingers to mine.

I got a sudden urge to lean in and kiss him. To see if I could coax his perpetually rigid lips to soften beneath mine. I wondered what he would feel like; what he would *taste* like. Probably earthy and sweaty. Which were...not normally attractive things.

But a pleasant *ziiing* shot through my muscles.

I tilted my head toward him. Just to see what he'd do.

He slowly turned his toneless eyes toward me. And they lingered, unblinkingly, on my face. With anyone else, this thousand-yard stare might've been creepy. But with him...

Hot. *Hot.* It was hot AF.

Because his gaze wasn't toneless at all. It was pondering, sad, confused, enthralled...*intense.* The emotions were there, no matter how hard he tried to hide them.

Now I *really* wanted to kiss him and see what else hid behind those emerald eyes.

My skin tingled—both with nerves and excitement. Fuck, when was the last time I got *nervous* over a possible kiss?

When was the last time I got excited?

Cheriour leaned closer, turning his head at *just the right angle,* so I felt the tickle of his breath against my lips. My belly did a full backflip.

CRASH!

Across the room, Maddox teetered, sending a wooden bowl clattering to the floor.

Cheriour was on his feet in an instant, leaving me sitting there, my head reeling.

What...the *fuck*...had just happened?

33

POLARIS

Time is a fickle thing, is it not?

For example: the afternoon sun had still been high in the sky when I began ~~righting~~ writing this tale. But it has long since set, and now the moonlight is decreasing as well. I've sat here for a full day, but it seems as though only mere moments have passed.

I dread what these next days will bring; perhaps another reason time is fleeing from me. I'm worried I won't have enough of it; that I will expire before I ~~right~~ write everything I want to say.

My years at Darfield had been the opposite: each day so dreadfully tedious that an hour seemed like a year. A year seemed like a decade.

And yet, as I walked along the river and found myself in

unfamiliar terrain, my time at Darfield seemed little more than a long night's slumber. The memories of those years were more akin to a dream; too muddled and disorienting to have been real. But those long and very real years had taken a hard toll on me.

A chill seeped into my bones. I trembled so forcefully, my body ached—a deep, gnawing pain that throbbed ~~incessintly~~ —incessantly when I was still and wailed when I moved. My feet burned, even though I wrapped them in stalks of grass to protect them from the elements. Walking drove sharp pinpricks of pain into my knees.

The riverbank steepened; the grass slickened. Twice, I nearly slid into the water. After the second time, I cried. I was so cold. The prospect of plunging into the icy water terrified me.

And my tunic was already saturated. I'd started sweating quite profusely, even though I shivered.

"It's not a fever," I said as my teeth chattered.

But it was.

I refused to acknowledge it as I crawled away from the river.

"It's *not* a fever."

Terrick was not here to press cool cloths to my fevered skin, or nurse me through the worst of the illness, as he'd done when he first found me in the woods. A fever would almost certainly mean death.

Perhaps it was what I deserved. But I feared it. My last memories of Mama, with the cough ravaging her lungs and the fever burning her from the inside, were still vivid. Terrifying.

"It's not a fever!"

I dragged myself into the shelter of the nearby forest, certain I would feel warm and steady once I left the eternal chill of the water.

Breathing *hurt*. I became winded after only a few minutes of movement.

I wanted to stop. To lie down.

I was alone, frightened, and weak. But instinct drove me endlessly forward.

Instinct...and Terrick's shadow.

For I heard his voice that day. Clearly. As though he was standing beside me. Guiding me. Protecting me.

"Find shelter, lass. The weather can turn quicker than a horse rounding cattle. Even if it seems calm, you'll want to make sure you're prepared for the worst."

"The worst has already happened," I said.

"It's not so bad as that, lass." Came Terrick's warm response. *"We'll do it together. Remember what I've taught you."*

Terrick and I had lived in the woods for months before arriving at Swindon. And, upon realizing I did not know the basic skills necessary for surviving in the wild, he had been all too eager to teach me.

Terrick *loved* teaching.

"Look to the trees. If their branches are thick, they'll shield you from the worst of the wind and rain."

My knees trembled as I raised my eyes upward. Most trees had shed in preparation for winter, but a great oak still clung to its leaves. They'd turned blood red, and would fall soon, but they'd provide some measure of protection for the night.

"Well done, lass."

Though the tree was only a short distance away, it took me several minutes to reach it. I was thoroughly winded as I lowered myself against the expansive trunk.

A leaf fluttered to the ground. For a moment, my fever-addled brain believed the red foliage to be a droplet of blood. I envisioned Terrick's body suspended in the branches above me, blood seeping from his blistered flesh.

I pressed a hand to my churning stomach, fighting back a cry. But when I glanced up, I saw only the branches as they swayed in the breeze, making soft, creaking sounds. It was gentle. And rhythmic. A lullaby.

Through the crimson leaves, I stared at the starry sky. And I remembered the night Terrick and I had lain beneath the moon and stars on a warm summer's eve, a full month before we would arrive at Swindon.

"Ah, lass," Terrick said, *"you see there, the brightest star in the sky?"*

At the time, I couldn't see what he was pointing at. But I nodded.

"That is Polaris," he traced his finger around the constellation. *"The Guardian. You'll never be lost, as long as he's watching over you."*

The stars blurred before my teary gaze. But Polaris, hanging high in the sky, still shone more brightly than the rest.

Yet I'd never felt more lost.

My chest ached. For all his faults, Terrick had cared for me. I was certain of that. Everything he'd done in the last years of his life had been to help me.

He'd *loved* me. And I him.

But his love had gotten him killed.

I wished he had never rescued me from the depths of the pond. Drowning may have been an ~~excrutiating~~ excruciating death, but the discomfort would have only lasted a few moments. It certainly would have been less painful than living.

And Terrick would have been free to spend the rest of his days surrounded by his books at Swindon. He could have had many more mornings whistling his happy tune as he strolled to the market. His eventual death would have been peaceful, with the warm touches and well-wishes of friends sending his soul on its final journey.

Instead, he'd spent the last years of his life driven from his home, forced to work a job that took too much from his aging body, and struggling to contain an uncontrollable hybrid.

The fire did not take his life that night. But my presence, my existence, had robbed him of the happiness he'd deserved.

"I am happy." Terrick's warm voice filled my brain once more. *"I'll never leave you, lass."*

The words were mere memories, but they were all I had left of him.

"This will pass. Rest. Do not fret."

As much as the words comforted me, they also intensified my sorrow.

I sobbed until my throat was raw and it felt as though someone were driving an iron through my skull. All the while, the big oak tree continued to sway above me, singing its mournful lullaby.

34

MOUTHFUL OF FEATHERS

ADDIE

Sometimes liking a person was a bad fucking idea.

That hill was steep. And you couldn't walk down it. Nope. Once the descent began, you'd roly-poly all the way down. Sometimes you'd get lucky, and the bottom would be a straight patch that'd bring you gently to a halt. Other times? You got rocks. Big-ass boulders. And you'd smash a few bones before you came to a stop.

I knew that dizzying plummet well. And I clearly hadn't learned my lesson because I'd started the downslope again.

I stared at Cheriour's back as he jogged his horse a few yards in front of me. He was talking to Kaelan. Or, rather, *Kaelan* was talking to *him*. Cheriour had only said a few words. Meanwhile, Kaelan babbled apologetically about something. I couldn't hear the entire conversation (too much noise coming from the other riders), but it had something to do with drinking. And...*other* depravities.

Sounded like Kaelan had snuck out to attend a rave at Sanadrin.

Crazy, right? Especially given the situation.

It'd been three days since the battle at Sanadrin. Hundreds of people had died—I kept trying to steer my gaze away from the hordes of riderless horses being ponied back. Because when I saw one I recognized, like Moira's bay stallion, I got this fluttering sensation in my chest. Not a *good* twittering. More like a wicked heartburn and gas pain combo.

But then I looked at Cheriour and got the other kind of fluttering, so...basically, I was all aflutter. Har, har, har.

Anyway, despite the grueling battle we'd been through and the losses we'd endured, there was Kaelan, sheepishly admitting he got smashed at a party.

Even when they were badass warriors, putting their lives on the line, kids were still kids.

And Cheriour looked so...*relaxed.* He rode with one hand on the reins, the other resting on his thigh. He had a damn good seat on a horse. No bouncing or arm flailing. No teetering (although I was the only rider guilty of that). He sat still, moving only to keep his body in rhythm with his mount.

A spattering of laughter broke out in front of me, drawing my attention away from Cheriour. A cluster of soldiers— mostly men—rode four abreast across the field. One of them was in the middle of an obscene joke. Something about an elephant asking a naked man how he breathed...

It didn't take much imagination to find the punch line there.

Another group on my right side talked about a newborn child. "The babe has more hair on her head than you, Rubert," a woman screeched gleefully, jerking her finger at a tall man with a big bald spot in the center of his head. "And he's naught but a month old!"

Rubert ran his hand over that shiny patch of scalp, smiling ruefully. "Perhaps I should ask if I could borrow some, eh?"

Normally, I would've dived right into one of these little chit-chats. But today I kept staring at Cheriour, replaying the conversation we'd had a few nights ago, and getting a fresh surge of rage for the family who had left him behind.

I also felt an outpouring of sappy, jittery emotions. Because we'd gotten so close that night. On an emotional *and* physical level.

That almost kiss had left me with some very confused and horny dreams.

But I'd seen a whole new side of him. And I itched to find out more.

"You're quiet today, aren't you?" Garvin's voice jerked me out of my thoughts.

"Yeah," I muttered. "I think I'm just tired." Not true. I felt like a caffeine addict who'd discovered spiked espresso: full of restless energy. Yet my mind was buzzy, the way it got when I drank too much alcohol and had sailed past the loopy *whoo-hoo, shots!* phase and into the *OMG, I'm gonna hurl!* stage.

"It's been a long week, hasn't it?" Garvin sighed.

He rode beside me, although not too close. Because I was back on Sacrifice, who'd gotten some wicked cuts during the battle, but was okay otherwise. And, y'know, Queen Bitch liked her personal space.

"It has," I mumbled.

Another burst of laughter drifted back toward me. But this one made my heart spin upside down.

I jerked my head up to find Cheriour's shoulders shaking as he chuckled at something Kaelan had said. Kaelan flushed and flailed his arms, as though trying to justify his statement. Cheriour kept laughing.

A few nights ago, I'd wondered what that laugh would sound like.

It was deeper and raspier than his voice. Almost a little breathy. Not what I expected. But so undeniably his.

My stomach did a tingly *swoop-swoop*.

Crap, crap, *crap!* I was *not* falling head over heels for a stanky warrior from Viking Land. Right?

Right???

"Addie..." Garvin said.

"Hmm," I mumbled, still giving Cheriour a creeper stare.

"Addie! Watch out!" The high-pitched tone in Garvin's voice pulled me out of my slightly-stalkerish thoughts.

"What's—Jesus Christ!" I screamed when something heavy (and fleshy) bounced off the back of my head. "What the *hell—*"

The sky was suddenly full of birds—squawking, shrieking, flapping birds. One by one, they plummeted to the ground.

The laughter surrounding me morphed into panicked cries.

I yelled as birds pinged off my back and the top of Sacrifice's head. She snorted and danced sideways.

The birds kept falling.

Their bodies were deformed. Most were missing feathers, their skin covered in blisters and boils. Some had almost no flesh left. It was like a scene out of a horror movie

"What's happening?" I asked.

"It looks like Elion's disease, don't it?" Garvin grunted, struggling to keep his horse still.

"How the hell would I know?" I clutched at Sacrifice's mane as she made a warbled noise and did a sideways cat leap.

"Go!" Belanna and Braxton yelled, almost in unison. "For feck's sake, GO!"

People hurtled in every direction.

"Addie," Garvin called before he wheeled a sharp right, "come with me!" He nudged his horse into the woods.

I tried to follow, but Sacrifice had turned into a wriggle

worm; the more I tried to straighten her, the more she zig-zagged. I kicked her to go forward, she flew backward. "Go!" I drove my heels into her side.

She rose instead, teetering on her hind legs. "Oh, fuck," I whimpered. A bird plopped off the top of my head. Another caught Sacrifice on the tip of her nose. And that was her final straw. When her front feet hit the ground, her back feet came up in a massive buck that pitched me straight over her neck. Down I went, face-planting into a pile of dead birds.

Yep.

Got a mouthful of feathers too. Tasted like fucking battery acid.

I gagged. Sacrifice bolted.

Fan-fucking-tastic.

The rest of the army abandoned ship. And I was horseless, unable to follow anyone.

"Addie!"

I glanced up, still choking on feathers, as Cheriour pulled his horse to a halt beside me.

"The bitch dumped me," I mumbled.

"I saw." Cheriour stretched a hand out, even as he fought to hold his panicked horse steady. "Come on."

He wasn't intending for me to hitch a ride with him, was he? There was no room up there!

"Addie! *Now!*" he bellowed.

And that got my attention. Because in the time I'd known him, he'd never yelled. He'd given commands, sure, but never raised his voice. Not like this.

I stood, fighting the urge to wipe my clothes off—bird guts...*yeck*—and wrapped my fingers around his. I jumped. He pulled. Pretty sure I accidentally whacked him in the ribs as I shimmied behind his saddle.

Cheriour gave me no time to adjust before he spurred his

horse into a gallop. "Eeek!" I squealed. The horse's rump muscles rolled beneath me. It was slippery and impossible for me to wrap my legs around anything. I had to grab onto Cheriour—giving him a full-on bear hug—to keep myself from sliding backward. "W-what the *h-hell* happened to those birds?" I yelled as we thundered through the woods.

"Elion," Cheriour called back.

"That's the disease guy, right?" My stomach curdled.

"Yes." Cheriour clicked his tongue, urging his horse over a downed log.

"Jesus!" I dug my nails into Cheriour's side. The freaking log was the size of a house!

Okay, not really.

But being on the butt of a horse when it took an enormous leap was *not* fun.

With a grunt, the horse touched down on the other side. My chin whacked Cheriour's shoulder. Hard.

"Sor—" I started. And then I screamed.

We had jumped headfirst into a trap.

A dozen Wraiths sprang from the bushes.

Cheriour made a noise—might've been a muffled *"fuck,"*—and tried to spin around. But his horse, freshly landed from a big jump, couldn't get its legs sorted fast enough. And the Wraiths were too close. Too quick. One yanked the reins out of Cheriour's hands.

"Addie, get down!" Cheriour reached for his knife.

He didn't need to tell me twice: the jump and sudden stop had knocked me 90% of the way loose. As soon as I let go of his waist, I hit the ground. Landed right on my ass too.

Meanwhile, Cheriour chucked a blade as he swung out of the saddle, and he still landed on his feet. Motherfucker was almost too graceful for his own good.

And the blade he threw? Went right between a Wraith's eye.

The Wraith holding Cheriour's horse turned, watched dispassionately as his comrade slid to the ground, and chuckled. "Well done." His voice was raw. Guttural. Like a barking cough. "But you don't have enough knives for all of us."

More Wraiths swarmed into the clearing. There had to be twenty, at least. And most wore those spiked helmets, so Cheriour wasn't likely to get another headshot in.

Twenty of them. Two of us. Well...more like one-and-a-half, since I sucked at fighting.

"Ugh," I hissed when my back collided with the trunk of the tree we'd just leapt over. I hadn't even realized I'd been scooting backward.

The Wraith holding Cheriour's horse (the head honcho of the group) turned his milk-white eyes toward me.

Creepy mofo...

"Look at her." Head Honcho smacked his gray lips as his gaze hovered hungrily around my midsection.

Cheriour shuffled sideways, arm outstretched, shielding me.

"I'll allow you leniency," Head Honcho said to him, "if you hand the woman over."

"She'd make a fine meal," a female Wraith cackled.

God-fucking-damnit. Why did everything in this stupid world want to eat me?

Oh, right. Fat equaled flavor. Har, har.

Freda used to say that all the time when she baked or cooked. And I'd bet my left arm the Wraiths held the same philosophy toward their *meals*.

"Addie." Cheriour kept his gaze focused on the Wraiths. "Go."

Head Honcho laughed. "She won't get far—"

Cheriour tossed another knife.

Head Honcho yanked the horse's head forward, shielding himself.

I let out a horrified rasp as the blade sank into the horse's throat. The animal squealed. Snorted. Swayed.

"And now you've one less blade." Head Honcho ripped the knife free.

"Addie," Cheriour dropped into a semi-squat, prepping for an attack, "go!"

"But—"

With a wet, bloody snort, the horse collapsed. Laughter rippled through the crowd of Wraiths.

"GO!" Cheriour insisted.

Where? Where the *fuck* was I supposed to go? And how could I leave him? He was facing off against twenty Wraiths. It didn't matter how good a fighter he was, the odds were shit.

Would me being here make them better? Heck no. But running wouldn't help either. I'd be caught in thirty seconds. Easy.

But if I stayed...

I reached back, sweat burning the blisters on my palms as I freed my poleaxe from its binding.

Cheriour couldn't win this fight. Not being so outnumbered. And he knew it. Perspiration trickled down his face as he plucked another knife from his holster.

If I stayed, at least he wouldn't have to die alone. I mean, there wasn't a *pleasant* way to die. But it was better to go down with a friend. Right?

I sure as fuck hoped so.

Cheriour did a double take when I moved to stand beside him. "I said go," he hissed.

"And I'm saying no." At least my voice was somewhat steady. Unlike my hands.

"So it's a fight you're looking for, eh? We'll oblige." Head Honcho raised his arm, a cold grin unfurling across his face as his lackeys shifted into position behind him. "Kill the man," he called. "Leave the woman alive. *For now.* We shall feast on her flesh tonight."

35

CRISPIER THAN KENTUCKY FRIED CHICKEN

ADDIE

The Wraiths charged.

Cheriour (the freaking badass) killed six of them with a few knife throws. I hit a seventh on a lucky crotch shot.

But the Wraiths were ruthless. Relentless. Hitting them didn't always take them down. Even my crotch shot only stunned the female for a few seconds. Then, privates still bleeding, she snapped right back into the fight.

Cheriour flung a blade into her throat.

If paired with a halfway decent fighter, Cheriour might've had a chance. But I was too inexperienced. And the Wraiths had taken the command to *"leave me alive"* to heart.

"Cheriour!" I yelled as gray-skinned hands closed around my arms, legs, and torso, dragging me backward. They tore the poleaxe from my grasp. "Cheriour!"

The Wraiths clustered around him, blocking him from my line of sight.

I dug my heels into the ground, muscles straining, lungs getting ready to burst as I struggled against the iron grip pulling me back. "Get off me!" I bellowed. "Cheriour!" Why couldn't I see him? *"Cheriour!"*

I thought of Moira, dead on the battlefield. My imagination replaced her face with Cheriour's. I saw his beautiful green eyes staring blankly at the sky.

It hurt. An actual, physical pain lanced my chest as I realized I might never see him again. I'd never get to run my fingers through his curly hair, or—

"Cheriour!" I gasped as he burst through the circle of Wraiths, swinging a short sword. He pivoted, twirled, swirled, stabbed...bled. Like, he bled a *lot*. It ran in rivers down the side of his thigh, soaking his breeches.

"Get off me!" I flailed against the hands holding me. My skin prickled and itched as my blood boiled. *"Get off me, you fuck—"*

One of them shoved a wad of cloth into my mouth. A wet, putrid cloth that smelled like shit—*human* shit. Another hand gripped the end of my braid, ripping my head back.

I watched, horror-struck, as a Wraith plunged a knife into Cheriour's right shoulder. And then something solid connected with the right side of my head and I passed out.

FIRST THING I realized when I returned to the land of the living? I was in my birthday suit (aka, buck naked). A chilly breeze brushed against my ass cheeks.

Second thing? The voices.

"Is the fire going yet?"

"Don't overcook her thighs. You *always* overcook them."

I groaned as I clawed my way back to consciousness. The

memories came flooding back: Cheriour...blood...the knife sinking into his shoulder...

A zing of panic shot through my belly.

Wake up! Wakeupwakeupwakeup!

Easier said than done. It felt like someone had kicked a massive hole in the side of my head. So. Much. *Pain.* It shot down my neck and across my shoulders. Opening my eyes? Ha! I might as well have put a vise around my temple and squeezed until my brain leaked through my nostrils...

Oh, man. Concussions were no fucking joke.

When I finally wrenched my eyelids apart, I stared at a canopy of trees as the dim, late-afternoon sunlight poked out from between the branches. Hands wrapped under my armpits and behind my knees, keeping me suspended in the air.

"No, no, no," a hoarse voice grunted. "Does that look like it'll hold 'er? You need sumfing bigger!"

My head lolled to the side; it was too much energy to keep my neck locked in place.

And...

Aw, fuck!

Cheriour lay curled in a fetal position a few feet away, his back facing me. His clothes were ripped, and his hair matted in a frizzy, blood-stained halo around his head. The toe of his left foot pointed at his ass—a broken ankle. Definitely.

He breathed. Shallowly. But he was *alive.*

The fogginess around my brain cleared.

Headache? What headache? I was right as rain. I *had* to be.

"Oi! I think she's waking!" a Wraith called.

Oh, buddy. I was *wide* awake.

I bucked my hips. Kicked out with both legs. Tried to yank my arms back to my sides, but nothing worked. No matter how much I thrashed and struggled, I couldn't break free.

"Let me go!" I bellowed. "You stupid, fugly bastards. Let. Me. GO!"

They started walking.

I let my head fall back to see where we were going. "Oh, *fuck* no!"

An immense bonfire awaited me. It was the size of a mother-freaking pickup truck. Flames stretched four—no, *five feet* into the air.

"This should hold her. Tie 'er down. Quickly." A Wraith walked over with a seven-foot-long stick. It looked like a sliced tree trunk. Another Wraith approached with ropes.

"Don't you *dare!*" I spat.

Too late.

They pressed the stick against my back and tied me to it. I couldn't do *anything*. They were too strong. I made a bunch of statements that sounded tough, sure. (*"When I get free, I'll ram this stick so far up your ass, you'll choke on it."*). But they were empty threats. And the Wraiths knew it.

There were only six of them left. *Six.* Cheriour had single-handedly taken down almost three-quarters of their group. But I didn't stand a shot in hell against the rest of them.

I was so fucking helpless.

Tears poured down my cheeks as the last knot was tied, securing me to the stick. My heart galloped at a breakneck pace —I'd put some serious mileage on this organ over the last few weeks. Probably aged it at least a decade.

Not that it mattered.

My heart likely wouldn't beat much longer.

The Wraiths hoisted my stick up, shifting it over the fire.

I was going to be roasted like a pig on a spit...*literally.*

Something tight coiled in my chest. I cried, my throat making a low *hic-urgh-hic-urgh* sound as I struggled to breathe.

Jesus Christ, of all the ways to freaking die!

"Addie!" My mom's phantom scream returned, making my ears ring.

I shivered so hard, my teeth ground together. Pain shot through my jaw.

This would be a very *long* death, hovering over a fire until my skin was crispier than Kentucky Fried Chicken.

I howled as the Wraiths placed the stick several inches above the tip of the fire. Heat washed over me. It was dry. And...kind of pleasant? Like sinking into a steaming bath.

"That's too high. She'll never cook like that," one Wraith grunted.

The stick lowered a few inches and shifted sideways, exposing my entire right side to the flames. The heat intensified, sizzling the rope, but it still wasn't painful. At all.

My skin should've been *frying*. And yet...

A Wraith gave the stick a hard shake. "Oi! What is this?"

"Flip 'er over." Another suggested.

Shit. Now I was facing the flames.

And still not burning.

Maybe I was in shock? Too numb to feel my skin crisping?

But that theory got blown out of the water a few minutes later when someone gave my stick another unhappy rattle. "Why isn't she cooking?"

"I told you the wood was too damp for a proper fire," one of them whined.

"Lower her down again," another said.

I squeezed my eyes shut as they rammed the stick into the flames. This was it. Pain. Death. Scorched skin.

Or not?

I wrenched my eyes open.

I was fully submerged in the fire now. Flames licked every inch of my skin. But I didn't burn. It was *relaxing*: the soothing heat, the tickle of fire cascading over me, the gentle hiss and pop of the wood below.

But *why? How?*

A quiver of fear shot through the group of Wraiths.

"It can't be—" one started, but the thunderous sound of hoofbeats cut them off.

My heart somersaulted—excitedly, at first. Because it had to be one of our riders coming to rescue us. Right?

Wrong.

"Oh hell," I groaned.

A riderless Púca barreled into the clearing, its reins and stirrups flailing through the air.

The Púca looked at me, those red-slitted eyes flickering in the firelight. Eyes that seemed *too* intelligent to belong to an animal.

No...freaking...way!

This couldn't be the same Púca.

Could it?

"Hey—" I started to yell. But, with a *crack*, my stick snapped in half. And I landed, face-first, in the fire. Got a mouthful of ash and burnt wood and mashed my nose on the impact, but I still didn't burn.

"You! Catch the Púca!" A Wraith shouted. "You! Don't let the woman escape. We'll eat her raw if we must. And—has no one been watching the man? He's waking."

Cheriour.

I sat bolt upright, ripping the fraying binds off my wrists.

Cheriour was, indeed, awake. He'd flipped onto his back, his head tilted toward me, eyes unfocused. Alive and awake, but not in good shape. At all. He needed help. ASAP.

I wrenched the rope off my ankles and stood. Get help. I could do that.

But how?

Okay, step one: *get out of the freaking fire!*

I moved, wincing as the splinters of not-quite-incinerated wood stabbed the undersides of my feet.

Step two...

Well, the Púca was helping me with that.

As four of the Wraiths approached the animal, attempting to restrain it, the Púca lunged. There was an audible *click* as its fangs snapped. The Wraiths ducked and drew their weapons.

"Don't you *dare* hurt that animal!" I staggered out of the fire, groaning when the cool, muddy ground soothed my bleeding feet.

I expected the Wraiths to pivot and attack. Instead, they bolted. *Away* from me.

Ha! *Look at that!* I hadn't even done anything and they were scared! I just needed a few dragons to drape over my shoulders and I'd be ready for my *Game of Thrones* cameo.

Scratch that.

Dragons were old news. Venomous horses acting as bodyguards? That was the new trend.

The Púca thundered around the fire, fangs flashing. It got three Wraiths in quick succession. One in the arm, another in the shoulder. The third was the bullseye: the Púca bit his left asscheek.

I had to laugh. *Had to.* "Yes! Get that booty!"

But the humor died when those Wraiths collapsed thirty seconds later. They initially convulsed and foamed at the mouth, then went still and rigid as the venom raced through their blood.

I winced and looked away.

Our odds were better now with only three Wraiths still standing. But they were armed to the teeth. And they'd scattered, forcing the Púca to hunt them down.

I needed to do something.

But where was my poleaxe?

And where the heck had they put my clothes?

I spun around but still didn't see my weapon. "The fu —*ooof!*" Something solid rammed into my back. A gray-skinned hand clapped over my mouth and nostrils, fingers digging into my cheeks hard enough to bruise. "*Mmmph!*" I yelled. My back flattened against the metal-coated chest of a Wraith. "*Hmmm mpphkin bastbmp!*" (English translation: *You fucking bastard*).

"I know who you are," the guttural voice rasped in my ear.

"Mmmph?"

"Immune to fire you may be," the Wraith hissed. "But you are still mortal." He raised his other hand, flashing a curved knife in front of my face. "You still bleed."

"Nphm."

He angled the knife, aiming the tip at my stomach.

Without thinking, I threw myself forward. *Into* the knife. Dumb move, right? But it knocked him off balance. (Of course it did. I was 160+ pounds of pure blubber).

We nosedived straight into the fire. I crushed my nose on the charred wood (*again*) and the blade sliced my stomach, slightly above my left hip. But the Wraith's wail drowned out my angry roar.

My skin somehow, *magically*, repelled flames. His did not.

"You stupid..." I grabbed a handful of embers and smashed them into his face as he writhed in agony..."fugly..." Another handful went into his mouth..."*asshole!*" I shoved embers into every orifice. I even thought about yanking his pants down and ramming them up his ass. "You fucking *stabbed* me! Prick!" He'd stopped screaming. Probably because I kept pushing ashes down his gullet. "I *HATE* you!"

Dark shadows moved in my left peripheral.

I sprang to my feet, snatched a flaming log out of the fire, and brandished it at the two approaching Wraiths. "Back the fuck up. I am not playing anymore. *Back up!*"

Amazingly, they did.

The Púca gleefully jogged over and sank its teeth into one Wraith's neck. The other tried to split, but I dove forward and walloped him across the face with my burning log.

And...that was that.

I stood, breath rattling in and out of my lungs, as I surveyed the scene around me. They were down. All of 'em. Not all dead but dying. Or paralyzed. The only creatures left moving were me, the Púca, and...

"Cheriour!"

36

LAMEX

LASS

It was the tree that woke me in the wee hours of the morning.

I'm well aware that trees are ~~non-centient~~ non-sentient beings, incapable of thought, rather rational or irrational. But there was, and still is, a part of me that believes the tree had attempted to warn me of approaching danger.

A twig snapped and fell, landing beside my left ear. It sounded like a whiplash in the otherwise quiet wood.

For a moment, while I remained in the disorientating stage between dreaming and waking, I imagined myself back at Detha, listening to the crack of a Wraith's whip. Until I opened my eyes and stared at a foggy sky. The air was cold enough to turn my breath to smoke.

My fever had broken during the night, but my muscles were still raw. My stomach was unsettled—especially when I heard the voices in the wind.

"I 'eard it was Seruf," a man said.

"Seruf?" Another exclaimed. "Have you lost your senses? The message said it was a *child*."

"Aye, but Seurf is quite small, isn' she?"

"How would you know? You've never seen her."

"Old man Rogers has. And 'e swears Seruf is small enough to pass for a child."

"Rogers? That man don't see anything that's not directly under his nose. It's not Seruf, you bloody dolt."

I rose and immediately tensed when my belly sloshed and rumbled.

Leaves crunched underfoot as the men drew closer.

"What if Seruf went and made 'erself a 'ybrid?" one asked.

His companion scoffed.

"And ye think it's only Raphael who's capable of creating 'ybrid?"

"No. But Ramiel and his lot have Wraiths. Why would Seruf weaken her power to give it to a human girl?"

"To trick us," the man said darkly.

I needed to leave.

My legs trembled and the sloshing sensation in my belly made it nearly impossible to move.

~~Salivia~~ saliva filled my mouth as a deep, foul-tasting hiccup rose from my chest.

"Oi! Darragh!" One of the men shouted. "It's 'er."

I glanced over my shoulder. But the men were nowhere to be seen.

"Where?" The second man huffed.

"Ye'll see her in a moment. Quickly. She's workin' up the strength to run."

I bit my lip, swallowed against the increasingly rotten flavor coating my throat, and stood, calling upon my trembling legs to give me all the strength they possessed.

I made it only two steps before I crashed headlong into something solid.

A man suddenly appeared before me.

He was a hybrid—a Traveler, with the ability to dematerialize from one area and re-materialize in another.

According to Terrick, Travelers were rare, and their power took a great toll on their bodies.

This man certainly confirmed Terrick's teachings. He swayed, struggling to keep his feet beneath him.

I turned, hoping his dizziness would give me time to escape, but he grasped the front of my tunic. "It *is* you," he hissed. "This garment is as they described."

There was something cold in the man's golden eyes as they meandered over my body. Something hateful.

"Let me go!" I shouted.

At the same time, the other man's call echoed from behind me. "Left!"

This warning came as I swung my left hand toward my captor.

The golden-eyed man seized my wrist before it connected with his cheek. I stared at him, stunned.

"Do *not* touch 'er hands!" The other man bellowed.

As the words left his mouth, flames danced over my fingertips. The golden-eyed man shifted his hold to my upper arm. "You'll not so easily kill us." His lips curled over his teeth. "Jaxon is a Foreseer."

A Foreseer—one of the rarest hybrids. And one of the most limited, as they saw mere seconds into the future. Nothing more.

If I moved quick enough, perhaps I could ~~thawrt~~ thwart Jaxon's ability...

"Right foot!" Jaxon called.

Again, his words sounded as I lifted my right leg, intending to strike the golden-eyed man's crotch.

The man wasted no time reacting.

I screamed as his mammoth foot crushed mine.

The rancid taste in the back of my mouth grew as my heart made rapid fluttering motions. "Please..." Fire swirled across my knuckles. "Please, I don't want to hurt—"

The man smacked my cheek.

The pain was sudden. And blinding.

"Darragh, no!" Jaxon screamed. "Ye've made it worse!"

Tears stung my eyes. Tears of shock. And hurt. And fear.

Darragh's grip bruised. The fire traveled along my arms, drawing dangerously close to his knuckles...

"I don't want to hurt you!" I whispered.

He drew his other hand back.

I stared at his face, at the vein pulsing in his temple, the look of disgust in his eyes.

"Ye'll need to stun 'er, Darragh!" Jaxon galloped through the trees, breathing heavily.

"Please," I started. "Hel—"

Darragh's fist connected with the side of my head.

Sadly, he was an inadequate fighter. The blow sent a searing pain throughout my skull, but it was misplaced and did little more than daze me.

I vomited, the clear bile spilling down the front of my shirt. My vision swam. I reached for something, anything, to grasp onto.

"Ach, no!" Jaxon called. "Darragh! Don't—"

Darragh cursed as I clutched his tunic. My fire consumed the fabric, singeing his skin.

"—let 'er touch ye." Jaxon's voice was frantic. "She'll kill ye!"

"You monster," Darragh hissed.

His next blow was much more effective.

THE TOWN I was taken to was called Lamex. But it was so similar in size and appearance to Swindon, I at first thought I'd been brought home.

I felt a twinge of excitement as I walked the streets, even as my hands were bound in iron shackles, and chains encircled my ankles. I'd traveled for days like this, hardly able to walk, pushed at a grueling pace anyway. But, for the first time in years, hope blossomed in my chest as I surveyed the town. My head swiveled every which way, trying to absorb my surroundings, hoping I'd find familiar faces amongst the sea of strangers.

But I had no friends in this town.

It was early morning. The streets bustled with market life. Vendors called out prices. Buyers argued the costs were grossly unfair. Children ran and laughed, chasing each other around the shops.

My hands trembled.

I'd been like those children once. Not very long ago.

Jaxon yanked on my chains when I stopped to watch a dark-haired boy share his apple with a bulbous pig. The shackles cut into my raw wrists, and I cried out.

The little boy looked up and startled when he glimpsed my chains. "Mama!" he cried, turning away from the pig and darting to his mother's side.

She'd been deep in consultation with a vendor about a spool of fabric. But she stopped at the sound of her son's distress and drew him against her bosom.

A smug smile stretched across Jaxon's lips. "The boy is

wise," he said to me, his voice light and conversational. "'e wanted to come over 'ere to speak with you. I'm glad 'e decided otherwise."

I found myself envious of the boy, wrapped in his mother's loving embrace.

"Don't," Jaxon snarled. "She's no' interested in what ye have to say."

I ignored him. "Please," I whispered to the boy's mother.

Jaxon tugged on my chains.

"Please!" I yelled.

A hush fell over the market. Children returned to their parents' sides. Many of the adults gawked at me, looking horror-stricken. But no one reached for a weapon. They did not know me; they hadn't seen my power.

Perhaps I could convince them to spare me kindness...

"Be quiet!" Jaxon hissed in my ear before he straightened and addressed the townspeople directly. "The girl is a prisoner. She may be workin' with Seruf—"

"I am *not*." I tasted salt on my tongue. Tears. "I'm merely a hybrid—"

"*Seruf's* 'ybrid," Jaxon interjected.

"*No*, I'm—"

"The girl killed more than a dozen people in Darfield," Jaxon spoke over me.

"Accidentally!"

"I'll ask that ye give us a wide berth, for yer own safety. We'll be takin' her to Byron, and she'll be dealt with accordingly."

"I'm not a monster!" My chest hollowed as people began vacating the market streets. "I don't want to *hurt* anyone. Please. I'm a hybrid—I don't know how to control—I need *help*."

No one listened.

The hollowness in my chest spread. I supposed I couldn't blame them for their wariness. Had I been in their position, watching a grimy girl beg for help while walking through the streets in chains, I might have chosen caution too.

"Please," I repeated as we continued our trek through the streets. *"Please."*

It would have only taken one person to change the course of my future. One gentle soul to step forward and offer a helping hand. But no one did.

They watched me as we moved toward the center of the town. Their gazes were cold. Frightened.

I stared at my battered, trembling fingers.

"If ye loose yer power here," Jaxon warned. "Ye'll be getting more than a lump on the head. Ye understand? I'd rather keep ye alive, but I'll not hesitate to kill ye if ye hurt anyone." He tapped his thumb against the knife in his belt.

"I can't control it!" I said, for what must have been the umpteenth time.

For the umpteenth time, he ignored me.

"For a Foreseer," I hissed, "there's much you refuse to comprehend."

Jaxon didn't spare me another glance.

Darragh walked behind me, the sharp edge of his sword pressed against my back. He would use it if I stopped again. Darragh had never refused an opportunity to hit me. Indeed, every time the men believed I was at risk of using my powers, I was struck ~~unconcious~~—unconscious. Which was a rather problematic way to travel, considering neither they nor I understood how my power worked.

Jaxon saw too much; too many instances where my power could come to life. He couldn't rely on his foresight to help him. So the men reacted to every noise or movement I made. I'd been struck for sneezing or coughing too loudly—the same infraction my kin at Detha had once been whipped for. I had received a blow to the head when I stubbed my toe on a tree root and had moaned in pain. Another blow had come when I'd swatted a fly that had been biting my ear.

Their harsh treatment was not without consequences.

Throughout our journey, as my head was repeatedly struck, my vision ~~deterated~~ deteriorated. I saw clearly when an object was in front of me. As soon as it shifted to the right or the left, it became fuzzy and unfocused. For example, while walking through Lamex, I could only discern faces if I turned my head and stared directly at them. Otherwise, they were blurred, shadowed shapes in my ~~perhiferal~~ peripheral vision.

It is a disability I still bear. To this day, I still relish the idea of encountering Jaxon and Darragh again and using blunt force to rob their sight. The way they had robbed mine.

Although their harsh treatment paled compared to what awaited me. The leader of Lamex had no plans to shatter my bones or pummel my skull, as my captors had. He sought to destroy my heart, my soul, the very fiber of my being.

And he nearly succeeded.

37

FREDDIE FUCKING HAWKINS

ADDIE

"Cheriour!" I dropped my burning log and stumbled over to him. My knees popped as I slid into a kneeling position. "Cheriour! My *God...*"

Sweat dripped from his brow even as he shivered. His eyes focused hazily on my face. "Addie," he choked.

"Shush. I need to concentrate." I touched his cheek. His skin burned. Fever. Not good. Not surprising either. "Jesus freaking Christ, how many cuts do you have?" Blood seemed to be coming from everywhere. His clothes were soaked.

"Addie." Cheriour made a huffing noise that sounded almost like a laugh. "You...the fire...you *are*—"

"Dude, I really need you to be quiet. I'm trying to think... *crap!*" I'd been attempting to undo the straps on his leather holsters, but my fingers kept shaking. "And if you were about to call me a hybrid, stop. *'Don't you put that curse on me, Ricky Bobby!'* I'm... that...it wasn't a real fire? Or something...ah!" The leather finally came undone. "Lift your arms. Come on." I snapped my fingers when he was slow to respond. "I'm saving your ass here. Give me at least a little cooperation. There we go." He sluggishly sat partway up, enough for me to yank his shirt over his head. "Okay, now... *fuck.*" This situation got 10x worse. He had gashes all over his arms, shoulders, and chest. But one laceration below his right ribcage went *deep.* I couldn't tell if that was his innards poking out, or jagged pieces of muscle. I didn't *want* to know either.

"You're bleeding," Cheriour mumbled.

"I'm not...*ouch!*" I slapped his hand away when he brushed his fingers against the knife slash above my hip. "Okay, I *am* bleeding, but not as bad as you. This is...*purugh.* I have no idea what noise I just made, but that about sums it up. *Bandages!* I need bandages." I wrung out his blood-soaked shirt. "Well, I won't be able to use this. Where the *hell* are my clothes?" I sprang to my feet, surveying the clearing.

The Púca watched me, tail swishing as it greedily guzzled Wraith blood.

Unfortunately, the Wraiths wore armor. Couldn't make bandages out of metal. And I had *zero* desire to see if the creepy mofos wore boxers or briefs underneath.

"Seriously, where are my clothes?" I saw my poleaxe, propped against a tree a few feet away from the bonfire. But no clothes.

"You've gotta be fucking kidding me..." I stomped away, throwing a frazzled, *"Don't move!"* over my shoulder at Cheriour. He grunted, his eyes already closing.

With a wet snort, the Púca abandoned its buffet and fell into step beside me. I tried not to shiver when its hot breath fanned across my shoulder. It smelled like a rotten meat medley.

Disgusting freaking animal.

But it had saved my life. More than once. So I gritted my teeth against the odor and kept walking.

Around the clearing I went, stumbling over Wraith corpses

and discarded weapons, and staying far, far away from Cheriour's dead horse.

My clothes were still MIA.

"They better not have chucked them into the fire," I snapped.

The Púca snorted again, spraying my arm with bits of mucus and blood. "Yo! C'mon, I don't even have anything to wipe..." I trailed off when the Púca stopped and pawed at the ground. A very *muddy* section of ground.

And guess what was speckled through the muck?

"Oh no," I groaned.

My clothes were covered, *covered*, in sludge. So they'd be perfectly sterile and okay to use for wound treatment.

Not.

"My luck freaking *sucks*," I grumbled as I squeegeed the worst of the mud off my shirt.

Behind me, the Púca grunted, as though agreeing.

I whipped the shirt against my knee, beating the remaining sludge off. Each wet *slaaaap* was punctuated with a pissy *fuck*.

Angry didn't even *begin* to describe my state of mind.

My bra was ruined...not much of a shock there. Those Neanderthals probably hadn't seen anything like the modern bra before. So they'd sliced between the cups to get it off me. *Bastards!* Thankfully, my pants and boots were still intact, if filthy. And...

The heck was that?

A sliver of pink—no, blue—no, bluish/pink—fabric poked out from under the mud. I frowned, dug my hands into the soil, and pulled out a gorgeous...

Shirt? Or dress? Hmmm. It looked more like a shirt. But it would've made a cute short-skirted dress too. And it was *stunning*. The shimmery material pooled over my fingers—more like liquid than fabric. The long sleeves had gold cuffs. And gold laces crisscrossed over the V-neck front. This legit looked like a tunic a disgustingly rich and vain medieval king would tout.

It was so fancy, even the mud didn't want to soil it. After four hard shakes, the shirt looked brand-spanking new. Not a spec of grime to be found.

And the color...holy moly. Not only did it pop like a neon glow stick at a nightclub but it kept *changing*. From one angle, the shirt looked rogue pink. From another, it turned deep violet, almost blue. If I held it close to the sunlight, it morphed into a soft purple.

How in the hell did these rudimentary Viking people make a shirt like this?

And what tasteless *idiot* dumped it in the *fucking mud?*

A muffled curse yanked me out of my trance. I whirled around.

"Oh—fuck—no!" I sprang to my feet.

The Púca stood over Cheriour, its head lowered.

"No! Uh-uh." I ran toward them, whipping my clothes through the air to make a loud *whoosh-snap.* "Shoo! He's a friend! Not food! *Shoo!*"

The Púca backed up, shook its head, and made a beeline for the trees.

I dropped to Cheriour's side again, touching his shoulders. "Shit, sorry. It didn't—did it bite you? I'm *so* sorry. I mean, the horse has no interest in hurting me. For some reason. But I wasn't *thinking.* Of *course* it would wanna take a bite outta you. That's what they do, right? Cheriour?" My eyes flew to his face. He was out cold. "Oh no." I ran my trembling fingers over his torso. Okay...still breathing. Still *alive.* But had the Púca bitten him? I couldn't tell. There was *so much blood...*

My gut lurched.

I threw myself to the side, a safe distance from his prone body, and upchucked.

"Heh. That's an improvement. Last time I got puke on your shoes, remember?" I wiped the bile off my lips. "This time I aimed."

He didn't stir.

"Cheriour?" I touched his forehead. His cheeks. And carefully combed blood and (*bleh*) chunks of flesh out of his beard.

He had freckles on his nose. Lots of 'em. How had I never noticed before? "I'm gonna patch you up." Why did my voice sound so squeaky? "And you'll be okay. Okay? You're a tough guy. Little cuts like these won't bring you down."

I kept talking. Because annoying rambles were my specialty.

"So," I tore my shirt (the old shirt. *Not* the badass blue/pink one.) into strips, "you wanted to know my origin story, right? I left a lot of details out the other night. But, well, since you ain't going anywhere fast right now, you might as well buckle up and listen."

And I told him *everything*. The good, bad, ugly, and the downright macabre. The people who'd cared for me, and the ones who hadn't. And the ones who'd hurt me the most.

"Freddie Hawkins," I said while I pressed on Cheriour's stomach wound to stem the bleeding. Was skin supposed to squish like that? *Yeesh.* "Let me tell ya about that sonuvabitch. I was thirteen. He and his wife fit the unhappy suburbia type to a *'T.'* Y'know: *'Marriage isn't going well. Sex life is drier than a prune. So, let's get a kid!'* Word of advice: if you ever decide to strap into a relationship, and it starts sinking, having a kid won't save that ship. It never does."

I'd turned down a dangerous road with that last bit. Because now I wondered what Cheriour would be like in a relationship.

Infuriating. Oh my God, yes. When you asked, *"what do you want for dinner?"* he'd likely be the type to respond with a droning, *"whatever."* It drove me up a *fucking wall* when guys did that. He was also a slob. Honest to a fault; he'd have no qualms telling someone their outfit made them look fat. And then he'd probably be too freaking dense to understand why his partner stormed off. Domestic arguments with him would be *maddening*. Because he was almost *too* level-headed. But his composure would help quiet the disagreement before it blew out of proportion.

His calmness had always helped me. How many times had he pulled me back from the brink of a meltdown?

Tears stung my eyes.

I had to get off this topic. "Anyway," I cleared my throat, "Freddy Fucking Hawkins...most people don't get teenagers to fix their marriage. But it didn't take me long to figure out why they'd chosen an older child. Or why his poor wife was so sexually frustrated. Freddie...well...at thirteen, I was right in his G-spot. Ha, *G-spot*. Get it?"

Cheriour remained still. Unresponsive. Even as I prodded and poked his wounds.

It was getting harder and harder to fight back the tears. Snot dribbled from my nose. I kept talking, though. The conversation wasn't doing jack squat for him, but it helped me. As long as I was talking, I was breathing. As long as I was breathing, I kept moving.

"There," I tied the dirty strips of fabric around his torso, "you're all bandaged up now. Don't you dare bleed out on me."

There'd been barely enough material to cover all his wounds. And the big gash by his ribs still oozed, even though I'd pulled that binding tighter than a corset.

I muttered more nonsense as I shakily yanked my breeches and boots on. "That had been my *only* bra. And my boobs ain't small—oh my God, you *jerk!*" I squealed at him when I pulled the pink/blue shirt over my head. "You've been making me wear wool clothes when I coulda had something like *this* all along?" The hem of the shirt came down to mid-thigh, and the top was a smidge tight around my bust, even with the laces loose. But, otherwise, it fit perfectly.

And it was so freaking comfortable. Smoother and softer than silk.

In comparison, my breeches felt like sandpaper.

"You better stop bleeding," I said. "I am *not* using this shirt as a bandage. No way."

I kept talking as I hauled a Wraith out of the clearing. "Holy cow," I groaned. "What are these guys made of?" It was like trying to move a box of cinderblocks! I got the body to the trees before the (thankfully shallow) wound on my side started throbbing. My head also hurt. And my muscles were both jittery and rubbery. So...*nah*, I wasn't in the mood to finish the body clean-up.

But sitting idly by, watching as the sun sank and inky pools of shadows spilled across the ground, was also torture.

Because I couldn't stop thinking about Cheriour, and whether he'd be okay. Or I wondered how I'd managed to crash-land in the heart of that fire and walk out unscathed.

Was I actually a hybrid? Was being fireproof one of their powers?

"I don't want to be a hybrid." I sat beside Cheriour, knees drawn up to my chest, teeth chattering. "So can you do me a big favor? Pretend you didn't see any of...*that*." I waved an arm toward the smoldering fire. "And I'll pretend it didn't happen and no one will know any different, right? I'm not a hybrid. I'm *not.*"

Cheriour shivered, his breath coming out in short, pained bursts.

Above us, tree branches creaked and groaned as the wind tore through them. The temperature dropped. A lot. Because, *why not?* It'd been hotter than Heat Miser's ballsac since I arrived here. But tonight, with Cheriour so badly injured and me being a useless sack of shit, Snow Miser decided to puff cold air over us. Typical.

Even when I pulled Cheriour's shirt over his chest, he kept shaking.

No matter how many shards of wood I chucked at the fire, the flames eventually died.

"Screw mother nature," I said. "It better not rain." Stars twinkled through the gaps in the trees, so there weren't any clouds. *Yet.* But with the wind gusts, I wouldn't have been surprised if a storm exploded at some point.

"Okay, look," I curled against Cheriour's side, "I'm doing this to keep you warm. To keep *both* of us warm. So please don't be offended when you wake up." I flung an arm over his chest, above his wound, and draped my thigh over his.

Beneath me, his body vibrated with the force of his trembling. I scooted closer, covering as much of him as I could. What else could I do?

I rested my head against his shoulder. Sniffling. Monitoring the unsteady rise and fall of his chest.

"Just keep breathing." I traced my fingers along his collarbone, his cheekbones, and his lips.

I had this feeling in my stomach; like I was at the top of a drop ride, staring at the ground. Except this wasn't the normal *whoo-hoo* tingly sensation I got at amusement parks, but more of a sickening sense of foreboding. Because the plummet was inevitable, and I wasn't strapped in. Wasn't safe. I'd fall, and fall, and fall, until I *splatted* across the ground.

"Just keep breathing." My tears splashed onto Cheriour's shoulder. "Please."

38

AU NATUREL B.O. MUSK

ADDIE

Monitoring Cheriour's breaths had the same effect as counting sheep. One second, I hit number two-hundred-and-something, and the next I groggily woke from a deep slumber.

Dappled rays of sunlight bathed the forest floor. I'd slept straight through the night.

And, oh boy, it'd been a *painful* sleep. My right shoulder, still jammed against the ground, had that awful, prickly pins-and-needles sensation. The gash on my side burned. And I was soaked in sweat. Probably because I was slumped on top of Cheriour. Like, *Jesus*, it was a miracle I hadn't crushed him.

Oh, and y'know what made this situation even better? He was awake. And playing with my hair.

It was kinda nice, though. Lying there while his fingers rubbed my scalp. It almost lulled me back to sleep. But I needed to move, stretch and try to get some kinks worked out.

I shifted, wincing when my achy hips popped.

Cheriour's fingers froze.

"You don't have to st-stop," I stuttered around a yawn.

Silence. But his breathing changed. Deepened.

"Some guard I am, huh? Good thing we weren't ambushed while I slept on the job."

"I was listening," Cheriour mumbled. "I would have woken you if I had heard something."

"Who are you kidding? You were in fever dream la-la land all night." I pushed myself away from him. Damn. Every joint in my body creaked, popped, or crackled. I sounded like an eighty-year-old woman. Felt like one too. I groaned as I rolled my shoulder and got the blood rushing down to my fingers. "Aw, crap! It's like being jabbed with a million tattoo guns! Dude...you look fucking *awful.*"

Blood caked Cheriour's pallid, sweaty face. His hair was grimy and matted. But he was awake and alert, so...progress. Right?

"I'm still alive," Cheriour croaked. "For now."

"Dude, think *positive* thoughts. You made it through the night!" I couldn't quite muster my normal perky tone as I touched a hand to his ribcage, inspecting my shoddy bandage job. "It's not infected." I peeked at the wound. "I don't think? It looks like shit though." Understatement of the freaking year. It was like someone had blown a crater in his side. "But wouldn't it be redder or oozing pus if it was infected?"

"Not always right away," he grunted.

"Does it hurt?"

He huffed.

"That's not an answer. Put it on a scale of 1 to 10. One being a small ouchie, and ten being *I think I'm gonna hurl because it hurts so much.*"

"Three."

"Hmm, that smells like bullshit." I tapped my finger against the outer edge of the wound. He hissed and flinched.

"I'm no doctor, but that looks more like an eight or nine," I said.

Cheriour swiftly changed the subject. "You shouldn't stay here."

"Well...do you think you can walk?"

He didn't answer. Just stared at the sky, jaw clenched.

"Then I'm not leaving."

"Addie..."

"This isn't up for debate."

"It's not safe—"

"It's not safe *anywhere* in this shithole world," I snapped. "So what difference does it make if I'm here, or at Sanadrin, or Niall? People get attacked every day that ends in Y. Since you're still alive—*for now*—I'm staying. If you kick the bucket, I'll leave. But I will *not* walk away while you're still breathing. Understood?"

He tilted his chin down, his brow furrowing as his gaze dropped to the hand I still had resting against his chest. "What are you *wearing?*" He blinked, as though noticing my outfit for the first time.

"This?" I plucked the collar of the shimmery blue/pink shirt. "I dunno. I found it buried in the ground."

Cheriour traced his fingers along my upper arm. "Impossible."

"No, that's definitely where I found it. The bastards dumped my clothes in the mud, and this," I tugged on the laces, "I guess belonged to their last meal?"

"No, it's impossible this garment exists here. Or it *should* be impossible." His fingers moved back and forth along my arm. It tickled, even through the fabric. "Do you know what this is?" he asked.

"A shirt?"

He shook his head.

"A *fancy* shirt?"

"No. This is a garment from the Celestial City."

"Oookay. Do Wraiths deep fry Celestials too?"

"No. They'd never be strong enough to..." Cheriour trailed off, his frown deepening. "You...last night, you emerged from the fire unscathed."

My skin prickled as he studied my face, and a nervous laugh bubbled out of my throat. "That's crazy talk."

"I saw it."

"You were fever dreaming."

He grasped my hand and pulled my shirt sleeve up, inspecting my skin. "You're not burnt."

"No. Because I wasn't *in* the fire..."

Cheriour gave me one of his patented indiscernible stares. "Stop lying."

"I'm not."

"I know what I saw, Addie. You *threw* yourself into the fire with a Wraith."

The prickling sensation intensified. But I didn't know if it was the conversation causing it, or a reaction to the tender way he held my wrist.

"You are immune to fire," he persisted.

"No, I'm not. And I'm not a freaking hybrid either! Don't you put—"

"That curse on you...Rickety Body?" he finished.

"*Ricky Bobby,*" I corrected. "And, crap, you *remember* me saying that?"

"Yes. What is a Ricky Bobby?"

"It's just a saying." I so wasn't in the mood to explain the wonderfully intricate story of *Talladega Nights* to someone who wouldn't appreciate it.

Cheriour sighed. "Addie, fire cannot burn you—"

"Stop—"

"You *are* a hybrid."

My eye twitched. I could *feel* my face reddening as my blood pressure rose.

"But it's more than that," Cheriour continued. "You—"

"I said *stop!*" I bellowed. God, why didn't he get it? "If I'm— I'm *not*, but if I *was* a hybrid...well, I guess that'd explain why I survived that goddamn house fire, huh? But where did that land me? In a fucked-up childhood where fucked-up people revolved in and out of my life and did fucked-up things. And then when I finally, *finally* got my life somewhat on track, I got booted here. Only to find out the reason I outlived my parents was because some mother-fucking Celestial *experimented on me!* I'm not a hybrid. I *refuse* to be one."

"Addie," Cheriour whispered.

"Shut up!" My throat ached. Had I screamed that whole tangent? Probably.

Cheriour stared, his eyes still and quiet, focused only on me.

Hic-hic-heeze went my unsteady, painful breaths.

He released the sleeve of my shirt and trailed his hand along my arm.

And then he fucking *massaged* the inside of my wrist, kneading his fingers into muscles I didn't even know were sore until he soothed them. And he was *good* at this, applying the right amount of pressure to each pain point.

My stomach squirmed. Not from fear or anger this time— oh no. This was the fun kinda squirm.

"Is it okay if I kiss you?" I blurted. Super romantic. But I didn't have the patience for light teases and gentle caresses. Not when my emotions were already frazzled. "After the other night...well, I figured I'd ask. It gets the awkwardness out of the way, y'know?"

Cheriour didn't laugh or scoff at my blunt statement. He

studied my face, his thumb rubbing an aching spot on the inside of my palm, and nodded.

Yes, yes...oh *hell* yes!

I kissed him. Hard. Actually, I think I *bit* him—I wasn't sure if my mouth even made contact with his, or if I just sucked his lips between my teeth. Not that I wanted to hurt him. Never. Pain play was not my kink.

But I wanted to get away from my jumbled emotions. And sex—*especially* rough sex—usually got my brain to shut down.

So, yeah, I threw myself at Cheriour like a cat in heat.

But then he touched my cheek, stilling me.

"Shit," I hissed, my blood going cold. "I'm sorry! Did I—"

Cheriour released my hand, lifted himself onto his elbow, his face briefly tensing in pain, and kissed me. In a long, languid, lingering way that perfectly matched his style.

I devoured.

He savored.

And, y'know...first kisses were meant to be savored.

His calloused fingers were rougher than nail files as they curled around my chin, but I'd *never* had a guy touch me so tenderly. Carefully. Like I was a crystal sculpture that would shatter beneath too much pressure.

I shivered as he traced the corner of my mouth with his thumb.

Goddamn, how long had it been since I'd last kissed a man? Six months? A year?

Way too freaking long, apparently.

My body was in some kinda kiss-withdrawal shock.

Cheriour's lips were soft. Butterfly light. Almost a smidge unsure—which was *adorable*. And the taste of him: salty and zingy. No minty fresh breath, remnants of coffee, beer, or any of the other flavors I was used to sampling on a guy's mouth.

Cheriour's was so uniquely his. Even his earthy (and slightly oniony) scent seemed sweeter than any cologne.

He paused, inhaling shakily.

But before I could draw back to give him (and me) a second to breathe, he angled his head, his mouth gently, so *freaking gently*, massaging mine again. And those little pecks, the brief seconds of hesitation, and the feel of him so close, his hand caressing my face...I *melted*.

His tongue cautiously brushed against mine. I shuddered. He stroked my neck, the shell of my ear, and my hair. Goosebumps exploded over my skin.

Kiss withdrawal had to be a real thing. *Had to be.* Because I was currently suffering through it. My stomach was in my throat, my muscles had that warm, ooey-gooey sensation, and my brain flashed a 404 error.

And this kiss was only a light tease! I needed to amp it up. And stat!

I leaned further down, deepening the kiss. It was uncomfortable, to be crouched over him this way. My back screamed in protest. But I didn't care.

He tilted his head and nipped at my bottom lip. *Delicately.* But that prompted a full-body shudder from me. I returned the favor, nibbling on his mouth, stroking the hard lines of his neck, and tugging on his hair, until his breathing turned unsteady. And the throaty whimper he made...

God-freaking-damnit if this wasn't one of the best kisses I'd ever had. Easily top five material—might've even cracked the top three if it hadn't been for his beard (which was still crusted with blood...*bleh*).

I pressed myself against him, wanting, *needing* more.

His hand tapped my shoulder, as though to get my attention. And, as my brain rebooted, I scrambled back with a gasping, *"crap."* Because my blubber had probably been crushing the poor bastard.

Cheriour panted, although some color had blossomed across his cheeks. Not much, but he looked like less of a corpse now. And a smile stretched across his lips. Which had my heart turning somersaults because I'd never seen him smile like that before. And it was *so freaking cute.*

I sat back, giving him more space, trying to ignore the way my mouth still tingled, and how cold my neck was without his hand there. "That—"

At the same time, he started, "I—"

We stared at each other. He wheezed. I trembled.

Ummm...*awkward.*

A raspy chuckle burst out of Cheriour's throat. But it sounded more like a rumbling cough. Beads of sweat formed along his brow.

The zingy, happy feelings from the kiss withered and died. "We shouldn't have done that. You still have a fever."

"I'm aware." He droned, laying back as I began fidgeting with his bandages again. I didn't know what else to do. If there was a stream nearby, I could've gotten water and tried to flush the cut out. But I didn't want to leave him and go trudging through the forest looking for one. I'd get lost. It wasn't like there were signs to help direct me: *Sludge Lake 1.2 miles ahead. Next exit: Bug Infested Bushes, 2.0 miles.*

Besides, even if I found water and made it back here, what if the Wraiths returned while I was gone?

"Addie." Cheriour touched the back of my right hand, stilling my fidgeting. "I apologize for upsetting you."

I scoffed. *"Upsetting me?* That kiss was amazing."

"I'm not talking about that."

"Ah." I kept my gaze focused on the bandage, which

blurred as my eyes watered. "Well, it's no biggie. It's not like it's the first time I've been upset."

"This was different. I saw it in your eyes. But I won't say any more about it."

I nodded but didn't look at him. Tears turned my vision into a blurred kaleidoscope.

My freaking hormones were going ape-shit. Was I due for my period? Had to be. I was likely a few days *overdue* at this point (trauma wreaked havoc on the body).

Cheriour slowly, tentatively, threaded his fingers through mine. His hand was burning hot, but I liked the warmth. And comfort. Especially when he ran his thumb over my knuckles. It made my stomach flip-flop.

But a dark, bitter sense of dread also curled around my gut.

I was getting pretty dang attached. And it was happening way too fast. "Jesus. It's only been a month," I scoffed.

"What?"

"It's only been a month. I've dated guys for *six* months and didn't get attached. The ones that made it beyond six months are a different story. But still," I swallowed when his hand clenched around mine, "it's not even like you're some drop-dead gorgeous hunk of a model that's got my panties twisted. Not that you're *not* good-looking. I didn't mean that to sound rude."

He didn't look offended though.

So I kept going.

"But you're not my type. At all. If I lined you up with my exes, you'd look like some redneck mountain man who crawled out of the woods and wandered into an upscale business park. I like guys in suits. Don't judge me." I added when Cheriour made a weird snorting noise. "And I'm really not trying to insult you. I'm...frustrated." Definitely *sexually* frustrated. Har, har. "And I don't understand why, after only a month, it seems like-like...fuck, I dunno. Like we..." I pulled my hand away from his. "We kinda went like this." I clapped my palms together. "Y'know? Like two magnets."

Cheriour's snort turned into a low laugh.

"I'm so glad you find humor in me trying to express myself." I grinned.

Cheriour grasped my hand again. "I thought I was alone in what you described."

"Oh no, you too? And I'm gonna guess you're not PMSing right now, huh?"

He said nothing. Just stared up at the trees, tracing his thumb over my knuckles.

"Didn't think so. But I always figured you found me annoying. Most people do."

He stayed silent for a moment longer before whispering, "Sometimes I wish you'd take more care with what you say. But I've never found you annoying. I...*understand* you."

"Huh?"

His lips twisted. "I'm not good at casual conversation. I find it infuriating." The words oozed off his tongue like molasses. I *itched* to dive in and help him, but I didn't. I bit my lip, held my breath, and stayed still, letting him sort his thoughts out.

"It always seems to me that each person speaks in multiple languages," he continued. "Their words say one thing, their body says another, and I'm meant to combine them to discern the truth. I often can't. And it's exhausting." He shifted his hand and rubbed the heel of my palm. "But you speak openly. *Freely.* I don't have to struggle to understand. I *enjoy* listening to you."

Oh. My. God.

That almost sounded like a love confession. Right? *Right??* Or was I losing my mind?

My emotions ricocheted all over the spectrum. I was scared. Excited. Heartbroken. Horny as fuck. Embarrassed. And I had the warm fuzzies. All at once.

I stared at Cheriour's bandages, although I couldn't see them. Not while I was having this allergic reaction to emotion. (aka, crying).

"Addie?" Cheriour prodded.

I wiped my watery eyes. "So you like the sound of my voice, huh? Luckily, I enjoy talking."

"Yes. You do." A slight tremor ran through his body. His fingers twitched against my arm.

"This is..." *too much.* And coming at the wrong time. Because if I lost him now, after having tasted his lips, and felt his hands on my skin, I'd have a massive hole punched through my heart.

"My head hurts. I'm lying down." I flopped against his side, burying my head into his chest, inhaling his *au naturel* B.O. musk. Which, for some unfathomable reason, still smelled better than most colognes.

The blows to the head must've recrossed some of my wires. Or maybe the horniness had knocked my body out of whack.

"I like you," I mumbled. "A lot."

A laugh rumbled through Cheriour's chest. The sound made my entire body tingle. "And I you," he said.

"Good," the word sounded warbled as it left my constricted throat. "We're on the same page. We've got a good thing started here. Don't die on me. Okay?"

Cheriour curled his fingers through my hair and rested his chin atop my head. He said nothing as he kissed my temple once. Twice.

I exhaled, trying to ignore the way his fever-hot skin burned beneath mine.

39

BYRON

On the edge of Lamex, a sizeable distance from the rest of the buildings, sat a hut. It was small—barely taller than Darragh and Jaxon—circular, windowless, and made entirely of stone.

My stomach curdled as Darragh shoved me through the narrow doorway. A candle sat in the center of the dark room, its miniscule flame casting more shadow than light. But I still saw the shackles nailed to the wall.

"Ah, excellent!" Darragh said gleefully. "So, Alexandra's told him then."

"Aye, well, Speakers have plenty of eyes in the forest, do they no'? *Oi!*" Jaxon shouted when I threw myself backward.

The sight of those shackles gleaming in the otherwise dim room created a strange sensation in my chest. A hollow, yet heart-quickening sense of urgency.

I was too weak to fight against two fully grown men. Darragh's sword pressed into my back. Jaxon yanked on the chains until my wrists screamed in pain. They threw me against the wall, clasping the new shackles in place, ignoring me when I screamed and thrashed.

I was trapped, my hands bound above my head, my feet strapped at an unnatural angle, forcing me to stand on my toes. For the first time, I beseeched my fire to come forth. But when I needed it the most, it had seemingly forsaken me.

"Is this her?" A third man appeared in the room. His deep voice seemed to shake the stone walls of the hut. He stood on my left side. And, as I was pinned to a wall with no room to move, I could not see him. He was simply a blurred figure at the edge of my vision.

"Aye," Jaxon said. "'Twas not easy, to get 'er 'ere alive. She kept trying to attack us—"

"I did *not.*" My lower lip quivered. "You perceived yourself in danger when you weren't and attacked *me* unjustly."

My words went unnoticed.

"And 'tis true, Byron," Jaxon continued. "She is a Firestarter. Like Seruf."

"She almost killed me." Darragh thumped the front of his chest, pointing to his ruined tunic.

"Perhaps if you hadn't struck me, you wouldn't have been burnt," I said.

Again, I was ignored.

"Thank you, Jaxon, Darragh," the blurred figure—Byron—said. "And well done. You may tell Lucia that she's not to take your coin tonight. Whatever you wish to eat or drink will be free of charge."

Jaxon and Darragh exchanged smiles.

Hatred burned inside of me as the men left, celebrating the pain they'd inflicted on another human.

But when Byron moved into my line of sight, my anger shriveled into fear.

Warped and wrinkled burn scars covered much of his face

and neck. He was missing his left ear and much of his hair, although a few blonde strands still clung to the right side of his scalp. His nose had melted into disfigurement as well. And his left hand was little more than a gnarled stump.

"Morning," he said cheerily, bouncing on the balls of his feet. "I'd offer a full greeting: *'good'* morning. But I'm not sure that's appropriate. It will not be a pleasant morning for you."

He paced as he spoke, continuously fading in and out of my limited line of sight.

"I'm *not* a Celestial." It took great effort to keep the tremor out of my voice.

"I know." Byron drew his sword, smiling when I flinched, and tapped the edge of the blade against my aching wrists. "You bleed red. Celestials bleed light. No, the claims of you being Seruf are, admittedly, laughable." He resumed his pacing. "I've seen Seruf." He ran a hand over his disfigured chin. "But most have not, so it's hardly a surprise they believed the rumor so easily."

"I am not working for Seruf." I gritted my teeth, trying to ignore the throbbing in my shoulders. "Nor have I ever worked for her."

"Now *that* claim," Byron raised his stump of a hand and pointed it at me, "is much more difficult to confirm."

"It's not," I snarled. "If you'd cease talking and *listen*—"

"You have her power," Byron interrupted.

"I am a hybrid," I said. "No different from any other."

"No different? There are no other hybrids with your power."

"You are merely unaware of their existence." My skin prickled.

"And you've seen others like yourself?" His brow raised. "Give me their names. Their existence will free you from those chains."

I glared at him, but I had no names to give. So I said nothing.

"*Lies*. As I thought." Byron crossed his arms over his chest, surveying me. "What is *your* name?"

"Lass."

"That is not a name."

"It's the only one I have."

"Well, then, Lass," my name sounded like a hiss as it escaped his mouth, "tell me... how did you get your power?"

"The same way other hybrids get theirs."

"You're lying."

"I am not." My palms itched. "I was taken by a Celestial after my mother died. I suffered the transformation and awoke alone."

"Lies."

"My words are only lies because you're *choosing* not to believe them." I wriggled my hands in the shackles, trying to alleviate the itch.

Byron's lip curled. "I'm not interested in listening to you spin a tale, no matter how well fabricated it may be."

"You're not interested in facing the possibility that you may be wrong."

"We have worked too hard, and lost too many lives, ridding Sakar of Ramiel's filth." Byron's jaw ticked. "Seruf was, admittedly, quite intelligent in choosing to send a child into our midst. Too many will forgive a child. Too many will care for one."

I thought of Terrick, my heart sinking. "I am a child no longer," I said. "And you are wrong. No one offered me forgiveness. I was driven out of Swindon and Darfield—"

"Because you murdered innocents."

"*Accidentally*. I can't control it. If you would only *listen*—"

"As you're still young," Byron spoke over me, "perhaps you

can still change. And I'd regret not giving you the opportunity to do so."

I yearned to spit in his face. I didn't like the way his colossal frame so easily dwarfed mine, nor how he stared at me; as though I was a disobedient colt who needed to be beaten into submission.

So I spat.

And felt the stinging pain as his palm lashed my cheek.

"That was rude." He wiped my spittle from his chin. "As I was saying, I have no desire to kill a child—no matter how despicable you may be—but I cannot allow you to leave and return to Seruf's side."

"I'm not—"

"So," he continued, his voice dull. Unenthused. "Shall we strike a bargain? If you begin speaking the truth—"

"I have been!"

"—and you tell me of Seruf's plans, I will release you. You'll be permitted to live in Lamex. Under supervision, of course. But it would be a free life. As long as you don't harm others, no one will harm you. You would have my word, as the leader of Lamex."

I swallowed. It was a grossly unfair situation. The idyllic life he described was the only thing I had ever truly wanted. But his promise was empty. That life was a dream.

"Continue lying," Byron's voice brightened, "and in those shackles you will stay. You'll spend the rest of your miserable existence, however long that may be, in this room."

A tremor started in the middle of my back, ~~ricoseting~~ ═ricocheting along my body. I stared at the dark, windowless room and the scarred man standing before me.

The itch in my palms grew.

"Ah, yes," Byron added, his deformed lips curling into a smile. "I should have mentioned...I had this building specially constructed for your maker." He stroked his scars. "Stone is quite immune to fire, is it not? And those shackles were a gift from the Celestial Ellard. A metal that cannot be melted by flames." He tilted his chin toward my right hand, where a flickering yellow light hovered above my fingertips.

The fire had returned.

But the shackles around my wrists remained cool.

My teeth clicked as the tremors grew. I was no stranger to fear, but the apprehension that festered in my gut as I stared at Byron's gleeful face was unlike anything I'd ever experienced.

Always before, my terror had been at the prospect of hurting others.

Now I feared for myself.

Byron was like a long night in the dead of winter. There was no warmth in him. No light. Only darkness, and bitter cold.

He was a being more akin to Wraiths than humans.

And, once I realized what he could do, I understood why.

"So, what will you choose?" Byron asked.

My voice quivered. "C-considering you won't believe me when I tell the truth, I suppose I'm staying here."

He clapped his hands, delighted. "Very well."

I expected him to use his sword—to slash it against my skin until I was raw and bleeding. Instead, he pressed his fingers against my temple. His hand was hot, his skin ~~callised~~ —calloused. For a moment he stood still, smiling at the fire that danced over my knuckles.

A wave of emotion crashed over me.

Fear.

No, fear is not a strong enough word to describe it. But, alas, I may have difficulty spelling words that would do it justice. ~~Constornation~~—consternation. ~~Trepadation~~—trepidation. *Terror.* The sort of fright that soured one's stomach and turned one's muscles limp. The sort of horror that, embarrassingly, made one lose control of one's bladder and bowels.

My heart felt as though it were being squeezed with an invisible fist.

Byron withdrew his hand as I found the breath to scream.

I slumped in my shackles, my muscles aching, my soul sore and battered.

Byron panted as heavily as I, but he smiled merrily. "Are you sure you'd prefer to stay here?"

I said nothing. My voice had abandoned me.

I didn't understand then what he had done; how he had induced such a hysteria within me. It wasn't until years later that I learned what he was, and had a name to accompany his powers.

Manipulator. A hybrid able to control the emotions of others. Byron could make me experience happiness, peace, fear, anger, hate, love, or anything else he wished me to feel.

Until my creation, Manipulators were considered the rarest hybrids. Only two were made. And their power wreaked havoc upon their minds.

In making me experience such a high level of anxiety, Byron had brought the same fear upon himself. His face paled as he drew a flask from his belt. His hands shook so violently, he had difficulty drinking. Indeed, it took him several tries to remove the cork, and he spilled some of the red wine down his front.

But it seemed he had developed a perverse love for darker emotions. Despite his trembling, he looked full of life and vigor. Whereas I was so feeble, my restraints were the only things keeping me upright.

Byron pushed the cork back into his flask. "Whenever you change your mind, you only need to say so." He stepped toward me again.

I tried to draw back, but I could go nowhere. My head struck the wall.

Byron laughed. "In the meantime, you and I will get to know each other quite intimately." He pressed his fingers to my temple. This time it was not fear he forced me to experience, but pain. Specifically, the agony of sorrow, of a broken heart.

And, even as I screamed and cried and thrashed against my bindings, I couldn't help thinking: perhaps this was what I deserved.

40

ABBY NORMAL

ADDIE

"The fuck?"

Barely ten minutes after I'd laid down, I sat bolt upright again, scrubbing tears from my cheeks. A god-awful squealing noise pierced the air. Sounded like a pig being slaughtered.

Beneath me, Cheriour flinched.

There were hoofbeats now. Lots of 'em, accompanied by the distinct *mowow* of a Púca.

Well, this was fantastic, wasn't it? We were sitting ducks, and about to be turned into Duck à l'Orange.

Cheriour's palm brushed against my back. "Where is your poleaxe?"

I got to my feet, trying to remember where I'd left it.

Oh...haha. It was still leaning against the tree. Easily a dozen feet away. Because why did I need to keep a weapon close while living in this super peaceful world?

I turned back to Cheriour, who gave me an exasperated look and hissed, "Hide. But take your poleaxe with you."

"I'm not leaving you," I said through gritted teeth as I moved toward my poleaxe.

And then I let out a bellowing, *"Holy shit!"* when a burly black body burst through the trees, its red eyes flashing.

A Púca.

My Púca. I knew those eyes well now.

The Púca squealed, kicking up its back feet as it came to a halt at the end of the clearing.

"Is that—?" Cheriour tilted his head back, staring at the Púca. But more hoofbeats rumbled toward us and we were suddenly surrounded by riders.

Human riders.

"Addie! Cheriour!" Braxton stopped his horse and leapt from the saddle.

Relief hit me like a battering ram. My knees turned to goop and I would've fallen on my ass if Braxton hadn't rushed over and pulled me into a bone-crushing hug.

"You have no idea how fucking happy I am to see you," I muttered, gripping his shoulders for dear life.

"And I ye." Braxton pulled away with a shaky smile. "We've found too many bodies today. It's nice to see ye both still alive." But his grin faded when he looked at Cheriour.

"Yeah," I said, following his gaze. "He's hurt pretty bad. I did what I could, but..."

Cheriour tapped his fingers against my ankle. It was a soothing gesture. Almost like he was saying, *it's okay.*

"Aye, I see that." Braxton knelt at Cheriour's side, touching a hand to his shoulder. "How bad is it?"

Cheriour didn't answer.

Braxton turned to me. And the unsure expression on his face...

My stomach plummeted to the soles of my feet.

I knew Cheriour was in rough shape. But I figured if help

arrived, he'd suddenly be a-okay. A silly notion, but it'd been my only hope. And now it was blown to smithereens.

Braxton sighed. "We'll need to get ye two on a horse. Navigator has the smoothest canter. And he's no' a complicated fellow, Addie, ye should manage—"

The roar cut him off.

I spun around.

Three armed soldiers had launched an assault against the Púca. But they'd fucked around and found out. Because my Púca was *pissed*.

"Shoot it, Tiernan!" A man shouted.

"That's no good. You're too close!" A woman called.

With another bellow, the Púca lunged. Its teeth snapped with an audible *clink* around the woman's sleeve.

"Bastard!" She flew backward. "Tiernan! *Kill* the wretched thing!"

"Don't you *dare!*" I didn't even realize I was running until I'd body-slammed into a man with a piddly little bow.

The Púca flung its head into the air, emitting loud cackling sounds.

"Don't!" I yelled when the woman pulled a knife.

"Bloody thing tried to kill us," she snarled.

"Ummm, it looked like you were trying to kill it first. That was all self-defense." I stepped forward, placing myself in front of the Púca. "Did you get bit?" I asked the woman.

She ran a hand over her torn sleeve. "Almost."

"Almost doesn't count. If it didn't break skin, you're fine. And maybe that close call will teach ya *not* to harass innocent animals."

"Innocent?" Tiernan said with an angry *harrumph*. "The bloody Púca chased us, scared the horses half into their graves, and—"

"Led you here," I said.

"A mere coincidence."

"No. It wasn't. The Púca was here before. Last night. It killed the Wraiths, *saved* us—"

"Impossible!"

"—and led you here. These horses are fugly bastards, no denying that. And they're venomous and..." I inhaled as I thought of Moira. "I get it. But this one *saved my life*. He's off limits." I glanced over my shoulder.

The Púca stared back at me, ears pricked.

Everyone else, Braxton included, looked at me like I'd sprouted five heads.

Well, Cheriour didn't. "She's right," he croaked. "About the Púca."

"That's—" Braxton's gaze shifted between me and the horse. "Addie, Púcas aren' animals."

"Yeah, yeah, I know. They're more like hybrids. Right?" Hadn't Belanna told me that?

"They're blood-thirsty monsters," Braxton said. "They can' be controlled. Not fully. Look at the equipment they wear. The Wraiths use pain to..." He trailed off, eyes widening.

The Púca had stepped forward. Its warm breath wafted across my back. A chill ran up my spine, but I forced the shudder back. "This one's different," I said.

The Púca draped its head over my shoulder, licking its lips, but showing zero sign of aggression.

"They're all the same." Braxton gripped his sword, his eyes locked on the Púca.

"Well, I dunno. Maybe this one's got an abby normal brain." I reached up and touched a hand to the horse's cheek. It felt like snakeskin. Freaky.

There were a dozen sets of eyes on me now, watching my every move.

And because I was me, I had to rub it in that this snake-scaled venomous horse had, for some odd reason, chosen to be my protector. So I reached up again and unbuckled the bridle. The Púca stood stock-still, moving only to spit the bit out when I pulled the headpiece over its ears.

The knife-wielding woman gaped at me. "How?" she asked.

"No idea." I ran a hand down the horse's scaly neck. "But it's kinda cool, right?"

"The horse stays," Cheriour grunted. "Addie," he tilted his head back to look at me. "It's your responsibility to restrain that animal. If it harms any member of this army, it will be killed. Understood?"

The Púca's eyes closed as I rubbed an apparently itchy spot at the base of its wiry mane. "Understood," I said. "He attacks someone, he's out."

"*She,*" Braxton corrected.

"What?"

"If *she* attacks someone. That Púca is a mare."

I ran a hand down the Púca's muzzle. "Well, ain't that perfect? Miss Abby Normal. Abby and Addie, that shouldn't confuse anyone, huh?"

The mare sighed, resting her head more fully against my shoulder.

By the end of the day, Cheriour looked like a corpse.

He'd managed to get on a horse. And he was able to ride unassisted once he got the initial weeble-wobbles out and had his kankle (aka, his broken ankle) secured to the stirrup. For a few minutes, he'd almost seemed like himself again.

But an hour into our trek through the woods, Cheriour's face had gone from pale to chalk white. Sweat saturated his clothes. He shook, swaying more and more in the saddle—and we'd only been walking. The forest was too dense for a canter. Or so Braxton said. He was probably using the cluttered woods as an excuse to keep the pace slow for Cheriour's sake.

And mine, considering I was leading my Púca on foot.

Well, I wasn't *leading* her. She'd thrown a holy fit when I'd tried to slip a rope halter over her head. She'd thrown an even bigger tantrum when I took the saddle off. I'd managed to, but only after she'd bolted and nearly dragged me through the forest.

"Ye sure ye don't want me to kill her?" Braxton had asked.

"Positive," I'd gritted my teeth and yanked the saddle off, tossing it to the ground. Abby Normal's back had immediately clenched into a violent, painful-looking spasm.

Braxton frowned as he watched her muscles twitch. "She's *hurtin'*, Addie. Might be a mercy to kill her."

"Absolutely not."

"And how are ye proposing to bring her with us if she can' be haltered?"

"Errr..." I'd stepped forward, reaching for the discarded halter again.

With a loud huff, Abby Normal had taken the same step.

Interesting.

I'd taken another step, and another, and another. She'd followed each one.

"*That's* how." I'd beamed at Braxton.

My venomous bodyguard plodded docilely next to me as we navigated the forest. Occasionally, she played with the end of my braid, nipped at the shaft of my poleaxe, or fiddled with the straps on the holster. Like an oversized, affectionate dog. Which, on any other day, would've given me the warm fuzzies.

But, to be honest, I wasn't paying much attention to her. Not when Cheriour looked two seconds away from keeling over.

And the bits of conversation drifting back from the other soldiers did *not* help to ease my mind.

"Elion was *there...*"

"Cayden led a group south. I think they went right into Elion's trap."

"He infected the *birds.*"

"How long was he planning this?"

"He *wanted* us to flee into the woods."

"Braxton, have you heard any news of the rest of the army?"

"I have not," Braxton answered the last question with a sigh. "Elion brought terror to this forest. The animals are hidin'."

Things were *really* looking peachy keen around here.

And it only got better when we found another section of our army. About thirty people. Or more. It was kinda hard to tell, considering their body parts were strewn in a dozen different locations. Arms stuck out of bushes. Legs draped over tree roots. Torsos filled large ditches. And heads sat atop tree branches, their blank eyes watching as we trudged by.

My stomach churned. There was *so...much...blood!* Crimson droplets splashed onto my legs as I stumbled through the puddles.

"Keep your eyes forward, Addie." Cheriour turned in the saddle, his gaze finding mine. A bead of sweat trickled down the side of his face. "Don't look at them."

But I did. And I pictured his body on the ground with the others.

Pain lanced my chest. *Do not chase that rabbit,* I scolded myself. *He's a tough guy. He'll make it.*

But as the hours wore on, he continued to deteriorate.

At dusk, we found a small stream. Braxton and I helped Cheriour off the horse and guided him over to the edge of the water.

"Addie, do you want me to do this?" Braxton stared grimly at Cheriour's blood-soaked bandages.

"I've got it," I said. "But I need more fabric."

"Aye." he turned to the rest of the group. "You heard her. Whatever cloth you can spare."

And they took that to heart. I got pieces of shirts, bits of blankets, some strips of saddle pads, and...

"Is this *underwear?*" I chucked a pair of dingy, cream-colored pants to the ground. Why? Because there were goddam *skid marks* lining the seat! "Who *the fuck* handed me dirty underwear?"

No one answered. But everyone sniggered. Including Braxton, who got red-faced and very, *very* focused on pulling burrs out of his horse's mane.

"Har, har, har...*asshole*," I mumbled.

But I totally laughed. Even Cheriour, pale and sweaty and breathing like a winded rhino, cracked a tiny smile.

Sometimes a shitty joke was the perfect balm for a shitty day.

I took the clothes (minus the poopy underwear) into the stream and scrubbed them within an inch of their lives. But when I pulled the old, bloody bandages away from Cheriour's wounds...

Well, clean bandages wouldn't make much of a difference at this point.

Yellow liquid oozed from the gaping laceration under his ribcage. A few other cuts were red. Swollen. Angry.

"How far are we from Niall?" I asked, trying (and failing) to keep the tremor out of my voice.

"A day," Braxton said.

"Three days, at the rate we're traveling," Cheriour countered.

"We need to pick up the pace." I blew out a shaky breath. "Right, well, I hate depriving people of a good drink, but does anyone have alcohol on them? Ale? Whiskey? Something? Do *not* piss in a bottle and try to pass it off as liquor."

Braxton's shoulders deflated. Like he'd been thinking of doing just that. "Aye," he laughed, "we have alcohol." He whipped a leather flask out of his shirt pocket.

Six other people stepped forward and handed me their flasks. I uncorked all of them, taking big sniffs of each one. Some smelled like flat beer. A couple were vinegary—probably wine that had gone a little sour. But Braxton had the worst offender.

"What the frick?" I sputtered. It was the same gasoline drink Belanna had given me a few weeks ago. "Dude, you and your sister have got some *awful* taste in drinks."

"Or, alternatively, we have good taste. And ye just can't handle yer liquor." Braxton winked.

"Get me some shots of something that's *not* gasoline, and you'll see how well I can hold my alcohol." I winced as I took another whiff. "Okay, since this is the strongest, it'll be the antiseptic. Cheriour, you hold this," I slapped one of the vinegar-scented concoctions into Cheriour's hand, "and take a shot. Or three."

"I don't drink alcohol," Cheriour said.

"You shitting me?"

"It addles the mind."

"That's kinda the point. Especially right now. This is gonna hurt like an S.O.B., so taking a few shots might help dull the pain."

He weakly pushed the flask back into my hand. "I won't need it."

"Seriously? *Fine.* Be all macho and suffer the consequences. No skin off my back. But I'm leaving it here, 'kay? Because *I* might need it."

And oh boy, did I need it when I was done.

Pouring alcohol into his smaller cuts? That was somewhat okay. Cheriour kept his eyes closed and only grunted once or twice. But the gaping wound had a *shit-ton* of debris inside, and dumping alcohol wasn't enough. I needed to get my fingers in there to clean it out.

There was a lot of yelling then. A whole lot of cursing too (mostly from me). Cheriour took the easy route and blacked out. Meanwhile, I had to finish draining pus-soaked leaves out of the wound (yum, right?). And, by that point, my fingers were jumping all over the place. Braxton had to take over while I stepped to the side, putting my hands on my knees, willing the forest to stop spinning. So yeah, I needed that vinegary wine. Every last drop of it.

Which meant I was almost relaxed (aka, tipsy as fuck) when Braxton led Cheriour's horse over to me.

"Ye think yer Púca—" he started.

"Her name's Abby Normal—" I said.

"—will follow ye while ye ride?" he patted the horse's neck.

I stared at the massive bay creature he was holding. And then turned to Abby Normal, who stood several feet away, watching my every move. "I guess we'll find out. Does it have to be *that* horse, though?"

"Navigator is a good mount."

"He looks like a mini elephant."

"He's gentle. And he'll take care of ye."

"Right. Well, I'm gonna need some help getting on him."

"Aye, I thought you might," Braxton chuckled.

Navigator's saddle was slightly above my head, and I

couldn't jump that high, so poor Braxton had to lift me onto the horse's back.

Abby Normal immediately pitched a fit. She pawed at the ground and made that awful *mowow*. Apparently, she was a jealous bitch.

"I don' understand the name ye've given that Púca," Braxton said as he watched her tantrum.

"Abby Normal." I shortened the reins when Navigator fidgeted.

"Are ye intentionally mispronouncing the word?"

"Yeah. But that's the point. Like, it's...well...it's a long story."

Braxton smiled. "Perhaps one day ye can tell me."

"When'll that be? While we're sewing someone's guts back in? Or in between battles? Nothing beats hearing a monster story while you're running for your life, right?" That came out way more snappishly than I'd intended. "Sorry," I amended. "It's been a long few days." I glanced over my shoulder. A still-unconscious Cheriour sat slumped over a saddle. He didn't even stir when another man leapt onto the horse behind him.

A sour feeling curdled in my gut.

Braxton gave my calf a light tap. "He's strong, Addie."

"Yeah, but he's in bad shape."

"Aye. No denyin' that. But he's survived worse."

"Define 'worse.' 'Cause, from where I'm sitting, there can't be many things *worse* than having a fucking crater in your stomach."

Braxton didn't answer. Just turned and patted Navigator's neck. "Ye should get along well with this fellow. He's a big ole fool who gets himself frightened over nothing sometimes, but he's lenient. And he'll do his best to be brave while yer on him."

And, with that, Braxton mounted his horse and gave the call for us to ride out.

I nudged Navigator into a canter and heard the thrumming of Abby Normal's hooves as she followed.

A few feet in front of me, a man held Cheriour steady in the saddle as his horse dashed through the trees. Cheriour's head flopped lifelessly back onto the man's shoulder.

41

MAJOR BITCH MODE

T he people of Niall watched us solemnly as we staggered through the streets. There was no music that afternoon. No laughter. No robust greetings. Just a lot of murmurs and worried glances.

My traveling crew was so small, battered, bruised, and dreary, we might as well have returned to Niall waving a neon banner that said: *We Fucked Up*.

And people *really* did not react well to seeing Cheriour injured.

A few gasped or covered their mouths. Multiple people cried, asking if he'd died.

"No," the man riding with Cheriour responded. "No. He is *alive*."

Alive, but unresponsive.

Quinn emerged from the castle to greet us. Like he had the first time I rode into Niall. Thankfully, he didn't lob a knife at my head this time. But he sure didn't seem happy to see me.

"What happened?" Quinn hovered by my elbow as I slid out of Navigator's saddle. He didn't shout. Or curse. But the fact that he directed the question at *me*, not at Braxton or any of the other soldiers...

This fucker was trying to put the blame on *my* shoulders.

Acidic hatred flooded my mouth. And I almost, *almost,* went right back at the slimy bastard.

Until I got a good look at him and saw the worry crumpling his face. The way his lower lip quivered, despite his best attempts to still it.

And, fuck, I hated being a softie. Because even though I wanted to scream and smack his fugly face, I couldn't. He was a raging asshat, yes. But he was also a man in pain. So I tried to rein my response back.

Tried.

"We were ambushed," I said.

"Aye. It was Elion, Quinn," Braxton added.

A vein pulsed in Quinn's temple. He stared at me, his forehead briefly puckering when he got a good eyeful of the blue/pink shirt, and then looked at Cheriour. "He protected you, didn't he?"

"No—"

"Don't lie—"

"I'm not."

"He was upset I sent you to Sanadrin."

"Well, that was a dick move."

"And I *ordered* him not to put himself in danger protecting you." Quinn's face turned a deep, vibrant red. Like a stop sign.

"Mind your blood pressure," I said, "before your head explodes."

"You are incompetent! And yet you stand there, unharmed, while..." he turned to the still-unconscious Cheriour and blinked once. Twice. As though fighting back tears. "And now you expect me to allow this *beast* into my city?" He jerked his head toward Abby Normal.

She stood a few feet behind the group, eyeing the city people warily. And they watched her like she was a ticking time bomb. A few drew weapons. One woman looked ready to hurl her meat fork into Abby Normal's neck.

"Oi! Quinn!" Braxton hopped down from his horse and snapped his fingers in front of Quinn's face. "That's enough, eh?"

"Where is your sister?" Quinn snarled.

"Not here." Braxton's face paled. "But if she's still alive, I'm sure she's on her way. And ye may be soon overrun with wounded, so how about ye stop throwing yer tantrum and help me get Cheriour into the castle? Afterward, perhaps ye should work on an apology. We wouldn' have gotten Cheriour here alive if it hadn't been for Addie and that Púca."

If looks could kill, I would've dropped dead from the vile glare Quinn tossed in my direction.

The twitch in my eye worsened. I 100% sympathized with his concern, fear, and anguish. But I would *not* be the punching bag he lashed at to make himself feel better. "How about instead of an apology, you treat me like a human being?" I snapped. "You don't like me. *I get it!* I don't like you either, but I've at least *tried* to be respectful. Whereas you've thrown toddler-level tantrums. Act your age, not your shoe size. 'Kay?"

"Quinn!" Braxton shouted, derailing Quinn's response. "Can ye heal Cheriour, or no'?"

With great reluctance, Quinn turned away from me and studied Cheriour. "I don't know." Quinn's hands trembled. "His wounds are deep, and my ability," his jaw ticked, "has been stretched thin. Bring him inside. I'll do what I can."

He gave me an evil, *I want to chop your friggin head off* glare and turned away.

Such a friendly, heartwarming guy...

"Alright, dude. You've been lying on your backside for three— er—" I looked out the window, at the sun crawling over the horizon. "Almost four days. At some point, you *have* to wake up."

I hoped.

Cheriour lay on his bed. Back safe and sound in his pigsty of a bedroom at Niall. And he hadn't moved since we arrived.

Er, no. That wasn't entirely true. About an hour after Quinn partially healed him, Cheriour had opened his eyes and emitted a grumbled *eerrghuh* before he puked all over himself. And, since I'd been in the middle of re-wrapping his bandages, guess who got sprayed with rancid, pea-green soup? Me.

"Y'know what," I'd said, mopping bile off my shirt, "we're even now. I got my bodily fluids on you, you got yours on me. And we haven't even *slept* together yet. Just took a beeline right to the gross stuff."

He'd closed his eyes. Out for the count again.

And now, as the sun creepy-crawled its way into the sky, I jiggled my knee, rattling Cheriour's thin mattress. "I've got, like, ten minutes," I said. "Before Quinn's awake and on the prowl again. Sure would be nice if you'd wake up before I go. My day would be filled with a lot less anxiety."

No response.

I sighed. Not that I'd been expecting anything to happen, but it would've been nice.

I wasn't *forbidden* from leaving my room and wandering the castle anymore. Quinn had honored his promise to remove all restrictions and guards. But I avoided Quinn like the freaking plague. No *way* I'd chance getting trapped in a dark corridor with him. *Hell. No.* Thankfully, even heartless bastards needed their beauty sleep. So I was generally safe roaming the halls and visiting Cheriour's room, between midnight and dawn.

But, with the sun up, it was time to GTFO.

I blew out a long breath and pressed my fingers to Cheriour's cheek. His fever had burned out yesterday. And his wounds were healing. Some of the smaller ones had scabbed over. His broken ankle looked normal. No more kankle. The crater in his ribcage was still red, still ugly, but it had stopped seeping yellow pus and was starting to close.

"I guess you want me to worry today, huh? Spend the afternoon *pining* for you? 'Cause I'm gonna." I brushed my fingers over his cheek, trailing them over his crooked nose, brushing them over his lips...

Fuck me. I'd had so many dreams about those lips. *Hot* dreams.

Most of the time, at least. Sometimes the horny moments dissolved into horror scenes. Because, y'know, my brain liked to get me all hot and bothered and then torment me with images of him dying in my arms.

But I couldn't stop thinking about that stupid fucking kiss. I remembered every second in full 8K detail. I wanted to kiss him again. Properly. I wanted to make him shake and moan and whimper—there was nothing hotter than a guy's desperate whimpering.

But more than that, I wanted to see his gorgeous eyes again. Hear his slow drawl. Without his steady, quiet presence at my side, I felt like I couldn't take a full deep breath anymore; my chest hurt too much. Almost as though...

As though I was *mourning*.

Crazy, right? I'd only known the guy a month. I shouldn't have been *this* upset over potentially losing him.

Too much shit has happened recently, I kept telling myself. *I've been off the pill, and I'm due for my period. My emotions don't know which way is up anymore.*

I brushed my fingers against Cheriour's cheek one last time and left the room, my chest heavy.

Abby Normal was not a happy camper.

Probably because she'd spent the last four days confined in a chintzy round pen. She was basically like a hamster on a wheel, running around in circles. And, with the six-foot-high fencing, she didn't have a shot at jumping out.

Or maybe her accommodations weren't the problem, and she was pissed that people hurled curses and brandished weapons at her every time they came close to her pen. And "*close*" meant anywhere within a general mile radius.

Or maybe she was bitter because her meals were runty pigs or cows. Y'know, the slaughterhouse rejects that had zero meat on their bones. She didn't get much blood from them. Definitely didn't get any *fresh* blood, since the carcasses were long dead by the time they got tossed in her pen.

If I were in her shoes—er, *hooves*—I'd be in a major bitch mode too.

I leaned against the coarse wooden fence, watching as she ran around. And around. And—oop, she changed directions. Now she went around to the right.

A dead pig lay in the center of the pen (aka, her breakfast) but she'd taken one whiff of it, roared in disgust, and started her angry sprinting. An hour later, she was still going. Her scaly body didn't sweat, but white lather foamed around her mouth and between her back legs.

I couldn't even open the gate to let her out. I wanted to. It would've been easy: undo the latch, swing it open, and watch her sail off into the sunset. The problem? She was being kept several hundred yards from the stables, but well within sight of the barn, the castle, *and* the city. If anyone saw her running loose, she'd be shot down. Instantly.

"I'm sorry!" I said as she thundered by. "You'll never save my ass again, huh?"

In response, she skidded to a halt in front of me, spraying grass and mud through the fence, before she pivoted and zoomed off in the other direction.

"I guess I deserved that," I mumbled as I wiped the gunk off my pants. My nose itched and my eyes blurred. I was crying because my horse was being mean to me. Could I get any more ridiculous?

But Abby Normal had been nice to me at first. She'd let me comb my fingers through her wiry mane and smooth my hand over her scaly body. Truthfully, she'd felt like the only friend I had left. And now she hated my guts.

Quinn may not have had guards on my ass 24/7 anymore, but the people of Niall gave me a wide berth. Probably because I'd been the one to bring the demon horse into their town.

Or because they believed I put Cheriour on his deathbed.

As for my *human* friends...

Braxton barely spent any time at Niall, preferring to use his days searching for survivors. I didn't blame him. There'd been a few times I'd thought about joining. But, y'know, I was a shit fighter and would've done more harm than help.

And there *were* survivors. They'd trickled into the city over the last couple of days. But their arrivals weren't always cause for celebration.

Belanna had brought a large group back with her two days ago. A hundred people, or close to it.

When I'd seen them heading toward the castle, I'd *run* to greet them. Me. Running. A rare freaking sight. But I'd been so *happy* to spot some familiar faces.

Belanna had turned to look at me as I skidded to a halt, wheezing, beside her group. She'd tried to grin, but it had looked more like a pained grimace. "It was Elion," she'd told Quinn.

"Braxton told me about the birds." Quinn hadn't even noticed me; his eyes too busy scanning the somber, petrified faces of the soldiers in Belanna's group.

"Aye. He tortured those precious..." Her lip had trembled. "But he also found our group."

Quinn's shoulders had sagged. "H-how many?"

"I can' say. He hides himself too well. Perhaps all of us."

So, yeah, that entire group of people now waited to see who'd get sick. The incubation period took up to a week. And once the symptoms started....

Well, I'd already seen what that disease did to people. It was a horrible fucking way to die.

Poor Kaelan returned the very next day with burns coating over half his body. Apparently he'd been partially cooked over a spit. And he was *not* a fireproof hybrid. His group had barely gotten him out alive.

I'd watched him get carted through the city, flopped over Sacrifice's back (*nothing* took that tough little cookie down). And the sight of those boils and blisters covering his once-handsome face...I'd cried. A lot. The poor kid didn't deserve that kind of pain.

All in all, we had less than a thousand soldiers return to Niall.

Two weeks ago, nearly *two* thousand soldiers had left on our ill-fated rescue mission.

It had been a shitty couple of weeks. A shitty month, really.

Abby Normal had been the only *good* thing in my life. So her sudden rejection stung. A lot.

I sighed as Abby Normal came to a halt on the other end of the pen, panting.

"You done?" I reached my hand through the slats in the fence.

She squealed and turned her back to me. Horse language for, *"fuck you."*

I sighed and turned my back to her, sinking to the ground and leaning against the fence. "I'm sorry," I whispered. But why should she believe me? I was the one who'd led her into this pen.

And how could I explain I wasn't the bad guy? That I was an outsider too, and as trapped as she was? Neither of us belonged here, but we had no option to go home. It was either live in this hellhole or die.

"Death's looking like the better option," I mumbled.

"Don't say that."

I jerked back, cursing when I whacked my head on the fence post. "*Ouch!* Motherf—" I glanced up, rubbing at the back of my head, as Cheriour knelt beside me.

42

THE MANIPULATOR

I hung limply in my chains, my arms quivering, wrists aching as the shackles dug into my skin. Tears streamed down my cheeks. No matter how hard I bit my lip or tongue, I couldn't stem the sobs. Byron's doing, of course. My grief was so strong, it was as though he'd physically reached into my chest and crushed my heart.

Then he touched my forehead again, and I was giddy. Full of life and laughter. My muscles yearned to run. To play.

Another touch left a hollow pit in my stomach, my chest once again gnawing with sorrow.

On and on this went. Happiness. Sadness. Happiness. Sadness. Until Byron finally drew away, his hands trembling, his face as pallid as mine surely was.

I sagged, the shackles biting into my wrists, forcing me to stand upright. My legs had grown weary; the muscles in my thighs and calves cramped.

I had toiled in that small, windowless room for several days, unable to move, sit, or lie down.

I was given provisions; scraps of moldy bread and ladles of

gritty water that were tossed ~~unceremonsiouly~~—unceremoniously into my mouth. I choked up more than I swallowed. And, as I could not leave the wall, even to use a privy...well, a body's natural functions couldn't be denied, could they?

So I stood in my own urine, with wedges of barely chewed food coating the front of my tunic, while my emotions withered in utter turmoil.

Byron suffered as well.

He staggered into the wall, his hand quaking so violently, he almost couldn't raise his arm to rap his knuckles against the door.

But he managed. And, at his summon, a woman entered the hut.

She had a round, kind face, and a wild mass of steel gray hair, which she kept twisted in a long braid. She spoke gently to Byron.

"Here you go," she pressed a flask into his palm. "That'll steady your nerves again. Tsk," she clicked her tongue when Bryon raised the flask to his mouth, his unsteady hand spilling much of the wine down his front. "Poor lad." She used the hem of her shirt to clean the mess. "Somedays I swear it's a curse the Celestials left you with."

She turned to look at me. Burn scars wrapped around the left side of her throat. Both her hands also bore puckered blemishes. "It's good work you're doing, Byron." Her eyes held no warmth as she studied me. Only revulsion.

Byron spilled more wine but consumed three large gulps. His shaking quieted. "Is there news from Darfield?" he asked.

"Very little," the woman said. "But there was an attack..." She paused, turning her cold eyes on me again, as though unsure whether to divulge this information in my presence.

Byron did not ask her to continue. He nodded, took another long sip of wine, and straightened. "I am fit to proceed."

The woman nodded, glowered at me once more, and left.

Byron drank from the flask again. And again, before he turned back to me. "What are Seruf's plans?"

I stayed silent.

"Why did she send you?"

I said nothing.

"Why did she create you?"

The only response was my ragged breathing.

"If you would tell me—"

"I can't give you the information you're looking for," I said. "How many times must I explain this?"

"You *won't* give me information."

"There is a difference between 'won't' and 'can't.' Perhaps you should educate yourself on the definition of those words."

His eyes narrowed. "Why do you protect her? It seems she is no longer inclined to protect you. Give me the information I seek, and I will release you from those chains."

He simply wouldn't hear the truth. Unless I fabricated a tale that suited his vendetta, he would ignore anything that came out of my mouth.

So we began the torment again. Sadness. Happiness. Rage. Joy. Despair. This continued for minutes, perhaps hours, the ever-changing emotions twisting my insides until Byron's unsteadiness forced him to stop. Again, he went to the door. Again, the woman brought him more wine and waited until he steadied before she departed.

My head lolled as Byron suckled from his flask. Much of the drink sloshed down his front. The rancid scent of alcohol filled the room and burned my nostrils.

But, oh, how I wished he would offer me a drink. I would have gladly exchanged food for a few sips of wine. The moldy bread did little to ease the niggling pain in my belly, but perhaps the alcohol would have granted me a few moments of sleep.

Instead, I hovered in the foggy area between sleep and waking, unable to fully rest while chained to the wall. I dreamt. Or, rather, my addled brain conjured memories to trick me into thinking I was dreaming.

As Byron slopped his wine, I found myself transported to Terrick's bookshop in Swindon.

"And this one," Terrick's *eyes gleamed as he pulled a tome off the shelf, "has dragons—great winged beasts who breathe fire! Oh, but they're not real, lass." He laughed when I stumbled away.*

"They're not?" I asked.

"No," he said. "They're fiction stories." He waved his arm, gesturing to the ~~colums~~ *columns of books and parchments. "They all are. But sometimes the most effective stories contain a grain of truth."*

I was dragged from the fuzzy, albeit pleasant, memory when Byron spoke.

"Wouldn't you prefer to lie down and sleep?" he asked. "Are you not yet tired of those chains?"

Sometimes the most effective stories contain a grain of truth.

Could I spin a potent tale around the truth? Would it be enough to end my torment?

Hope fluttered in my battered heart as I willed strength to return to my fatigued body.

"You're a fool," I spat, "if you believe Seruf has lowered herself to confiding in a human."

Byron smiled. "So, you're finally admitting—"

"I know nothing," I said. "But this is my truth. I was born in Detha—"

"Detha?" Byron's red-rimmed eyes widened. He sniffled. "That is in one of the islands of Uchen."

I ignored him, as he'd ignored me these past days. "I became a hybrid and was brought here when I was five—"

"Is that when you began working with Seruf?" his eyes bulged. He reminded me of the fat toad—my first kill.

My palms prickled. Itched. "I was a child. Do you think a cosmic being such as Seruf has the time or desire to rear a child?"

Byron straightened; his nostrils flared. For the first time, he was listening. *Truly* listening.

"I have never interacted with her, as I have said," I continued. "I know nothing of what she is planning, as I have *also* said on numerous occasions. But she created me." The lie rolled easily off my tongue. Perhaps because it wasn't a falsity. It was something I'd suspected for a long while. "Therefore, she must have a plan for me. Perhaps she was waiting for me to come of age. And if such a plan exists, she'll not be happy when she learns of my confinement, will she?"

A flicker of uncertainty crippled Byron's face before he raised his gnarled stump of a hand, gesturing around him. "As you can see, we're amply prepared should she decide to pay a visit to Lamex."

"Amply prepared?" I barked out a laugh. "You have one room and a single set of chains. Tell me, mighty ruler of Lamex, when Seruf comes to save me, how do you propose to contain *two* Firestarters?"

"You're human," he said, although his statement sounded more like a question. "And easy to kill—"

"And ending my life will only incense her further, will it not?"

Byron opened his mouth to speak, but nothing came out.

"I have no wish to harm anyone."

His jaw closed with a snap. "No wish to harm? How can

you make such a claim when you've already murdered innocents?"

"*Accidentally.* As I, again, have repeatedly stated. I cannot control my power, but I truly do not wish to harm humans. In fact, I'm quite tired of watching you pathetic creatures die."

Again, my words seemed to have made an impact.

Byron turned away, running his fingers over his scars and staring at the ground as he paced. His breathing grew short and agitated.

He stopped, stared at me, and resumed his pacing. For a moment, he said nothing. Until his mindless wandering brought him back to my side. "Your tunic doesn't burn," he said. "Material from the Celestial city?"

"I don't know. It was a gift from—" My stomach turned to rot as I pictured Terrick's kind smile.

"A Celestial?" Byron supplied.

"No. A friend. Terrick. Perhaps you know of him; he was a hybrid who fought in the war."

"I was a child when that war was fought," Byron said. "Did your *friend* tell you where he got that tunic?"

"He purchased it from a merchant in Darfield."

"Lies."

"No. I invite you to tear a strip of this fabric and take it to Darfield. The merchant displayed this tunic in their window for years and priced it exorbitantly. They were quite proud of it, no matter how they obtained the fabric, and I've no doubt they would verify my claim."

Byron's jaw closed again. He turned away from me, tension roiling across his back. "And what happened to this friend of yours?" he asked. "Why is he not here to defend your innocence?"

"He's dead. *I* killed him."

Byron's jaw twitched, but he turned away, saying nothing.

More tears rolled down my cheeks. I hated the way tears felt; rather like ants crawling across my skin.

For several moments, there was silence, broken only by my grating breaths, and Byron's low, unintelligible murmurs. His hands ran restlessly over his scars, nails digging into flesh, as though trying to recreate the pain those burns had once inflicted.

I thought of the pockmarked woman who brought him wine. "Seruf has been here before."

Byron remained facing the door. "Yes. A long time ago."

"What did she do to this town?" I asked. "To you?"

"Sakar was not always peaceful. You were not yet born when Ramiel ruled here." Byron gave his scars another vicious scratch.

"I lived the early years of my life in Detha," I said. "I think you'll find I'm well-~~aquainted~~ acquainted with the harshness of a Celestial's rule."

"And Detha is within the borders of Idril—Ramiel's home —is it not?" Byron asked.

"I'm not certain."

"Did you ever see him?"

I had to ponder this; the early years of my childhood seemed like another lifetime. "No," I said. "Only his Wraiths."

"Unsurprising. Ramiel cares little for humans. Some say he finds us revolting. Seruf does not share this view." He turned to face me; his eyes flooded with a dark, raw terror. "You were incorrect in saying Seruf wouldn't have the time or desire to raise a child. Seruf has a *great* desire for children."

He watched me expectantly. As though waiting for me to rebuke or agree with his statement.

When I remained silent, he pivoted and left the room.

I DIDN'T EXPECT him to release me. I was merely hoping for an end—even if it meant him driving his sword through my heart. When Byron returned a day later and began loosening my shackles, I feared I was dreaming.

His eyes were cold as he yanked on the chains with unnecessary force. "I believe you," he said. "You truly do not know Seruf. But I do. She would not have permitted a child to leave her side. Yet, you have never been with her."

"As I've said. *Repeatedly.*" I gasped as blood returned to the fingers of my newly freed arm. It felt as though there were spikes inside me, clawing at my skin.

Byron wrenched my other arm away from the wall. "Your separation from Seruf was likely a mistake. And it seems she has returned to Sakar to remedy it."

I winced when he tossed the chain away from my left wrist, sending the heavy metal slamming into my side.

"Against my better judgment," his lips curled over his teeth, "I'm setting you free, but you cannot stay here. I'd advise you to enjoy your liberation. It's not likely to last long."

43

WHAT HAPPENS AT THE HAIR SALON STAYS AT THE HAIR SALON

ADDIE

My hormones were officially out of control.

I burst into tears as soon as Cheriour knelt beside me.

He recoiled and searched my body, as though looking for injuries. Because, y'know, he wasn't used to his soldiers bawling over nothing.

I'd never, *ever*, be mistaken for the stoic warrior type.

"Addie," Cheriour started.

"What are you *doing* here?" I screeched. "It's a long walk from your room. And I'm 99% sure you shouldn't be moving that much yet. Don't you dare," I hissed when he opened his mouth to say something. "You're about to say, '*I'm fine,*' right? *Bull...fucking...shit.* You've been on your deathbed for days. *Days.* No one is *fine* after that. Are you *trying* to put yourself in a grave?"

Cheriour slowly sat beside me, looking utterly flummoxed.

And utterly *not fine*.

Yeah, he'd returned to the land of the living. But he had big, dark rings beneath his eyes. Like a raccoon. Those rings *clashed* with his otherwise colorless complexion. A rumpled, dirty shirt sat crookedly over his torso. He'd probably grabbed the first shirt he'd stepped on. His hair hung loose upon his shoulders, the first time I'd ever seen it out of a ponytail. And, my God, what a freaking rat's nest.

"Turn around," I snapped.

His nose wrinkled. "What?"

"Never mind. I'll go around you." I stood, walked behind him, and plopped back down.

From this angle, I saw Abby Normal over his shoulder. She still had her back turned to me, but she'd cocked her head in my direction, her ears splayed. She looked as confused as Cheriour.

But neither of them were as befuddled as me. I had way too many emotions swirling inside me. Hello, PMS mood swings. With a healthy dose of PTSD mixed in.

I touched the top of Cheriour's scalp.

He jerked in surprise. "What are you doing?"

"Fixing your freaking hair." It was so damn matted. I needed conditioner. Detangling spray. Hell, a decent comb would've been a godsend. But all I had were my fingers. And...

I glanced at Abby Normal again. "Aha!" She had a water bucket in her pen! "Hang on." I sprang to my feet, ducked between the slats of her fence, ignoring her when she pinned her ears, and snatched the wooden bucket.

"What are you—*urrgh*," Cheriour grunted when I sloshed water over the top of his head. Not all of it, but enough to get his hair damp.

"Addie..." he started as I knelt behind him and ran my fingers through the tangles. Right off the bat, I hit some knots that had him grimacing.

"Sorry!" I said. "But, y'know, this wouldn't hurt as much if you brushed your hair once in a while."

He sighed but said nothing else as I set to work.

I didn't have the power to wave my hand and make his injuries go away, but I knew how to fix snarled strands. And the process of holding a small section of hair, working it with my fingers until the knots gave way was therapeutic. Calming. It was like I'd been transported back home. Back to my old job. Even as my knees ached from kneeling, and my hands cramped, I kept going, lost in my work.

"You enjoy this," Cheriour said after a while.

"*Duh*. It was my job. Once. *Don't move!* I'm almost done with this part." I massaged his scalp, hoping it soothed the ache that accompanied hair detangling. "Y'know, I love your hair. With these curls, and the body, and the *color*—there are so many cool styles I could do! If I had the right equipment. Which, I don't. So you're off the hook."

"You miss it. This job you had," Cheriour whispered.

"Of course I do." I shoved a chunk of detangled hair over his shoulder. "I miss the work. The conversation. *Everything*. You wanna know how many fun stories I've heard over the years? People sat in my chair and *spewed* gossip at me. I swore they thought I was their therapist," I chuckled. "One time, I had a woman ask for an updo because she had a big date planned. Not an abnormal request. Until she told me her husband was away arranging his mother's funeral. The woman used the death of her *mother-in-law* to give herself a fancy night on the town with the guy she'd been fucking on the side."

A laugh rumbled out of Cheriour. It was so soft, so subtle, I almost mistook it for a sound of pain. Except, when I peered at his face, his lips were curled into a smile.

My hands suddenly jittered as I combed his hair. "What about you?" I asked. "This is as close to a salon chair as you're gonna get. Got any juicy secrets you'd like to share? I won't tell anyone. Scout's honor. What happens at the hair salon stays at the hair salon."

"I don't," he said, but his shoulders jerked.

"Liar. Everyone's got juicy secrets. I'd happily share more of mine with you, but our exchanges are always one-sided. My fault. I talk too much. So I'm giving you the floor this time. Fire away. Start with something simple if you're not ready for the heavy stuff yet. Like...your drawings. I won't ask about the Germany one...*yet*. But how did you get into art? Were you self-taught? Or did someone else show you how to draw?"

"Someone showed me."

"And...?"

Cheriour blew out a breath and shifted, stretching one leg out in front of him. "His name was Gowan. He owned a shop in the city where he taught art and sold supplies."

"You guys have an art studio?" I asked.

"We did. It's gone now. This world hasn't always been as you've seen it. People lived in peace, once. For a short time."

There was audible pain in his voice.

I kneaded his scalp, wishing I could do something more to take the hurt away.

"Niall thrived once." Cheriour leaned back, tilting his head toward me, enjoying his mini-massage. "Many of our buildings are now either empty or being used as housing. But they were once shops. Merchants here sold jewels, gowns, books, and art. We also had a dozen winemakers. More than any other city in Sakar."

"Jewelry and wine?" I asked. "You're making the old Niall sound like paradise."

He made that deep, rumbly chuckle again. "It was. During this Renaissance period, Gowan transformed his home into a place of teaching. To advertise his services, he painted a mural on the facade of the building: a field of lavender flowers. This very field," he inclined his head, indicating the dead-ish grass we were sitting on. "I..." There went his mouth again. Turning. Twisting. Searching for words.

I lowered my hands to the nape of his neck, rubbing at the muscle knot below his hairline (Jesus...he was, *literally*, all knotted up), and waited for him to continue.

"I admired the mural," Cheriour said after a long beat.

That word, *admired*, packed a ton of weight. Because there was clearly more he *wanted* to say. Maybe he wanted to wax poetic about how the stunning piece had moved him to tears, but he couldn't figure out how to make those words work. So he'd settled on one. *Admired.*

"Gowan noticed me and offered to teach me how to recreate the image. When I declined," a grin tugged at Cheriour's lips, "he brought his parchments and paints to the castle, where I couldn't refuse him."

"I like this guy." I grinned.

"As did I," Cheriour said.

The past tense word caught my attention.

"He died?" I whispered.

"Yes. Several years ago."

A sharp pang shot through my stomach. Poor Cheriour. His family abandoned him. A lot of his friends had died. He really didn't have anyone, did he? "How do you do it?" I asked.

"What?"

"I mean, look at me. I've been here a month and I'm an emotional wreck. How do you keep trucking along so calmly with all the shit that goes on here?"

"Life continues, even when tragedy occurs. You know this." He angled his head toward me. "Your life has not been without tragedy. I heard you. That night in the forest." His eyes met mine.

My hands paused. "You heard the Freddie Hawkins story?"

Cheriour nodded.

Shame flooded me. Sure, I'd spewed that info voluntarily. But I hadn't actually meant for Cheriour to hear it. "That was a long time ago."

"Perhaps. But it's a wound that still hurts you. And I'm sorry you had to suffer it." His lips contorted as he considered his next words. "We don't get to choose our tragedies. Only how we respond to them. I endure the atrocities of this world because I must. When I become overwhelmed, I draw. It gives me a few moments of peace. Much like fiddling with my hair has calmed you. Although," he grimaced, touching a hand to his side, "have you finished?"

"What? Oh, yeah. Sorry!" I withdrew my fingers from his hair and scooted beside him. "How bad is the pain?" I asked. "Put it on a scale of one to ten again. But give me an *honest* answer this time."

"Six." He winced as he leaned back, unfurling his other leg.

And Cheriour's six was probably an average person's fifteen. No wonder he was still chalk-faced. "Well, your hair looks fabulous, at least." I rearranged the curls over his left shoulder. "Considering I didn't even have a comb, I did a damn good job. Y'know, you should let me braid this." I twirled a strand around my finger, trying to hide how hard my hands shook. Because Cheriour's normally restless eyes were, once again, focused only on me.

Not that I *disliked* the attention. Shit, I'd once done everything short of performing carnival tricks to get him to focus on me. But I'd never considered how *intense* his stare was. How it would make my skin prickle and my insides squirm. Cheriour's eyes didn't just roam over flesh. He didn't ogle me because of my booty and boobs (although I sure *hoped* he liked my assets). His gaze went deeper. Like he was trying to read my mind, feel my emotions...get to the very core of who I was.

It was thrilling. And terrifying.

So I rambled. Trying to distract him and myself. "The braids would keep your hair off the back of your neck. Plus, you'd have the added bonus of looking like a Viking."

Cheriour's eyes moved, traveling along my arm, stopping for a moment on the sleeve of my blue/pink tunic. "You're still wearing this?" he asked.

"Uh, yeah. Did you think I'd go back to itchy wool shirts after having this bad boy on? Hell no." My stomach flipped and flopped, as his gaze roamed over my face, halting on my mouth.

There was a dramatic pause. Like the kind in a sappy romance movie: he stared at me, I at him. The air got all emotionally charged. He had a slack-jawed expression on his face. I trembled.

I leaned in. He swallowed, tongue moistening his lips, and tilted his head...

A full-on electric *zing* shot up my spine.

He drew back.

Bloody bastard.

"I've not told anyone about your immunity to fire," he said.

"Aw hell. You killed the mood to bring *that* up?"

Cheriour grinned. A *full* one this time. A smug-as-fuck, shit-eating grin.

"You jerk," I whacked him lightly on the shoulder, my stomach tingling when he laughed. "You're teasing me, aren't you?"

"A bit." God, he had such a nice smile. The way his eyes crinkled, and those little cheek dimples peeking above the edge of his beard...*swoon*. And he had some seriously decent teeth, considering he lived in a world without toothpaste. Like, his teeth were both whiter and straighter than mine—how was that fair?

"I won't say anything," he continued. "Not until you're comfortable discussing it. This applies to...other things as well."

He didn't elaborate on that last bit. But he didn't need to. The Freddie Hawkins story had probably left him with a gazillion questions.

"Thank you." My stomach quivered. Fluttered.

Cheriour reached out, trailing his rough fingers over my cheek. "I don't understand the appeal of this." He brushed the backside of his knuckles over my arrow industrial earring.

"It's cool. *That's* the appeal."

"But I do like this." He dropped his hand to my left arm, fingers rolling up my sleeve, exposing part of my tattoo. "I don't understand the images," he trailed his thumb over *Iron Man's* helmet, "but I like the colors against your skin."

"Yeah, well, I'm glad I have it. I miss movies. And it sucks that you guys don't know *anything* about these characters, or —ummm..."

Without warning, Cheriour leaned in and brushed his mouth against mine. It was a maddeningly soft kiss. Barely more than a peck. But...oh my God, *yes!*

His fingers were feather-light as they stroked my cheeks, my hair, the sides of my neck, my spine—

I made a (slightly mortifying) gasping noise.

Back rubs had always, *always,* been a weird, non-sexual G-spot for me. I was kinda ticklish there (especially along my spine) so having it caressed made my muscles flutter and left a little *whoosh* sensation in my stomach. I freaking *loved* it. And once Cheriour realized this was my erogenous zone, he didn't let up. His fingers pressed and stroked and scratched, forcing me to arch into him as my body went haywire.

I dug my hands into him too. My left wrapped around the back of his neck, nails grazing his scalp. I smiled when he shivered. The other hand I kept on his face, tracing along his high cheekbones, carding through his beard, circling his ears, cupping his jaw...

"Hmmm..." A shudder ripped through him as a strangled sound escaped his mouth.

Whoomp-Whomp, my heart stuttered.

I'd grabbed a proverbial live wire with my bare hands. My belly quivered; my hands jittered. Cheriour was so damn responsive. So wriggly. So easy to make shudder. I wanted to see what he'd do when I put my mouth and hands on other parts of his body.

The screech made us both jump.

Abby Normal strolled up to the fence and shoved the pig carcass through the slats. A carcass she'd mauled while Cheriour and I were kissing. The pig was in six big, meaty, bloody chunks.

She flattened her ears at me and turned away again.

"You cock-blocking bitch," I murmured.

But the laugh that came out of Cheriour—even if it was cut a little short by a hiss of pain—was so fucking *perfect:* deep, breathy, and masculine. The kind of laugh you could listen to over and over and over again.

I was *so* fucked.

THE THING ABOUT KISSING? It was an addiction. Something about the *swoop-swoop* sensation that left me dizzy for more, or the taste of another person that left my insides knotted and gnawing.

When we walked back from Abby Normal's paddock (after

Cheriour arranged for a plump, live goat to be served as her dinner), I couldn't stop myself. I jogged to Cheriour's side and kissed him again.

I stole another kiss inside the castle.

He stole one in the stairway.

And another in the hallway.

And my lips were still locked on his, even as we entered his bedroom. Where I should've unglued myself and exited stage right.

Because, first of all, the dude was barely back from the dead. Second...his room was major *ick.* And with the way he'd started kissing me back; still gentle, still slow, but with a firmness he hadn't had before...it seemed kinda inevitable we were gonna do *ick* things in his *ick* room.

But I had *some* restraint left. Not much, but enough to steer me away from the bed, which would've been way too tempting (despite the grimy sheets).

I backed against the wall, cursing when I rolled my ankle over some discarded object on the floor, and coaxed Cheriour to lean against me. He dropped his brow to mine, letting his lips touch the tip of my nose, and rested a hand on my hip, his fingers kneading the top of my ass.

Slowly, carefully, I ran my hand over his chest.

His *fine-as-fuck* chest.

I hadn't really paid attention to his body before. Even when he'd had his shirt off, the gaping crater in his side had stolen all the thunder. But Cheriour was *built.* There wasn't an inch of fat to pinch on him. He was all muscle. Not bulky, but long, lean, hard, practical muscle. And *damn* if it wasn't thrilling to run my fingers over the sharp planes of his chest.

He exhaled against my lips as I found his left nipple through the fabric of his shirt and circled my thumb around it. His hips bucked into mine, and his grip on my ass tightened.

He'd braced his other hand on the wall beside my head, but I saw his fingers digging into the stone.

Oooh, he'd be so much fun to get undressed and in bed.

The thought of him, naked, red-faced, straining, squirming...my thighs quivered. There were *things* I wanted to do. I wondered if he'd consent to being tied up. Or blindfolded.

He flinched.

Aw, snap! Had I vocalized my dirty thoughts?

But, no, my hand had just wandered a little too far down his body.

I mean, I couldn't blame it for having a mind of its own. Cheriour's abs were fucking *glorious*. Not the chiseled, washboard abs you'd see Chris Hemsworth touting, but they were firm. And six-packy.

And too close to his injury.

Reluctantly, I let my hand slide away, wrapping it around his lower back instead.

"Listen..." I pitched forward off the wall, ducking my head to the side, evading his kisses so I could nip his earlobe. "If it hurts, or you don't like it, say something. Got it?"

I was so close to him, my lips now wandering down the side of his neck, I felt him gulp.

"Only if you do the same," he said.

"Well, we won't do *that* much." I dragged my teeth along the chorded muscle in his neck, reveling in his shudder. "I don't want Quinn hunting my ass because you had a heart attack during sexy—oooh. Damn, that tickles!"

Cheriour wormed his hand in between us and made a slow pass over my stomach.

He wouldn't find a six-pack there. I was more like the Pillsbury Doughboy: squishy and pokable.

A low laugh reverberated through Cheriour before he *fucking poked* me. Right above my belly button.

Because *of course* I'd blurted the Pillsbury thing out loud.

So, to keep my disobedient mouth occupied, I latched my lips to his neck and sucked. Hard.

I felt his groan. That sucker came all the way from his toes. It was deep. Low. Almost a little pained, but not in a *bitch, you're smashing my wound* kinda way. More like he was straining for something just out of reach.

Hot. Hot. Hot.

I nipped at him, savoring the salty tang on his skin, the way his beard and hair brushed against my face, and his earthy scent—which was sweeter than it'd been before. Less oniony. He'd likely taken a quick sponge bath after waking up.

Why did that thought turn me on goddamn much? Why did *everything* about him turn me into a horndog? I was trying to give *him* the world's biggest hickey, but *I* was the one shaking. Sure, Cheriour responded with low grunts, letting me know what he liked, and what he *really* liked. But he was still mostly steady.

As for me...my muscles vibrated so hard, I wondered if they would burst out of my skin.

I gave him one more not-so-gentle suck, reveling in the strangled sound that reverberated through his chest, and pulled away.

It was meant to be an *okay, time for a breather* moment. But he interpreted it as his turn. And how could I tell him no?

I smacked the back of my head against the wall as Cheriour turned his mouth to my neck, very obviously mimicking what I'd done to him. But softer. Slower. He suckled deeply, but not harshly. His teeth never did more than scrape. Everything was light. Measured. Careful. I'd left marks on his neck, but he would leave none on mine.

And it was *insane* how quickly I lost my mind.

"*Fuck!*" I raised a hand to my brow, my fingers clenching

my own hair as he pressed kisses to the outside of my ear. His beard tickled. His mouth burned. And his eyes kept watching me in that intense/impassive way of his. Like he was studying something under a microscope.

Or, more likely, he was trying to figure out what *I* liked.

It was too much.

But also...not nearly enough.

Jesus, I needed to get off this fucking wall before I lost my shit...

Cheriour suckled along my collarbone while his hand slipped under my shirt.

Too late. My shit was lost.

I made an embarrassing moan when he twirled his callous roughened fingers over my belly button. I wanted him to dig those fingers in. And move them. Up or down, I wasn't fussy.

He nipped at the curve of my shoulder, that laugh rolling through him again when I made another awkward noise.

I stood up on my tiptoes, itching to shove him toward the bed.

Instead, I tugged at my hair again, relishing the pain. The distraction.

That live wire I'd touched earlier? My hand must've gotten glued to it. Because the shuddering wouldn't stop. Electricity ran in currents through my veins, needing, pleading for an outlet for...for...

I bucked my hips into his, heard his sharp intake of breath, and I couldn't stop. My hands twined around his back, grabbing at his hips, his ass, his upper thighs. Everything was rock solid. I might as well have been grinding myself against the statue of David.

Except, I didn't think the statue of David could make the same soft hums Cheriour made.

The statue of David also wouldn't be languorously humping me back, while suckling at my earlobe.

I whimpered when he hit a *good* spot.

He paused, his deep (and only slightly unsteady) breaths caressing my cheek, and cupped my chin in his palm, his thumb tracing my cheekbone.

And the fucking *look* on his face as he stared down at me...

The horny guy expression (pupils blown wide, jaw kinda slack, brows furrowed, stare all intense and smoldering) was always a major turn-on for me. I loved seeing a guy writhe.

But this was different.

Cheriour's eyes were placid. Happy.

I reached for him, caressing the scar around his left eye. The skin there was puckered. Rough. Almost leathery. And the scar ran right across his eyelid. Whatever had cut him had gotten *extremely* close to blinding him.

Cheriour leaned into my palm, his breath tickling the inside of my wrist, and closed his eyes. He looked less horny (despite the taut lower half of his body) and more ready to zonk out.

Relaxed.

He was *utterly* relaxed.

Cheriour never let his guard down. Ever. He'd fought tooth and nail to stay semi-conscious even when he was *dying*. It was overwhelming to see him lower those guards, even if only for a moment, while wrapped in my arms.

It almost made me cry.

Cheriour huffed, his laugh a raspy sound, as he kissed the heel of my palm.

And then he moved again. Again. And a fucking third time. It was just right, but also not even close to what I needed. He applied enough pressure to put me on the edge, but not enough to send me on the nosedive.

With another low chuckle, Cheriour lowered his head, nuzzled the collar of my shirt aside, and got a good (almost harsh) bite. All while driving his crotch into mine *yet again.*

"Fuck!" I hissed.

He smiled.

But he also flinched when I started to get too rough. When I tugged at his shirt, desperate to touch his skin, to lick every nook and cranny of his six-pack abs. To get my hands on his bare, statue-esque ass. And to definitely, 100%, get my fingers and mouth on his, *erm,* more private parts.

But his small, micro-flinch brought me up short.

I wanted *everything.* Like, I wanted to see if I could get him to yell.

But not because he was in pain.

And, if we kept going, he would be in pain. He'd try to hide it, sure. But he'd hurt all the same.

And rutting against the wall, while clothed, having to be careful not to hurt him...it wasn't how I wanted to do this. Uh-uh.

I touched his chest, my palm flattened. A *stop* motion.

He paused. And drew back.

"Okay, so apparently, it's been way too long since I've had sex." My laugh sounded forced, even to my own ears. "And PMSing gets my hormones all screwy. And I don't wanna hurt you. So this has to stop here. At least until you've healed. But, look, I don't want to leave you with blue—"

Cheriour's mouth covered mine, this kiss sweet. Calming. And then he stepped back, giving me space to move away from the wall.

But, before I could crack my terrible "blue-balls" joke, Cheriour asked, "Where is your poleaxe?"

It took me a second to process that one. Because my gutter

brain thought he was talking about some weird sex toy. "Er...huh?"

"Your poleaxe," Cheriour repeated in a bored, droning tone. "Where is it?" He wasn't even breathing heavily!

Meanwhile, I billowed like a racehorse and still daydreamed about him naked, strung up, and losing his composure.

Bad brain. Bad!!

"Um...I think it's in my room." I said.

"Have you cleaned or sharpened the blades?"

"Was I supposed to?"

"Yes. It does not take long for a blade to go dull. Go get it. I'll show you how to care for it."

"How is this what you're thinking about right now?" I gaped at him. "What're you, a freaking robot? You flip a switch and *bam,* horny time's over?"

He gave me an unreadable look.

And I knew him well enough by now to understand what that stare meant. "*Fine.* I'll go get it." I still felt too hot. Too winded. Too scatterbrained. And he looked too goddamn composed. I *hated* that.

I gave his ass a hard pinch as I walked by. His very *un*composed reaction was music to my ears.

44

FREAKING STUBBORN, MACHO MEN

ADDIE

Cheriour was a *total* snuggle bug.

He had one leg draped over mine, his arm over my chest and his chin on top of my head. His breath fanned my hair. Which was nice. I loved a good cuddling session. For a while.

But now I was roasting.

Sweat dripped down my back, plastering my shirt to my skin. But Cheriour looked so freaking adorable. I didn't want to push him off me.

He'd fallen asleep with his arms convulsing, trying to pull me closer (not possible). And now he had this little grumbling snore going on. Which was super endearing coming from a guy usually so schooled, strict, and regimented. So, yeah, I didn't want to ruin the moment. At least not yet.

Dim moonlight spilled through his bedroom window, casting shadows over the piles of clothes, weapons, and papers sprinkled across his floor.

His pigsty room was even more chaotic than normal. After our horny wall-hump session, Cheriour had tossed more shit around, searching for something to sharpen my poleaxe with. Because, y'know, that took priority over him resting.

My poleaxe had freshly sharpened blades. So did his knives. And his leather holsters had all gotten a good polish. The room was wrecked. But Cheriour was finally, *finally* resting (although he'd nearly passed out before I could convince him to lie down).

Freaking stubborn, macho men.

And now *I* couldn't sleep.

Cheriour's room was on a lower level, so it came with more city noise: people talking. Animals screeching, braying, or cock-a-doodle-dooing.

It wasn't the sounds that kept me awake, though.

I stroked the back of Cheriour's hand, smoothing my fingers over his rugged skin. Small white scars scattered across his knuckles. His pointer and middle fingers had ugly black spots beneath the nails, and his ring finger had no nail. His thumb was crooked, like it had been broken, but not reset, and had healed at a funky, cock-eyed angle. He had the ugliest freaking hands I'd ever seen.

But I couldn't stop touching them.

He was, without a doubt, the stinkiest mofo I'd ever shared a bed with.

But I didn't mind the B.O. musk anymore. It suited him.

How the fuck had this happened?

I traced a scar on his wrist.

My heart kept doing funny things. Not the fluttering it did when I saw a hot guy. No. The organ seemed...*heavy*. Like it had somehow inflated and was now too big for my chest.

And the sound my pulse made in my ears, like a boiling teakettle...

Wait.

Shit, that wasn't my heart making those noises.

A sudden, chilling scream rose from the city streets. My blood turned to ice.

A moment ago, the light coming through the window had been dim and gray. Now it morphed into a bright, flickering haze. The faint scent of smoke curled around my nostrils.

Fire.

"Cheriour..." I had to swallow a few times to get my voice working. "*Cheriour!*" My hand shook as I jiggled his shoulder.

He lazily opened his eyes, took in the murky orange light splashed across the walls, and untangled his limbs from mine.

More shrieks filled the air.

Cheriour said something as he pulled his boots on, but his voice seemed far away. Meanwhile, the yells grew louder and louder and...

"Addie." Cheriour gave my arm a rough shake. "Put your boots on. Now." He plucked them off the floor, pressing them to my chest, before he turned and peered out the window.

Outside, a man yelled, "Get the 'orses out!"

Another man bellowed, "The roof is collapsing! We can't get to 'em!"

I envisioned horses swirling in their stalls, whinnying in fear as flames drew closer.

White spots flashed before my eyes. I didn't realize how much I was swaying until my ass smacked the ground—I'd slid right off the bed.

"Addie." Cheriour's hands curled around my upper arms.

"W-what's—" I started.

The harsh clang of a bell had me sucking in a sharp, unsteady breath.

"*Seruf!*" Someone bellowed. "She's here!"

Seruf. I'd heard that name before...

"They call her the Firestarter," Cheriour said. "She's a Celestial."

How the *fuck* was he calm right now?

My hands shook so violently, I couldn't get a grip on my boots. But his fingers remained steady as he took the shoes from me and pulled them over my feet. He spoke with a droning, placid voice. "Addie, listen to me...Niall is going to fall tonight."

"W-what?"

"Seruf is here. The city *will* fall. You need to leave. If you can." He moved about the room, gathering knives and swords and strapping them to his vest. Then he flung my holstered poleaxe over my shoulders.

Outside, a woman wailed.

Her voice blended with the ringing in my ears.

I swayed, knees sagging. Cheriour gave me a not-so-nice tap on the cheek. "Addie. *Focus.* I can't help you escape. I must lead the soldiers against Seruf."

"But—you—you told me Niall's going to fall!"

"It will."

"Then—ain't that a suicide mission?"

"Yes."

I gaped at him. He was so nonchalant. *"Oh yes, I'm gonna lead a group of people straight to death's door. No biggie. Just a regular Thursday night."*

"If we all flee," Cheriour said, "we all die. But if we slow her down, some may survive. You are going to run."

"Run," I scoffed. "Run *where?*"

"Sanadrin."

"Okay. And? Did you forget *they* got attacked last week? What happens when Seruf rolls from Niall to Sanadrin?"

"You keep running." Again, a very blasé response. "Keep living. For as long as you can." Cheriour grasped my wrist. There was a slight tremor in his fingers now, but I wouldn't have noticed it if he didn't have such a death grip on me.

Before I could say anything else, he charged out the door, dragging me behind him.

It was stiflingly hot outside. Probably because, y'know, the *entire fucking city was on fire.*

Orange flames reached the sky. Houses blackened and crumbled. People dashed, desperate to either save loved ones or rid themselves of smoldering clothes. The piney odor of smoking wood filled the air, combined with the potent scent of pork chops. Anguished wails ricocheted off the stone streets.

My breath stung like acid trickling down my throat. The ringing in my ears intensified—although it didn't drown out the cries of a mother who'd lost her child.

"Eanna!" the woman screamed, crawling on her stomach toward a collapsed house. Her legs were mottled and blistered, burnt right to the bone. "Eanna!"

A man lifted her off the ground, pulling her away from the blaze.

"My son!" she kept saying. "Don't make me leave him! *Eanna!*"

Now it felt like acid was burning a hole in my gut.

I knew her pain well. The fear and isolation of being unable to do *anything* while a loved one perished. Sometimes I swore it was better to be the one burning alive. Because that excruciating pain had an end. But surviving a fire, and watching someone else die, was an agony that lingered forever.

"Blake!" Cheriour galloped down the castle steps, shouting instructions. "I need you to organize a group and go to the eastern side of the wall," Cheriour told the tall man. "Do *not* let them pass through—force her army to the main entrance. Mollie! You do the same with the western side..."

He turned his back to me. Because he'd already given me my order: *run.*

But how could I?

Hundreds, *thousands*, would die tonight. These were *good* people. Brave people, willing to fight even when they had no hope of winning. Because their sacrifice would (maybe) allow others to live.

Meanwhile, I was gonna run? To save my own ass? Was I really that selfish?

"I suppose this is goodbye, then." Belanna rushed by me, securing her bow to her back with short, jerky movements. "It was nice to have met ye, Addie," she said as she hopped down the rest of the stairs.

"Belanna!" Cheriour spun to face her. "I need you and the rest of the archers to stay back. It's too late for you to be on the wall—"

With an earth-rumbling groan, a nearby building collapsed. It'd been a three-floor house. The sounds of terror from the people still inside were swallowed up in the rest of the pandemonium.

Fire destroyed everyone and everything.

Except me.

And I suddenly knew what I had to do, even if the notion scared me shitless.

"Oh fuck it all to fucking hell," I hissed as I stormed down the steps.

"We've done this before. None of you are novices!" Cheriour continued calling commands to the group of stoic, but frightened soldiers in front of him. "Anyone with a polearm needs to be *in front*. Addie—that does not include you. Addie!"

I steamrolled past him, marching toward the first house in the city.

How fireproof was I?

A bonfire had been one thing. But could I walk into a burning building, with no protection, and emerge unscathed?

404

Only one way to find out, right?

Don'tpukedon'tpukedon'tpuke.

My stomach crawled up my throat as I unsheathed my poleaxe and barrel-rammed it into the door. It took only two hits for the charred wood to give way.

Flames billowed around me, dancing across my skin. Smoke tickled my nostrils. But I didn't burn. Or choke. Actually, breathing seemed easier now. Like the vapor nourished my lungs, rather than damaged them.

I moved further into the house, watching as tongues of fire creepy-crawled up the walls and across the floor.

"Hello!" I yelled. "Is anyone in here?"

For a few seconds, the only response was the low hiss and pop of disintegrating wood.

But then someone started hacking up a lung.

I turned. A man crawled on his hands and knees toward me.

"Hey! I'm here!" I ran to him, using my poleaxe to knock debris out of my way. "I've got ya, buddy. Hold on." The man yelled when I grabbed him beneath his armpits and hauled. He gagged once, twice, vomiting all down his front.

I gulped to keep my stomach in place. "You're alright, buddy," I said as I hefted him toward the door. "Just a little more...yeah, keep coughing," I added when he sputtered. "You inhaled a shit ton of smoke. Gotta hock it all up. Ah, look at that! We're already at the doorway. You're gonna be okay. Some cool compresses and aloe vera'll work wonders for those burns."

Out the door we went, the man going limp as I pulled him to the center of the street. "C'mon, dude." I released his arms and hit his cheeks, hard, until his red, teary eyes opened. "You're safe! Don't die on me now—"

Hands closed around my arms, whirling me around.

Quinn's shocked face was only inches away. He stared at me like I was the Oogie Boogie.

"You might wanna do your Vulcan Mind Meld thing," I said, my voice only a little shaky. "This guy's alive, but he's in bad shape."

Quinn opened his mouth. Closed it. Opened it again. Closed it again. "You—you—" his eyes looked ready to bulge out of his head.

"Yeah, yeah. Looks like I am a hybrid after all," I said. "Whoop-de-fucking do. But it means I can help. I can get people out of these buildings."

Over Quinn's shoulder, I saw Cheriour, still assembling his soldiers by the castle steps. He turned to look at me, a brief smile touching his lips, and nodded.

Quinn's hands slid away from my arms. "Go," he said.

I didn't need to be told twice. The quicker I moved, the sooner I could put this hell night behind me. Right?

Right??

I sprinted from building to building, busting down doors, walking through flames, and searching for signs of life. If I found people alive, I dragged them to the street, where Cheriour had assembled a group of soldiers to help me.

"I've got her, Addie." Braxton took a little girl out of my arms. Poor kid. She wasn't in bad shape, but her mother...

Well, tearing a terrified child out of her dead mother's arms wouldn't go down as the highlight of my life.

"Bless you, Addie," a bald guy said a few minutes later as I handed a heaving man over.

I didn't know how long this rescue mission took. Minutes. Hours. I was trying not to think about it. Thinking would've led to fear. Or doubt. And I didn't have time for that shit. So I pushed myself forward. Even as my boots and breeches went *poof*, putting my pearly white legs out on full display. The leather harnessing had bubbled away, but my poleaxe was still intact, although the blades were a-cookin'.

But my blue/pink shirt? Still cool to the touch.

Celestial-made shirts were the freaking *bomb!*

I'd have to ask Cheriour what this thing was made of. Assuming, of course, we both survived this nightmare.

"Hey, kiddo...what'ya say we get out of your parent's hair. Huh?" I plucked a toddler out of his cradle. His parents were in the other room, both dead. The little boy was unconscious, but still alive. His shallow breaths brushed against the side of my neck as I clutched him to my chest and booked it out the door.

"Gah!" I grunted when my toe caught on something solid. And mushy. And wet.

A body lay in a crumbled heap in the middle of the street. Blood pooled around it, still warm. My bare feet slipped as I staggered back.

I knew this body.

My gut churned.

"Garvin?" I whispered.

His head sat two feet away from his torso, but it was him.

"*Fuck.*" I clutched the little boy closer to my chest as I peered through the black smoke, looking for a Wraith, or a hellhound, or...

"So, they sent you after all."

A woman's voice drifted over to me.

I spun, nearly falling on my ass when I lost my balance, as a figure emerged from the smoke. A woman—and a damn pretty one at that. Perfect hourglass figure. And she wore a gauzy scarlet dress that accentuated *every...single...curve.* Shimmering black hair lay over her shoulder, twisted into an intricate braid. Her red-painted lips curved into a coy smile.

It would've been enough of a red flag to see this runway-ready model strolling through a medieval slum. But y'know what made it ten times worse?

Two expansive red-and-black wings unfurled from behind her back. Those suckers had to be at least fifteen feet from tip to tip, if not more.

"You've gotta be fucking kidding me." How was this my luck? *How?*

The woman—obviously a Celestial—smiled again and took another step toward me. "Welcome home..." She paused. Beamed.

And, as I opened my mouth to shoot a snarky retort, she shocked the *hell* out of me.

"Adelaide." My name, my *full* name, sounded like a purr as it rolled off her lips.

45
RUN

Darragh and Jaxon returned to escort me out of Lamex. I saw them for only a moment, staring at me in repulsion, before Byron pulled a burlap sack over my head.

"Take her into the forest," Byron instructed as he tied a rope around my hands.

"How far?" Jaxon asked.

Byron tugged at my arms when I reached for the sack, attempting to free my mouth. "You'll leave that on if you want to stay ~~concious~~—conscious," he hissed before saying to the men, "One day's walk. Be sure she doesn't know how to return to Lamex."

"And if she looses 'er power?"

"Do what you must to ensure she doesn't."

For twenty-four hours, we walked. Jaxon, again, held my bound hands. Darragh kept a sword pressed to my back. Neither spoke, and their tension seemed palpable.

"This should be far enough," Darragh said after the long stretch of silence.

The sound of his voice startled me.

"Ach." Jaxon, mistaking my flinch for an attempt to flee, jerked on the rope. "No, ye don'. Ye'll be free to go soon, mind, but we'll no' have you followin' us through the forest."

The rope around my wrists tightened with a painful snap. My knuckles scraped against hard tree bark.

"Ye'll have to untie yerself," Jaxon said. "Or simply use yer power and burn the rope away. But know ye'll be noticed, and hunted, if ye destroy the forest."

They left me tied to a branch of that birch tree.

And, as my wretched flame never appeared when I most needed its help, it took more than an hour of fiddling to undo the knot.

I was left with a three-day ration of food and water. Nothing else. No weapons to hunt with, no additional clothing. Not even a pair of boots.

Thus, I walked.

I had no destination in mind; merely the notion that moving was preferable to standing still.

And I was hunted.

Even when I delved deep into the forest, where the thicket of barren trees barred the sun from casting its light upon the ground, soldiers relentlessly pursued me.

I LAY flat on my belly, hidden beneath a bush, while two women roamed the clearing.

"Byron's a fool," one said as she knelt to inspect the ground. Looking for my footprints, no doubt.

Fortunately, my bare feet left shallow impressions that were quite easy to cover up.

"He fears Seruf," the other woman commented. "And did not want to bring her wrath upon his people." Her fingers cast a luminous glow in the dark wood. She was a hybrid—an Illuminator.

The light tore at her skin, creating shallow fissures that oozed blood. But she did not allow her power to dim as she searched through the tree branches.

I flattened myself to the ground, burying my nose into the soft soil, struggling to keep my breathing even and slow.

"But he had her *contained*," the first woman spat in disgust. "If he'd *questioned* her, perhaps he would have found a weakness—"

"We do not yet know the connection between Seruf and her pet." The Illuminator's light seeped through the foliage. "Likely Byron thought freeing the girl would draw Seruf's gaze away from Lamex. Perhaps he chose the right course of action, perhaps not. Time will tell. I only hope the girl is found before—"

The light pierced my bush, nearly blinding me. But my whimper of fear was suppressed by the Illuminator's cry of triumph.

"She's here!" The Illuminator tore through the spindly branches of the bush and grasped my tunic. She dragged me across the ground, ignoring me when I yelled and thrashed and pleaded.

"Cara!" She called to her companion. "Hurry!"

My skin prickled. The ~~salivia~~ saliva evaporated from my tongue. "Don't do this!" I begged. "Please!" The itch grew sharper. Burning. Maddening. As it always was before the flames emerged. "I don't want to hurt—"

But it was too late.

As the other woman rushed forward, her sword raised over her head, my skin burst into flames. The more I writhed, desperate to distance myself from the women, the more incensed my fire became.

My flailing arms brushed a strand of the Illuminator's dark hair. She howled as the flame latched on, spreading across her scalp and down her face. The other woman faltered, lowered her sword, and rushed to her companion's aid.

"Leave me!" The Illuminator wailed. Her skin bubbled. The sulfuric scent of burnt hair filled the air. "Get the *girl!*"

My fire roared across the ground, ~~ravenisly~~ ravenously devouring everything in its path.

Including the two women.

In the aftermath, I sat beside their smoldering remains, shaking. The fire had long abandoned me, but it still pulsed through my veins. Impatiently awaiting its next meal.

MEN AND WOMEN continued to roam the woods, searching for me. The Firestarter, I'd been dubbed. The *"girl wearing a Celestial's garment."*

As my beautiful, shimmering tunic did not blend with the colors of the forest, I rid myself of it. Burying it, because I could not bring myself to destroy it.

It pained me to throw dirt over the beautiful fabric; Terrick's gift to me. The only thing I had left of him.

I stared at the swaying trees encircling the tunic's resting place. "Guard this for me. Please," I beseeched them. "Keep its location hidden. Safe. I'll come back for it one day."

I memorized the clearing, and the path I took away from it, fully intending to return.

But I never did.

Of course, burying the tunic may have helped conceal me from my hunters, but it further exposed me to the elements. Thankfully, the weather remained mild; winter had not yet taken a firm hold of the land. But insects feasted on my blood and left painful welts all over my body. Some plants were coated in poisons that left me covered from head to toe in hives.

"Look at the leaves, *lass,"* the memory of Terrick's voice gently chided. *"The ones that shine or grow in clusters of three mean you harm."*

I'd forgotten much of his teachings. I'd been so young when we spent that summer in the woods. The memories had mostly faded, but they began to trickle back as I navigated the forest, desperately evading my captors.

Days passed in a slow trickle.

And my hunters were never far away.

"So you 'eard the story from Charlie, who 'eard it from Lola —who 'appens to be a scandalmonger, mind," One man called out as he stood beside the fallen log I'd burrowed myself into. Quite an ingenious hiding spot: the thick oak wood concealed me. I'd only be discovered if a person dropped to their hands and knees and peered into the shallow opening, which was partially submerged in a muddy puddle.

The unfortunate aspect of being so close to a pool of stagnant water were the bugs. Small insects hummed ~~incessintly~~ ═incessantly around my ear. And this man, so intoxicated he could no longer speak without slurring, had decided the puddle was a perfect location to defecate. The putrid odor rising from his feces made my eyes tear.

His companion, too far away for me to hear clearly, responded.

The man beside my log laughed. Rather perfect timing, as my stomach chose that moment to give a tremendous heave in protest of the stench. But my soft, dry gag went unnoticed.

"You can drink fresh, running water, lass." Terrick's voice echoed in my mind. *"But the water from a stagnant pond will make you ill."*

I'd never fully comprehended how revolting a stagnant body of water was until that moment. For there were no waves or currents to remove the feces. It merely stayed where it landed, festering, and contaminating everything around it.

"Has Seruf truly arrived in Sakar?" the man asked, still chuckling. "Or is Lola merely spreading 'er rumors?"

The conversation from that point onward centered on Lola, and the way she used her plentiful bosom when she wanted to beguile soldiers into giving her information. There was quite a bit of talk of her bosom. At least until the man finished spewing his toxic odors and stood, pulling his trousers over his hips.

I saw his knife fall, and I stopped breathing as it landed with a *plop* in the murky water.

"For feck's sake!" the man knelt to retrieve his blade. His eyes flashed as he caught sight of me, huddled in the log. "You bloody—" he snatched my legs. "Hiding now, are you? Waiting for—*oof.*"

I swung my arm, my knuckles catching the side of his throat, winding him. As he wheezed, I slithered out of the log, landing in the water with a splash.

Water. I gasped in relief. The itch rippled across my skin as the fire thundered in my veins. But it did not emerge. It couldn't. Not while I was submerged.

"You fecking *bitch!*" The man seized a fistful of my hair, dragging me out of the puddle.

"Stop!" I clawed at his hands. "Leave me in the water!"

The man shoved me backward onto the ground and wrapped a lock of my hair around his fist. "Hmmph," he grunted as he twisted my neck back. "They didn' say you was pretty."

I disliked the hungry look in his eyes as he gazed upon my bare flesh.

His hand stretched toward my chest. "If ye can keep that power of yours contained for five minutes, I'll let you leave. Ten minutes, and I'll hide your trail." He winked.

His ~~callis~~—callous-roughened hands hurt when they touched my skin. His breath smelled of ale and decay.

The fire inside me roared.

"Remember, lass," Terrick said, *"When you hunt, be sure to kill the animal quickly. If your initial wound wasn't fatal, find the beast and end its misery. There's no need for any creature to suffer."*

I burst free of the man's hold and grasped his face in my flame-wrapped hands. And I felt no remorse when he cursed and bawled. Instead, the sounds incensed me to keep clutching onto him until he perished.

A quick death. As Terrick had taught me.

There was also no shame in me when I repeated my actions with the man's equally odious companion.

So this is to be my fate, I thought glumly in the aftermath.

To be hunted. To kill those who wished to kill me. And to repeat the horrendous process each day until I perished.

THE NEXT DAY, I took shelter inside a yawning tree hollow as yet another group of hunters approached.

"It took Seruf a mere *hour* to breach Darfield's borders." A boy said in a hushed whisper as the soldiers rode their horses past my tree.

Darfield.

I trembled as I pressed myself to the back of the tree trunk.

"How?" A woman asked. "Darfield has one of the largest hybrid armies in Sakar. *And* the protection of a Celestial."

"Aye. Maya said Ellard Fell," the boy said grimly.

Another woman gasped. "Is she certain?"

"She seemed to be."

"It—but—how is that possible? Without Ramiel—"

"Who's to say he's not accompanying Seruf? Even if he's not been seen yet," the boy said. "And with Seruf's hybrid on the rampage..."

I could barely hear the next words over my booming heart.

"We need to find that hybrid," the woman snapped. "Before she kills us."

But they didn't find me. Not that day.

My stomach soured as the riders continued their trek, and the nausea persisted even after they'd disappeared.

Darfield. It wasn't a coincidence Seruf had attacked my old home.

I wondered what had happened to the blue-eyed boy. Quinn. Had he perished in battle?

Tears filled my eyes. I hope he had—a quick, painless death. For that was preferable to being turned into a Wraith, the fate that surely awaited any living soldier defeated by Seruf's army.

MORE DAYS PASSED. The cooling autumn breeze carried whispers of pain. And fear. The animals must have sensed it too. Birds stayed closer to their nests, no longer singing their morning tunes. Rodents scurried to safety, only emerging to gather food. Squirrels huddled in the trees. Deer traveled in tightly knit groups. Even the predators seemed reluctant to emerge from their dens and hunt.

On some afternoons, the sound of my bare feet shuffling through the leaves seemed deafeningly loud in the quiet woods.

A chill seeped into my bones. A deep, bitter cold. Accompanied by a pain I knew well.

Fever. Hardly a surprise, given the recent torment my body had endured.

Walking became a tremendous struggle. Each step was ~~monumentous~~—momentous, as though I were climbing a mountain, rather than trekking across mostly flat terrain. My vision worsened; even objects directly in front of me seemed unfocused. Breathing brought a sharp, stabbing pain to my lungs.

Soon, that pain turned liquidy (is this a word? Liquidy —*watery?*), as though someone had filled my chest with molten metal.

I began coughing.

The fits hit suddenly, with little warning, and often left me doubled over, struggling to inhale.

Still, I moved forward, choking on great mouthfuls of blood and mucus. The ~~flem~~ (goodness, is this a word? I believe it is).

~~Phlem~~—Phlegm filled my throat and airways, making it impossible for me to take a breath. And when air wormed into my lungs, it rattled the hot liquid inside my chest and created another fit.

My ailing body could go no further.

And that afternoon, as I lay shivering, despite the relative warmth of the day, my arduous journey ended.

Rough fingers clasped my shoulders. Metal coiled around my wrist. Hands scraped at my raw skin as I was flung into a saddle.

"If you burn my horse," a woman warmed me as she settled herself into the saddle behind me, "or *me,* I will slit your throat. Do you understand?"

I nodded as I stared at the horse's gray mane. "I don't want to hurt people."

The woman made a sound of disbelief.

"Truly. I-I—have you ever lost control of your stallion?" I asked. The horse's muscles quivered beneath me. He fidgeted and ground his teeth against his bit. All signs of a high-spirited animal. And given his impressive height and strong legs, I imagined he was a powerful runner.

"Javen is well trained," the woman said.

"Perhaps now," I said. "He wasn't always. I'm certain he's taken you—perhaps merely at a faster pace than you expected."

"Of course." The woman tightened the reins when the horse began bobbing his head in earnest.

"Then you're well-~~aquainted~~—acquainted with the sensation of having a beast that is both larger and stronger than you take any illusion of control you thought you had. That is how I feel when my wretched power surfaces." Tears sidled down my cheeks. "It is an unbridled stallion, wreaking havoc as it thunders through the land. And I am a rider, strapped to its back without the means to halt it. I've no wish to hurt people. But I cannot stop myself from doing so." I turned, although the woman remained a blurred figure on the outskirts of my damaged vision. "Kill me. Please. It's the only way to guarantee I won't harm anyone else."

"If it were up to me, I'd bleed you out here and now. You're a wretched creature who doesn't deserve to draw breath. But," the woman clicked her tongue and shifted her legs, urging the stallion into a trot, "we need answers about your master."

So I was to be tortured. Again.

The thought did not fill me with fear or dread. It only left me exhausted. "You're making a mistake," I whispered.

Of course, I didn't know the full gravity of that mistake. Not until several days later.

46

SHITFACED SHUFFLE

ADDIE

"How do you know my name?" I stared at the woman —Celestial—as she took another step. That sloshy, sea-sick sensation had returned to my stomach.

If she had called me *Addie,* I might've had a nonchalant *"who the heck are you?"* response.

But for her to call me *Adelaide...*

Only two people had ever called me by that name.

My mom. *"That's it! Go straight to your room, Adelaide. If it's not clean in the morning, you've lost your Kandy Kakes for a week."* That had been one of the last things she'd said to me.

And then Freddie Hawkins entered the chat; *"Adelaide. Such a pretty name. Rolls right off the tongue, don't it?"*

Otherwise, everyone called me Addie. I even used my shortened name on all legal documents (license, passport, etc.).

So how in the heck did this Celestial figure out my full name?

She didn't respond. Her wings shimmered in the flickering firelight as she smiled.

"Answer the damn question!" I bellowed.

Okay, so yelling at a winged creature wasn't a bright idea. Especially when I saw how she used those wings. I expected her to flap them; like a bird. And she did...*kinda*. But she didn't lift off from the ground. No. Her wings twitched, the glistening feathers made a soft ruffling sound, and she *poofed*—disappearing in a haze of black smoke.

Only to reappear two inches from my face.

"Gah!" I flung myself backward. But my feet got tangled around each other and I fell. Hard. Pain rocketed up my spine, shooting into the back of my head. *Goddamn.* Tail bone = broken.

But the bigger issue? I'd lost my grip on the kid and my poleaxe. The weapon clattered a few feet away. The poor kid hit the ground right at the Celestial's feet.

She scooped him up, clicking her tongue and tilting his head from side to side as she examined the burns on his face and neck.

"Put him down!" I scrambled back to my feet.

"Poor thing." She stroked the boy's cheek. "He's inhaled quite a bit of smoke. His lungs are damaged."

"We've got a healer," I said.

"Yes. *One* Healer. Tell me, Adelaide, do you think your healer can help all the injured here? All the dying?"

"Umm, yeah. All he's gotta do is tap his finger and *voila...* patient's all better." My belly squirmed as I lied.

The Celestial tutted in disbelief and glanced at the boy again. "I love children," she purred, stroking the boy's face.

That sounded...not right. At all. Way too sensual. "You a pedo or something?" I blurted.

"They're so innocent," she continued. "Naïve, even. Precious."

"Sounds like something a pedo would say." Disgust bubbled in my stomach when she pinched the boy's cheek.

"Children are the best parts of humanity," she said. "They embody everything you are meant to be. *Before* you age and sully yourselves. And I don't relish killing children, but sometimes..." she rested her hand against the kid's face. Gaudy gold rings glittered on three of her fingers. The ruby jewels on those bands seemed too big to be real. Like costume jewelry.

They glimmered when flames burst from her fingertips.

"No!" I screamed. But it was too late.

The little boy was incinerated. His skin blackened and his eyes melted. Juices seeped from beneath his still-closed lids. He never woke up. And I hoped, *prayed*, he'd already been too far gone to feel pain. Because, my God, what a horrible way to die.

Bile left a foul, metallic taste in the back of my mouth. "You're Seruf," I said. "The Firestarter."

"Goodness, do they still call me that? *'The Firestarter?'*" Seruf emitted a fake, tinny laugh before she opened her arms and dropped the tiny, charred skeleton to the ground. "There. he'll not have to suffer anymore."

"You fucking bitch—" I started.

Seruf was suddenly on top of me, one hand stretching toward my face.

"Don't!" I spat.

But she was too fast. Her (surprisingly cool) fingers brushed my skin in an almost gentle caress. Meanwhile, her other hand grabbed my arm, holding me still with a bruising grip. "The last time I saw you," her apple-scented breath fanned over my face, "you were barely older than that wretched boy. You were so *beautiful*. It's a pity you had to grow up."

"Age is a bitch, ain't it?" My words sounded steady, even as my brain zoomed at warp speed. The last time she'd *seen me?* I'd never laid eyes on this whacko before.

Seruf cupped my chin. A flash of orange danced at the bottom of my vision as flames erupted from her fingertips again. But the fire did not burn me.

Seruf smiled. "I knew we'd see you again, Adelaide."

"Seriously, what are you—"

She clamped her hand around my jaw, almost causing me to bite my tongue off when my teeth snapped shut. "Luckily," she tapped her fingers against my lips, "I saw you dashing through the fire. You would have been killed if I hadn't been here."

A movement over her shoulder caught my eye. Another figure slithered through the smoke. It was human-shaped, like the Wraiths, but twice as terrifying. Its neon-yellow eyes radiated through the smog. Greenish skin stretched across its gangly frame. And big ole pointy spikes stuck out from its shoulder blades.

"Isn't she fortunate, Gabriel?" Seruf turned to beam at the creature.

Gabriel didn't smile back, thank God. His dagger-sharp pearly whites were freaky enough when he *wasn't* smiling.

"He would've slaughtered you," Seruf continued. "But I stayed his hand."

Gabriel's right arm shook. I glanced down as he drew the bleeding appendage behind his back.

There was no hand there.

His left arm had a hand—a gnarled one with long-ass fingernails. The right didn't.

"You nixed his whole hand?" I blurted.

"It'll grow back," Seruf responded brightly. And then she chuckled. "That face... darling, is this the first Fallen you've seen?"

Fallen??? Fallen from where? *Zombieland?*

"Oh, it is!" Seruf chirped. "Gabriel, dear, come over here. Let her get a look at you..."

The creature shuffled forward. He looked even fuglier up close. The fluttering light cast dark pools of shadow on the dips in his craggy, pewter-green flesh. He was buck naked too; his junk wobbling lifelessly like a flag on a windless day. And he had a thick layer of angry-looking scars coating his skin.

He was terrifying.

But I pitied the poor bastard. No idea why. Maybe because of the way he walked; hunched over, eyes on the ground. He looked defeated. Depressed.

"This is Gabriel," Seruf said. "Our oldest Fallen."

Hang on...

My brain was running a little slow, but the gears started grinding. *Gabriel.*

Wasn't that the name of a prominent angel?

My insides soured. "He's a Celestial. Or he *was.*" A Fallen Celestial...just when I thought I'd seen all the weird shit this world had to offer.

Seruf's eyebrows shot up. "Very good." She gave my lips another affectionate tap. "It's quite fascinating to watch you think—do you realize you verbalize your thoughts?"

Aw hell. I needed to start super-gluing my lips together.

Seruf grinned and leaned a little closer.

Yeesh. Did she wanna kill me or kiss me? I was getting some mixed signals.

"I'll not kill you," Seruf murmured. Because (surprise, surprise) I hadn't kept my thoughts to myself. "But you'll also not receive another kiss from me." She winked.

"*Another?* What are you...?" I trailed off as another shadow moved through the streets, behind where Gabriel stood. Green eyes peered at me through the smoke.

Cheriour.

My racing heart hit the brakes. Hard. *No. No, please. Stay away!*

"Anyway, Gabriel..." Seruf turned.

Thank *fuck* Cheriour was quick. He scuttled out of her line of sight.

"Do you understand now why I reacted as I did?" Seruf asked Gabriel. "Look at her, my dear. Do you know who you nearly killed?"

Cheriour's shadow shifted again, crouched low to the ground.

Go away! I bit my lip, hard, to make sure I didn't start pleading out loud.

Sure, Cheriour was a phenomenal fighter, but he was alone. And already wounded. He didn't stand a chance.

I couldn't, *wouldn't,* watch him die.

I had to do something. Fast.

But what? Seruf stood right on top of me, her bony hips pressed against mine. I didn't even have enough room or leverage to bitch slap her. Besides, there was the fact that she was, y'know, *not human.*

Cheriour shuffled closer, still down in an almost animalistic crouch, his knife clutched in his right hand.

Do something! My mind screamed, even as I dug my teeth into my tongue. *What are you good at? Talking. Start freaking talking!*

"Where'd you get that dress?" I blurted.

Seruf's brow furrowed. "Pardon?"

"That dress." I dropped my gaze, letting my eyes travel over the gauzy material. "It's *gorgeous.* I mean, I wouldn't be able to pull it off. Clingy dresses aren't always flattering on us curvy people. But you've got the body for it! Hmmm. So where'd you get it?"

Seruf stared.

"Where I come from, this is a compliment," I blathered on. "It gives people a chance to show off. Especially if they're bargain hunters. Like, *'oh, I found this at the thrift store and it's a designer dress.'*"

Seruf's nose crinkled in befuddlement. Gabriel stood behind her, eyes still down. Neither of them had noticed Cheriour.

The problem?

He crept closer. And closer. They would eventually see him.

"Or!" I exclaimed. "Sometimes people like to open up about bad experiences. Like, *'yes, I got the dress from here, but...* stay away!' Y'know? Because some places sell pretty stuff, but they're dirty and they'll *rake you over the coals.* Literally."

Cheriour glanced up.

Okay. I had his attention. Now...

"Fuck!" I screamed when he threw a knife.

His aim was perfect; the blade sank between Seruf's shoulder blades, right by her wing joint. And, based on her reaction, that was akin to kicking a Celestial in the balls.

She doubled over, gaping. Like the wind had puffed right out of her sails.

"Bitch." I shoved her away from me and dove for my poleaxe.

Gabriel dove for me.

We collided and went down together. Him on top of me, the poleaxe just out of my grasp.

"Ekk...no!" I slapped the back of his knuckles when he dug his sharp nails into my stomach. "No...that's rude. You don't grab a girl without her—gah!"

He grasped my thigh, clawing at my bare skin.

"Don't harm her!" Seruf rasped as she stood upright. She ruffled her wings, knocking the knife (and a few feathers) loose. And then she *poofed* again.

"Cheriour! Look out!" I cried.

But, as Gabriel raked my upper thighs, Seruf reappeared beside Cheriour and kicked his legs out from under him. A nauseating *crack* echoed as at least one of his bones broke.

"Why do you fools do this?" Seruf shoved Cheriour down. He didn't cry out or give any indication of pain, but I saw it in his face. In the way he squeezed his eyes shut and cradled his mid-section as he hit the ground. And I couldn't go to him! Not with freaking Gabriel holding me down.

"We cannot be killed by your weapons. When will you learn..." Seruf paused with a strangled gasp when Cheriour looked up at her. "*Brother?*" she whispered.

Brother?

"Get off, get off!" I played whack-a-mole with Gabriel's fingers, smashing or biting at them every time he touched me. He never flinched, even when blood oozed from the lacerations I left on his knuckles. "Get off!" I yelled. "Fucking—*holy fucking shit!*"

Gabriel suddenly sprawled sideways when Seruf shoved him out of the way.

"What a night this has been!" She plucked me off the ground. I was no lightweight, and she held me by the scruff of my neck like I weighed no more than a kitten.

Her wings fluttered.

We *poofed* across the street—where Cheriour lay on his side, wheezing.

And traveling through the *poof*...holy crap, it was awful.

In one way, it reminded me of the night I'd stumbled upon a playground while doing the shitfaced shuffle from the bar to my apartment. Drunk me had been helpless against the allure of a twisty tube slide. The problem? I wasn't a kid anymore. Not even close. I *barely* fit. And the hard plastic squishing my body from all sides as my skin made a *squeeeak* sound...

Combine that, with the stomach-left-behind sensation you'd get from a drop ride, and that was how I felt *poofing* from one end of the street to the other.

I clenched my jaw as my stomach took a few seconds too long to catch up. "That would've been a ten-foot walk! Are you really that lazy?" I snarled at Seruf.

Seruf *tsked*, cupped my cheek again, and turned to Cheriour.

He'd pulled himself back into a crouch. Sweat trickled down his pale face. Blood oozed from the wound at his rib cage. A lot of blood.

"You know," Seruf curled a strand of my hair around her finger. "I don't believe you know who you are."

"The name's Addie Collins," I said through gritted teeth. "You want my dating profile? '*Likes fast food and fun times. Hates long walks outside. But is always up for sex on the beach—the drink and actual activity...*'"

"Darling," Seruf gave an overdramatic sigh, "I'm worried about where you've been these past few decades. You speak quite a bit of nonsense. Anyway," she trilled, "this has been a night of great fortune indeed! My brother is finally going to receive punishment for his crimes." She waved cheerily at Cheriour before draping her arm over my shoulders. "And I'll make sure he confesses to the nasty secret he's hidden from you."

47

UV BAR UP THE ASS

ADDIE

"Umm, *what?* Y'know what, just get *off* me!" I jabbed an elbow into Seruf's ribs.

With a melodic laugh, she tightened her grip on my shoulder. She didn't even flinch. "Shall I explain? Cheriour..." she stopped, frowned, and *poofed* to Cheriour's side, wrenching a knife out of his left hand. "That's quite rude, brother," she tossed the blade away and twisted his hand backward. The bones sounded like a freaking gunshot when they broke.

"Stop!" I screamed.

Cheriour drew in a sharp, whistling breath and closed his eyes. His face contorted in pain.

"As I was saying," Seruf *poofed* back to my side and grasped my shoulder. "Cher—"

I cut her off. "Cheriour?" I whispered to him.

He breathed raggedly, head bowed, shoulders shaking. He didn't look at me.

Pain lanced my chest.

"Yes, *Cheriour*," Seruf cooed. "*Tut-tut*, don't fret so much, darling. He won't die. Not really." Seruf's apple-scented breath tickled my nose when she turned to face me. "You see, he was a Celestial. Once." She let out an obnoxiously flirty giggle.

"The heck are you smoking?" I grunted.

"Hard to imagine, isn't it?" Seruf said. "He's quite pathetic now. But it's true."

I stared at Cheriour, expecting him to shake his head, huff and puff, or strike his *Lord give me strength* pose.

He did nothing. Said nothing. His eyes remained focused on the ground, his shoulders shuddering as he panted.

"Do you know what makes the Celestials what we are?" Seruf continued in her sing-song voice. "Essence."

"Like the makeup brand?" I blurted. "And here I thought you had naturally luscious lips."

Seruf gave a long-suffering sigh. "It's our *soul*; one personally crafted by the Creator, and far more potent than any human soul. Celestials without Essence are pathetic creatures." Her lips curled into a superior smile as she *poofed* back to Cheriour's side. He hissed when she combed her fingers through his hair. "They're *worse* than humans." She drew her arm back, whacking him across the scruff of his neck.

He crumbled.

My heart hammered. "Cheriour!"

Slowly, he pulled himself back into a sitting position. He still wouldn't look at me.

My mind raced through every interaction I'd ever had with him, combing over each minute detail. There was *nothing* to back up Seruf's crazy claim.

Except the drawing. The canal at Monschau, Germany. A place that didn't exist in Sakar. A scene Cheriour should *never* have been able to draw with such precise detail.

Unless he'd been there before.

"It's true, isn't it?" I asked.

A chunk of hair fell out of his ponytail, obscuring a part of his face as he nodded. He looked so damn small, huddled beneath the crumbling city. Vulnerable. Helpless.

A yawning pain stretched across my chest. Tears blurred my vision. "I don't care," I said, both to Seruf and Cheriour.

"Pardon?" Seruf was beside me again, tracing her fingers along my arm.

"*I don't fucking care,*" I snapped. "Did you think this big reveal would make me feel betrayed or something? We've all got dirty secrets. His are just...*different* than most."

Seruf shrugged. "I only wanted you to know the truth." She twirled around me, a smile dancing across her red lips, her fingers trailing along my collarbone.

"Yeah, right," I scoffed. "You *wanted* to upset me. You manipulative—"

Seruf abruptly reared back with an agonized screech.

Cheriour staggered to his feet, his broken fingers curled awkwardly around a second, teensy dagger. He yelled when he threw it—an animalistic roar of pain.

Thunk.

The dagger sank into Seruf's back. She howled and twitched, her feathered limbs flailing as she fought to dislodge the knife.

"Cheriour!" I darted to his side, wrapping my arm around his midsection as he swayed. My shoulder screamed as he leaned his full body weight into me.

"Gabriel!" Seruf screeched. "Go kill the insolent *bastard!*"

"Don't you fucking dare," I hissed as Gabriel shuffled toward us. "You creepy motherf—"

Hoofbeats thundered through the streets.

Gabriel and I both looked up. He scrambled forward with a croak but wasn't fast enough.

Abby Normal body-slammed him. It was actually comical

—like something you'd see in a movie: the villain blasted right out of his shoes.

But watching him getting trampled beneath her hooves was less funny, especially with the way he cried. And, when Abby Normal circled back to him, her red eyes rolling in their sockets, and buried her fangs into his chest...

Nope. Not funny anymore.

But Cheriour laughed. "Belanna," he slurred. "I asked...to loose Púca...before..."

"Dude, you're making zero sense," I grunted as he sagged against me, his body vibrating.

A few feet away, Seruf continued shrieking. Both of Cheriour's blades were jammed into her left scapula. She couldn't get either out, no matter how she flailed or thrashed.

Her blood glowed as it oozed along her feathers. Literally. The silvery liquid was as bright as any LED lamp.

"You need to go, Addie," Cheriour panted.

"Good idea." I hefted him onto my shoulder. "Let's get moving."

"You go," Cheriour hissed. "*You.*"

"I will. With you limping right along next to me."

"No."

"Brother!" Seruf bellowed. "How *dare* you—I'll make sure you suffer!"

Cheriour weakly shoved himself away from me. His knees buckled.

"Stop with this self-sacrificing bullshit." I snatched his torso, gripping his blood-soaked shirt. "I ain't leaving. Get that through your thick head, okay? I *won't* leave you."

His eyes rolled back.

"Shit!" I clutched at his shoulders, his hips...any part of him I could find. But he'd fainted. And I wasn't strong enough to carry him.

He hit the deck in a heap.

Seruf whirled toward me, her luminescent blood puddling on the ground around her feet. "Darling..." her attempt to revert to a sing-song voice backfired. She sounded like a demented wind-up doll. "I won't make...suffer." Her voice warbled and echoed, as though there were a dozen versions of her screeching at once. "... pain... no less than he deserves..."

Why was her voice doing that? She was talking gibberish!

"But you...attached...so grant...mercy." More unintelligible words. And her skin turned translucent, as though someone had shoved a UV bar up her ass and illuminated her insides.

"Step aside..." Seruf blathered. "...get it over...rise again..."

I scrubbed my hands over my ears.

My palms tingled. So did my ears. And the back of my neck. It was a burning itch that made me want to peel my flesh off. Like that time I'd used Nair and had an allergic reaction.

The fuck was happening to me?

I rubbed my wrists together, desperate to relieve some of the irritation.

Seruf stepped forward, stretching a hand toward Cheriour.

"Stay away from him." I shimmied in front of his prone body.

Now *my* voice echoed.

Seruf took another step, leaving glowy footprints on the ground.

"I said *stay away!*" I snapped.

At this, Seruf sighed, her happy-go-lucky facade slipping, and spewed more rubbish.

The light under her skin got brighter and brighter. And a sound pierced the air; a ringing in my ears, but worse. Because it was more like *shrieking.*

Pain ricocheted around my temple. The prickling itch under my skin intensified.

She moved closer, her wings still spasming.

I threw my hands out, instinctively trying to push her away. But then my hand sank through *her chest.*

"Gah!" I squealed when my wrist disappeared inside her glowing boob. "The f—"

A jolt of electricity shot through my veins.

The screaming got louder. Disembodied voices swirled around me.

"Seruf!"

"Please don't!"

"Help!"

"How were we defeated at Sanadrin? You had best fix this, Seruf—"

"You monster!"

"—or you'll join the humans."

"He was only a child!"

WHACK!

Seruf's hand connected with the side of my face.

I staggered back, my hand slipping out of her boob. My cheek burned. One of her rings had caught me beneath my left eye. Blood trickled from the wound.

"You—" Seruf's face paled. Her lips trembled. Tears glistened in her eyes. "How *dare...*"

She was so flabbergasted her mouth quivered.

I wasn't doing much better. My muscles jittered and my heart felt maxed out on caffeine and ready to have palpitations.

I stared at my convulsing hands. The fuck had just happened?

"Seruf!"

I whipped my head to the side when Gabriel cried out. He'd gone rigid; barely able to move his lips.

Abby Normal stood over him, her fangs buried in his chest as she lapped at his blood. "Seruf, please!" he called.

Seruf, breathing shakily, turned. Another fireball flickered above her palm as she gazed at Abby Normal.

No! Fear grabbed my stomach in a painful cramp. I didn't think twice before I shoved both hands into Seruf's glowing boobs. And I clutched on even as a proverbial nuclear bomb exploded in my chest, sending burning toxins through my bloodstream. Even as Seruf walloped my cheek again, and again, and again. I closed my hands into fists, held on, and went for the trippiest ride of my life.

I plummeted into a whirl of colors, sounds, and images.

Voices rang in my ears. Too many and talking too fast for me to understand. Figures danced before my eyes: people, burnt and dying. Crying children dressed in fine silks.

There were so many fucking kids.

A dark-haired man screamed as his black-and-red wings (identical to Seruf's) were hacked off with a knife.

And...*Cheriour!*

I saw him for a split second, but my heart almost did a full cartoon leap out of my chest. He was younger here and his curly hair was short, barely touching the tips of his shoulders. His face was clean-shaven too—he had a dimpled chin!

But then he vanished.

A young girl sat before me. Her honey-brown hair fell over her shoulder in one big, matted clump. She was buck naked, and almost skinny enough to pass for a Wraith. Her shoulder bones looked like daggers jutting out from under her skin.

She turned. And I gasped.

The girl had purple eyes. Almost exactly like mine.

"Who—" I started, but then she *whooshed* above my head and disappeared.

The dark-haired man returned. He huddled over his disembodied wings as he rocked back and forth.

His howl blended with a swirl of other pained cries that encircled me.

My stomach heaved. This was like a bad amusement park ride. No, it was like being *drunk* while on a bad ride. I didn't know which way was up, down, straight, or sideways. People twirled across my vision from all angles. The cries, shouts, and pleas swamped my ears. I had no freaking clue where they came from. Time escaped me. Had I been in here for seconds, minutes, hours, or days? No idea. I might've been trapped there for years.

I wanted off this damn ride. *Needed* off, before I upended my guts. But how? How the heck was I supposed to stop this? I didn't even know what *this* was.

A scream rose, shriller than the others. Clearer. Automatically, I moved toward it, wading across rows and rows of corpses. Waltzing beneath snarling Wraiths and galloping Púcas. Stepping on naked, wailing, terrified children.

Jesus. Guess what was gonna haunt my nightmares for the rest of my life?

Colorful wings brushed against my arms, feet, head, and shoulders. Glistening buildings sprouted above and below me.

All the while, the singular scream persisted, still rising above the cacophony of chaos.

Invisible quicksand ensnared my feet. But I grasped onto the shrill scream like a lifeline, pulling myself along, wrenching my feet loose...

"Don't!" Seruf's voice echoed inside my head as the scream reached a crescendo.

"Fuck off," I grunted. My thighs burned as I trudged along.

"I'll take you home!" Seruf exclaimed.

A sudden image flashed before me. One I recognized all too well: the (modern-day) New York City skyline.

I paused.

"Come back," Seruf pleaded. "I'll take you home."

"Why should I believe you?" I snapped, although the whirlwind stole my voice.

"You don't belong here," Seruf said. "And you needn't die here. Come back. Allow me to take you home."

Home.

I wanted to believe those words. Desperately. I *hated* living in Sakar. I wanted to get back to 21st century life, where there was edible food, good drinks, decent medicine, and coffee to go.

The step back was a lot easier than the steps forward had been. There was no quicksand behind me. Only in front.

I shifted back again.

Home.

No more fighting.

Home.

No more trying to treat critical injuries with dingy clothes and questionably clean water. No more sitting by someone's bedside, praying I'd done enough to keep infection away, but knowing I was probably going to watch them die.

I took another step back.

The shrill scream lessened and became lost in the noise.

The people dancing across my vision blurred, becoming more unrecognizable as I continued backtracking. Their voices faded too. Even the colors had muted.

But then I saw Cheriour again.

He was still young, but his long hair hung loose and dirty around his shoulders. A dingy gray shirt billowed around his thin frame. He staggered; his beautiful green eyes dull as they sluggishly surveyed his surroundings.

I stopped, reaching for him, but he *whooshed* to the side and disappeared.

"Darling," Seruf purred at me.

If I went home, Cheriour would die. So would everyone else in Sakar. I couldn't save them. And I knew that. But could I go back to my happy life knowing they had suffered?

"It's alright," Seruf cooed.

"Fuck this shit." I plowed forward through the quicksand.

The shrill scream grew again. It pierced my skull. Ruptured my eardrums. I squeezed my eyes shut, clapped a hand over my ears, and kept going.

"Don't!" Seruf moaned.

The quicksand thickened. Every step became a laborious effort. My lungs burned and my head seemed ready to split in two.

Around me, voices boomed, louder than before.

"Seruf, Guardian of Earth," a man called. *"You are accused of performing unspeakable atrocities on mortal children and using the gift the Creator bestowed upon you to harm those that oppose you. You are, henceforth, banned from the Celestial City, and your Essence will be removed..."*

"Darling," Seruf's frantic voice raked across my brain. "Stop! You don't know what you're doing!"

A man slithered in front of me, staying only long enough for me to glimpse his lush auburn hair and the blinding white wings protruding from his back. *"Our Brother's punishment was far too harsh,"* he said. *"You do not deserve to Fall, Seruf. Come with me. I shall help you right this wrong."*

"Adelaide!" Seruf screamed. *"STOP!"*

A claw wrapped around my skull, squeezing my brain through my eyeballs. I ground my teeth, took another step, and...

Silence.

I stood in the middle of a cavernous room. Sunlight spilled through the arched windows on the left side. The floor was a bright prism tile that got rainbowy in the light. The white walls twinkled. Silver rhinestones bedazzled the furniture. Even the slippery silk sheets twinkled. It looked like *My Little Pony* had spewed rainbow sparkle shit all over this place.

"Where?" I started, but a strangled sob had me spinning around.

A woman sat huddled on the floor by the windows. The gossamer curtains brushed the top of her head as a breeze trickled into the room.

"Who are you?" I asked.

The woman lifted her head.

Seruf.

Her red-rimmed eyes glowered at me. She had her knees drawn to her chest, hands clasped around them.

"The hell?" I mumbled.

Seruf scoffed. Sniffled. "Congratulations," she said hollowly as she rose to her feet. "You've won."

"W-what—"

"You've *won!*" she spat, flicking tears off her face.

"The hell are you—?"

Seruf lunged, her eyes rolling in their sockets, her pale lips drawn over her teeth in a grimace. "Do you know what happens to the Fallen? The ones that *lose* their Essence?" Spittle flew from her mouth. Before I could respond, she continued. "They're mortal. And then they do what all mortals do. *Die.*" A bitter laugh tumbled out of her. "The cough took Gabriel. *Tuberculosis.* After a mere two years. But as he's not human, he can't *truly* perish. He suffers, dies, and rises. Again, and again, and again. Gabriel is a wretched creature, trapped between life and death. *That* is the true curse of the Fallen." Her smile was pure evil.

A chill raced along my spine. I was suddenly seized with an urge, an *itch,* to dig my fingers into her face and rip her smug grin off.

"Once Cheriour's heart stops beating, he'll rise again too," Seruf gloated. "But he won't be the same. Oh no, no, no." Her eyes bugged out of her skull.

My breath hitched. "He's not dying tonight."

"If not tonight, then tomorrow." Her smile widened. "Or the next day. Death is inevitable. He'll join Gabriel before long."

"Shut up!" I yelled.

"He may not recognize you when he rises..."

"Enough!"

She barked out a laugh. "You humans love tragic love stories, do you not? Well, now you're living in one."

"I said *shut up!*" Black spots erupted across my vision as I pummeled her face.

She didn't stop me. Didn't defend herself. Just took the open-handed hit and cackled as she spat out a mouthful of radiant blood. "Do it again."

"I—what?" My palm stung. I had to shake my hand a few times to get the tingly feeling out of my fingers.

"Again!" Foam bubbled over her lips. "You have my Essence." She leaned back, arms stretched wide, gesturing to the Unicorn-Poop room. "*Destroy it.*"

"You are making absolutely no sense...gah!"

With a banshee scream, Seruf grabbed my ankles, her nails cutting deep into my calves.

"Are you fucking crazy?" I roared, stumbling back.

"Would you like to know about the children?" Her eyes rolled. Her teeth bared. She looked like a rabid animal. "You didn't like seeing them, did you?"

Ice slid into my belly.

"Didn't like their screams?" Seruf sank her teeth into my shin, cackling when I yelped. "Well, I *do*," she hissed. "There's nothing more erotic than a child's—"

Rage blinded me. I saw big, crimson blobs as I snatched Seruf's hair, ripped her head back, and smashed her nose. Not once. Not twice. *Three times.*

She laughed. And laughed. *And laughed!* Even as blood spumed from her broken nose, seeped from her eyes and dribbled out the corners of her mouth. "Well done," she rasped. "It's only a pity I won't get to see what this does to you."

A thunderous explosion rocked the room. With a *crrraccck,* the windows shattered, sending a cloud of splintered glass toward me.

"Holy shit!" I ducked, raising an arm to protect my face.

But the glass never hit me.

Instead, I stood on wobbly knees, staring at the smoldering remains of Niall's city. I didn't think I'd ever actually moved. Not physically, at least.

I glanced at the smoke-covered sky and ruined houses. Garvin's corpse still lay a few feet away. Abby Normal still hunched over Gabriel's rigid body, watching me speculatively, her ears pricked.

Cheriour was still behind me. Still breathing, albeit shallowly.

Panting like a winded elephant, I turned my gaze to Seruf. My hands were still inside her chest.

She stared blankly back at me, a white film covering her eyes.

"W-w-what was—*what the frick?!*" I squealed.

Seruf's skin shriveled. Her bones crumbled. She turned to dust, disintegrating right before my eyes.

I stared at my outstretched palms as black powder (her

ashes) swirled over my skin, some bits getting stuck in the hairs on the back of my hands.

What in ever loving *fuck* had just happened?

I didn't realize I'd spoken out loud. Not until an unfamiliar voice behind me answered.

"You destroyed her Essence."

48

VAPORIA

LASS

I was dreaming.

I stood in a smoldering city. Billowing clouds of smoke hung over the houses. The wind caressed my cheek, bringing with it the smell of ash and incinerated flesh. The scent of death.

These streets were unfamiliar, as was the majestic white castle that stood gallantly in the distance. Yet they *seemed* familiar, as though I'd visited this place before. Perhaps in another dream.

A woman stood before me, her golden hair cascading over her shoulder. I never glimpsed her face, as she kept her back toward me, but I approached her gleefully. As though she were an old friend, one I was intimately ~~aquainted~~—acquainted with.

This woman was a stranger.

Yet I was so excited at the prospect of seeing her, of speaking with her, that I sprinted the last few steps. Her name rested on the tip of my tongue—and I was certain it was her name, even if I'd never uttered the word before.

The wind blew again, harsher this time.

The golden-haired woman vanished.

But the odor of smoke and death only intensified. And soon the familiar sound of wailing accompanied it.

I lurched forward, crying out when I found myself falling, my body plummeting for what seemed like an eternity before I hit the ground.

Above me, a horse snorted, and the echoing sound of hooves against hard dirt struck close to my ear. The animal had very nearly trampled me.

Such a shame it missed.

"The girl!" Someone called, although their voice seemed far away. "The bloody horse ran off!"

I wrenched my eyes open and coughed, spitting out a mouthful of dirt. It took several tries to lift myself off the ground—my hands were bound, and my muscles weak. The change in height as I went from lying to sitting left me winded.

Smoke curled through the air. Heavy, black smoke, too thick to see through.

I squinted, a sliver of fear striking my gut.

I'd lost control of my power again, hadn't I?

The surrounding shrieks deafened me but I saw nothing through the plume. I didn't know how many people were suffering. Hundreds, perhaps thousands.

My stomach ached. Would the fire ever be satiated? Even my fever hadn't dampened its appetite.

A shadow caught my eye, and I turned as a woman staggered into me.

My heart leapt and I wondered—*hoped*—if this was the golden-haired woman from my dream. But sadly, 'twas not. This woman had a mane of dark hair. I recognized her.

My captor.

I'd spent the last three days riding with her as I drifted in and out of ~~consiousness—conciou~~—consciousness. Every time I woke, she threatened to kill me.

"If I see but a wisp of smoke," she had snarled, many times, "I won't hesitate." She punctuated her words by pressing the flat side of a steel blade to my throat. Even while riding on a briskly jogging horse and holding my prone body steady with her right arm, it took her a mere second to draw her knife.

Of course, when I asked her to follow through with her warnings, she refused. "We need you alive. But *I* want you to feel the pain you've inflicted on others." And then she would dig the edge of the blade into my neck, my shoulders, or my arms. The shallow cuts drew blood but were not enough to end my life.

I was, after all, labeled as Seruf's pet. An evil, inhuman monster that needed to suffer.

And now this woman, who'd once happily lashed at my skin, grasped onto my shoulders, her eyes wild with fear. She breathed almost as poorly as I—her every inhale a long wheeze.

"You should have killed me," I told her.

"What?"

"You should have killed me!" A salty tear splashed across my lips. "You buffoons simply won't *listen*. You insist on keeping me alive, threatening death, but failing to deliver it."

"What are you blathering about?" she snapped.

I gestured wildly to the vapors surrounding us. "How many times must I repeat myself? I *cannot* control my power!" Yelling made my lungs burn, so I quieted my voice. "Killing me won't save this place, but it will prevent this from happening again. Stop making empty promises and *do it*."

The woman opened her mouth but paused as the screams swelled around us. The noise seemed almost tangible; as though I could stretch out my hand and physically grasp a person's pain.

"This wasn't you," the woman said.

Surprisingly, her words did not bring relief. "It wasn't?"

"No. This is Seruf's work." Unshed tears made the woman's eyes glisten. "Vaporia's streets were ablaze before we crossed its borders. You didn't do this. But you do not burn. And you claim you are innocent. If you've no wish to harm people, *help* them." She knelt before me. The wind blew her hair across her face, causing several strands to stick to her tear-streaked cheeks. "The citizens of Vaporia are dying; many are trapped inside their homes. The fire spread too quickly. There was no time for them to evacuate. But you *don't burn!* You can save some of them. Prove your innocence," she whispered, "and I'll free you."

Truthfully, it was tempting to use my ability for something good. Perhaps the act of valor would have eased some of the guilt I'd been carrying with me.

Perhaps not.

Saving a life wouldn't change the fact that I'd taken lives. Many of them.

"And if I were to lose control, what then?" I fought to steady my voice. "Will you kill me? Or continue to make empty threats?"

She swallowed. "Well, you could hardly do more damage—"

"I certainly could." A bitter sensation coiled in my chest. "Some may yet have a chance to escape and live. I can ensure no one survives."

The woman's breath hitched. "You would damn them all to die?"

"You would have damned me to a fate far worse." My vision grew so blurry, the woman was reduced to little more than a shadow. "You used me as a scapegoat, an outlet for your own fears and shortcomings. You've hunted me. Tortured me. Despised me." I wiped the moisture from my eyes. "And now you want me to show compassion for people who would have gladly seen me suffer? I will not. I have *never* worked for Seruf. But I will not protect you from her wrath."

"You insolent wench!" The woman reached for her knife.

"Kill me. I'm begging you to," I taunted.

She paused, shaking her head. "No. I will not grant you that wish. I'd rather you *suffer*."

"Then leave me." I shrugged. "Or stay if you'll not be satisfied until you see me in pain. But I, as you already pointed out, will not burn in this inferno. You will."

She stood and stepped back, her eyes roaming around the towering flames encircling us.

"You all wished me to be a monster," I said. "And I'm tired of trying to convince you I'm not. So a monster I shall be."

A gust of wind caused glittering embers to rain down upon us. The cinders evaporated off my skin but left welts on the woman's exposed flesh.

She gave me one long, frightened look before she ran.

Her sudden departure wasn't a surprise. Death by fire is one of the most ~~excrutiating~~—excruciating ways to perish. Or so I've been told.

Perhaps I'd been foolish in letting my anger best me. Perhaps the woman would have upheld her end of the bargain and granted me ~~leinceny~~—leniency if I'd saved some of the townsfolk.

Even if she had, my freedom would've been short-lived. Because humans never changed. They feared what they didn't understand, and that fear drove them to cruelty.

My life stretched before me as an endless cycle. I would live in peace, for a time. But the fire would take control again. It would kill again. And I would be hunted. Until someone else made an offer of peace and began the cycle over.

I was tired of traveling around that eternal loop.

So I made it stop.

And I felt nothing as I listened to the people of Vaporia die.

Perhaps my body was too weary to process emotions. Or, perhaps, their accusations had been right, and I'd never been fully human. I was merely a creature with fire in my veins and a heart made of coal.

I sat, listening to their cries, their shouts, their pleas, and I watched as the fire crept ever closer to me.

Flames can be quite tranquil, can they not?

I'd never noticed before because I'd always regarded them with terror. But, as I sat there, in the middle of a dying village, I found peace. There was something soothing in the scintillating light. The smoke billowing around me seemed to be a healing balm. The more I inhaled it, the less my chest ached.

Time slid away. I might've sat there for moments, or hours. Or longer.

The wails of the dying faded. The crackling hiss of smoldering wood rose.

I tucked my legs into my chest as the flames drew ever closer, bathing my feverish skin in a glorious heat. I stretched my hands forward, desperate to feel more of its warmth.

The last time I'd reached for a flame, I'd been a child.

"You must never go too close to a fire, love," Mama had said as she placed a damp cloth over my burnt hand.

The scars from that day were still visible; small circles of puckered flesh on the tips of my pointer and index fingers.

Now, of course, the flames danced merrily over my skin, leaving me unscathed.

What would Mama have thought of me, if she'd lived long enough to see me become what I was? Would she have still loved me, despite the lives I'd taken? Or would she have turned on me, as everyone else had?

"Child."

The voice that spoke to me was gentle. But the smoke was now so thick, I could barely see the tip of my own nose. I certainly could not discern the speaker amongst the heavy clouds.

Anger coiled again. Had I not made it clear I wanted to be left alone? "As I've explained already," I snarled, "I will not save you from Seruf's fire. Your time would be best spent escaping the city. If you can."

A soft chuckle swirled around me. "Oh, my child, I have no wish for you to rescue the humans. You wouldn't be able to anyway. There is no one left to save."

Unease unfurled along my spine. The speaker was too calm —her voice filled with too much mirth. "Who are you?" I asked.

She didn't respond immediately. Instead, the smoke dissipated, as though it had been commanded to retreat. The swirls thinned, allowing me to glimpse the woman standing before me.

Except she *wasn't* a woman.

Two ~~volumous~~—voluminous black and red wings cascaded down her back, the feathers shimmering like a liquid pool. She wore a magnificent gown made of a silver material that radiated through the darkness. Her teeth, when she smiled, were rather unnatural—far too white and straight.

Something cold and dark grasped my insides. I did not need her to introduce herself. I knew who she was. "Seruf," I said.

"Indeed." She smiled as she surveyed my bare, unburnt skin. "My dear child...I thought I'd never see you again."

49

PRESS HERE TO DEACTIVATE YOUR STARK RAVING MAD ANGEL

ADDIE

I turned and the earth immediately tilted sideways on me. *Timber!*

My ass smacked against the ground. A ringing sound started in my ears, getting louder as the edges of my vision got fuzzier.

A man stood in front of me.

The dude was hunk-a-licious. Tall and broad-shouldered, with short auburn hair and azure blue eyes. He had some big ole dimples in his cheeks when he smiled. Add in his gray three-piece suit (complete with navy blue tie) and he checked all the boxes on my *perfect specimen I'd like to fuck* list.

Not that I *wanted* to fuck him. But he was the type I typically drooled over.

But y'know what ruined the whole package?

His dazzling, snow-white wings.

Did I want to deal with another Celestial? *Hell. No.* Especially after—

Well, I still had Seruf's ashy remains on my hands. I'd killed her. No clue how. But I had.

Addie Collins: Celestial Killer.

I turned my face into my elbow when the stale bread I'd had for dinner *squish-squashed* around my stomach.

"Adelaide," the male Celestial tucked his hands into the pockets of his slacks, "you're more magnificent than I dreamed you would be."

"Oh, fuck off," I slurred. A nasty, metallic taste seeped across my tongue and wouldn't go away, no matter how many times I swallowed.

"Do you know what you did?" The man had a thousand-watt smile as he hiked up the legs of his pants and knelt, looking me in the eye.

"Yeah. I 86'd your girlfriend." I rubbed my hands together, watching as a cloud of ash plumed into the air. It was meant to be a threatening gesture. Like: '*see, this is what awaits you if you don't buzz off.*' But it made my hands shake harder.

"You took her Essence. And then you *destroyed* it," he said. "I admit, I didn't think you'd be capable of it, but you far surpassed my expectations."

I frowned. "You stood by and *watched* me kill your girl-friend? Didn't even try to save her?"

His smile soured. "Seruf has been unreliable of late. The, well, the *small* pleasures she indulged in—"

"Oh, *gag me!*" I groaned as images of those scared, crying kids flashed before my eyes.

"—began to interfere with her work. This was her last chance for redemption. If you hadn't destroyed her, I would have taken her Essence myself."

His handsome face swam in and out of focus as the vise around my skull tightened. And I *recognized* him—he'd appeared at the tail end of Seruf's trippy glowing boob tunnel. "Who are you?" I asked.

His wings twitched, feathers gleaming, even in the smoky haze. "Ramiel," he said.

"Oh, fuck my fucking luck."

"Come now," Ramiel said lightly as he stood. "I'm not as terrible as the humans have made me seem." He turned, his eyes catching on Abby Normal. A drawling smile stretched over his face.

She made a nervous sound, her tail flicking, before she turned and bolted.

With a snobbish laugh, Ramiel moved to Cheriour's prone form.

"Don't!" I tried to stand, but my body said, *ehh, not a chance,* and I sat back down with a huff.

Ramiel bent, tapping Cheriour's shoulder. "Cheriour and I never saw eye to eye," Ramiel murmured. "He was Raphael's understudy, so I'm not surprised he still holds a disdain for me, but it is rather disappointing." He stood. "Let me guess: he painted a portrait of me as a mad king and told you to hone your powers so you could *'free the people from my oppressive grasp?'"*

"Er...kinda?" That conversation with Cheriour had been, what, a month ago? He'd said something about a feud between Ramiel and his brother, but I honestly couldn't remember the details. "But...Cheriour didn't even know I had powers until a few days ago."

Ramiel scoffed, putting his hands back in his pockets. "He knew. At the very least, he suspected."

My stomach squirmed. I couldn't think straight, not when it felt like my brain was being squeezed through my eyeballs. "You made the Wraiths," I blurted the first piece of information I could remember.

"I did. And you know what Wraiths are."

"People without souls?"

Ramiel made a face. Almost as though he was disappointed. "Wraiths are soulless humans, yes. They are humans who were dying, grieving, or in distress and had no wish to continue living. So I took their souls, had my healers mend their bodies, and—"

"And what did you do with those souls?" I couldn't see straight anymore. Two Ramiels floated in front of me, both smiling thinly.

"They're not in pain," he said.

"That's not what I asked."

"They're with me. Safe."

"With you? Hmm, I'm sure you're not carrying them around in your pocket."

"That would be impossible."

"Didn't think so." How many Wraiths were out there? Thousands, right? Ramiel had all those human souls stored away in that hunky body of his?

"You say it so disdainfully," Ramiel chuckled.

"Because there's nothing 'dainful' about stealing souls." Was *dainful* even a word? Eh, whatever. It was now.

Ramiel made a soft, amused sound. "I ease a person's suffering and I'm denounced for it. Raphael's hybrids live a life of agony, and the humans *celebrate* him. I'll never understand mortals."

The darkness around the edges of my vision crept inward. This conversation needed to be wrapped up. And stat. "Look," I dug the heel of my palm into my temple, "I don't *celebrate* your brother. As far as I'm concerned, you're a pair of immature assholes waving your dicks around to determine who has *the most girth*. Your whole *'woe is me'* speech won't win any brownie points here. Because the only ones I feel sorry for are the poor fucking bastards you put in the middle of all this. The humans, hybrids, Wraiths...all of 'em."

"You pity the humans?" Ramiel asked. "Even though they asked—nay, *forced* you to fight in their battles?"

"Okay, well, that was mostly Quinn," I said. "And he can fuck off too. But the rest of them—"

"Quinn?" Something dark flashed behind Ramiel's eyes. "That boy is still alive?"

"Unfortunately."

Ramiel's nostrils flared. A red tinge appeared on his cheeks. My heart plummeted. Uh-oh. The fuck had I done?

"Is he here?" Ramiel asked.

"Who?"

"*Quinn.*"

"Quinn? Who's that? You must be hard of hearing. I said *Finn*—"

Ramiel pulled his hands from his pockets, his wings lifting over his head.

Shit!

I hated Quinn's guts. No ifs, ands, or buts about it. That didn't mean I wanted to sic this deranged, soul-eating Celestial on him.

I needed to do something. *Fast.*

And, like a miracle from the heavens, it happened.

Ramiel's skin turned fluorescent-y, like Seruf's had. I didn't think twice. I staggered to my feet (nearly blowing chunks when my stomach *squish-squatched*) and thrust my arms through his chest.

Down I tumbled, into that tunnel of color and sound. Except Ramiel's was brighter. Louder. Harsher. My head almost split in two.

I couldn't hold on this time. So, I drew back, sobbing.

"You are brave, attempting to use *my power* against me." Ramiel's voice drifted over my head as I hit the deck again.

I looked up at him—or, at least, I *thought* I looked at him.

But my brain had gotten knocked loose. It sloshed around inside my head, mashing against my skull. Blinding me. I couldn't see anything around the black spots in my vision.

"But you should know better," Ramiel continued. "Did I not teach you to—"

"*Teach me?* Goddamn, I think all you angels are on crack. You make *no* sense. None."

Ramiel knelt, grasping my chin, ignoring me when I tried to bite his hand. He pushed my head back, his coffee-scented breath billowing over my face as he stared at me. "You don't remember, do you?" he asked.

"Remember *what?*"

Ramiel's hold on my chin tightened. "Well, that explains..." he cleared his throat, his other hand drifting toward my chest.

"Aw hell no!" I whacked his hand. "You perverted—*ouch!*" I gasped as he shoved my head back further, threatening to break my neck.

"Those memories are still there." Ramiel's fingers dug into my breasts. "My brethren buried them, but they can't be fully expunged from your soul. So..." he squeezed harder. Fucker felt like he was trying to push my boobs into my spine. "Let's see what secrets your soul is hiding, shall we?"

The pressure at my chest changed. It was as though an unyielding metal hook had fitted itself around me. And it yanked me, hard, down, and down, and down...into that swirling, awful, trippy tunnel.

But the colors, sounds, and figures weren't random figments this time.

They were memories. *My* memories.

Nineteen-year-old me shook with fury as Tom (aka, the twenty-eight-year-old "love of my life") slammed his fist into the wall above my head.

"Goddamn you, Addie! Do you ever think of anyone but your-self?" he bellowed.

"You don't want kids. Neither do I," I spoke through clenched teeth. "So I took care of it."

"You murdered it!"

"It's better than the alternative. Trust me."

I got wrenched down again.

Fifteen-year-old me sat behind the wheel of a junky 90s Camaro. Tears clogged the back of my throat. My hand trembled like a leaf as I clapped my palm over the bleeding gash above my left eye. A gift from Mark (aka, foster mom #5's boyfriend). I'd thanked him by stealing his precious P.O.S. car and taking it for a joy ride.

No surprise I'd gotten pulled over.

"Kid," the pudgy cop said as he leaned against the driver's side door, eyeing up my busted face. "If you tell me who hit ya, I can try to help."

"Your wife," I slurred. "She's got some kinks, let me tell you..."

"Otherwise," the cop rubbed the back of his neck, "I'm gonna have to take ya in. Call your parents..."

"Ha! Good luck with that. They've been dead 10 years."

"Or guardians," he continued. "And have them come sort this out."

I shoved my hands out the window. "Cuff me, baby," I mumbled. "I'll even call you daddy if you want."

I gasped when the hook thrust me into another memory.

Freddie Hawkins stood over me, shoving my bloody underwear in my face. "Stupid bitch," he snarled. "You couldn't wait another year or two to start this shit?"

Because, y'know, a girl had full control over when her period started.

Adult me would've taken that underwear and smeared it all over his nose.

But thirteen-year-old me simply cried.

Stop! I yelled, although I had no voice. *Jesus fucking Christ. STOP!* I thrashed, busting my ribs against the hook, but I couldn't loosen its grip.

"It hurts, doesn't it?" Ramiel's voice drifted through my mind as I got hauled out of that wretched memory and shoved into a new one. "Your soul has known darkness. More than you're even aware of."

Five-year-old me wandered down the carpeted stairs, still hiccupping from my earlier tantrum. Black shadows enveloped the house.

My blood immediately ran cold.

I'd relived this evening *hundreds* of times in my nightmares. The night my parents died.

But this time, everything was different.

Before, I'd gotten a late-night snack and returned to my room, where I stayed until after the fire had blown through the house.

This time...

The candle flickered in the dining room. Pine scented. My parents had forgotten to blow it out. And, when I snuck into the kitchen, the flame caught my eye as it twerked away in the dark room. A pool of melted green wax swirled around the wick. To my dumb kid brain, it looked like a mythical mermaid pond.

I stuck my hand in.

The flame brushed my palm as I dipped my finger into the molten wax. It didn't burn me, but it consumed the sleeve of my Disney Princess PJs and traveled up my arm. The more I panicked, screaming, the faster it spread.

Like, it spread faster than a normal *fire should've been capable of. But nothing about me, or that night, was normal.*

I dashed up the stairs, crying for help. Everything I touched burned. And, in trying to get to my parent's bedroom, I'd inadver-

tently trapped them in the inferno. The fire ripped through their open door, rippled across the floor, and set them both ablaze.

They'd been awake already. Awake, and out of bed, likely to see why I'd been screaming. And then they burned.

Mom howled.

Dad smashed his melting body against the window, fighting desperately to escape.

I cried, the scent of pork chops swirling around my nostrils, and made a beeline for my room.

"No!"

The wail came from adult me, not five-year-old me. Why? Because I was suddenly *fucking terrified*. Like, heart in my throat, cold sweat, stomach-churning, *terrified*.

This memory is wrong! It's not mine!

"Oh, but it is." Excitement colored Ramiel's voice. "My brethren attempted to replace these memories, but your soul hasn't forgotten the truth. We're almost there now, Adelaide..."

The hook dragged me to a gaudy, circular room.

Gold covered the walls, the furniture, the carpet...everything. It looked like some rich S.O.B.'s hideous mansion.

I'd never seen this place before. Ever.

Yet I knew every nook, cranny, and secret hiding spot.

The sprawling king-sized bed had a hollow post on the left side; perfect for stashing small objects. A knife was concealed beneath a loose slab of stone next to the fireplace. Letters were tucked away behind the ornate mirror that hung above the mattress. And the full-length mirror beside the door had a secret 6x6 room cut out behind it.

A woman was ushering me into that very room.

A girl, really. She was little more than a teenager, although she had the gnarled, rough hands of an eighty-year-old.

Those sand-papery hands grasped my arm. Tightly.

I drew back. The sight of that mirror had me breaking out in a nervous sweat.

Noise rose from outside: metal objects clanging. Loud booms.

I started to cry, but the girl turned, holding her finger to her lips, shushing me.

Her wide eyes were purple—almost the same shade as mine. And everything about her: the caramel brown hair that cascaded down her back, her heart-shaped face, her small, wiry frame...it all seemed familiar. As though I'd seen her before. Somewhere. Maybe in a dream, or on a TV show.

But before I could try to place her face, the woman shoved me into the secret room.

I cried.

She slammed the mirror shut as another woman called, "Lasair!"

A few seconds later, a series of ear-splitting shrieks rose.

Some of it came from the purple-eyed woman.

Most of it came from me.

Stop! I yelled.

The hook tightened again, pulling me downward, into another memory of the golden room.

NO. I dug my heels in, grunting when the pressure cracked another rib.

"We're nearly there," Ramiel said.

I'm not going. I threw myself in the opposite direction, ignoring the crushing pain in my chest, churning my feet through the invisible quicksand.

"It would be easier..."

I said NO! And I didn't budge. Pressure closed around me, shattering my bones and tearing my skin to bits. But I didn't give in. I didn't want to know what had happened in that lurid room. I would've preferred to *die* than find out.

The pressure vanished.

I was back on the stone streets of Niall, staring into the smoky smog.

Ramiel rose to his feet, beaming. I crumbled, my breath rattling in and out of my lungs.

"As always, I commend you for your tenacity," Ramiel laughed. "But this didn't need to be so painful."

"Pain's my fucking kink." Blood oozed from my mouth when I spat.

Ramiel's feet shifted into my line of sight. And his shiny black dress shoes *really* chapped my ass. They were pompous and obnoxious. Like the man himself.

My vision swam.

Ramiel's feet moved closer to me.

I stretched a hand out, searching for something, *anything*, to use as a weapon. I almost cried in relief when I sliced my finger against the blade of my poleaxe. Sucker was twisted like a pretzel, but still sharp.

"We'll try again," Ramiel said. "Once I bring you to Idril and—*argh!*"

I drove the warped tip of my poleaxe through the polished patent leather of his left shoe. And his small, surprised yelp was music to my ears.

But then he went sprawling sideways.

I blinked, staring at my misshapen poleaxe, as Ramiel hit the ground a few feet away. He didn't move.

"Oh snap," I laughed, even as my skull throbbed. "Did I find the magic button? *'Press here to deactivate your stark raving mad angel—'*"

"Adelaide."

"*Fuck!*" I hissed.

The new voice made me jump, which sent pulsing pain down the back of my neck and caused my vision to go totally black for a few seconds. I drew shallow breaths, my teeth clenched, and waited for the sensation to ebb before I opened my eyes.

Another goddamn Celestial knelt before me. A woman, swathed in a white dress, with radiant blue wings. She had a long, golden staff propped on the ground and was leaning her left hand against it, while her right brushed my shoulder. Her curly, flaming red hair cascaded to her waist.

And her electric blue eyes...

"You—ooh, you *bitch!*" I slurred. "You coulda at least let me eat my pizza before you sent me here..."

The woman's face was blank. Not a hint of remorse. Or any emotion. "If it were up to me, you would have stayed where you were. You were much less dangerous there."

"*Dangerous?*" I started, and then yelled, "Oh, you pizza-depriving *bitch!*" when she grasped my shoulder with one hand and lifted me to my feet. My ears made a heavy *whomp-whomp-whomp* noise.

"Understand this," the woman held me steady when I swayed, "my brethren did not want me to intervene. I am here against their orders."

My eyes watered. I couldn't keep them open anymore. "Did you kidnap me against their orders too? Or e-e-erase my memories?" I pitched forward when my knees gave out.

The woman thrust her staff under my chest, propping me back on my feet. "It seems I'm the only one of my brethren who learned from past mistakes," she continued, ignoring my comments. "I cannot take you away from here this time. But I can give you a warning."

"A warn—"

She didn't give me a chance to finish. "You may have destroyed Seruf's Essence, but you also absorbed a piece of it."

"H-How?"

461

"Souls and Essences, are...well, to put it crudely, they're rather like gum."

"Gum? Like...*bubble gum*?" I snorted.

She sighed. "Yes. When you trod on gum, you take a piece of it with you. The same thing happens when you touch a soul: it leaves a residue, one that will damage *your* soul. If you use this power too often, you *will* change. That is my warning."

As I attempted to work out what the heck that meant, she grasped my shoulders again, spinning me around. "Because I am alone," she continued, "I cannot hold Ramiel indefinitely. But I will give you time to escape."

A horse snorted in my ear.

I cracked an eye open as Abby Normal nuzzled my arm. "You're nuts," I told the woman. "I can't ride...you don't know *anything* about this horse."

"No, *you* know nothing about her," the woman said.

Before I had time to squeak out a protest, I was flung across Abby Normal's scaly back. I grunted, whimpered, and grasped onto fistfuls of her wiry mane as she shifted.

"The humans—those still alive—have fled into the forest and are en route to Sanadrin," the woman said. "The Púca will take you to them."

"Wait!" I cried when Abby Normal moved forward. She stopped, pawing uncertainly.

"Did I not just say I can't hold—" the woman started.

"Cheriour," I rasped.

"My brother is close to death."

"If Quinn's still alive, he can fix him."

"It would be better if you let him go," the woman insisted. Her voice wasn't exactly gentle, but it had softened. A smidge.

"Not happening," I said.

"When he dies—"

"He'll rise. And he won't be the same. I got that whole spiel already," I snapped. "But *I don't care*. He's fought so hard—he *wants* to live. And...I need him." A salty tear trickled into my mouth. "You've taken everything from me. *Everything*. Don't take him too. Please."

She said nothing. Every time I opened my eyes, my vision swam, and the dim light from the dying fire seemed as bright as a thousand-watt bulb. "Really," I huffed when she stayed silent for a few seconds too long. "You're *really* gonna ignore me. You bi—*oof.*"

Cheriour's body flopped over my lap. He was out cold. And it was awkward to have him in this position, dangling horizontally across Abby Normal's back, his torso pressed against the tops of my thighs.

I grasped his shoulders, feeling the unsteady rise and fall of his chest, while my hands trembled.

"Now go," the woman said.

With that, Abby Normal was off, her hooves clip-clopping against the stone streets.

I grasped onto her mane with my right hand, Cheriour with my left, and held on.

After several agonizing moments, the terrain shifted. Abby Normal's feet now thundered over grass.

Just a bit further, I kept telling myself as the *whomp-whomp-whomping* in my ears got louder.

Just a bit further.

My brain bashed against my skull. Stars erupted behind my closed eyelids. I wouldn't make it much longer.

I almost cried in relief when I heard voices.

"It's a Púca!" someone shouted.

"Wraiths!" another cry rose.

"No, wait," came Braxton's voice. "Addie?"

And that was the last thing I remembered.

50

SECRET SECRETS ARE NO FUN

This had all started with a fucking pizza.

And now I couldn't even remember what it tasted like.

I tried. Lord, had I tried. Since arriving at Sanadrin two days ago, I'd racked my brain, trying to recall the aroma and flavor of my favorite ooey-gooey cheesy meal. Nada.

Other things I remembered with *too* much detail. Like the fake-pine scent that rose from a cheap department store candle. Or the low *sizzle-sizzle* of flames gobbling cheap, made-in-China cotton blend pajamas. Or the odd sensation of dipping my fingers into hot wax and having the molten liquid cascade *away* from my flesh. It didn't stick. Didn't dry, the way it would've on anyone else.

These were memories from *decades* ago. Memories that hadn't existed in my head until Ramiel forced them there. And now I saw, heard, and smelled everything in full 8K resolution.

But pizza? No idea what it tasted like anymore.

I lowered my head to my knees, closing my eyes.

And then immediately opened them again, snapping my

head back against the wall when an image of the purple-eyed girl filled my mind. A girl I knew but didn't remember how.

Unless Ramiel had fucked with my head and *tricked* me into thinking I knew her?

I wasn't sure. And the only person who could give me answers (*maybe*) was lying on a bed a few feet away, doped up on pain.

Not pain *meds*. But apparently severe blood loss and extreme agony gave you the same loopy-brain side effects as drugs.

The fever sure didn't help.

Cheriour shifted, mumbling nonsense like "Creator," or "I won't eat it," or "East wall," or, my personal favorite, "Cheese!" Usually barked like a harsh command. *"Give me the cheese, damn it!"*

Dude was having some interesting fever dreams.

He'd had some moments of lucidity the last few days. Not many. Some of his injuries had healed. Not many. Not enough.

The door on the other end of the room creaked as it opened. Maddox's eyes peered through the darkness. (Pretty sure it was mid-day, but Sanadrin had ten windows. Total. And they were all up in the towers. The mid-level bedrooms were swathed in darkness 24/7).

Maddox's gaze lowered until he found where I sat on the floor, huddled against the wall. He sighed as he replenished the almost burnt-out candle sitting on the shelf by the door. "I've left you more candles," he said.

"The dark doesn't bother me." I would *never* light a candle again. Ever. The one Maddox kept lit had already given me a couple of panic attacks, and I stayed far away from it.

"And I can get you bedding..." Maddox continued.

"I don't need it."

Maddox sighed and stepped into the room. "How is he?"

I tilted my head as Cheriour let out a garbled, "I will *not!*"

"'Bout the same," I mumbled. "How you holding up?"

Maddox looked like a walking zombie: big, dark rings encircled his eyes. He'd dropped weight quickly, and his clothes hung loose around his body.

When I'd seen Quinn earlier, he didn't look much better.

They were both stretched too thin. There were too many wounded.

"I'll be alright." Maddox touched Cheriour's side.

The bed shook as Cheriour flinched and let out an animalistic snarl.

"Can you hold him down, Addie?" Maddox asked. His hands trembled. He didn't have the strength to suppress an ant.

But neither did I.

I hadn't been injured in my encounter with Seruf and Ramiel. Not physically, at least, except for a few bruises. But my body hadn't gotten that memo. *Everything* hurt. My joints creaked as I walked to Cheriour's bed. The ache in my head had dulled, but it was still there, always pulsing behind my eyes.

Maddox said I needed rest. That my pain likely stemmed from emotional and mental trauma. But every time I closed my eyes, I was back at my parents' house, watching them die. Or trapped in the gaudy gold room with the mystery woman. So, yeah...sleep wasn't coming easy these days.

I perched beside Cheriour, grasping his arms, pressing my body into him as Maddox lifted the bedsheet and inspected his wounds. "It's healing," he said, lowering the sheet back over Cheriour's naked body. "Slower than I'd like, but...I..."

Maddox and Quinn had self-imposed a hard rule. They did enough healing to keep a person's heart beating. No more. It was the only way two healers could save the thousands of dying that had fled to Sanadrin after Niall's fall.

Maddox touched two quivering fingers to Cheriour's forehead.

Cheriour thrashed again, nearly bucking me off him, and almost knocking poor, wobbly Maddox on his ass. "He *is* getting stronger," Maddox said. "I gave him a little more..."

"Maddox," I sighed.

"...it might be enough to break his fever." Maddox staggered when he walked away from the bed.

"You need to be more careful." I wanted Cheriour better. Desperately. Didn't mean I wanted to see Maddox go down.

"I am." Maddox's teeth flashed in the dark as he smiled. But then he swayed again.

"You wanna sit?" I asked. "You can shirk off your duties for a bit. I won't tattle."

"I can't." He leaned against the wall, pinching his nose between his forefinger and thumb. "The symptoms of Elion's disease have started."

Ice clanked around in my belly. "H-How many are sick?"

"Over a hundred."

The whole freaking group. Just as Belanna had feared. "So... so...what do we..."

"We'll keep them comfortable," Maddox said. "For as long as we can. It's all we can do for them now."

"A-are you setting a room up for them? Do you have enough beds? I can—"

"Addie," Maddox gave me a sad smile, "you need to heal too."

"But—"

"The infected aren't going anywhere. You'll be able to help them once you've gotten some of your strength back. Not before." He pushed himself away from the wall. "By the way," he chuckled, "your Púca is making an excellent guard. She hears refugees approaching before our watchers in the tower can see them."

I cracked a grin at that.

Abby Normal carrying Cheriour and I to safety had convinced some people (not all, unfortunately) that she wasn't evil. So she'd graduated to a paddock. One with a stunning view of the mountains. And she was happier for it. "She's a cool kid," I said.

"She still won't let any of the stable hands close to the fence, though."

"Well, I didn't say she wasn't a bitch," I laughed. "I'll go down a later and...I dunno. Try to teach her manners."

Maddox nodded and then jerked his head toward Cheriour. "He may wake up soon. Find someone to fetch me or Quinn when he does."

And, with that, he left.

I stayed perched on the edge of the bed, staring around the dark room. Which was depressing AF and only made my dreary mood worse. But, whatever. Not much would make me happy at this point anyway.

Except a large, extra cheese pizza. With mushrooms. And olives. I'd take a slice; a *sliver* of a slice, even. Just to remember what it tasted like.

This time, when I closed my eyes, trying to recall the warmth of the pizza box in my hands as I walked to my car, I saw the red-headed woman. The Celestial with the electric blue eyes.

...it leaves a residue, one that will damage your soul.

Had I lost a part of my soul at Niall? Was that why my memories were messed up? But what did a soul even *feel* like? How did you know when you damaged one?

If you use this power too often, you will change.

What did that mean? Would I keep losing memories? Turn into a deranged serial killer? A monster?

Behind me, Cheriour shifted, kicking out at some invisible enemy. I turned, watching as his face pinched with pain, and then dropped my head into my palms.

A million more questions swirled around my brain. Ones only he could answer.

How does an angel fall? What, exactly, will happen to you when you die? Is it like being a zombie? Worse? Who was the blue-eyed angel who saved me (and also freaking kidnapped me)? Is what she said about me true? How did I get these powers?

I sniffled.

Did I kill my parents? Were those memories real?

And, if you knew about this, why didn't you tell me?

Something brushed against my back. I jumped, wincing when my neck cracked, and turned.

Cheriour's heavily bandaged hand touched my lower back again. "I'm sorry," he slurred. His half-open eyes were more alert than I'd seen them in days. "For not telling you."

"You're—wait, was I talking?"

A low, pained laugh rumbled out of him. "You're *always* talking."

"Sorry."

His shoulders jerked, almost like a shrug. "I like your voice," he mumbled. His hand tapped my back again. "And...I should have told...you. But...I didn't want...to hurt...you. Sometimes it's better...not knowing..." His slur became more pronounced as his eyes closed.

The back of my throat got that clogged, cottony sensation again. I mean, he wasn't entirely wrong. I'd've gladly lived the rest of my life (however short it would be) without knowing the things I knew now. And I wasn't angry at him for not telling me. Not really. Well...maybe a smidge. But would I have listened to him if he'd tried to explain upfront? Hell no. I would've told him to lay off the shrooms.

"Well," I cleared my throat, "secret secrets are no fun. Y'know?"

Cheriour opened one eye when I touched his cheek.

"You get a pass this time. Because I like you," I murmured. "And because you were trying to protect me. But no more secrets, 'kay? I won't forgive you next time."

His lips twitched, and he nuzzled my hand before he breathed out a long sigh and drifted back to his fever dreams.

My heart clenched.

"You and I are gonna have a long talk once you're better," I whispered, tracing the scar over his eye.

Although, to be honest, the prospect of that conversation terrified me.

It was gonna hurt. Secrets usually did when they surfaced.

I hoped I was strong enough to bear the pain. And to meet whatever other nightmares this shithole world had to offer.

51

SERUF

LASS

The vague childhood memories I had of Seruf were faded and distorted. I'd long envisioned her as a winged Wraith: warped and inhuman. A horrifying sight to behold.

But Seruf was merely a winged woman. She seemed unthreatening. Especially as she stared at me, her dark eyes gleaming with joy and relief.

I did not fear her. Truthfully, I did not seem capable of feeling *anything.* My heart churned away inside my chest, but it had turned into something resembling a clockwork mechanism, like in Terrick's fiction books. A device that mimicked life but was incapable of truly living.

"My child." Seruf folded her knees into a crouch as she surveyed me. "What have they done to you?"

I stared at her but said nothing.

Around us, the smoke continued to clear, revealing rows upon rows of debris-covered streets. Burnt remnants of humans and beasts crisscrossed along the road. This had been a rather large town, once, if the ruins were any indication. Easily twice the size of Swindon, and likely housing twice the number of humans.

Those humans were all dead.

I wanted to pity them. But I didn't.

"I heard you had returned to Sakar," I said to Seruf.

She beamed at me. "For you," she said. "I returned for *you*."

"So it's true." My stomach turned hollow. "The accusations—"

"Accusations?"

"That I was created by your hand."

"Ah," Seruf's smile stretched, if possible, even wider. She looked rather comical, with her too-white teeth glinting in the dying fire. "Of course it's true." She raised her hand. The tips of her fingers (the nails, to be more accurate) were painted a dark shade of red.

It looked as though she'd dipped them in blood.

She shifted her fingers and summoned a tongue of fire. It hovered, still and quiet, above her palm.

She closed her fist, extinguishing the flame.

I envied how easily she accomplished that. How many times had I fought to banish the fire from my skin? How many times had I lost control over it? And yet, she made controlling it seem as simple as...well, as closing her fist.

"I am the last fire elemental to live in this wretched place. My brethren sided with Raphael," Seruf said. "Imagine that. We were bonded; closer than—well, there isn't a human equivalent to describe what we were to each other. Closer than kin, certainly. And yet they *left* me."

"So you killed them."

"I would have," Seruf laughed. "Sadly, they chose to flee. Except for Ellard, of course. Although he's little better than a human now."

"And I suppose you created me to ease your loneliness?"

Seruf's eyes widened, but her smile never faded. "My, my, you're more tempestuous than I thought."

I glared at her, my brain at war with itself. One part—the rational side—argued that I should choose my words more carefully. This was not a human crouched before me. Nor was it a hybrid. Seruf was a Celestial. Ageless and powerful.

The other part of me, the side that was battered, tired, and had grown a prickly defensive shell, told me to keep going. To see how she would react to my provocation. After all, what would she do in retaliation? Kill me? I no longer feared death.

Turn me into a Wraith?

Considering how ~~callisly~~—callously I'd viewed the destruction of this town, the transformation would hardly be traumatic. It didn't seem I had much of a soul left.

"I'm not tempestuous," I said. "Only truthful."

"Oh yes?" Her eyebrows raised. "You are a child. What truths do you know?"

"You created me," I said. My mind rolled back, and back, and back, recalling everything that had happened since Mama died. "Perhaps you intended to keep me, but something went wrong." I remembered the day of my transformation and the second Celestial who took me away. "I was brought to Sakar, where you were barred from going. And, for more than a decade, you did not try to reach me."

"Perceptive!" she exclaimed. "A true marvel! Yes, child, I abandoned you here, didn't I? It was not intentional, I assure you. When Ch—well," an angry twinge crossed her face, but she quickly smoothed her expression. "My brother will be dealt with...in due time, of course. But I was led to believe you had perished."

"'Led to believe?'" I repeated. "But had no desire to confirm?"

Another ripple of annoyance briefly marred her face. "I did not believe I was being lied to. And you cannot fathom my relief upon hearing you were alive."

My skin suddenly seemed stretched too taut over my ~~skelton~~—skeleton. It was uncomfortable. As was the churning of unease in my stomach. "Why did you not create another hybrid to replace me?"

"Creating hybrids is no simple task, my child."

"Why? Does it deplete your powers when you give a human a piece of it?"

Seruf straightened, her wondrous wings ruffling as she stretched and began to walk, allowing my question to go unanswered.

"Your shoes are terribly impractical," I said. She did, indeed, have the most ridiculous pair of boots I'd ever seen. The tops were open, exposing her foot to the elements. And the heel was so elevated, it forced her to stand on the balls of her feet. It was a wonder she could walk.

"Perhaps for these rudimentary human streets." Seruf wrinkled her nose in disgust as she scraped the toe of her silly boot across a patch of dirt. "But in Norhall, where our roads are even and well-paved, these shoes serve me quite well. You will adore Norhall, child. It's modern. And clean." Her lip curled as she regarded the ruined town.

"I'm sure this town was clean as well. Before you destroyed it."

Seruf made a small *hmming* sound. "A *clean* town? Where humans sleep side-by-side with their livestock—"

"Animals are great company."

"Child," she knelt before me again.

I tensed when she twirled a lock of my hair. Not because I feared her attack. But because her touch, unwelcome as it was, made my skin prickle, a sensation that usually accompanied the emergence of my power.

My apprehension was rather silly, of course. She was the Firestarter. My fire would not harm her.

In all likelihood, she would harm me.

But she didn't seem inclined to do so, as she worked the knots and snarls out of my hair. "Poor thing," she murmured. "What is your name?"

"Lass," I answered.

"*Lass?*" Seruf scoffed. "Oh no, no. My dear, that is not a *name*. That won't do at all."

My skin itched again. I could still hear Terrick's voice as he rolled my name off his tongue. "I've no desire to be called anything else."

"Well," Seruf combed her fingers through a freshly untangled section of my hair, "may I make a suggestion? What do you think of the name 'Lasair?' Do you know what it means?" she asked when I started to protest.

"No," I said.

Seruf smiled. "'The Bringer of Light.' *Lasair.*"

I turned the word over in my head. *Lasair.* It was similar to what Terrick had affectionately called me but more sophisticated. A better fit for an adult, perhaps.

"It's not all that different from Lass, is it?" Seruf said, as though she'd heard my thoughts.

I didn't want to admit I rather liked it. So I stayed silent as she combed my hair.

And perhaps I was a fool. Perhaps I was simply starved for a touch of kindness, but I relaxed beneath her ministrations. My breathing steadied. My tense muscles loosened.

She drew back, cupping my chin in her palm. "Would you like to see Norhall, child?"

I swallowed. *No.* The only word out of my mouth should have been *no.*

But I said nothing.

Seruf continued. "You are my protégé and you would be given the finest accommodations, afforded every respect and comfort. We have soft clothing." She traced a hand over the cuts and hives on my bare shoulders. "And warm, scented baths you can indulge in whenever you wish. And the *food*... have you ever tasted chocolate? Sweets?"

At my blank look, she tapped her fingers against my chin. "You will sample them," she assured me. "As many as you'd like. What say you?"

Bile rose in my throat.

At the time, I didn't understand why. She had shown no abhorrence, no inclination toward violence. Only a friendly, soothing demeanor.

Yet her touch, her presence, and the sweet apple scent that wafted from her skin made my stomach roil in rebellion.

Despite her caring words and gestures, there was no warmth in Seruf's eyes.

Aside from the power we shared, Seruf had no bond with me. She did not care for my well-being. If she had, she would not have assumed me dead so easily. She would have continued searching for me until she saw my corpse with her own eyes.

It's what Terrick would've done. For all the mistakes he made, Terrick never gave up on me. He cared too much to let me go.

Seruf didn't care.

She only wanted the fire that flowed through my veins. The fire that had come from her own blood. She wanted the piece of herself that she'd given up returned.

I would find no love if I accepted her proposal.

But perhaps I could find peace.

Seruf, far more powerful than I, would certainly not fear me, or look at me in repulsion as the humans had done. Could I live freely beneath her tutelage? Could I, perhaps, learn to control the fire that had long terrorized me?

A fluttering sensation rose in my throat. A peaceful life. It was all I'd ever wanted.

But what would that peace cost me?

The rolling sound of hoofbeats drew me away from my ponderings.

No less than a dozen human soldiers rode into Vaporia. They drew their snorting, panting horses to a halt, and grimly surveyed the debris surrounding them.

Seruf turned, her wings spasming as a flicker of annoyance crossed her face. The soldiers, likely blinded by the billowing clouds of ash and smoke, did not immediately see her.

"We're too late!" a man said as he dismounted his horse.

"Search the buildings," a woman called. Her horse shied when a smoldering ~~skelton~~—skeleton of a home collapsed, sending embers into the sky. The woman snatched the animal's reins, steadying it. "Move quickly. And bring the wounded to Quinn."

Quinn.

In my chest, the heart I thought had turned to coal fluttered.

There he was. *Alive.* Dismounting from his horse, his face ashen. He laid a comforting hand on the red-headed woman beside him as she shifted rubble off the burnt remnants of a child.

Quinn's brilliant blue eyes surveyed the rest of the ruined town. They paused when he caught sight of me. Widened. Realization dawned on his face.

"Seruf!" he shouted. "She's still here!"

Immediately, the red-headed woman drew her bow and fired her first arrow. Her aim was true: the head of the arrow struck Seruf's right shoulder. The wound oozed a silvery light —the same substance Seruf had forced me to drink when I was a child.

Seruf did not flinch when she wrenched the arrow from her shoulder and tossed it aside. Her irritation boiled; I could almost feel its heat.

She would kill them.

And I felt no remorse for them. Except...

Quinn stood still, even as those around him drew their weapons. Even as the red-headed woman fired three more arrows. Seruf avoided two. The third pierced the side of her throat but, again, she did not flinch.

Quinn still did not move. He seemed rooted to the spot; his eyes affixed to my face. The hurt and confusion in his gaze made my insides burn with shame.

Quinn had been the only human, except Terrick, who had not believed me to be evil. He helped me when others would have harmed me. And now he saw me with Seruf and was likely regretting he'd ever spared me a moment of benevolence.

But his kindness, passion, and even his arrogance had been the few dim rays of light in the bleak well of despair my life had become since leaving Swindon. I'd not known Quinn long. I'd not known him well. But, for some inexplicable reason, I cared for him. And I couldn't bear to see him perish.

He had saved my life once.

Now I would save his.

"Yes!" I said, even as another arrow hurtled at Seruf. This one missed her but clipped my left ear. I relished the aching sting it left behind.

Seruf turned to me.

"You asked if I wished to see Norhall," I said. "My answer is yes."

With a gleeful chuckle, Seruf pressed a lingering kiss to my temple. "You'll adore Norhall, child. Now, allow me to extinguish these pests..."

"Must you?"

"They shot an arrow at me. And at you."

"You were left with barely a scratch." Her wound had already healed. "Against your power, humans are little more than insects."

"You pity them?" Seruf raised an eyebrow.

"As anyone pities a trodden insect, yes. Humans are wretched creatures, but they know no other way of being, so the fault does not lie with them. And..."

Quinn drew his sword. Unlike the other soldiers, who handled their weapons with ease, Quinn fumbled, nearly dropping his blade.

"I've grown tired of trodding on insects." My lower lip quivered. "I ask that you spare them. If only to spare me the revulsion of seeing yet another trampled creature."

A long, ~~eggaerated~~ exaggerated breath escaped Seruf's lips. "Very well. For you, my darling, I would do anything." She combed my hair, her fingers lingering against my scalp.

I tried to ignore the sticky sensation that coiled in my gut when she touched me. Tried.

"Lass!"

Quinn's voice pierced my heart.

As Seruf wrapped her arms around me and spread her wings, I caught a final glimpse of him. He'd forsaken his sword and was sprinting toward Seruf, ignoring the shouts and commands from his fellow soldiers. "Lass! Don't!"

I closed my eyes when Seruf flapped her wings.

And, thus, my time living amongst the humans came to a close.

My time with the Celestials began.

TO BE CONTINUED....

ACKNOWLEDGMENTS

It's time to get sappy, y'all!

My adventure with Addie and the crew began when I was 18—nearly 15 years ago! I'm not sure when I got so old, lol. And the idea came from a mix of things:

A.) I've always loved epic fantasies but didn't always love reading them because the writing tended to feel a bit dry for my taste (looking at you, *Lord of the Rings*).

B.) I've always skewed toward campy/cheesy humor and wished more fantasies utilized that (like *Xena: Warrior Princess*, which is 100% as campy as it is epic).

C.) I was a Catholic school brat (from a surprisingly non-religious family...but that's a story for another time, lol) and angel mythology fascinated me.

Long story short: I wanted a dark/epic fantasy with badass angel lore and oodles of campy jokes. And that was...not what I wrote when I was 18, LOL. The plot was a mess, the characters were cardboard cutouts, and I hadn't found my voice yet, so the writing had as much personality as a slug. But I did the thing and wrote an entire long-winded book, so kid me gets an A for Effort. And that dumpster fire of a book was the very first step on the long-ass stairway that led to Fires of the Forsaken. Because as awful as my original version was, it lived rent-free in my head for *years*. Because I *knew* my idea was solid. It just needed better execution.

Fast forward *many* years later, and this story was still bouncing around in my head. So I decided to dig in. I re-read my originals, tossed the garbage, kept what worked, took the time to build the world properly, and flesh out my characters (impatient 18-year-old me did *not* do this). And, *voila*, the kickass story known as Fires of the Forsaken was born.

But I couldn't have reached this point without help.

First and foremost, I have to thank my mom. She read (and loved) the original dumpster fire version of this story and she's been my cheerleader through every step of this rewrite.

I've also gotta give a huge shoutout to my beta readers: Hannah, Stephanie, and JoJo for taking a chance on this wild story and telling me when I was running the plot in confusing circles. (And to anyone who might've read the original version *way* back in the day...thank you. It's been a while, and my memory isn't great, so I'm sorry I can't give you a personal thanks. But I am deeply appreciative of the feedback I got in my teenage years. It helped me find my writing voice.).

I can't do an acknowledgment without casting the spotlight on all my fellow Midnight Tide Publishing authors. Publishing is a hard industry that has more downs than ups, so having a support system is crucial. You need people you can vent to, bounce ideas off of, cry with, and who will celebrate your success with you. MTP has given me that group, and I'm super thankful for it.

My editor, Meg, is a flipping rockstar. I dumped this book and 20ish pages of notes on her on New Year's Eve. I was like an unhinged and over-caffeinated creative sliding into her DMs in the middle of the night, lol. But she muddled through my ramblings and, as always, provided crucial feedback to whip this story into shape.

Lastly, I have to thank YOU, the reader, who picked up this book knowing it was going to be weird as hell. *Thank you*, a million times over, for taking a chance on me and this wild story. It wasn't exactly lighthearted fare, but I hope you enjoyed the journey. And I know I left all my characters hanging in some rough spots, but they'll be back. I promise.

ABOUT THE AUTHOR

As a child, Stephanie E. Donohue roamed Narnia with the
Pevensie siblings and rode the Hogwarts Express with Harry
and his friends. She never tired of discovering new and magical
worlds through the pages of a book. And, when the yearning to
explore still wasn't satiated, Stephanie turned to writing. With
a pen and a few sheets of paper, she learned to craft new
worlds, and vibrant characters to explore with.

That passion has never died. Stephanie still enjoys writing
stories that take readers on exciting, and sometimes dangerous, adventures.

When she's not writing, Stephanie can usually be found cuddling with her two cats, obsessively re-watching The Office, or rocking out to a Pound Fitness class.

Linktree:
https://linktr.ee/stephanie_e_donohue

OTHER BOOKS BY STEPHANIE E. DONOHUE

Standalones

Windsong (2022)

The Across Time Series

Fires of the Forsaken (2023)

Ashes of the Earth (TBD)

MORE BOOKS YOU'LL LOVE

If you enjoyed this book, please consider leaving a review.

Then check out more from Midnight Tide Publishing.
https://www.midnighttidepublishing.com/

Of Loyalties & Wreckage by Lou Wilham & Christis Christie

Sometimes, family is found in the most unlikely of places.

Born with horns that set him apart, Prince Ander is an outcast in his own mother's court. Unwilling to stay and suffer it any longer, Ander leaves to try to make his way in the mortal realm. However, even amongst the humans, tragedy follows the half-muse.

Orphaned before she was given a name, Mab Duchan has never known a real family outside of those paid to care for her. Just when she thinks she's found one, the arrogance and jealousy of a hateful noble nearly destroys her. When all hope seems lost, the most unlikely of heroes arises.

Now it's Ander and Mab against the world, but the stronger their bond as a family, the more life seeks to break them apart. Can they hold on to the ties that bind, or will love be the one thing that finally tears them apart?

Burnout by Devon Thiele

Her boss would call it a 'strongly encouraged leave of absence.' Quinn Brennan would call it her last chance.

Quinn, as the leading magical analyst for the Arcanum—a renowned organization advancing the world's knowledge and use of magic, as well as defending against its darker forces—, is no stranger to life-or-death decisions on the front lines in the battle against magic. Driven to advance her career in the Arcanum to fulfill a promise to her parents, Quinn has always put work first. When one decision goes awry, it costs Quinn her career, two of her closest friends, and her self-confidence. Now placed on leave from the job she once loved above all else, she is determined to prove that she still has what it takes to be number one.

Her interest piqued by reports filed by the town of Beteville located in magic's hot zone, Quinn uses her leave of absence to conduct an investigation of her own. What she finds is a mystery that was decades in the making.

When townspeople begin disappearing without a trace, eerily like those thirty years prior, Quinn must use her Arcanum experience. Assisted by the lone survivor of her last botched mission, Quinn must put a stop to the Beteville Beast for once and for all or lose her last chance at redemption.

CPSIA information can be obtained
at www.ICGtesting.com
Printed in the USA
BVHW060932220323
660885BV00001B/4